LITTLE MEN, BIG WO

Ben Reisman, veteran columnist for the *Journal*, is bored. So when he stumbles across a reference to a character known as "De Ark," an underworld person who seems to operate without anyone knowing about him, he is intrigued. "De Ark" is in fact Mr. Orral Wanty, Arky to his friends, the right hand man of the Mover, the man who really runs the city. Arky's control is so tight, even Commissioner Stark, the zealous law-and-order crusader, has never heard of him. But Arky's hand is everywhere. He's the man Leon Sollas, front for the syndicate, makes his weekly payment to—and he's the man who Sollas goes to when he wants out. But Arky's got problems of his own. The big city boys want to move in. His woman, Anna, wants a baby. And somewhere, hot on his trail, is a newspaper man in search of a story…

VANITY ROW

Police Captain Roy Hargis is the Administration's fair-haired boy, only answering to Chad Bayliss, the city's political boss. Most of the officers are in awe of him. Hargis can do no wrong. He knows how to cut to the heart of a case and bring the facts home to the D.A.'s office. So when rich lawyer Frank Hobart is shot down in cold blood, it looks open and shut. Hobart had been fooling around with a babe named Ilona, but things got out of hand, and she's accused of killing him. But Hargis doesn't figure it that way—not after he meets Miss Vance. Because Ilona Vance is a force to be reckoned with, not merely beautiful, but so desirable it almost hurts. Hargis will go to any lengths to get her off, but he's up against it this time. The syndicate wants to see her burn, Bayliss wants a quick conviction, and Hargis is finding his tough shell has been thoroughly cracked.

"His novels are not mysteries, but crime novels, powerful, accurate cynical explorations of criminals in their own environment: at their best they are important additions to the honor roll of hard-boiled fiction."
George Grella, *20th Century Crime & Mystery Writers*

Little Men, Big World

Vanity Row

W. R. Burnett

STARK
HOUSE

Stark House Press • Eureka California

LITTLE MEN, BIG WORLD / VANITY ROW

Published by Stark House Press
1315 H Street
Eureka, CA 95501
griffinskye3@sbcglobal.net
www.starkhousepress.com

ISBN: 1-933586-67-2
ISBN-13: 978-1-933586-67-0

Book design by Mark Shepard, shepgraphics.com
Proofreading by Rick Ollerman

First Stark House Press Edition: March 2015
FIRST EDITION

They Can't Really Win: The Start of W. R. Burnett's "Urban Trilogy"

by Rick Ollerman

"A writer has to have an imagination—that's what makes a writer. He has to be able to put himself imaginatively in the position of whatever character he selects. And I have a very good grip on reality, which I inherited from my father, so I pretty much know the limitations of humanity and the possibilities in life, which aren't very great for anybody. You're born, you're gonna have trouble, and you're gonna die. That you know. There's not much else you know."

W. R. Burnett,
from an interview with Ken Mate and Pat Milligan,
Backstory 1: Interviews with Screenwriters of Hollywood's Golden Age,
University of California Press, 1986

William Riley Burnett, known professionally as "W. R. Burnett" but as "Bill" to his friends, was born in 1890's Springfield, Ohio, on November 25th. He went through school, lasted just one semester at the College of Journalism at Ohio State University, and "knocked around at various jobs" until he eventually ended up with a political job as a statistician for the state. The job gave him the opportunity to write, and by the time he was too bored to continue with his government career, before he finally "escaped" to Chicago, he'd already decided on making a literary life for himself. He said that he wrote during this time without the slightest encouragement from anyone other than his wife, Marjorie, who was helpful in every way. For eight years he worked like this, never selling a line, but he persisted, he said, "either through stupidity or determination, I've never been able to decide which."

Burnett needed a change. "Disgusted," he said, he "threw up his hands and went to Chicago. Unwittingly, I'd done the very thing I should have done." From his time in Ohio, he'd written five novels, hundreds of short stories, and a few plays—none of them published or produced.

The city of Chicago was what he needed. There was a bigger-than-life Al Capone to help turn him around, help him develop his style. Not directly, of course, but when Burnett started meeting lower level mob guys, he began a whole new education. On his first night in Chicago, while staying at a fleabag hotel, Burnett was awakened by an explosion that came from directly across the street. Windows rattled, the floors shook, and this was followed by two more just blocks away. Turns out things had gotten rough among garage owners, to the point where they were throwing "pineapples" through the windows of each other's shops and blowing holes through brick walls. To the rank and file, this was just business as usual. To Burnett, this was excitement. "The city made a tremendous impact on me," he said.

This was toward the end of Prohibition, at a time when Capone went from being a man of the people, the local hero who was just giving the people what they wanted—booze and more booze—to a violent, murderous criminal, the force behind the St. Valentine's Day Massacre.

Corruption was rampant. Violence was everywhere, and accepted by the people on the street. Burnett called it "ostrichism," the notion of the populace that this stuff was just so much newspaper copy, that nobody ever really saw actual gangsters. Burnett already knew better.

He met a man who was a police reporter and gradually the idea for a book began to take shape, something Burnett originally called *The Furies*. At this time, Burnett was still trying to write what we'd think of as "literary" novels today, though in the past there was no such distinction. He said that had that title stayed, the book wouldn't have been a hit—it was too far removed from the street. As it was, the novel became a seminal and vastly influential book, not just in literature but in Hollywood. It became *Little Caesar* and it made not only W.R. Burnett, but when the movie version came out, it made Edward G. Robinson, as well.

Burnett published over 35 books in his life and worked on many more screenplays for Hollywood. The result is that he had a deep and lasting revolutionary effect on two major media industries: literature and movies. Many of his screenplays were adaptations of his own work, both novels and short stories.

Little Caesar told the story of Rico Bandello, a gangster rising in the Chicago ranks before inevitably and tragically falling. Second possibly to the great Orson Welles line from *Citizen Kane*, the whispered "Rosebud...", Robinson delivered his great finale, speaking of his character in the third person, "Is this the end of Rico?" It has become an enduring cinematic moment.

The book didn't come easily to Burnett. Under the title of *The Furies* he felt it was too high-brow and he couldn't get a handle on either the characters or the story. Then the revelation hit: the book needed to be not only about the gangster Rico, but it had to be written from his particular worldview:

> Suddenly one night it came to me. The novel should be a picture of the world as seen through the eyes of a gangster. All conventional feelings, desires, and hopes should be rigidly excluded. Further, the book should be written in a style that suited the subject matter—that is, in the illiterate jargon of the Chicago gangster. I threw overboard what had been known up to then as "literature." I declared war on adjectives. I jettisoned "description." I tried to tell the story entirely through narration and dialogue, letting the action speak for itself. I also jettisoned "psychology"—and I tried hard to suppress myself and all of my opinions.

Burnett had met a man, a North Side barber shop owner who also turned out to be a pay-off man for one of the largest mobs in the area. Burnett was impressed by his "practicality," his lack of conscience when it came to the necessity of murder, or of a "rubout." You try to reason with a guy, he doesn't go along, well—he's made his choice. The guy has to go.

> I must say that when I first started to talk with John my understanding was clouded by many old-fashioned notions. I was under the impression that murder—or, as John would have said, a rubout—was morally wrong and that the murderer was bound to suffer pangs of conscience and remorse. I even said something like this. John stared at me in consternation, then almost choked laughing. Was I kidding? Do soldiers in a war suffer stuff like that?

> What was the difference if a guy rubbed out Germans or "impractical" business rivals? I must be nuts.

> In short, I gradually and painfully acquired from John an entirely new and fresh way of looking at the world. It was not a pretty way; it was more than a little frightening; but it was certainly "practical" and was later taken over lock, stock, and barrel by all the tyrants—all the little Caesars—of Europe. Better yet, although only realizing it little by little, I was getting exactly what I needed to make a real book of the manuscript I was laboring over: a picture of the world as seen through the eyes of a gangster.

For the first time an author had given readers an inside view, a book with the perspective—an all too human perspective—of what it was like to be in and of the world of organized crime. It wasn't *about* the mob, it *was* about the people that made up the mob. It was this sense of literary realism that Burnett brought to the crime genre that would be his trademark style throughout the major novels of his career. The mob guys were real people, doing real things with real hopes and real dreams, but doing them from the wrong side of the law. Right and wrong is blurred, if it exists at all. Legal or illegal may be more appropriate terms. The local government is corrupt, the police are corrupt, the gangsters are corrupt. And as long as the public was relatively safe and able to get a snootful of gin or whiskey when they wanted it, people could go along with the mob action all around them. They didn't have to see it. They didn't want to see it.

Still, *Little Caesar* didn't just jump out of the gate. The legendary Maxwell Perkins rejected the manuscript and into the trunk it went. Burnett's father, who had read the pages and liked the book, told his son that he was 27 years old and had been wasting his life bent over his typewriter. He was no longer young, it was time for him to get wise. He gave him a job in the hotel business, where the elder Burnett had been taking over the running of foreclosed hotels.

Burnett initially went along but he said he hated this more than the statistician job back in Ohio. He said he felt like he wanted to "walk into Lake Michigan" until his "hat floats."

Before he allowed himself to get that wet, he took *Little Caesar* out of the trunk, read it again, and liked it more than before. He sent it off to The Dial Press and that's when it became an almost instant smash. Burnett had arrived, though he still had some doubts to overcome:

> …I was afraid I was giving birth to a monster. But then a consoling thought came to me—out of the blue or the subconscious, as you prefer—my leading figure, Rico Bandello, killer and gang leader, was no monster at all, but merely a little Napoleon, a little Caesar.

Little Caesar was clearly Burnett's novelized take on the legendary figure that was Al Capone. After the breakout success of the book, Hollywood came calling, and they came strong. They wanted Burnett to work on screenplays but he didn't feel he knew what he was doing. He gave them what he thought was a huge figure, assuming they'd laugh and leave him alone. Instead they hired him at a thousand dollars a week and his boss later joked at this, saying he would have paid twenty-five hundred a week to get Burnett on board.

One of the first films he worked on was the classic 1932 Howard Hawks movie *Scarface*, starring Paul Muni. This was even more blatantly inspired by Capone and came from a short story by Burnett. In the same way *Little Caesar* was a revelation to mob literature, *Scarface* continued what had begun with the film *Little* Caesar: they created the modern gangster movie, offering us glimpses on the inside life of this sort of mobster.

Burnett was one of five classic crime novelists that had an enormous effect on the film noir movies of the forties. There was Dashiell Hammett, whose *Red Harvest* was published the same year as *Little Caesar*; Raymond Chandler, who also served time as a Hollywood screenwriter, perhaps most famously on *The Blue Dahlia*; James M. Cain, whose source work for movies like *The Postman Always Rings Twice* and *Double Indemnity* fit the form perfectly; Cornell Woolrich, father of psychological suspense, whose novels and stories have been filmed perhaps more times than anyone else's work in the genre; and Burnett, who ended up actually writing more movies than he'd penned novels.

Burnett had credits on John Ford's *The Whole Town's Talking*, 1935; Raoul Walsh's *High Sierra*, 1941 (from his own book), in collaboration with John Huston; Frank Tuttle's *This Gun for Hire*, 1942 (from the great Graham Greene novel); John Farrow's *Wake Island*, 1942, which earned him an Oscar nomination; and John Sturges's *The Great Escape*, 1963, sharing a credit with *Shogun* author James Clavell, and which earned him another Oscar nomination.

He also wrote the screenplay for John Huston's *The Asphalt Jungle*, 1950, from another of Burnett's "big three" of novels: *Little Caesar, High Sierra* (starring Humphrey Bogart in the movie version), and *The Asphalt Jungle*. None of these books are mysteries; they're crime novels, powerful, accurate examinations of criminals in their own environments. Tightly written with a terse, close style, careful attention is paid to the observed reality of modern urban society, giving the books—and the movies that stemmed from them—a distinct cinematic urgency.

Early on Burnett's works called for comparisons to Hemingway but Burnett himself said he was "but little influenced by him." Instead, he was affected mostly by European writers whom he read in translation. There was Prosper Mérimée, Gustave Flaubert and Guy de Maupassant from France; there was also Pio Baroja from Spain and Giovanni Verga from Italy. Former *Time* magazine editor T. S. Matthews said that Burnett's style spoke of his "mature and keen technique" and said that he "gives the impression of never interfering—either with us or his characters."

Along with *The Asphalt Jungle* in 1949, *Little Men, Big World* (1952) and *Vanity Row* (1952) came to be known as Burnett's "urban trilogy." The three books share minor overlapping points—they take place in the same city, one mentions the police commissioner from the previous book, the same tailor makes suits for hoods and cops alike—but the real key to these books is seeing the themes Burnett uses. They don't need to be read as a series, or even in order. Each one shows a different facet of crime and the reason for its ultimate downfall, related by the strengths but ultimately the weaknesses of the criminals involved. Hoods are people, Burnett shows us, complex and plagued with the same differences in personalities, the same sins and vices, as everyone else.

Years later, Donald E. Westlake would create his Parker series, about a man who worked with "professional" crews to put together capers that would set each of the members up for a period of time. In every book something would go wrong and it was up to Parker to make things right, at least for Parker. These books are very oriented toward a central character whereas Burnett's books are very much ensemble productions. Lionel White, another "caper novel" specialist, wrote similar plots to *The Asphalt Jungle* but the emphasis was more on the suspense generated by the crime itself, not on the tension taking place among the principals and the individual flavors of their vices as well as the crime.

In *Asphalt Jungle,* along with Riemenschnieder, we have three people working with him on the actual heist, a safe cracker, a driver, and an enforcer. There's a crooked lawyer bankrolling the operation in advance of getting the merchandise to a fence, a bookie, and a cast of cops that are intent on finding Riemenschnieder and preventing whatever it is they feel he must be planning.

Every participant has a strength, every participant has a weakness. In the end, one by one, it's these weaknesses that take them all down. The wealthy lawyer who is supposedly fronting the operation has an eye for young, beautiful and expensive ladies. He's broke, only no one knows that, so when Riemenschneider approaches him, he sees a double-cross as an opportunity to get out from under.

Riemenscheider himself has an unhealthy obsession with young ladies, and in the end, when he could have finally eluded the police net that was strangling the city, his inability to break away from flirting with a young woman at a diner leads to his arrest and the ultimate undoing of the biggest heist the city had ever seen.

Burnett's showing us these characters, especially Dix Handley, the enforcer, indicates not only how each crook is different but also shows us how each of them sees life. His writing is never flashy and, as always, Burnett gives us this kind of insight into each of his characters:

> Emmerich and Craven both burst out laughing. What a character, this Farbstein! He could go on like that for hours and never repeat himself. And yet there was something sad about him, too, as if long ago he'd discovered the limits of cleverness, but, having no other approach, persisted in it, like a man butting his head against a stone wall. His sharp tongue had earned him many enemies; and his brilliance, many ill-wishers. His lack of success, however, when so much had been expected of him, lost him no friends. Those he had, swore by him. Emmerich was one of them.

The book is written in clear pieces, which must have made it easy for filmmakers to see the possibilities of a filmed version. This came out in 1950, directed by John Huston, and starred Sterling Hayden as the muscle, James Whitmore as the driver, and even a young Marilyn Monroe as the lawyer's girlfriend. This was a small part for her but she impressed the studios and it led to a new contract for her, helping to ignite her foundering Hollywood career.

The book is a staple of the film noir world but where the book reads more like a human tragedy, the movie comes off more as a "crime doesn't pay" morality tale. The strength of the book is actually the weakness of the movie. In print, there is no single, strong character guiding the story. The ensemble characters, each with their own motives but working toward a common goal, fall like dominoes as a single breakdown leads to the gradual unraveling of what could have been a perfect plan. Human foibles take down what should have worked. The movie version seems to tell us that no matter how perfect the scheme, its criminal nature doomed it from the start. Law may not always beats crime, but people just might.

Even though the stories in both book and film are the same, this is why it works better in print. Riemenschneider is often at the center of the novel's plot, but he doesn't work as well as the center of the movie. The ensemble nature of the book is much stronger than the centralized movie version. The fact that Hayden received top billing for being only one of the robbers, and perhaps the least important to the crime, seems odd because the movie is no more about his character than it is about four or five others.

Perhaps a more entertaining but less true film version of the book is *The Badlanders* from 1958. This movie stars Alan Ladd and Ernest Borgnine and was made as a western, again with a strong lead character as opposed to a more balanced ensemble cast. It isn't noirish at all, and the motivation for Ladd's character has more to do with him having been wronged in the past as opposed to having an inherently criminal disposition. He chose his path not because he was a career criminal but because he was righting a perceived wrong, what the character likes to call "poetic justice."

The book was filmed in a similar loose fashion twice more, with 1963's *Cairo* starring George Sanders going after the jewels of Tutankhamen, and 1972's *Cool Breeze*, a blaxploitation movie about robbing a bank in Los Angeles.

In the second book of the trilogy, *Little Men, Big World,* we're back in the same city as *Jungle* and the old police commissioner has moved on, leaving behind the great stickler Commissioner Hardy. We also have newspaperman Ben Reisman who has now made the big time as a columnist but who can't quite leave his investigative reporting instincts behind.

Burnett gives us a bookmaking operation under control by the mysterious and mostly anonymous Mover, as administered by his underling, Orval Smith Wanty, known as Arky (he's off the farm from Arkansas). Reisman's chance hearing of the name "de Ark" sets him on the trail of this unknown bigwig, though he's not quite sure what to do about it. Meanwhile, organized crime from out of town tries to take a stake while Arky and his boss have to fend them off. In the end, justice—absolute justice—is levied by the force of will and conviction of a single man.

The Asphalt Jungle was about a singular crime that fails due to a bad piece of luck and the individual faults and weaknesses of the individuals involved. *Little Men* is about a crime ring that fails due to a piece of bad luck and the notion that stubbornly single-minded men like Reisman (as a reporter) and Hardy (as an idealist) can, admittedly temporarily, clamp down on what they think is wrong. Where *Asphalt Jungle* is an ensemble story, *Little Men* focuses much more on the viewpoint of Arky, similar to how *Little Caesar* illustrated the life of Rico Bandello.

Little Men, Big World was televised as an episode—written by Burnett—in 1952 of the *Studio One in Hollywood* program as "Little Man, Big World."

"Commonwealth Street was short and peculiar. It ran for only five blocks, from the west bank of the river to a deadend one block beyond Blackhawk Boulevard. Near the river, Commonwealth was filled with commission houses, fish markets, and cheap saloons; then, as it traveled westward, came pawnshops and employment offices with blowsy bulletins; then two and three storey brick rooming-houses, with dim lights and crooked blinds, stretched almost to Blackhawk, where they were overshadowed and blotted out by the forty-storey Commonwealth Building. Beyond Blackhawk Boulevard and on to the deadend, Commonwealth really blossomed, and was referred to as Vanity Row.

Vanity Row ran for one block. In this block were three exclusive clubs—Cipriano's, the Gold Eagle, and Merlin's; there was also one of the finest and most expensive restaurants in the state—Weber's; and there were two beauty parlors where, as Wesson said, you were looked out unless you were a debutante or dowager from Riverview, or a mink-bearing Vanity Row whore. Glassman's, the Tiffany's of the Midwest, was at the corner of Blackhawk and Vanity Row. On the other corner was a Cadillac sales-room.

At night, the stylized neons of the Row glittered like expensive jewelry: rubies, emeralds, star-sapphires, diamonds. Just a glance at the façades kept most yokels out. If not, the headwaiters, and other major domos, soon had them in the street, suffering from feelings of awe and humiliation."

This is Burnett's *Vanity Row*, right from the book. A different sort of human condition is played out against the backdrop of the baser ones of society at large. We have love vs. institution, and the institution supplies the job for the torn protagonist. The system may be crooked, but up to now it has provided for the investigator at the center of this story.

Of the three books in the "urban trilogy," this one is the most human. Amidst the greed and depravity of serious crime we find the unexpected emotion of love, not fully explained perhaps, but when is that true of love, really? This is the book that doesn't end in outright disaster for the protagonist; in the end he is saved by something he doesn't understand, despite the crime, despite the bucking of the establishment that provides his livelihood, despite the way he's always lived his life. This is new. This is the pressure. This is the city.

And is he really saved? We'll never really know.

Vanity Row is the only book of the trilogy not to feature outright criminals as the main characters, although readers get the feeling that according to Burnett, anyone not an over-the-top personality like Commissioner Hardy from *Little Men, Big World* is corrupted to some degree. This was probably especially true for urban dwellers during the Prohibition era.

This book isn't so much about people trying to get away with a crime, but rather about people trying to solve a crime. They need to do it their way, not only so it works in their best interests but more importantly in the best interests of their bosses, too. The goals of the players only intersect and touch off each other in differing places, so the reader is kept off balance, and again, Burnett's depiction of a human nature at war with itself is what provides much of the drama and tension. A crime doesn't fail because of a criminal's personal issues, a crime is solved despite someone else's. Burnett puts the crooked shoe on the other foot.

Burnett held a mirror to the post-Capone mob era in Chicago and showed how the rural fellow, the immigrants, drifted to the big city to work their crimes before the big boys from back east took over. There were no farms among the burgeoning skyscrapers, and if you wanted out of the dirt, you bought into the grime—and crime—of the city.

Readers begin to root for the bad guys in some of Burnett's work. You empathize with the characters without admiring them. *Jungle's* Louis has a wife and kids... he's real, not a cartoon character stick-up man. You root because the capers are puzzles the characters are trying to solve and the reader, too, naturally tries to solve the puzzles. It's the natural instinct or curse of the crime fiction reader.

This may be Burnett's greatest gift as a storyteller. He tells complex stories peopled with even more complicated characters. Rarely, if ever, is anyone all good or all bad. Burnett makes them real, and that makes them compelling.

In an interview with David Laurence Wilson, Burnett had this to say about his writing:

WRB: I deal with crime but I don't deal with the freaky, crazy crime, like we have today. I was only interested in crime as a social phenomenon, as a left-handed form of normal endeavor. They're just businessmen who don't abide by the rules.

DLW: But they don't win.

WRB: No, they can't really win. Criminals can't win if authority is any good at all. The only way they can win is Number One—if authority is weak; Number Two—if it's corrupt. If it's neither they haven't got a chance. But that's the problem.

This is what Burnett gives us in these three books: we get his number one option, we get his number two option, we get variations of them both. Crime isn't any simpler for the criminals than it is for the people trying to stop them. If there's a lesson to take from Burnett's trilogy, this would be it. And if we don't want one, it serves as great background for wonderfully real characters placed in the dirty milieu of a broken city in a corrupt time. This is Burnett's world, the one he lived in once he moved to Chicago, and the words he gave us paint the characters that are among the most poignant and unforgettable in crime fiction.

—January, 2015
Littleton, NH

Sources:
Burnett, W.R., introduction to reprint of *Little Caesar*, The Dial Press, 1958
Interview with W.R. Burnett by David Laurence Wilson, 1981
Twentieth Century Authors: A Biographical Dictionary of Modern Literature, ed. by Stanley J. Kunitz and Howard Haycraft, The H. W. Wilson Company, 1942

Little Men, Big World
by W. R. Burnett

For Whitney Again
And for the Same Reason

1

It was a gray day. Dark rain-clouds moved slowly in from the west, grazing the tops of the tall buildings downtown. The huge, sprawling Midwestern city by the river looked dirty, bleak, and ugly under a steady drizzle. When from time to time the drizzle stopped for a moment, bubbles of moisture, streaked with soot, danced in the heavy damp air. Tugs moaned on the river.

Ben Reisman was bored, depressed, at loose ends. Today he'd really hit bottom. Why else would he be hanging around the old 17th Ward, trying to revive the past? Twenty years ago he'd been a police reporter and this had been his beat. Now he was the fair-haired boy of the *Journal*, the envy of the other newspapermen. His new column, "Day In, Day Out," was catching on, and one by one other Midwestern papers were picking it up, even in Chicago. He was a big man in the city—a success!

Lately he'd been able to move into a nice house in a nice suburb and his wife, Sarah, noted for jumping the gun, was already talking about sending the oldest girl to private school. Private school, yet! Six months ago, Sarah had been hanging the Monday wash out on the fire-escape to dry.

Sudden success, some people said. Sudden success, after twenty-five years? And was this success? How about the plays he'd intended to write, the novels? Reisman groaned and stared into his glass of Vichy water. The others were drinking whisky. He, too, liked whisky, and some nights he even got drunk. But the doc told him it would kill him and sometimes he was afraid. Why did he have to have ulcers? Young Downy did not have ulcers. Young Downy had pink cheeks and optimism. Not much in the way of brains. But what are brains? A liability.

Reisman and the police reporters from the Pier 7 Station House sat staring out the bar window, watching the rain fall on the bricks and asphalt of the filthiest slum in the whole city, even worse than Paxton Square.

The others seemed depressed, too, and looked to Reisman for some entertainment. What was he doing hanging around the 17th Ward, anyway? That stuff about nostalgia he'd been talking in the station house was strictly the bunk. A shrewd one, Ben Reisman. Probably knew where it was buried. A guy's gotta have an angle or he don't get no place. Be funny, Reisman, they wanted to say. For Christ's sake, be funny!

What kind of a life was this? Life at its worst, of course—life in the 17th Ward. Life full of rape, drunkenness, thievery, slugging, unwanted babies in drains, old drunks dead in the alley, young punkeroos trying to be tough—life at its worst all right, but not even interesting. Just dull, dull, plain dull.

"Who was that woman I seen you with the other night, Reisman?" asked Joe

Pavlik, hopefully.

"That wasn't no woman," said Reisman with a sigh, "that was the managing editor."

There were wan smiles. Reisman was not himself today. Even Downy, his boy Friday, was looking at him critically.

They turned and watched the rain. It was making streaks on the sooty buildings. Blackish brooks ran in all the gutters.

"April is the cruelest month, breeding..." Reisman began, but somebody interrupted him.

"It's May!"

Reisman glanced at the interrupter with distaste. "Once upon a time," he said, "there was a fellow named T. S. Eliot. He was a real slugger. He finally got into a World Series game as a pinch-hitter but struck out with the bases full. Eliot Agonistes."

Only Downy beamed. The rest merely stared, not understanding the allusion. Was this supposed to be funny? What was it—double talk? Reisman was getting goddamned superior since Mush Head broke down and let him have his say in a daily two-column spread. Christ knows he'd been around long enough. Should be managing editor by now with all his brains. Or *was* it brains? Wasn't it just a kind of superficial cleverness?

Reisman began to speak again and they all listened. Their quick attention warmed him a little and he ordered a bourbon and water, making the mental note: This, I'll be sorry for!

"...It's not only the rain," he said, "and the sad and dirty city that lowers my blood pressure and makes me a prey to the hoo-hoos. This morning I came down to breakfast feeling pretty good, for *me*—which wouldn't be good for *you*, Downy—my egg was cooked right for a change—it didn't drip goo or I didn't have to strip it out of the shell with a reamer—the coffee was adequate—I always like an adequate brown coffee—and the toast had been well scraped by my oldest daughter—almost all the charcoal was off of it...."

There was soft laughter and Joe Pavlik raised his eyebrows at the others as if to say: You see?

"... All was right with the world. Okay, it was raining. I got rubbers. I got an umbrella. I even got a closed car. My wife looked like hell across the table, but I'm no Pinza, myself, so...? A good world. Then I pick up my morning paper. Japanese Communists marching on Tokio. Okay. Communists are always marching on something. A new secret weapon—it makes the atom bomb look like a firecracker. This time you don't have to worry about radioactivity. They won't even find one of your pants buttons. I pass on, scared. So? A woman's body found in a wicker basket, minus the head. My egg don't taste so good now. Child abandoned in a stolen car in a vacant lot: child dies. Four killed in a traffic accident. I almost drop the paper. I know one of the guys. Like me he's got three kids and damn little insurance. I turn the page. Noted businessman drops dead. Apparently in perfect health. His age? Forty-two. My age? Forty-six. And I ain't in perfect health—far from it. So what do I do now?"

"You turn to the sports page," said Joe Pavlik.

"No," said Reisman, "first I argue with my wife about reading the paper at the breakfast table. To shut her up, I give her the woman's section so she can read about all the coming-out parties in Riverview and what Old Family is being joined in indissoluble bonds to what other Old Family. A thing of deep interest to the Old Family of the Reismans.... Then I turn to the sports page—man's refuge in an evil world: and what do I see? Dames. Nothing but dames. The famous ice skater, little Miss Frozen Pants—caught by the camera in a position she didn't learn in finishing school. Famous girl bowler in the tightest pair of slacks I ever saw, bending over, of course. A bevy of swim cuties in French bathing-suits. This is the *sports page?* But where is Ted Williams? I turn to the horse-racing news. Ah—a picture of Citation, my favorite horse. But I can't see him. Why? Miss Racetrack of 1950 has got such a broad keister she blots him out...."

Joe Pavlik was rocking in his seat now. Reisman broke off and stared suspiciously down at his bourbon and water, then he drank it fearfully, and waited. Was that a premonitory quiver of the pain to come he felt running along the wall of his stomach? But no: probably only gas. He felt better at once, ordered another bourbon and water.

There was a silence. Everybody looked more cheerful now, except Reisman. And it was an act with him, they all were sure: that long, sallow face—the unsmiling funnyman—the Pagliacci of the press room, according to Red Seaver.

Reisman sighed and looked out at the rain. Down at the end of the street he could see the worn brick buildings abutting on what used to be called Death Corners. "In the twenties," he said, "when I was working this beat we used to have some real excitement. The bootleggers used to shoot each other around here just to see each other fall. This street was like a penny-arcade shooting-gallery. I used to duck by instinct when I got off the streetcar to go to the station house. A motorman got clipped by a stray bullet right in front of this bar. It was a speak then. Don't anything ever happen?"

"You're wasting your time here," said Joe Pavlik. "No copy—except the juvenile delinquents. Them young girls—brother! Run for your life. They try to peddle it in broad daylight—and all of fourteen."

"Look at the circles under Joe's eyes," said somebody.

"I could name names," said Joe indignantly, "but the old Riverview name of Pavlik would not be among them."

"They shifted the guy from the *Examiner* on account of it," said Downy.

"And you better watch it yourself, Downy," said Joe. "I saw you talking to that big kid with the bushy red hair."

"She asked me for a cigarette, goddamn it!" shouted Downy with unnecessary heat. "Is it a crime to give a girl a cigarette?"

"If she's a minor—yes."

"Show me that law."

"Right here in my pocket," said Pavlik. Then he turned to the waiter. "Buster, would you mind giving me a little whisky with my water next time?"

The waiter called Joe something under his breath and shuffled to the bar.

Reisman rose, leaving almost half of his second drink. A faint pain was nagging at his stomach. "If I only had less brains and more strength of character!" he murmured sadly.

"Don't give up so easy, Ben," said Joe. "Sit down. Something may happen yet. Brannigan on the desk always calls us."

"I'm not looking for anything," said Ben. "That is, anything Brannigan could call you about. Gentlemen, I was merely looking for my youth. You'll all understand about things like that later. For Downy—twenty years later."

"Okay, pappy," said Joe. "Come back again in a decade. We don't get many celebrities around here—and it brightens the place."

Downy rose to accompany Reisman—at least to his car—the obsequious disciple. But Joe snapped his fingers at a sudden thought.

"Say," he called, "you get around, Ben. You're not buried like we are. Hear anything about George Cline moving back in?"

Reisman showed a flash, then lowered his eyes. He remembered Cline well. A big boy ten years ago. But they'd run him out. At least that was the story. Leon Sollas, the new boss of the vices and rackets, had run big George out. George had gone west and prospered. Las Vegas. Reno. Some place like that, if there *were* any other places like that!

"No," said Reisman. "Haven't heard a thing."

"We only hear rumors," said Downy, defensively, afraid Reisman might be sore at him for not mentioning such things.

But Reisman ignored him. "I don't know, Joe. Such stories are always floating around. Leon's been running the thing for ten years. Last time I saw him at the fights he looked mighty smug and healthy."

"Leon's a front and you know it," said Joe. "The boys in the background call the turn and pull the strings. Leon merely takes the rap and gets all the unfavorable publicity. Public Enemy Number One. That crap."

"You know maybe who the boys in the background are?" asked Reisman ironically.

"If I did I'd be the biggest man on Newspaper Row. But the rumor is, things been rocky with the boys lately and there have been complaints that the set-up can't deliver any more."

"I wouldn't know," said Reisman. "I am now merely a columnist."

In spite of what he said, however, Reisman felt a sudden quickening, a sudden interest in life. His stomach crawled slightly, as in the old days, and this time he was sure it was neither gas nor his tried and true friend and companion, the ulcer; it was instinct warning him, some kind of sixth sense that had made him a top reporter on the crime beat.

Things were at sixes and sevens in the city. He knew that. There were rumors and rumbles—had been since old Commissioner Hardy, elected to Congress, had left for Washington and had been replaced by his friend and protégé Thomas Stark, who was zealous and able but not quite another Hardy. Bookies had been prosecuted and heavily fined—something unheard of in the old days. A famous escort bureau—the biggest call service in the city—had been put out of business, and Mrs. Lansing, the most famous madam of all, was now serving a term in the Winona Women's Prison. But Reisman had ignored all this. Stark's intentions were of the best, but you can't sop up the ocean with a sponge.

Sollas was the boss—at least, he was considered to be the boss, and he'd got credit for running George Cline out of town. If Cline tried to move back in, there'd be real trouble. Or would there? The crime climate had changed greatly since the wild and lunatic twenties. The big hoods were now businessmen and owned hotels and summer resorts and distilleries. They all wanted to be "gentlemen," and winced away from the word "crime." All on the legit, now. Of course, occasionally somebody got the blast put on him—but only as a last resort, strictly as a last resort.

"Well," said Reisman, "if George wants to move back he and Leon will probably kiss and make up. Plenty for all is the new motto, more or less, wouldn't you say, Joe?"

"I guess so," said Joe. "The sale of kid gloves has gone up like hell the last twenty years. You don't find guys in alleys with pennies in their hands any more. Ah me. I was born too late. It must have been lovely in those days."

"It was just ducky," said Reisman, then he turned and went out, followed by Downy.

"He was nosing around all right," said Joe to the others. "Looking for his youth, eh? Him only forty-six and going like a house on fire."

"What do you mean, *only* forty-six?" demanded a chubby-faced kid reporter. "My old man's just forty-seven."

"You must have been one of his earliest mistakes," said Joe.

Young Downy opened the car door for Reisman. "Ben," he said, "can I ask a favor?"

"Sure," said Reisman, glancing in mild surprise at the handsome youth.

"Couldn't you put a bug in the Old Man's ear for me? I hate this place. It makes me sick at my stomach. I have nightmares."

"You kidding?"

"No, Ben. I'm serious."

"I thought you were going to be a writer. This is life in the raw. Great copy."

"It's not for me. I can't stand all this dirt and filth—every kind. And these crazy young kids, and these poor beat-up old winos, men and women. I'm getting the jumps. Is this what life is?"

"Oh! A reformer!"

Downy hesitated, got hold of himself. "Well, I just thought you might...."

"I will, kid, if that's what you want. But don't get sore if they send you out to cover flower shows and ping-pong tournaments."

"Thanks, Ben."

"And keep your ears open about these rumors. You know?"

"Oh, sure, Ben, sure," said Downy, flushing slightly, embarrassed, feeling derelict in his duty toward his idol.

Reisman still felt quickened, unusually alive, like a hound on the scent. Actually it was none of his goddamned business. He had his column now and that was a full-time job, a heart-breaker. They kept telling him he was too conscientious about it. But how could you be too conscientious about your bread and butter with three growing girls to feed and a wife to clothe and appease? Mush Head, the editor, had said to him: "Jesus, Ben, you don't have to sparkle every day—just now and then. It gets monotonous. Anyway, you know as well as I do that the dullest columns get the most readers and the most dough in the end. Get your sights down. You're not writing for *The New Yorker*." "How do you go about being dull?" Reisman asked. "Read the editorials," said Mush Head, with a dirty laugh.

No, it was none of his business. But he couldn't let it go—for two reasons. One, his old training: it nagged at him. Two, he was in love with Commissioner Stark—that's what Sarah said. Sarah resented his interest even in a man.

Yes, in a way, Reisman was in love with the new Commissioner. He admired him and felt sorry for him. He was in a spot, subbing for Hardy, and besides, he was like the Dutch boy trying to stop the dike with his finger. But in the case of the Commissioner, the dike had a thousand holes in it, and he only had ten fingers.

Reisman decided to look up an old source of information: Bat Riggio, an ex-pug with a broken nose, eyebrows bulged out with scar tissue, and a tin ear. He had always looked punch-drunk but wasn't—far from it. Reisman hadn't seen him for about a year and then he'd run into him at the fights by accident. He'd looked prosperous, said he was managing a couple of pretty good boys.

He found him in a stinking gymnasium, smoking a big black cigar and grimacing in disgust at the antics of a couple of sad-looking palookas who were belting each other around with the big gloves.

Bat was pathetically glad to see Reisman. They went into his little office and sat smoking. Riggio was pushing fifty and liked to talk about the past, when things were really "hot," as he put it. They talked about the past for quite a while. Occasionally the phone rang and Bat grunted into it: "Okay. Don't bodder me." He grew more mellow and relaxed as the time passed and finally Reisman observed out of nowhere:

"I hear George Cline's coming back in."

His defenses down, Bat laughed and grunted: "Nobody's coming in. De Ark's too tough."

Before Reisman could say another word, Riggio came to himself with a start. He reddened, and a look of fear showed for a moment on his beat-up, subhuman face.

He got to his feet. "I didn't say nuttin, Reisman. You woimed it outta me."

"Relax. Relax. It's only a rumor. None of my business anyway. Just trying to make conversation."

"You're a liar, Reisman. Here I am doing great, getting hot; now you come messing me up wid your sweet talking, you louse." He said this sadly, his chin trembling.

"Off the record. Off the record. What do you think?" said Reisman. "Anyway, the hell with it. I'm a columnist. I don't print police news."

"You'd print de crucifixion wid all de nails in it, you louse. You tink I don't know? I didn't say nuttin. You go home now, Reisman."

Reisman went back down the dirty stairs, walking on air. *De Ark!* What the hell did the old pug mean? Riggio was no cream-puff and had always managed to look after himself in a racket as tough as they came. But he'd showed fear—real fear.

"April is the cruelest month, breeding..." Reisman mused, as he walked slowly across the littered pavement toward his car. It was still raining, and a damp wind blew up the street, pasting a torn sheet of newspaper against his leg. He kicked and kicked, but couldn't get rid of it. Unlocking his car, he went on: "... breeding Lilacs out of the dead land, mixing Memory and desire, stirring Dull roots with spring rain...."

He drove off down Wharf Street. Ahead of him he could see the ugly vistas of Paxton Square, blurred and misty in the spring rain. The tall clock-tower was little more than a dark penciling on the gray sky.

"*De Ark*," he said aloud, trying it over and over. Could he have misunderstood Riggio's grunted jargon? If so, it was too bad. The next time, Riggio would run from him.

Halfway through a page on his typewriter, Reisman suddenly remembered his one-time friend, Harry Radabaugh. They'd got into a thing over an item that had somehow managed to get itself printed in the *Journal*, a very hot item, and Harry had blamed Reisman. Harry was a tough boy and took a poke at Reisman, but big Red Seaver had clipped Harry from behind, knocking him down, saying at the same time: "Hitting a reporter, eh? That's arson!"

Nobody argued with Red, especially after he'd had a few drinks; not even Harry Radabaugh, who had a bad record on the force for using his gun and billy too freely. In fact, Herman Frick, the Chief of Police, had finally kicked him out of the Police Department, during the big clean-up last summer when Commissioner Stark demanded action so loudly that even the lethargic Frick was forced to do something, *anything*, to make a showing. Harry was one of many who had got the gate. He was now a special investigator for the district attorney's office, and he got around and the hoods liked him because he never fingered anybody big, only the small ones, principally the out-of-towners who drifted in, looking for pickings.

"Too bad we are not on visiting terms any longer," mused Reisman. "Too bad I am always making social blunders and gaucheries and alienating people."

Nevertheless, after a moment's thought, he picked up the phone and called Harry. Things had changed now perhaps. Reisman was no longer a loose-footed reporter—nothing, in short. He was a columnist. Which was like being a god to some people. They'd lick your boots just to see their names in a widely read column. Did I say boots?

Yes, things had changed. Harry was very friendly on the phone. It was Ben, old boy!

"I'm just sitting here getting drunk," said Harry. "Got that ulcer tamed yet? A fellow gave me a case of Johnny Walker Black Label this afternoon and I'm working on it. I want to drink it up before some of my bum friends find out about it. But you're special—even if I did strike you in anger once." Harry laughed hollowly. "I was younger then."

Reisman grimaced to himself. He could just see some magnanimous fellow giving Harry a case of Johnny Walker! Harry had muscled it some way—a great little muscle artist, not above blackmail, or so Reisman had heard.

"I'm a bourbon man, myself," said Reisman. "And I ain't tamed the ulcer. It's practically tamed me. But I might drop over. Things are dull. Got any ideas—I mean for my column?"

"Do I get my name mentioned, yuk, yuk?" cried Harry, sounding like some jerk trying to be the life of the party.

"Could be," said Reisman. "It would be easier if I was running a Love Life column, though. Like what broad you're now sleeping with. Your love life used to be pretty extensive, if my memory does not fail me and it seldom does—except when Sarah asks me to bring something home for supper."

"I just drink now, and think about it. Saves me a lot of trouble. You coming over?"

"Yeah. Be right there."

Reisman tiptoed out of his workroom. The house was quiet, the kids and Sarah asleep. Maybe he could slip out once—just once—without questions or yammering. He put on his hat and raincoat and did not take time to find his rubbers and his umbrella though it was pouring outside. *"Il pleut doucement sur la ville,"* said Reisman as he opened the door inch by inch. "Ah, Verlaine! What a stinking bum you were!"

"Ben!" cried Sarah. "Where are you going in that rain?"

The bedroom door was open about a foot. She was glaring at him. She looked kind of cute in that pale-blue crepe de Chine nightgown. Of course, the light was bad!

"I knew we should have bought a two-story house. Then you'd be upstairs."

"Shut up. Don't try to be funny. I'd still hear you."

"Who's being funny?"

"Where you going? You come back here. You're a columnist now. You don't have to go running around at all hours of the night."

"I just got a hot lead on a good story. Relax, Sarah. I'll come back to your arms safe and sound."

"And what good would that do *me*?"

"Please, Madam Reisman."

Sarah began to laugh. Reisman went back and kissed her. "At least," he said, "you got a pretty good idea I ain't going out looking for nooky."

"Such vulgar talk. Maybe you should put it in your column and not use it around the house."

"That's what Mush Head keeps telling me at the office. I'll be back shortly."

"Bring me some ice cream."

"You'll be asleep."

"I'll wake up any time for ice cream."

"How about the kids?"

"Bring plenty. Couple quarts, anyway. They're up listening now." She raised her voice. "Aren't you, kids?"

She was answered by faint giggles. Reisman flinched slightly.

"So you see," said Sarah, "you better stop that vulgar talk."

Harry's apartment was on a slope just off Italian Hill. Reisman had lived in the vicinity for years, in fact, he'd just moved to the suburbs recently: Lakeside Village, the place to raise your family; all the most modern conveniences, lawns, shrubbery, even a lake where you can take the family boating and drown Junior some Sunday morning when he wakes you up at six a.m. Reisman had missed the noises of the city at first. But now he never gave them a thought. One place was like another. Changing places meant nothing at all, though some people thought it did. No matter where you went you always took the same old burden with you—yourself: the same fears and worries and responsibilities. You could not run out from under them, shake them off, or pass them to a friend. Even the lake, with real water, and boats and little piers, helped but slightly.

Harry's eyes were bloodshot. He was a big, tough-looking fellow with curly dark hair. He had a hard chin and big shoulders but there was something wrong with his mouth—something flabby and unformed, something babyish.

He didn't exactly fawn on Reisman, but he came close. Reisman begged off on the drinking, though he felt that he needed a drink, and they both sat down and talked about things in general. Both were very much interested in baseball and they raked the local team over the coals and plaintively wondered when the team was going to get a decent manager and some ball players.

"What humpty-dumpties!" said Harry, shaking his head. "This big hitter they got—I saw him bust one up against the fence in the far right corner and only get a single. He runs like he's got a man on his back."

They shook their heads over this for some time, then Reisman gradually led the conversation around to what was going on along the Front. "I saw Leon at the fights the other night," he said. "Front row as usual. Where does he get those ankle-length polo coats he wears?"

"Sam Brod, the tailor, makes 'em for him. Two-five-oh! Some coats," said Harry. "They went out with the bustle, didn't they?"

"On him they look good. He was smiling from ear to ear."

"Why not?"

"Why?"

Harry tapped his chin and studied Reisman for some time. "Well," he said at last, "he figures to smile a little at the fights. The Bat dug him up a pretty good boy. A middleweight. The kid might go some place. And you know Leon. A frustrated fighter. He's been trying to find a champ for fifteen years. I don't say he has. But the Bat's pretty high on the boy, and he's no clunk when it comes to fighters. You know Riggio?"

"Oh, sure," said Reisman.

"Well, that's why he's always smiling at the Arena. Shouldn't he smile?"

"I'm asking you."

"Look, Ben. This ain't column stuff. This is why guys leave town—by request."

"You're an officer of the law, my boy."

Harry laughed sneeringly. "And you're a guy who spreads things for money that shouldn't be spread. Remember?"

"That wasn't me, Harry—as I tried to tell you." There was a brief pause, then Reisman added: "But it might have been."

"Well, Christ—at least you're honest, Ben. Look. Just write your column. Don't play detective. What for?"

"Curiosity. It's nothing I can print. You know that. But there are rumors flying all over the place. Who's *Ark*?" he asked suddenly.

Harry dropped his cigarette on the carpet and, stooping over, took his time about picking it up, keeping his eyes lowered. Reisman felt pretty sure that he might as well go buy the ice cream and hit for home. Harry seemed to know who "Ark" was all right, but he wasn't telling.

Harry composed himself, threw the cigarette in the ash tray, and lit another one.

"Ever hear of anybody called Ark?" Reisman persisted, just for the fun of it.

After a moment, his face blank, Harry shook his head slowly. "Nope. Don't believe I ever did. What kind of a name is that?"

"As in Noah's, I guess. Or maybe I heard wrong. Sometimes I think my hearing's not so good—slipping."

"It used to be good enough, Christ knows," said Harry. "The boys all called you rabbit-ears."

"Well," said Reisman, "since you don't seem to know as much as the guys kicking the rumors around I might as well go back to my little nest. It's been so nice."

"What rumors?"

"About George Cline."

Harry grimaced. "A dead one, that's for sure, Ben. I been hearing it for five years."

At the door, Harry hemmed and hawed for a long time; finally he asked, flushing slightly: "Say, Ben, couldn't you put a line in your column about the way I handled the Nansen investigation? I did pretty good. But no publicity, and publicity helps at the office. The boss is a ham."

"Be nicer if I mentioned him, too, wouldn't it?"

"Oh, sure. Sure," said Harry, grudgingly.

Reisman walked to his car in the pelting rain, talking to himself. He still felt excited. He was on the heels of something. But what? One thing for certain: he'd have to stop asking questions. No more questions. It would get around. Everybody would shun him.

He was almost to Lakeside Village before he realized that he'd forgotten to buy the ice cream after all. Cursing quietly, he drove back through the rain toward the blurred lights of the big town. Everything closed in the Village by nine. Like living in No People, Oklahoma.

2

It was June now. People were already hitting north to the Great Lakes for their vacations; the baseball team was back off the road for a long home stand; and a fairy-blue sky was arching over the city, making the hulking, soot-streaked buildings uglier and more conspicuous than they were under the gray skies of winter. Pale sunshine showed in all the city canyons and the lawns were green in the city parks by the river. A stiff breeze whipped the flag on the tall new Post Office Building and swayed the slender pole.

Reisman had reached a dead end. Nothing! Lost in thought, he drove through the heavy traffic of the financial district, turned over at the boulevard, cursing the pedestrians who ran from one traffic island to another like silly geese, and crossed to the western end of the city over the Pulaski Street Bridge.

Paxton Square looked old and tired and dirty in the pale sunshine. The 17th Ward looked even worse. It was a nighttime place, and seemed to shun the day. In the brick tenements and crazily leaning frame boarding-houses many worn crooked shades were still down at three in the afternoon. Just beyond Wharf

Street, and in violent contrast to it, the Front began—the Front with its big gam-
bling-houses, expensive supper-clubs, theaters, and restaurants; its many taxi-
stands, prowl-cars, and doormen in gold braid. But it was a nighttime place too,
and, deserted now, it slept in the sun, waiting for darkness and the unfailing rush
of chumps.

Reisman parked in a side street, and went into Henry's Bar. The boys from
Pier 7 Station House hadn't showed up yet, and the place was deserted except
for a couple of young hoodlums standing at the bar, who eyed Reisman with
suspicion and contempt, noting his baggy navy-blue serge suit, his white shirt
and dark tie, his dark shoes and the old creased and sweated Borsalino he'd won
on a bet from Chuck Morse—former sports editor of the *Journal*—God rest his
soul: he *would* drink gin and drive seventy miles an hour. A light standard met
him head-on one night: finis!

The young hoodlums wore long coats, pegged pants, and drooping keychains.
They were about eighteen. They looked out at the world coldly and arrogantly.
A tough place, chum! But we're tougher.

One of them tossed a remark at Reisman, which he didn't quite catch. But it
sounded like: "... a frigging square!" But the hard-faced, sad-looking bartender said something to him sharply and the kid immediately turned his back
on Reisman, who sat down and ordered a bourbon and water, but made up his
mind he wouldn't drink it; he'd just let it stay in front of him till young Downy
and the rest showed up. They'd be surprised to see him again so soon, surprised
and slightly suspicious perhaps; but he didn't care. He felt restless and at loose
ends, and he had an irrational hunch that if he hung around the Pier 7 district
he might find out something. What? He didn't quite know.

In a moment, Reisman drank his bourbon and water and ordered another one,
groaning to himself. Last night he'd been forced to sleep with the heat-pad on
his stomach. Sleep? Roll and toss! The afternoon before he'd read an article on
cancer in a national magazine. Take steps now. If you get it early enough,
you've got a chance. Symptoms? Everybody had such symptoms—one or two
of them at least, which meant that a million people would be scared white and
half a million would run, not walk, to the nearest doctor.

Fear was a great persuader. You may not know it, brother, but you stink, and
are probably a social pariah as a result. Dig down at once, brother—buy me, but
only me—reject all substitutes. Visit your doctor every six months, also your
dentist or suffer the consequences—lockjaw, tuberculosis and fits! Pay your
taxes or rot in jail. What are you doing about old age, my friend? Have you
thought about it? Do you want to spend the twilight of life in the pogey? Now
our new insurance policy…. What about an Eternal Resting Place for yourself
and family? Don't hesitate! Buy one of our Choice Plots at once while the sup-
ply lasts. It's later than you think.

Reisman began to sing: "Enjoy yourself! Enjoy yourself! It's later than you
think…."

He picked up a tabloid from another table and turned to the sports page. In a few minutes the boys came in whooping, but Downy was not with them. Joe Pavlik stopped and stared at the sight of Reisman.

"Hello, Ben. I wish I had an idea what you're chasing."

"Just my tail, like a bored fox-terrier," said Reisman. "Where's Downy?"

"He's over at Arky's joint."

Reisman knocked over his glass, spilling his drink all over the table.

"You see what I mean?" he said. "Jumpy."

"Yeah," said Joe, eying him suspiciously.

"Downy be here soon?"

"Don't know," said Joe. "He and Babe have taken to betting the beetles—two here, two there: they even had a four-horse parlay going for them yesterday. How stupid can you get? A man's lucky if he can drag one in."

"Parlays are for hoosiers," said somebody in the background.

The hard-faced bartender mopped up Reisman's table without comment. The others sat down and ordered.

Finally Reisman said: "I've got to see Downy and get back. Where will I find him, Joe?"

"Down at the Corners. Remember the old pool hall? That's it. Bookie joint in back. Cigar store in front. Pool tables in between. And get a load of the character in there."

"What character?"

"The Syrian that manages the joint. They call him Zand. He's a killer." Joe and the other boys laughed.

Reisman eyed them steadily. "How do you mean?"

"Sharpest dresser in town. Poiple shoits! He'll moidah ya—ya bum!"

Reisman felt cold, then hot, but tried to keep his face controlled. "I thought you said it was Arthur's joint, or something like that."

"Arky," said Joe wearily. "He owns it. Nice fellow. Country boy, but pretty much wised up now and citified. Must have an 'in' some place. Even the coppers from the station house bet with him. A solid guy!"

"But a small-timer, eh?"

"Oh, sure. Definitely. Small book—nothing. Why?" asked Joe suddenly.

"No reason," said Reisman as if slightly irritated with Joe and his suspicious nature. "Except—Downy. He's a kind of protégé of mine, and I don't want to see him in any trouble. He shouldn't be hitting the books on his salary."

"He's free, white, and twenty-one. But the books won't get him. If anything gets him, it'll be some of these young bums around here—these teen-age chicks. They whistle at him. Literally. I'm not kidding. If he could only sing he'd be the Vic Damone of Pier 7."

"Girls whistling at boys, my, my!" said Reisman as he went out.

"Whistling's nothing in this neck of the woods," said somebody in the background. "I could maybe write a book, with pictures yet!"

There was nobody in the cigar store, only a tired looking blond woman at the counter, but back beyond, through an arch, Reisman could see a crowded poolroom with all the tables going and a flock of young hoodlums sitting in high chairs, looking on. Long horizontal strands of tobacco smoke moved lazily under the hooded lights.

The blond woman looked him over apathetically. "You're a new one, eh?" she said.

"This used to be my beat in the old days, dear," said Reisman, stepping up to buy a cigar. "But that was long before your time."

"Get right, chum. Get right," said the woman. "I don't go for that magoo."

"You look young to me."

"With all that fuzz running loose in the streets? Mister, you need glasses."

Reisman took out his shell-rimmed reading glasses and put them on. "You look even younger with these."

"All right. 'E' for effort. Here's an extra cigar on the house. It's our buggy-whip special; one puff you see stars."

"Two puffs?"

"You drop dead."

Reisman burst out laughing and leaned on the counter. The world was a pretty good place after all when a poor knocked-out broad like this could give you a belly. What the hell kind of a life could she possibly have? Whatever it was, it wasn't funny.

Someone brushed Reisman lightly. He turned and looked at the top of somebody's head. As Reisman himself was far from tall, this was somewhat startling. A little dark-faced, hawk-featured man was staring up at him with sharp black eyes. His jet-black hair was carefully oiled and curled in three symmetrical waves; heavy dark eyebrows went straight across his face. He had on a purple silk shirt, and a white knit tie, and white suspenders, very wide and decorated with gold facing, held up his chartreuse slacks. On his feet were purple and white sport shoes. He looked like an Easter egg.

"You must be Zand," said Reisman.

"Yeah. Heard of me?"

"The boys at the station were telling me what a wonderful dresser you were."

Zand grinned. "They kid a lot, but they're envious, see? Look at the shoes. Ever see purple and white shoes before? Course not. I have 'em made. Everything tailored."

"Except his kisser," said the blond woman.

Zand rocked with laughter. "Lola—she kills me. That's my girl friend, mister. Was she giving you some of that gab?"

"Yeah."

"Ain't she a killer? Thousand laughs an hour. That's Lola."

"What can you do in a joint like this and with people like this, but laugh! Especially a girl like me brought up in one of the best families of the South. South Chicago."

Zand held on to the counter to laugh, then he turned to Reisman. "You new at the station, buster?"

"Yeah," said Reisman, "and I'm looking for a couple of friends of mine."

"They're in the back, waiting for the fifth to come through from Washington Park. You a betting man?"

"Now and then."

"We pay track odds. Only joint in this area. And no arguments, and no credit—unless the boss okays it. All cash."

"I thought *you* were the boss."

"Well, I am. I manage it, anyway. But I don't own it—only a piece."

"He works here," said Lola, showing irritation. "And so do I. And the hours are long, and my feet hurt."

They were interrupted by a loud argument in the pool hall. Two hulking young hoodlums were quarreling violently about some point in the game. They both had pool cues in their hands and looked as if they might use them. Reisman felt a sudden stab of apprehension. This was a rough neighborhood and a rough joint. A guy could get killed around here.

"Excuse me, mister," said Zand.

Reisman moved cautiously to the archway to see what would happen. Would the big, rough-looking hoodlums take this little man apart? Would there be a free-for-all with pool balls flying through the air and a call for the riot squad? But no. As soon as the hoodlums saw Zand coming they stopped arguing at once and when he went up to them they began backing away, one of them looking a little greenish.

"Didn't I warn you, Turkey?" said Zand mildly.

"Yeah," whined Turkey. "But he started it."

"Get out and don't come back," said Zand. "If you do, I'll open you up to see what you're made of."

"Aw, God, Zand..." begged Turkey, his tough face wrinkled up as if he were going to cry. "I don't want no trouble with you. I won't do it no more. Honest to God... tell him, fellows. I won't do it no more."

There were subdued and ambiguous murmurs, all eyes on Zand.

"All right," said the little Syrian, finally. "But next time I don't talk, see? I just start working on you."

The game was resumed, but there was a nervous quietude over the place now. Zand walked back to Reisman, smiling slightly.

"They don't mean no harm, them boys," he said. "But you got to be rough with 'em. It's all they understand." He seemed completely unruffled. Must weigh a quick one hundred and ten pounds, thought Reisman: hardly bigger than the average jockey. "You want to go back and see your friends now?" asked the little man.

"Yeah," said Reisman.

He followed Zand across the silent pool hall and out through a little door into a barnlike, ramshackle room with green tin shades over the lights and a line of blackboards along one wall. The place was packed with men sitting on folding-chairs. The air was blue and foggy with tobacco smoke. A loudspeaker was blaring the fifth at Washington Park.

Reisman saw Downy standing back against the wall, his face flushed, snapping his fingers excitedly, trying to urge his horse home. Finally the race was over. Downy sagged dejectedly.

Reisman slipped up to him unnoticed.

"Didn't your mother ever tell you you shouldn't?" he asked severely.

Downy started, stared, then grinned sheepishly. "Well, I've got to do *something* down in this God-awful place," he said. "Any chance on that transfer, Ben?"

"Yeah, I think so. But meanwhile go easy on this stuff. It's stupid, keeping a bookie on your salary."

"I'm through for the day."

"Let's sit down then."

Downy found a couple of chairs and they sat in a corner away from the others where they could talk.

"Ben," said Downy, "the fellows keep asking me—are you looking for something down here?"

"You mean you think it's any of their business? What did you learn in the College of Journalism at State, anyway?"

"I don't mean that. The hell with them. But they make me curious, that's all."

"Didn't I mention the rumors?"

"Oh, them. New ones every day. Cline's moving in. He's not moving in. Leon's moving out. Leon's not moving out. You know. I mean, are you really on a story? It must be an awful big one. Your time's kind of expensive now."

"Flatterer!"

"If you are, I'll be glad to help."

Reisman absent-mindedly puffed on his cigar for a few moments, then, holding it away from him, he studied it curiously. "I haven't dropped dead yet, but I'm close."

Downy gave a start. "What's that?"

Reisman threw the cigar away in disgust. "Nothing. Nothing."

He sat watching a broad-shouldered lout in a red shirt marking up odds on a blackboard. There was a buzz of conversation over the place, but on the whole it was pretty quiet, with no more hubbub or commotion than its equivalent downtown, a brokerage exchange.

"Pretty good business here."

"Small bettors," said Downy. "Mostly two dollars, except when they get to winning—then they chunk it in a bit."

"The little Syrian own the place?" asked Reisman innocently.

"No. Fellow called Arky."

"Anybody we know?"

Downy glanced at Reisman, tried to read his blank face. "A fellow nobody knows, I guess. Minds his own business. Nice fellow, I think. All the coppers seem to like him."

"They like the kick-in, no doubt. This place is only one jump from the station."

"Has to be a kick-in, of course. But you know those big coppers as well as I do. A kick-in doesn't make them *like* you. They seem to like Arky."

"Tough kind of guy?"

Downy glanced at Reisman again. What was it with the Master today? "Arky? Oh, no. Never raises his voice. Says hello to everybody. He's in and out. Never lights. Lives next door, I think. Or upstairs. Some place around. Zand does all the bossing. If there's any trouble, *he* handles it. Not that there is very much. Row in here, though, the other day. Arky never said a word. Just sat there. Zand came in and stopped it."

"Mild kind of fellow, eh?"

"I'd say so."

"In this neighborhood? Running a bookie joint full of thieves and hoodlums? A likely story, Downy; a likely story."

"Yeah," said Downy thoughtfully. "I never looked at it that way before."

"Well, look at it that way. And another thing. No transfer. You stay here in the 7th."

Downy's face clouded, then brightened. He even slapped Reisman lightly on the back. "Okay, Ben. Okay."

"And let this slip out," said Reisman, "especially to Joe Pavlik. I'm running down a big story about narcotics."

Downy chuckled to himself. Narcotics were always dynamite. Joe's ears would whirl. Downy felt a rising excitement. Something big was up. Something very big. And he was in on it. Suddenly he gave a slight start as a door opened in the back.

"There's Arky," he said.

Reisman turned his head slowly. At first he couldn't pick out the man from the others near the door. Had he been expecting a country boy from the Ozarks in overalls and a checked shirt? Arky was over six feet tall and slender but strong-looking. Maybe about forty. He was wearing a loose but well-cut double-breasted suit of some fine gray material; a white linen shirt with long collar points and a loud but fashionable tie. He looked almost like the clothing ads you saw in the papers: he had the right build—lean, narrow-hipped, wide in the shoulders, and the suit accentuated it. The face did not seem to go with the suit or the build, however. In spite of the clean shave and the short, fashionable haircut, it was a country face, lean, a little bleak, homely. His hair was dark brown and getting a trifle thin at the temples, his eyes were small, blue, and of a triangular shape, and surrounded by squint-wrinkles like the eyes of a cowboy or an explorer. His mouth was wide, thin, and firm.

He smiled and nodded as various men spoke to him, then he glanced over at Downy, moved toward him.

Reisman was struck by a sudden thought. "Don't name me," he said to Downy quickly.

Downy merely glanced at Reisman as a sign he'd heard, then he said: "Hello, Arky."

Arky paused and smiled, including Reisman with a quick pleasant look. "Hello, son. How the horses treating you?" He spoke with a faint Arkansas accent blurred by big city overtones: he'd apparently been away from home for a long time.

"Not so good."

"They never do," said Arky. "But guys never learn. You can beat a horse-race but you can't beat the horses."

"Knocking down your own game?" asked Reisman.

"It's a game you can't knock down, mister. It's like women and liquor." He turned to Downy. "He a friend of yours?"

"Yeah."

"Reporter?" asked Arky, smiling.

"Yeah."

"They sure flock to the 17th. I'm getting right smart trade from 'em at the present time. Well, see you around." Arky made an easy gesture. Reisman noticed the strong-looking, well-cared-for hands; the French cuffs, the garnet-and-gold cuff links; then Arky smiled and passed on.

He paused at the far door to say a few words to a knot of men clustered there, then he went on into the pool hall.

"You know something?" said Reisman.

Downy had been waiting for Reisman's opinion. "No. What?" he demanded eagerly.

"There's a lot of sartorial consciousness for a joint like this. First, Zand. Now that Bob Burns character."

"Arky? Dresses swell, doesn't he? But Zand—he's a big yuk."

"Sartorial consciousness just the same."

"That mean something?"

"Maybe. But I don't know what." Reisman turned to go. "Stick on the job for a little while, Downy. None of this may come to anything. Week or so won't hurt."

"Okay. Any leads?"

"I wish I had one."

Reisman wandered out, baffled. Arky had seemed like a nice friendly fellow all right. No doubt about it. And yet....

"Yet me no yets," said Reisman to himself.

Was he following an imaginary lead through boredom? Possible. One time he'd read a story, a true story, about a scientist who had spent ten years doing research on nonexistent rays. Was he himself doing research on a nonexistent Ark? Was it Park? Dark? Clark? Mark? Why hadn't he thought about that before? Could Harry Radabaugh, nervous, have misunderstood him? Worse still, and more likely, could he himself have misunderstood the Bat? He was sure the old fighter had said "De Ark," but he might have said "Dark." He might have said "Constantinople," for that matter. What a mush-mouth!

Nothing made any kind of sense. Imagine George Cline afraid of a 17th Ward, small-time bookie. Imagine Riggio afraid of him, or even Harry Radabaugh.

"Ben J.," said Reisman to himself, "I think you were born with a loose screw and it is getting looser."

Nevertheless, he wandered down to the huge, battered old station house. It was as usual: sagging stairs, and stinking of mortality and cheap disinfectant. He was lucky enough to find Precinct Captain Carl Dysen in his office. The Captain, about fifty, was six foot three and weighed two hundred and sixty pounds. His iron-gray hair was cut short and stood up steeply from his round skull. His heavy face sagged like a bloodhound's, dragging the lower lids of his eyes down. He was a very tough boy and for ten years had been known as the "tyrant of the 17th."

"Hello, Ben," he said. "What is this, second childhood? I heard you'd been hanging around."

"Looking for my lost youth."

"You guys never know when you're well off. You're a big man now. It don't look good you hanging around this jungle."

"I'm living in Lakeside Village. Boats and everything. Closes tight at nine. The other day somebody stole a lawnmower. Brother, what an uproar!"

The captain laughed in his deep bass voice, and the paper knife on his desk vibrated slightly.

"Yeah. I know. I live in Locust Grove."

"I been down to Arky's watching the hoosiers toss their dollar bills around."

The captain's face darkened. "I manage *my* ward *my* way, Reisman."

"Who's complaining?"

"You been running to Commissioner Stark. So I hear. Don't run to him about *my* ward. Understand?"

"Third degree? The hose? Bright lights? Go to hell, will you, Dysen?"

The captain showed anger, then composed himself and chuckled. "All right. *Run* to him. We close 'em up. They open the next day. They've got a fix going and you know it."

"Don't you ever read the papers? They've been sending the boys up."

"In the downtown area. Here and there," said the captain, wearily. "Look, sharpshooter, the commissioner's got one set of principles; I got another. My business is crime: armed robbery, rape, thievery, arson, murder. My job is to see that people are safe. Is gambling a crime? Are bookies criminals?"

"According to the law, they...."

"Stop being funny. Look. I got the biggest and the toughest ward in town. I also got the Front—most of it. So what do I do? Let the white-tie tramps do what they please on the Front and close up on the poor guys around here with two bucks?"

"Captain, I didn't know you were a social philosopher. But you're having an argument all by yourself. I didn't come down here to make you any trouble. You got my word for it."

"Then why *did* you come?"

Reisman sighed and stood up. "Okay, I'll stay away. I think you got something there."

He went out. An old turnkey who hadn't seen Reisman for twenty years yelled at him, but Reisman, self-absorbed and not hearing, hurried on. He felt depressed, useless, and the late-afternoon pain was beginning to nag at his stomach.

The hell with it! All a mirage. Not a flicker of anything—guilty knowledge or even resentment—when he mentioned Arky's name. All the captain was worrying about, apparently, was his policy of letting the bookies run. And Captain Dysen knew the big town in and out.

3

Young Downy had been given a few days off. He was not yet twenty-five, he had money in his pocket and a new car, so he was in a big hurry to hit the road north for Half Moon Beach, which was full of vacationing shopgirls and secretaries at this time of year: dancing on the pier to a good orchestra with the moon overhead and little motorboats coming and going across the dark, still water of the bay... wonderful! No city smoke, no soot, no stench of printer's ink, no crime!

All the same, eager as he was, he stopped at the Greet Memorial Hospital on his way out of town to see Reisman.

He found him sitting up in bed, smoking a cigarette, reading the *Sporting News,* and listening to the rebroadcast of an important Eastern baseball game. There was a sickly smell of flowers in the room, but no flowers. Reisman looked awful.

"Hello, Ben," said Downy, hesitating a little. He disliked and feared hospitals, illness, middle age. He wanted things to be smooth and happy as in the travel and automobile advertisements: one big smiling family in a big smiling world, no problems.

"Thank Christ you didn't bring flowers," said Reisman. "This morning I woke up and the joint was full of flowers. They'd given me something to make me sleep. I didn't hear all the moving around. I began to yell. The nurse came running. She's a Swedish kid with nice knockers but no brains. I been kidding her and she thinks I'm crazy. I yell at her: 'Get these goddamn petunias out of here. I ain't dead yet.' She went for the doctor. She always goes for the doctor. He goes for her, too... but that's another story."

Downy was somewhat overwhelmed by this torrent of words coming from one who looked so tired and spent. He began to stammer.

"I didn't even think to bring *anything*, Ben. I'm sorry. But....''

"Transfer came through, eh?" Reisman demanded, breaking in.

"Yes. Thanks to you. And I think I'm going to be assigned to sports. I hope so. They gave me a few days off. I'm on my way to Half Moon Beach."

"Lucky guy," said Reisman. "Don't suppose the place has changed much. I haven't been there in fifteen years. They used to call it the Riding Academy."

Downy blushed and laughed faintly.

"Don't look guilty about it," said Reisman. "It's natural."

There was a pause. A plump blond nurse wandered in and wandered out again; then she put her head in the door and looked at young Downy.

"I didn't know you had a visitor, Mr. Reisberg," she said. "Everything all right?"

"Does it look like everything's all right, you schnook? I'm sick in bed, ain't I?"

"Oh, you!" she cried, giggling, then she looked at Downy again and went out.

"You see how our lives hang by a thread?" Reisman demanded. "That's my nurse."

Downy cleared his throat uncomfortably, not knowing what to say. Finally he spoke. "I was talking to Red Seaver. He told me they weren't going to operate. Is that right?"

"Yeah," said Reisman. "As a matter of fact I seem to be in better shape, according to all the tests, than I was five years ago. The ulcer, I mean. Otherwise, I'm all run down. Need a rest. Low blood-pressure. Mild anemia. Getting on for fifty, in other words. Also I'm in for observation. Whatever that means. Looks like a cinch I'm here for a couple weeks more."

"Fine, just so you're all right. How about the column?"

"I write it. I'd write it if I was dying. Elsa, the nurse, will be my inspiration. She don't know nuttin about nuttin, like a lot of my readers. She'll be a big help—the right slant."

Downy hemmed and hawed before he spoke again. "That big story—nothing happened on it, is that right?"

Reisman laughed ironically. "I'll tell you about that. When I was a police reporter I used to have a kind of—what'll I say—intuition? I don't know. Anyway, I made my best beats riding silly hunches. It used to hit me like a pain or something. This time it was a pain. And here I am."

"Sorry to hear it. About the story, I mean." Downy shifted from one foot to the other. He was excessively nervous and ill-at-ease in these surroundings. He wanted to get out into the sunshine and shake off the cloying smell of flowers and disinfectant and illness.

Reisman observed him ironically for a moment, then he said: "Why don't you sit down? Stay to dinner? If I get lonesome, I'll have them put a bed in here for you."

Downy couldn't suppress a quick look of dismay, then he grinned sheepishly. "I guess I'm kind of fidgety. I'm sorry, Ben. But...."

"Go on," said Reisman. "Beat it. Thanks for coming."

Downy smiled with relief. "I'll give you a ring when I get back, and if there is anything I can do...."

"Remember me in your prayers."

After Downy had gone, Reisman lay for a long time looking at the ceiling. Making a conscious effort, he began to fight off feelings of hopelessness and despair. A big story might have helped. Now what?

4

Night seemed to drift into the 17th Ward from Paxton Square to the north. Lights came on along the river and were reflected upside-down in wavering zig-zags. Tugs moved toward their home moorings, whistles moaning for the landing. The garish neon lights of the Front sprang on and a purplish glow showed above the brick tenements. Juke boxes began to play in bars and the denizens of the 17th began to come out from their caves and prowl the dim-lit streets. The first police siren of the evening wailed down by the river. Trouble already?

Arky listened to the siren absent-mindedly. To him it was a mere pin-prick of sound, having no significance. Slowly smoking a cigar, he sat in the deserted and littered bookie room, wondering about Anna. Something was bothering her. What? As a rule she was calm and placid and amenable, a big blond woman who smiled, dismissed trouble with a shrug, and took things as they came. A damned good-looking big broad, when you came to that, maybe a little too plump for the average taste. "But not for mine," said Arky with distinct satisfaction. "She's got it where it belongs."

Yeah, something was bothering her and Arky did not like it. He trusted Anna maybe more than a man should trust a woman: she knew a lot, perhaps too much, and it was quite a load to carry.

When he first met her, ten years back, Anna used to smoke cigars. It merely seemed funny at the time—a big handsome blond with a cigar in her mouth—

then it began to irritate him; finally it annoyed, and even revolted him, to such an extent that he got into a row with her about it. Why not chew, too? So Anna quit smoking cigars. Except once in a while... when she was nervous or upset.

Tonight, when he'd gone home to change his clothes, the place had reeked of cigar smoke, and Anna had all the windows open in spite of the damp wind blowing in off the river.

"That boy friend of yours," he'd said, "he really smokes El Cabbago. Better put him on cigarettes."

Anna had said nothing. She'd laid out his clothes, as she always did, helped him knot his tie and set his tie-clasp, and held his coat for him.

"Okay," she'd said finally. "I was smoking a cigar."

"Anything wrong?"

After a long pause, she seemed about to tell him something, then she spoke hastily. "No. Maybe the meemees. I don't know."

Anna was always talking about them getting married, or at least thinking about it. Arky didn't get the idea at all. It didn't figure. If he got married it wouldn't be to a broad named Anna Hunchuk—or to a broad who had been around the way she had. Where's the percentage? But maybe that was what it was, bothering her again. The thing was bound to come up from time to time. Women always had to have something to complain about. Anna had picked marriage as a good subject! But if that was the case why hadn't she come out with it? She wasn't tongue-tied—far from it.

Arky sat smoking and listening to the distant wail of the police siren. These were touchy times with things the way they were. It wasn't that he could ever think of Anna as wishing him ill. But mistakes could be made. Pressure could be brought a hundred ways. Words could slip out and then be regretted. Anna liked to talk, just for the sake of talking. She had a friendly, expansive nature.

The door opened behind him, but he didn't turn. He knew it was Zand.

"It's getting around eight," said the little Syrian.

Arky got up, took off his coat, walked to a desk, unlocked it, then got out a shoulder holster with a heavy automatic in it, and strapped it on. Zand helped him back into his coat.

"Did Lola talk to Anna today?" asked Arky.

"I don't know," said Zand. "She's always running up to see Anna when she gets a minute. Gab, gab. Yackety, yack. Dames!"

"Tell Lola I want to see her."

Zand stared. "Look, Ark. We ought to be going."

"He can wait," said Arky, disdainfully.

"Anna never tells Lola nothing, Ark, if that's what's worrying you. Lola minds her own business. Don't know anything. Don't want to know anything. Smart."

"Well, Anna's got something in her craw."

Zand looked at Arky for a moment, then he went back to get Lola, who seemed a little pale and nervous under the hard lights of the bookie room when she entered from the pool hall. Zand stayed outside. Lola glanced over her shoulder as if she wanted his support, then she came up slowly to Arky who was sitting on the edge of the desk, swinging his foot.

"Did you talk to Anna today, Lola?" Arky asked quietly.

"Yes, I did. Why?"

"What's biting her?"

Lola hesitated before she spoke. "Something biting her?"

"I'm asking you."

Lola hesitated again. She seemed to be struggling with some obscure emotion, then suddenly she burst out into hysterical giggles. Arky's lips tightened.

"What's so funny?"

"Kill me and I won't tell you, Arky. But you got a surprise coming." Lola turned away to laugh, and finally stuffed her handkerchief into her mouth.

Arky watched her for a moment, then he said: "Something funny, eh? Real funny. Nothing serious. Is that right, Lola?"

"That's right. I'll give you my oath, my affidavit, cross my heart. Nothing serious."

"Okay," said Arky, getting down from the desk.

He wasn't worried any longer. It was probably just some silly woman-business of one kind or another. No, he wasn't worried, but he was curious. It must be something pretty funny to break up a tired broad like Lola. He'd go into it with Anna first thing when he got back.

Lola went out, still trying to suppress her giggles. When she opened the door Zand, who was just beyond, stared at her with marked surprise and curiosity. What was so funny? But Arky did not enlighten him. He'd have to pump Lola later that night.

They went out the back door, locking it after them, and got into a nondescript, well-aged Ford. Zand drove down the alley to Wharf Street, and turned on Pier Avenue toward the Front, the lights of which were blazing against the night. It was early yet, except for the theater crowds, and the traffic was not the irritating snarl it would become later.

"There's a show I want to see," said Zand.

Arky said nothing.

"Don't you like shows, Arky?" Zand persisted.

"Not much."

"What do you do for excitement? I never see you do nothing."

"I got a private life."

Zand leaned over the steering-wheel to laugh. "Yeah, yeah," he said, but did not go into the matter further. Sometimes Arky was inclined to be touchy.

Zand turned off the Front near Erie Street and drove up a wide, well-lighted alley. Above them flared the huge and famous gold neon sign which lighted pilgrims the way to the Club Imperial, the biggest, gaudiest, and most expensive clip joint on the Front. It was a quarter past eight and the rear parking-lot was empty. Zand drove into a stall marked Private—Club Imperial, which was only a few feet from a huge padded door.

Arky got out. Zand stayed in the car. A colored parking-boy in gold jumpers with an embroidered crest on each pocket came in from the alley, stared at the car for a moment, then disappeared.

Leon's chartreuse-colored Cadillac convertible was parked in stall 1, which was marked Owner—Stay Out—Yes, You!

Arky smiled slightly. "That Leon fellow—he sure likes to be inconspicuous. Even *you* don't wear them sunrise suits when you go out."

Zand was wearing a dark-blue turtle-neck sweater and an old pair of blue slacks.

"Yeah—but I feel naked," said Zand.

Arky chuckled, absorbed in the convertible. "Goose-turd green, practically," he mused. "At least that's what they'd call it down home. I'd sure like to drive up to the farm in that."

Zand leaned forward to laugh. "It'd be great for hauling manure. Boy, I'd love to see you on a farm once, Arky, in your pin-stripe gray suit."

"Ought to see me pick cotton. I could beat any brother I got—and the old man, too!" He grunted and seemed to come to himself. "Got plenty gas?"

"Yeah," said Zand. "Just filled her."

Arky nodded and disappeared through the padded door. Zand hesitated, then got out of the car and went over to examine Leon's convertible. Had everything in the world on it and he'd heard it'd set the guy back eight G's. That wasn't exactly eating-money!

Arky passed back through a long dark corridor filled with cooking odors from the big club kitchens just beyond, went through an employees' door, and came out into another corridor, a very different one, with a thick, sumptuous carpet on the floor, a crystal chandelier, glittering mirrors, and huge divans. It was deserted. A piano tinkled in the bar at the end of the corridor and Arky could hear a girl singing blues in a low, husky voice. Sounded nice. He had an impulse to go take a look at her: a sexy voice—but all put on more than likely, the old come-on, like everything else on the Front. It sounded nice, it wasn't, and brother, it cost you—*how* it cost you!

He turned away from the bar, opened the door of Leon's office and went in. A tall, shapely cutie with cropped black hair was sitting on the desk in the ante-room, reading a magazine. She glanced up at Arky with no expression in her eyes and jerked her thumb toward the inner office.

"My little ball of fire," said Arky.

"You again?" she said in a flat toneless voice, resuming her reading.

"What is it, babe—low blood-pressure?"

"Hiccups," said the girl.

"All the time?"

"No. Just when I see you."

"What's wrong with me?"

"My mother was raised on a farm. She told me all about you farmers."

"Don't the suit help at all?"

"It hinders."

Every time he came, it was the same thing. A very irritating girl. One of Leon's many, masquerading as office help. Sure must cost him. She thought that Arky had money in the club and that his name was Johnson—not that she seemed to give a damn, one way or another. Most indifferent girl he'd ever seen in his life. With Leon she was the same, or seemed so. Maybe he kept her around for laughs, or maybe periods of rest. It was a scandal the way the dames threw themselves at Leon: old ones, young ones, any kind you could name. You'd think at least some of them would be leery of Leon, considering all the bad publicity he got, but it didn't seem to work that way.

Arky pushed open the door of the inner office and went in. Leon was pacing the floor behind his big carved desk. He looked at his watch, but made no comment. He was of medium height, but very husky, with broad, bulky-looking shoulders and a thick, powerful neck. He had curly black hair slightly streaked with gray and cut rather short, and an almost startlingly handsome face with regular features and large dark heavy-lidded eyes. His manner was smooth and pleasant as a rule, but tonight he seemed nervous. Arky noted the double-breasted pale-blue lounge coat with the silver buttons, the doeskin slacks, and the cream-colored suede shoes. A killer, Leon. Like Zand, only not so funny.

"Sam make that suit for you, Arky?" asked Leon abruptly.

"Yeah," said Arky, sitting down opposite the desk. "Like it?"

"It's a little Riverview for me. But he's a good tailor. Didn't I tell you?"

Arky grunted. Leon paced back and forth for a moment or so with his hands behind his back. Then he went to his desk, took out a long, thick, sealed manila envelope and tossed it to Arky, who caught it, slipped it into his pocket, and made a quick acknowledging gesture with his thumb and forefinger.

"It's a little short," said Leon.

"It varies," said Arky mildly.

"It's ten thousand short."

"That's a hell of a variation, my boy," said Arky, the amiable expression leaving his face for a moment and his blue eyes showing a sudden cold flash.

"I know. I know," said Leon, hurriedly. "But there is over forty G's there. Forty G's a week is not exactly what you would call marbles. Forty times fifty-two will give you over two million. In one year, it's not bad."

"And it ain't good. Come on, come on, Leon. This money has to go to a lot of places. Do I have to tell you the facts of life over and over?"

"Don't get tough with me, Arky."

"Aw, for Christ's sake, stop trying to be the boss. I work for somebody and you work for me. Now shut up that kind of talk."

Arky lost his tenseness after a moment, relaxed, and lit a cigarette. Leon sat down at his desk and took his handsome head in his hands.

"We're slipping, Arky," he said. "And you know it as well as I do."

"Don't start that again."

"Twenty convictions last month. You read the papers. How long do you think the boys are going to keep on paying when we can't deliver?"

"We been delivering for a long time. They got no kicks coming. I talked it all over with the Mover on the phone. Some of the boys have got to hold still for a conviction now and then, especially downtown. It gets headlines and the Commissioner'll begin to think gambling's being cleaned up."

"If Stark was out of there, maybe in a better job, things would be rosy. If the Mover was smart, he'd get him promoted, or run him for office...."

Arky showed a wilder flash. "If the Mover was what?" he shouted. "Why, you two-bit, dame-chasing, pretty-boy hoodlum—if it wasn't for the Mover...."

Leon was quailing. "All right, Arky. All right. I didn't mean it that way. But couldn't it be done?"

"If it *could* be done, it *would* be done. You just don't understand the Commissioner. He don't want nothing—not a thing. And how can a guy be handled when he's like that? He's just a conscientious old coot. One of them reformers you get once in a while. Damn seldom, however."

Leon ran his fingers through his thick curly hair and sighed; then he got up, lit a cigarette, and began to pace the floor, pretending to ignore Arky. He'd dealt with some bad boys in his day, but this lint-head was the only one who had ever actually given him goose-pimples. Why didn't he go back to Arkansas? Wouldn't listen to reason. Wouldn't let you try to contact the Mover. Dared you to, in fact. Things were coming to a pretty pass when a hayneck like this...! He turned.

Arky was moving toward the door.

"Ark," he called.

"Yeah?"

"Suppose I told you it could be done. Suppose I told you I maybe had a guy could do it."

"It's all up to the Mover. Give me the facts."

"No use. The guy won't make a play unless he can talk to the Big Man himself."

"Who is this trying to cut in? Not George Cline. Not that again. All I say is, don't go behind my back."

"How can I if I don't know who the Mover is?"

There was a brief pause, then Arky spoke in a deadly voice. "But you do, Leon."

Leon stared at Arky, shaken. "What are you talking about?"

"You know what I'm talking about. You've tipped it half a dozen times in the last year or so."

"Tipped it?"

"Yeah, in your conversation. You know, all right. So be careful, Leon. If anything should accidentally happen to him...."

Leon hurried over to Arky, his face pale. "What are you trying to say? You insinuating that I'd...?"

"I'm not insinuating. I'm just saying—*don't*."

"You're getting crazy, Ark."

"Look, Leon, I've known about you for a long time. You've given plenty guys the double-shuffle. And you might do it again—but it'll be the last time."

Leon, showing a flash of something Arky didn't quite comprehend, grabbed his arm. "You better wake up," he shouted. "We're all on our way out unless something's done. So something's got to be done. The Mover's got to talk to somebody. I'll arrange it. It's for his good as well as ours. Why are you so pigheaded? The Mover's not God, is he? He's a man, and living soft while we worry."

Arky shook Leon off, then grew calm. "If the guy's got real angles, I'll talk to him, then we'll see. But don't go behind my back or maybe the Mover will throw you out in the street... like he did George Cline when George got too big."

Leon stood lost in thought for a long time, then he sighed and said: "You sure make it tough, Arky. All right. I'll see if this guy will talk to you, and he's not George Cline. That's all nightclub gossip."

"Just keep the Mover out of it. Too bad you know who he is. It puts you in a spot."

"You're saying I know. That don't prove it."

Arky merely looked at Leon, then went out. Leon closed the door after him, hurried to his private phone, and dialed a number, but after a long try, nobody answered. Leon slammed down the receiver, jumped up, and began to pace the floor.

Oh, well. Things had been nice for a long time. You couldn't have peace forever.

They drove in silence along the upper reaches of the River Road, passing the tall gateways of huge estates; many lighted windows glimmered faintly in among the trees, and music drifted out to them from some of the big houses.

"Saturday night," said Zand. "The rich tie 'em on, too, eh, Arky? I'll bet Pier Street's roaring by now."

Arky made no comment. He was worried, and anxious to get to the private phone at the cottage where he could talk in peace. After a moment, he said sharply: "Step on it a little, will you, Zand? Or give me the wheel."

Zand glanced at him sideways. "I'm doing fifty-five, Ark. These curves are bad."

"Pull over," said Ark.

Zand did not like to think about the rest of the drive: the memory of it was a nightmare. The wind screamed in the wind-wings, the tired jalopy swayed from side to side, and the tires shrieked on the curves. Glaring headlights came out of nowhere and disappeared at once. A couple of cars honked at them in fear.

When Arky finally drew up in the dooryard of a fashionable cottage on the upper river, Zand felt cold and clammy all over.

"You better go back to picking cotton," he said.

Arky jumped out without a word and in a moment disappeared into the shrubbery in front of the dark cottage. Zand heard a door close softly; then he saw a dim light in the windows. He sighed and lit a cigarette with shaking hands.

A little man in his late fifties with a bald head, a tired smile, and shell-rimmed glasses had let Arky in and they were now walking down a dark hall-way toward a brightly lit study at the far end. The little man was known to hundreds of phone contacts merely as the Paymaster. The paying off was generally done by special messenger and not over half a dozen men in the city had any idea that the Paymaster was anything more than he was supposed to be: a retired lawyer who'd cashed in his holdings and his retirement insurance and was now spending his declining years in a nice cottage on the upper river. He seemed to have a vague connection with several big law firms downtown, especially Dighton and Black, who handled considerable underworld business, particularly the business of the "king pin," Leon Sollas and associates. But this was perfectly legitimate.

His name was Gordon King. He was a bachelor, had one servant, an old colored man, and spent his spare time collecting ultra-modern paintings, which covered the walls of his cottage and never failed to startle Arky when his glance happened to fall on one of them. Nightmares, cockeyed stuff. The guys that painted them must have been on the weed. And although he liked King very much, he never felt exactly right about him since he'd noticed the pictures. How could a normal guy live, day after day, with stuff like that staring him in the face?

As they entered the study Arky handed King the envelope and explained about the shortage.

King shrugged wearily. "Well, in that case, we spread the shortage around."

"You'll get complaints."

"I'm used to them."

"Plenty complaints?"

King nodded. "Never fails. And besides, the hungriest ones are always thinking up other people who have to be taken care of. 'Little fellows,' you know." King snorted with contempt.

"I want to use the private line," said Arky. King nodded, tossed the manila envelope into an open safe, and went out, closing the door after him.

Arky smiled to himself as he dialed the number. King knew the Mover better than he did himself: they were close friends, in fact: but the Paymaster was cautious, smart, wary; not like dark-faced Leon, who wasn't satisfied with his chartreuse convertible, his Club Imperial, and his harem, not to mention the awed respect of hoosier hoodlum-lovers, and café-society columnists—no, he wanted to be the Big One in fact as well as fancy—he wanted to know everything, pull the strings, tangle them up even if there was no other way for him to feel big. Leon was a wrong one. The Mover knew it all right. The Mover knew everything. But he always worked slowly and cautiously, like the Paymaster.

Arky got no answer. The Mover's private phone rang no place but in his study. All the same, it was pay day, the Mover knew the time and that Arky might call. Arky began to sweat. Could something have happened to him?

Arky kept trying and finally heaved a long sigh of relief when he heard a premonitory click. Finally the Mover came on. His voice always gave Arky a feeling of pleasure, of warmth; as soon as he heard it he knew that his worries and fears were baseless, and that things were going to be all right. It was deep, sure, genial.

"Ark? Something wrong?"

Taking a deep breath, Arky explained at great length.

The Mover did not interrupt. It was almost as if the phone were dead. Finally Arky concluded and, taking out his handkerchief, mopped his forehead.

First, the Mover laughed; then he said: "Arky, I've told you a hundred times you take that fool too seriously. Of course he knows who I am. That doesn't matter. Leon is not dangerous. He might cheat you. In fact, he's cheated everybody he's ever been connected with...."

Arky paled and broke in. "You mean about that shortage? Why, I'll...."

"Wait! Wait! I don't mean the shortage. That has a perfectly legitimate explanation, as you know. I mean Leon is a cheap chiseler and a coward. He is not physically dangerous—not unless he's cornered and thinks he is in for it. Then he might be. Any man might be. Understand? No, Arky. We've had this trouble before. Somebody is always trying to move in. Naturally. This is one of the biggest gambling cities in the country. The take is bound to be big. So the wolves gather on the outskirts. We'll keep them there."

"You bet we will, sir," said Arky.

"Any talk about controlling Stark is ridiculous. As for getting him a better job in the city, *what* job? As mayor he'd be worse. As director of public safety he'd turn the city upside down, and you can't elect a congressman every day! Quite a fellow—Stark!" The Mover chuckled at the other end of the line. "Arky, you know, you can't help admiring a man like that. I don't suppose you ever heard of Don Quixote...."

"No, sir. I didn't."

"Well, never mind. And as for removing him... hopeless. They love him at City Hall now. They can point to him with pride. Very funny." The Mover chuckled again. "Very, very funny. However, Arky, talk to this friend of Leon's. Play it straight. I want to know all about him. Understand? It might be a Big City bunch trying to move in. It's been done in other places. And it never works out. The locals end by taking a financial beating, the real money goes out of town, and pretty soon the shooting starts. Now we don't want any shooting, do we, Arky?"

"I ain't so sure," said Arky.

"Come, come now," said the Mover. "Shooting is for idiots, Arky. Haven't I taught you anything in all this time?"

"You sure have, sir."

"Well, profit by it. And here is a thought: there is one hope of getting the Commissioner out. On the whole he's had enough of the Bench. But the State Supreme Court's another matter. Such an appointment would be hard for any man to resist, even me." The Mover laughed.

"That's where you ought to be, sir; and not where you are." Arky bit his tongue and turned pale.

There was a long silence at the other end of the line, then the Mover spoke in a different voice. "I'm going to ignore your insolence, Orval. Just this time. But I don't want to hear any more of it."

"Yes, sir," said Arky, sweating. "It just slipped out. I mean, you could handle it, sir. Nothing you couldn't handle."

"...And never mind the flattery. You're not talking to Leon now. Anything else on your mind?"

"No sir. I'll have Leon make a date for me to talk to this character. Then I'll call you."

"Check with the Paymaster and he'll set up the time for your call. I'll be right by the phone. I'm a little curious about this. Good night, Orval." The Mover hung up.

Arky kicked himself under the chair. When the Mover was really annoyed with him he always called him Orval. "Why can't I keep my big mouth shut?" groaned Arky. "What the hell business is it of mine whether he's on the Supreme Bench or where he is? He knows what he's doing." He lit a cigarette and sat thinking about the past. He'd been the Mover's chauffeur for five years in the early thirties.

In a moment, the door opened and King came back. He glanced at Arky, noted his long face, wondered, but made no comment. Arky looked up at him, then something beyond the little man caught Arky's eye. It was a new picture on the wall: a horror, like something you'd see after going to bed on a full stomach. He winced slightly. King followed his glance.

"I see you noticed my new picture. Just came yesterday." He studied Arky ironically.

Arky stood up and stretched. "Yeah," he said. "Some picture. What's it supposed to be?"

"It's an abstraction."

Arky nodded as if he understood what King was talking about, then he said: "Well, so long. See you next week."

"Good night, Arky."

5

All evening long Arky had not given Anna a thought; he'd forgotten that he'd been worried about her earlier in the day and that Lola had promised a surprise of some kind. Business had driven every other consideration from his mind.

But as he undressed for bed in his big old ramshackle apartment over the pool hall, suddenly he remembered. But the place was quiet; Anna was sleeping heavily in her bedroom—he had opened her door on his way in and listened for a moment to her heavy breathing—it was just no time of night for explanations, arguments, or surprises. Tomorrow was soon enough.

He put on his pajamas, turned out his light, lit a cigarette, then went to the window and stood smoking and looking out at the city. Pier Street rose steeply from the tug landings at the river's edge, and the Corners, where the pool hall stood, were about midway up the slope of Riker's Hill. Arky had a good view, across acres of dismal rooftops and dirty stacks and chimneys, of the wide, dark pavement of the river with its many trembling reflections and all the tall buildings of the downtown area beyond. The Pier 7 Bridge was a mere garland of yellow lights stretching to the far shore. It was after two a.m. Sirens wailed in the city. Far off to the southeast, Arky could see the glow of a big fire. A faint damp breeze touched his face lightly from time to time and stirred his short hair.

He'd been in the city for a good many years now but it had never seemed like home to him, only a way-station... but a way-station to what? No place? He just didn't seem to belong anywhere, didn't fit in. Too countrified for the city, and too citified for the country. The Mover had said that to him once, and the Mover was right, as he always was. Maybe *nobody* seemed to themselves to fit in. The hell with it, anyway!

The moon began to rise over the downtown section across the river, looking a little pale above the glare of the city lights. Faint music drifted up from a dance hall on the west bank at the end of Pier Street: a stinking hole with six bouncers, but from this distance the music sounded nice.

Somebody began to yell down below; then there was the sound of running feet, the shock of bodies—and a fight was on. Smoking quietly, Arky listened to the sounds of the struggle indifferently. Young hoodlums full of cheap whisky or maybe weed. There were always fights at night in the 17th. There were curses, blows, screams of rage. Somebody was knocked down and yelled for help. The sound of running feet again: then silence, and finally loud laughter and jeering from a distance. "I'll get you yet, you yellow bastard!" somebody shouted to a chorus of jeers, then there was nothing more except the footsteps of a single person passing under Arky's window. Whoever it was, was dragging his feet. He'd probably been belted around a little.

Arky yawned, tossed his cigarette out the window, and got into bed. He liked to sleep alone. This was another one of Anna's beefs. She said it wasn't natural: they were as good as married, weren't they? She was gregarious, he a solitary. It made trouble between them. But he'd be damned if he'd change the ways of a lifetime just to keep her quiet. You'd think she'd be used to it by now. But no; every once in a while it came up, like that marriage business. Arky lay wondering if Zand had any trouble with Lola that way. Probably not. Lola, in spite of her wisecracks, seemed too tired to argue or resist. She just took things as they came. But there was nothing tired about Anna. She was full of health, vinegar, and hell in general. Arky laughed quietly to himself.

Strong as a horse, she was always moving the furniture around, never satisfied with how it looked. The apartment was a showplace as it was—though you'd never think so from the outside. This gave Arky quite a kick. You'd come up those dark stairs from the pool hall, open the door, and there you'd be in a seven-room apartment that looked like a choice suite in a downtown hotel. All Anna's doing; of course he'd furnished the money, plenty of it.

Arky turned over, still thinking of Anna, and tried to go to sleep, but he felt nervous and a little jumpy, and after slapping his pillows around and turning over a couple of times he finally realized that he was going to have trouble tonight, as he often did. Rolling over on his back, he decided to put his sleep system to work. It didn't consist of counting sheep, but it was something like that. He took the major-league baseball teams one by one and tried to remember the batting orders: it was tough to do, even for a dyed-in-the-wool fan like Arky; he always had the most trouble with the Browns, the White Sox, the Senators, and the Cincinnati Reds—and he saved them till last. The Browns last of all, especially this year when they had practically no holdovers. He had got as far as the White Sox, and things were growing very muddled in his mind, when a faint alien sound in the apartment that he couldn't account for brought him straight up from his pillow.

It was some kind of animal sound, a little like a cat mewing but different somehow... very different. The sound stopped. Arky lay back and waited; the silence went on and on; and finally he began to wonder if, dozing, he hadn't imagined it. In a few moments he closed his eyes and returned to the batting order of the White Sox: he had just reached the clean-up spot, Gus Zernial, when the mewing started again, followed by faint thin wailing, like some kind of ghost or spook. Arky's hair stirred slightly and he felt a chill along his spine. Cursing, he sat up, swung his feet to the floor, and groped for his slippers.

The thin wail continued. Sounded almost like a baby. But what the hell would a baby be doing...? Now he heard vague thumping sounds in the rear of the apartment, coming from the spare bedroom where nobody ever set foot. At last he found his slippers and switched on the light to look for his robe. He thought he heard Anna's door open, and opening his own door quickly, he peered out into the hall. But it was dark. Anna's door was closed.

Silence returned to the house. Arky stood listening. "What the hell's wrong with me?" he demanded aloud. "I got the fantods, or something?"

He put on his robe, lit a cigarette, and began to pace back and forth in front of his open bedroom door.

The wailing started again, and suddenly a crack of light showed far down the hall under the door of the spare bedroom.

"I'm damned," said Arky, stumped.

Moving quickly down the hall, he opened Anna's door. Her bed was empty. He ran to the spare bedroom and turned the knob; the door was locked. The wailing was much louder now. It was a baby, all right. What else could it be? He raised his fist to knock, changed his mind, and pressed his ear to the door. Anna's voice came faintly to him, punctuated by wails.

"Keep him quiet, will you, for God's sake? Ark's home in bed. We'll tell him tomorrow."

Another female voice spoke at some length, but Arky couldn't make out a single word and suddenly he realized that the second voice was speaking in a foreign language of some kind.

Exasperated now, he beat on the door with his fist. In a moment, he heard the key turn in the lock, the door swung back, and he was face to face with Anna. Beyond her he could see a fattish, towheaded girl, who couldn't have been over sixteen, holding a baby in her arms. On a stand was a big market-basket with what looked like a horse-blanket in it. The girl showed all the signs of intense fright and seemed unable to make up her mind whether to run or faint. The baby wailed louder than ever now, and Arky could see it waving its tiny fists.

"Will you stop making so damn much noise?" cried Anna. Then she gave him a push. "Get out of here. Go back to bed. I'll talk to you tomorrow."

"You'll talk to me now. You think I want a zoo made out of my apartment? Who's that girl and whose kid is that?"

The girl jabbered despairingly over the thin baby-wails.

"Never mind, Milli," said Anna. "He just makes a lot of noise with his mouth. Arky, go back to bed. I got to get the kid's bottle. We were hoping he'd sleep through, but...."

"Maybe I'm crazy," said Arky, barring her way. "But who said blondie could bring that kid in here?"

"I did. She's my niece, and she's got no place to go."

"Christ, another Polack, and a little Polack on top of it. Ain't there enough Polacks in the world?"

"Maybe. And there's enough white trash, too. Get out of my way."

Furious, Arky grabbed Anna, pulled her out into the hallway by the wrists and slammed her back against the wall. In the spare bedroom, the towheaded girl began to wail a duet with the baby. "I tole you, Anna. I tole you," she stammered.

"Don't get rough with me," said Anna, her blue eyes glaring icily at him. "I'm not scared of you, if everybody else is." She tried violently to wrench herself away from him and finally he let her go.

"The poor kid's hungry," she said, calming down a little. "He ain't et for five hours and he didn't eat good then. I'd've fed him later if I'd known when you were coming back."

"Talk sense, for Christ's sake. What do I know about feeding kids—or care? What I'm saying is, what's he doing here? You know I have a hard time sleeping. Why drag a kid in to make it worse?"

"Will you let us feed the baby? Then he'll go back to sleep, and I'll tell you about the whole thing."

"It better be good."

Anna flounced away from him and disappeared into the kitchen. Scratching his head in irritation, Arky glanced into the bedroom. The towheaded girl was staring at him with the eyes of a whipped dog. The baby had stopped crying and was now hiccupping.

"I tole Anna, mister," she said. "Please... I don't like bodder nobody."

"Ain't the kid got a father?" asked Arky curtly.

The girl didn't seem to comprehend and looked at Arky blankly, her full lips dropping open.

"I don't like bodder," she said. "I take him 'way."

Arky ground his teeth in irritation. What was a kid like this doing with a baby, anyway? She looked something like a baby herself.

"Where's his father?" he asked.

"Please?" said the girl. "I don't understand."

"All right. All right," said Arky, then he turned and went back to his bedroom. But he knew there was no use trying to sleep. It was after three now. At four it would begin to get light. At five the tugs would start blasting on the river. He knew the schedule by heart. Swearing to himself, he got out a deck of cards, sat down at a table, and laid out a game of solitaire. He heard Anna go back down the hall, heard the door of the spare bedroom close; a few faint wails, then silence.

Finally Arky spoke quietly to himself. "Well, this is pretty good. Dragging a little bastard into the house without even asking me about it. That's too much crust—even for that big Polack."

He mussed up the solitaire layout, then picked up a paper and tried to read. All of a sudden, he felt sleepy. He could hardly believe it. Getting up quickly, he locked his door, turned out the lights and got into bed. Somebody started yelling in the street below; then hard heels hit the asphalt as somebody ran up an alley. Arky listened hazily to the running footsteps. The last thing he heard was the wail of a police siren, coming nearer and nearer.

Arky woke with a start. It was broad daylight, and somebody was knocking on his door. He rolled over groaning, and looked at his watch. Noon! What a sleep!

"Arky, are you dead?" called Anna's cheerful daytime voice. "I got your breakfast."

Arky got up yawning and stretching, half asleep, and finally managed to get the door open. The towheaded girl came in, carrying his tray. She glanced at Arky shyly and rather fearfully, as if expecting a blow or a kick. Anna, looking placidly cheerful, had the baby in her arms. Arky stared, suddenly remembering. Then glancing at the girl, he hurriedly put on his robe.

"Look at him, Arky," said Anna. "Ain't he a doll-dear? He brought you good luck. That's the best sleep you've had in months."

Arky threw a grudging glance in her direction. The kid had reddish-blond hair, a fat face, and round blue eyes. He looked like a baby, just a baby, *any* baby.

"He's only six weeks old, but look how big he is. And strong! He's already grabbing at things, and swinging his fists at you. Ain't he a doll-dear?"

"What's his name?" asked Arky, feeling slightly embarrassed due to the baby's steady blank stare.

"Thaddeus," said Anna.

"That's a hell of a name," said Arky. "Who thought it up?"

"It's Milli's father's name."

The baby raised its arms in what looked like a shrug, its smooth little face puckered for a moment, then it gave a loud belch.

Arky started slightly and stared at the baby in disapproving surprise.

"Oh, nice burp for Aunt Anna. Nice big burp. Got another burp?" said Anna, cooing.

"Take that kid away, will you?" said Arky. "He's spoiling my breakfast." Arky sat down at the table where Milli had put the tray and began to eat. He was hungry as a wolf and Anna had cooked him mush and ham with good thick ham gravy. Fit for a king!

The baby belched again, then cooed, and seemed to laugh.

Milli spoke to Anna in Polish and Anna nodded. "Look at him laugh," said Arky. "How do you like that!"

"He's not laughing. That's gas," said Anna. "We tried a richer formula. Gave him gas."

"What do you mean, formula?"

"What he eats."

"Don't he eat milk?"

"Yes, but.... Oh, never mind."

Arky turned to Milli, who seemed to be trying to hide. "Why don't you nurse him yourself?"

"I don't understand," said Milli.

Arky turned to Anna. "Don't none of your relatives speak English?"

"Milli came over only three years ago. She's my sister's oldest girl. How do you expect her to speak English when she only just got here? Can you speak Polish?"

"Well, Milli don't have to speak English to nurse the baby, does she?"

"Her milk's no good. Anyway, they don't nurse babies any more."

Arky cleaned up his plate, rose, and taking his coffee cup with him, walked over to the window. Milli grabbed up his tray at once and went out with it.

"She's trying to help, Arky," said Anna, irritated. "Didn't you notice? She helped me cook breakfast. She's going to do the dishes while I look after the baby. She's a crazy kid but she means well."

Arky turned and looked at Anna, searching her face for her intentions. Finally he asked: "When's she leaving?"

"Can't she stay?" asked Anna quietly. "She's got no place to go." The baby gave a few preliminary whimpers, then a long yell. Anna tried to soothe him.

"What the hell's wrong with him?" asked Arky, staring at the baby.

"Gas, I told you. He's got to be burped better." She turned and went out.

Arky called after her. "When I get back this evening I want that kid and her baby out of here."

He got no reply.

Irritated by Anna's attitude in regard to the baby, and by the questioning looks he kept getting from Zand and Lola downstairs, Arky decided to go to the afternoon game at the ball park. He called up a ticket broker he knew and got a single box seat along the first-base line, then phoned Leon's office at the Club Imperial. Roberta, the indifferent one, answered his ring. There was never any use trying to talk to Leon until six p.m. or after—Leon went to bed about dawn, sometimes later, and had his breakfast when other people were beginning to think about supper—but Arky wanted to set up a call.

"What time you expect him, ball of fire?" he asked.

"Oh, is that you, hoosier? He said seven thirty. That means any time up to ten thirty. He drove out of town last night and didn't get back till nearly eight this morning."

Arky thought this over, wondering. "If you don't hear from him by six, ring his apartment, honey. Tell him Johnson wants him to be in his office at eight."

"Oh sure," said Roberta. "Would you like to talk to Anthony Eden at nine? I'll have him rush right over."

"Better tell him, honey. I call his office at eight. Don't slip up. Or you'll have to wear the same old mink next year."

"Did you buy it? Look, hoosier, just because you own stock in the company...."

"Don't slip up, honey. Maybe Leon owes me money, or something. You never know." He hung up.

This was not his idea of how to handle Leon; it was the Mover's. Respect his privacy, the Mover had told him: so Arky had never even asked Leon for his apartment phone number; in fact, he didn't even know where Leon's apartment was. Of course, that was no problem. If he wanted to find out, he'd just have Zand tail him. An Indian couldn't shake Zand off, and Leon was no Indian, far from it; a blind man could follow him, almost, in that goosy-green convertible.

After the call, Arky went into the pool hall, handed Zand a slip of paper on which was the location of his box at the ball park, just in case he might get a hurry-up from the Mover, then he walked down to Putnam Boulevard, a wide through-street, and grabbed a taxi.

All the way out to the ball park, Arky and the taxi driver talked baseball, but Arky's mind was not on it and some of his replies were awkward and made the driver turn to look at him. Arky was wondering why Leon had driven out of town. Was the guy Leon had been talking about "hot" one way or another? And was he stashed? Arky did not like the sound of that!

Besides, the locals made three errors and lost a dull, one-sided game.

It was nearly six when Arky got back to the 17th. The cigar store was deserted except for Lola, who was leaning wearily on the counter, putting dark-red polish on her nails; and there were only a handful of customers in the pool hall, all merely lounging but two.

"Zand's looking for you," said Lola. "He's back in the cleaning establishment." Lola considered this designation of the bookie room funny, but Arky ignored the quip.

"Why didn't he call me?"

"He just started looking. Knew you'd be on your way."

The bookie room was packed, a lot of the patrons hanging on for late results from a California track. Zand, in a Kelly-green shirt and white slacks, came over to him at once.

His eyes were dilated; he seemed nervous. "The Paymaster called," he said. "You're to call the Big Man right away. He's waiting."

Arky said nothing. Turning, he walked leisurely back through the bookie room, nodding and smiling to men here and there, then he went out the back door and as soon as it closed behind him he took the stairs to his apartment three at a time, let himself in with a key, hurried to his bedroom, and shut the door.

The Mover answered his call at once. "Arky? I have some news for you. Not very good news, I'm afraid, but nothing too startling. I have good reason to believe that Leon is trying to deal the Big City boys in. One of them has already bought a place on the Front through an intermediary: the Bandbox. I've talked to the Officer. He'll close it up sometime this week. No big rush. Just a sudden raid, you know; and he can always blame the Commissioner."

Arky laughed appreciatively. "Nice going, sir."

"It will cause trouble, but the right kind. So stall with Leon."

"I've got a call in for eight, figuring to make a date with that clunk of his."

"No dates, Ark. Cancel it. Pretend it was a mistake. Ignore Leon till next week. We'll sweat him a little."

"He can stand it. He's got too much lard around his belt."

There was a chuckle from the other end. "That was a very tactless remark, Arky," said the Mover. "Perhaps you'd better sweat me, too."

Arky wanted to bang his head against the wall. His big mouth! The Mover was a large wide man and had quite a belly, although you could hardly notice it the way his clothes were cut. Anyway, Arky never thought of him as fat. He was a firm, solid-looking man. Leon, much slimmer—not fat at all, as a matter of fact—looked soft. "You know what I mean, sir," said Arky. "I didn't mean...."

"Oh, stop it. What's the matter, no sense of humor? All right. Ignore Leon. We may have some leads later. I've got a very smart young man working for us in the Big City at the moment. He informs me that George Cline is there, and that he's been talking to the boys, persuading them that things are such here now that they can move in. I don't know what George's idea is. Because if they did move in, they'd certainly shove George back out of the way in a hurry."

"Maybe he's teamed up with Leon. They used to be friends."

There was a long pause at the other end; finally the Mover spoke. "Arky, if things keep on the way they are going, we may have to start looking around for a new front man."

"That suits me fine."

"I know. But they are not so easy to find. Anyway, that's for the future. But cancel your call. Let Leon sweat."

Arky told the Mover about Leon being out of town the night before, and the Mover said: "Sounds like a Big City boy. They like to stay out of sight. He's probably at some little Lake resort, or a private home. All right, Ark. Goodbye."

The Mover was like that: he'd talk and talk, and even make jokes, then suddenly he'd hang up.

Arky felt a grim satisfaction in regard to Leon. He didn't like the guy, never had; nothing about him. It would be a pleasure to sweat him and sweat him good. In Arky's opinion the Mover was maybe a little too easy with Leon. It wasn't that he was criticizing the Mover. Who was he to criticize a man like that? But the Mover had never met Leon, judged him only by his actions and his repute. Leon needed a strong hand.

Still smiling to himself, Arky took off his coat and loosened his tie. He decided that he would not change his clothes before supper, as he usually did; then suddenly he observed that Anna had forgotten to lay out fresh clothes for him... and then... he remembered the baby!

He stood listening. The apartment was very quiet, but wasn't that a faint whiff of steak broiling that he caught? Somebody was cooking and it smelled good.

He had just decided to investigate when his private phone rang. The Mover again? He picked up the receiver, smiling, ready to speak in his most polite voice; but it wasn't the Mover at all, it was Leon. Arky glanced at his watch. Not much after six. Why the rush? Why the call, for that matter? Leon hadn't called him twice in two years.

"About that call tonight..." Leon began.

"What call?"

There was blank silence for a moment at the other end of the line. "You called me today, didn't you? Roberta said...."

Arky had a sudden inspiration how to sweat Leon. "No, Leon. I didn't call you. Maybe Roberta's been drinking."

"She said you called and you were sore. Wanted to set up a call for eight."

"I don't get it," said Arky.

"Look, for Christ's sake, Ark," said Leon, "stop kidding. Stop playing games. Robbie's a sharp girl, even if she doesn't seem like it. What *is* this?"

"You know as much about it as I do," said Arky indifferently. "Look. I'm busy."

"Wait a minute," said Leon, his voice sounding strange. "How about tonight? I can deliver this guy about eight. My office."

"What guy?"

"Why... the guy we talked about. You know."

"I'll have to check with the Mover. See you next week, same time, same station." Arky hung up, laughing to himself. Leon sure sounded bewildered.

Arky was in a wonderful humor and the smell of steak made him feel even better. Whistling, he walked down the hallway and looked into the kitchen. Milli was bending over the stove, wrestling with some saucepans. Hearing something, she turned, saw Arky in the doorway, screamed, and dropped one of the pans.

"Oh, Christ," said Arky to himself, "what an animal!" Then he turned and walked down the hall to the spare bedroom, opened the door, and went in.

Anna, wearing a while smock and looking like a dentist's assistant or a masseuse, was leaning over an article of furniture Arky had never seen before, working on the baby, who was kicking around, waving his little fists, and chortling.

Anna glanced over her shoulder at Arky, but said nothing. By the bed was a beautiful new basket, lined with padded blue satin and decorated with fine lace. Arky noticed a huge pile of baby clothes, a basket of bottles, three pale-blue blankets, a humidity gauge and thermometer in one, several jars of nipples and caps, and even a couple of small toys—all new.

"Poor little devil," said Anna, "he didn't have nothing, nothing at all. He was sleeping in a market-basket."

Arky made no comment; he was staring at the naked baby in wonder.

"Lord Almighty," he said, "look at the pecker on him."

Anna flushed violently and, turning, swung at Arky with the diaper. "You dirty thing!" she cried. "That lovely baby. You get out of here."

Arky roared with laughter, sank down on the edge of the bed and held his sides. Anna turned to look at him several times as she pinned on the diaper, then she began to smile, then to laugh.

"I was just surprised, that's all," explained Arky. "Them Polacks!"

"He can stay, can't he, Arky?" Anna demanded all of a sudden. "She can't look after him, hasn't got sense enough—and all she's worrying about is that damn fool boy friend of hers. He hates the baby: ran away and left her on account of it. Course he's only eighteen—just a kid."

"He a Polack, too?"

"Yes, but his name's Chuck."

"Chuck what?"

"She didn't tell me."

"Probably don't know. Probably the kid didn't even take his hat off."

"They're married," said Anna, loftily, throwing a triumphant look at Arky. "She's got the license."

"Did you see it?"

"No, I been too busy. Look at all the stuff I bought."

"Yeah. I notice. Listen, the guy's name will be on the license, unless he stiffed it."

"I don't care what his name is. All I care about is this little love. Look at him, Arky. How cute can you get?"

"He looks just like another fat baby to me."

"Come here and feel how strong he is."

"No, the hell with it. Babies are for women."

Anna turned and looked at Arky for a long time. "You know," she said at last, "I been trying to make myself believe that once upon a time you was a cute little baby like this, but it's no use, I can't do it."

"You know something?" Arky demanded. "You look mighty cute in that white thing you got on. Mighty cute."

"Supper's almost ready," said Anna. "Anyway, I got to look after the baby. Why don't you go change your clothes or something? Read the paper?"

Arky took out a cigarette and lit it, then comfortably crossed his legs. "Why don't the kid take her baby home?"

"She's got ten brothers and sisters, all sizes. No room. Anyway, her old man kicked her out. Thad's awful strict."

"But they're married."

"They got married since; then the kid run off and left her. Couldn't stand the baby."

"Well, she can go home now, can't she, now she's married?"

"Thad won't even speak to her. He beat her with a stick. They had the police. It was awful, I guess."

"Fine thing," said Arky, staring at the end of his cigarette. "Don't the old Polack know it can happen to anybody?"

Anna laughed appreciatively, then she lifted the baby up and showed him to Arky. He was dressed for sleeping, in a little blue gown.

"Look at him, Ark. He can stay, can't he?"

"Well," said Arky, "I don't want to see him out in the street, nor the animal in the kitchen either. But... look; can't you get her a room in the neighborhood or something? I don't want that kid crying and waking me up, for Christ's sake!"

"I tell you she hasn't got sense enough to look after him. She gets impatient with him when he won't eat fast enough, and shakes him. When he's got gas she just lets him cry. She's only a baby herself—sixteen. Just."

Arky sighed. "God, I don't know. Funny things sure happen to a fellow."

"We might have had one ourselves. You never know. Then what?"

"You ain't been."

"It could happen."

Arky stood up and stretched. Just as he was going to say something Milli came slinking in with her hands behind her back, glancing at Arky fearfully. She hesitated for a moment, handed Arky something quickly, then ran out.

"What the hell is this?" Arky demanded, staring at the piece of paper.

Anna came over and took it. "It's her marriage license. You see?"

"What's the father's name?"

Anna studied the license. "It's... Aloysius Sienkiewicz."

"It's what?" asked Arky, staring.

Anna repeated it, then turned to the baby. "That's you, darling. Thaddeus Sienkiewicz."

Arky went out in disgust.

In a few days Arky got used to the baby, and even showed a faint interest in it at times, but he couldn't get used to Milli, who never relaxed for a moment when he was around. She always got as far away from him as possible; when he spoke to her she became completely tongue-tied, and no longer even muttered something in Polish or said: "I don't understand."

Anna tried to explain the situation to Arky. "You see, you're the head of the house, Arky, and she thinks you're like her old man. He belts the kids around pretty good. Not because he's mean; he ain't. But because he wants them to grow up to be decent people. That's why he gave Milli such a beating that time...."

"He was a little late, wasn't he? The barn was empty; the horse'd already been stolen."

"Never mind the hick talk. I'm trying to tell you something. So you see, she thinks you're like Thad. She's figuring she'll do something wrong without knowing it and you'll cuff her around. You may not realize it, Arky; but you got a mighty mean look in those small eyes of yours at times."

"I don't look mean at her. She just irritates me. What an animal!"

"You ought to be ashamed of yourself talking that way. She may be dumb, but she means well. You weren't so smart when you were sixteen, I'll bet."

"I'm not so smart right now," said Arky. "But that Milli, she don't know her ass from a slippery ellum."

"There you go again. Long as you've been out of the bushes, and you still talk like a hillbilly radio show. Why don't you talk to fit your suit?"

"You wouldn't go so well in Riverview yourself."

"My old man still can't talk English. Neither can my mother. Neither can some of my cousins, or even my own sister. I think I do pretty good. But you! All your folks been here God knows how long...."

"Since the Revolution, by Christ," said Arky. "I had three great-grandfathers in the Civil War."

"Who won?" asked Anna.

"Go on, Polack. You wouldn't know about such things. All your folks were living in huts along a river someplace at that time. Or maybe in trees."

"That's why you won't marry me, isn't it, Arky?" asked Anna suddenly, her face serious.

Arky was slightly taken aback, and flushed. "Who says so?" he blustered. "I never did marry anybody yet, and I knew plenty of girls in Arkansas and here, too, before I ever saw you."

"All the same," said Anna, "that's the reason. You can't kid me. You think foreigners stink."

To Arky's intense astonishment, Anna burst into tears and ran out of his room, slamming the door after her. In a moment he heard her bedroom door slam down the hallway. Arky had been sitting on a straight chair; he jumped up and kicked the chair around the room. Then he went out and down the stairs to the pool hall, cursing to himself.

"Women!" he cried under his breath. "Dames! You can't satisfy 'em. Here she spends a couple hundred bucks on that damned Polack kid and I don't say nothing, nothing at all!"

He stopped before the door of the bookie room to compose himself. When he entered, his face was blank, but it didn't matter because everybody had gone home except a couple of young roustabouts who were sweeping up the litter—and Zand, who was sitting on the counter, reading a tabloid. He looked tired and his yellow Chinese-silk shirt was all sweated under the arms, but his black eyes flashed when he saw Arky, and without a word he handed him the paper.

A headline read: NOTED FRONT CLUB RAIDED.

"Bandbox?" asked Arky.

Zand nodded, grinning. "Yeah, and it says they busted up ten thousand dollars' worth of gambling equipment."

"The Officer did it up brown."

"Yeah. Says the proprietor's going to sue."

"Does it name the proprietor?"

"Yeah. Augie West." Zand's face clouded. "Say, ain't he one of ours?"

Arky glanced across the room at the roustabouts to be sure they weren't trying to listen, then, reassured, he said: "Used to be."

"He's the one who sold out, eh? I wasn't just sure."

"Well, he gets credit for it, anyway. Good friend of Leon's, though."

Zand raised his eyebrows, but made no further comment. Arky handed Zand a cigarette, took one himself; they lit up and sat on the counter swinging their feet. Finally Zand turned to Arky.

"How's Buster coming?"

"The kid? Fine. Growing already."

"Sure got Lola all upset."

"Dames are always upset. But how do you mean?"

"She wants to have a kid like Buster."

Arky almost fell off the counter. *"Lola!"*

"Yeah? Can you imagine a knocked-out broad like that? Good kid. Sure. But she's been round the wheel, brother—and shows it. I says to her: 'Be yourself, will you? We ain't even married so how can we have a kid?' 'It's done every day,' she says, wisecracking; but she was serious all the same. Can you beat it?"

"The older I get the less I understand about women."

"It's not that I'd mind marrying Lola," said Zand. "But I'm out of the habit now. I was married when I was seventeen. Syrian girl—my cousin. She was too Syrian for me. I'm an American, Goddamn it!"

Arky glanced at Zand sideways, but made no comment.

"Yeah," Zand went on, "I'm just out of the habit."

The buzzer from upstairs sounded under the counter and Arky got down.

"Anna, I guess," he said. "Now what?"

Zand laughed and waved ironically. Arky hurried out and up the stairs. Anna was waiting for him on the landing.

"Telephone," she said. "Leon."

Arky threw her a surprised glance, then a smile of satisfaction began to spread slowly over his rugged, homely face. He went into his bedroom, closed the door, picked up the phone and said: "Leon? What's with you?"

"Where you been? Why haven't I heard from you?" Leon sounded both worried and irritated.

"I'm not due till tomorrow night. Something wrong?"

"I thought we were going to get together. I can't keep this guy waiting around forever, Ark."

"Well, send him back to the Big City then."

Dead silence at the other end for a moment. "I wish you'd stop playing horse, Ark. This is serious."

"Sure is."

"I'm only trying to do what's right, and what'll help us, Ark. You know that."

"Oh, sure, sure," said Arky with exaggerated irony.

"Have you contacted the Mover?"

"Tried to. But he's been very busy. He'll get around to it sooner or later. Keep your shirt on."

A pause. "We better get some action, Arky. And not only on this business. How about the Bandbox? There goes five hundred a week."

"I heard a funny thing about the Bandbox," said Arky. "Did you?"

A pause. "What do you mean, Ark?"

"If you don't know, it ain't up to me to tell you. You should get around faster, husk a little more corn."

"Would you explain that last remark? I never been to Arkansas."

"It's a nice place if you like country. Anything else, Leon?"

"Anything *else!* We've got no place so far."

"I'll try to get in touch with the Mover before I see you tomorrow."

"All right. And say, try to find out what he's going to do about the Bandbox. That's serious."

"He ain't going to do nothing. He already did it."

"You mean he...."

"Look, Leon. Out-of-towners may think they are dealing with country boys. But sometimes country boys know the time of day, too." Arky hung up, grunting with satisfaction. Let Leon sleep on that one. Hundred to one Leon's guy would be waiting to talk to him tomorrow. He'd have to contact the Mover, see what he should do about it.

It was almost midnight. Arky was lying on his bed in the dark, staring up at the ceiling, at the shifting reflected pattern of light from the street. He felt lazy and contented. Anna had been with him for an hour and they'd had one of their good nights. These were getting fewer and farther between, but, no use to kid yourself, that was in the cards, because they'd known each other for years. Good gal, Anna. It was as if she'd been trying to make it up to him on account of the row they'd had. Arky began to sing, going away back absent-mindedly for a song:

> Possum in the treetop,
> Way up high,
> I'll get him down from there,
> By and by!
> Sweet potatoes cooking
> In the pot.
> Here I come, possum,
> Ready or not!

Anna had been feeding the baby. She came back laughing.

"You should have seen him eat tonight, Ark. Like a bear. Say, was that you singing?"

"Me? I don't know," said Arky with some embarrassment. "I was half asleep."

"Oh, that little doll-dear," said Anna, sitting on the edge of the bed. "I could squeeze him to death. He went right back to sleep. I got a song I sing him in Polish about good St. Wenceslas. He likes it. And when I call him Thaddeus he likes that, too!"

"I'd think the poor kid would puke. You sing to him in Polack and call him Thaddeus. That's a hell of a name for a kid."

"What's wrong with it?"

"This is America. That's no name for an American kid."

Anna began to get angry but restrained herself. Things were going so well with Arky and the baby right now, why spoil it? She decided to defer to him. "Well, what should we call him then?"

"I don't know," said Arky. "How about Elmer? That's my brother. Or Leeroy? That's another brother. I got one named Anderson, too; and another one named Tasker. But them's family names. Couldn't name him after the old man, either!"

"Why not?"

"On account of the name Grandma hung on him. Grandma was hell for reading the Bible. She hung a Biblical name on him."

"What was it?"

Arky hesitated for a moment, shifting. Finally he said, laughing: "Levi."

"*Levi!*" shrieked Anna. "That's a Jewish name."

"No, no," said Arky. "Lots of old-fashioned old fellows in Arkansas named Levi. Matter of fact, fellow named Levi Startle runs the drugstore at Dry River right now."

"Levi Startle! Dry River!" cried Anna. "Jesus! Sounds like you're making it up. But I got a better idea for the baby. We'll call him Orv, after you."

"Not after me you won't. He ain't my kid. Anyway, if we change his first name, might as well change his last name, too. Nobody can spell it or even pronounce it!"

"I want Zand to stop calling him Buster. I don't like it."

"It's better than Thaddeus."

"Move over," said Anna. "I'm coming in."

"You're going to get disappointed."

"Don't flatter yourself. It's cold out here."

Anna got into bed and pulled up the covers. There was a long silence; finally Anna said:

"I don't know what we're going to do about Milli. She cries herself to sleep every night."

"Why? Plenty to eat around here. Got a nice room."

"It's on account of Chuck. She keeps writing him letters."

"Does she know where he is?"

"No. She sends 'em to a place where he used to work. Somebody might know."

"I doubt it," said Arky. "Babies scare a lot of guys. Every once in a while down home some young fellow used to hit the road on account of a baby—or one coming, anyway. It's only natural."

"It's a hell of a way to act just the same."

"How about the girl? If she'd've behaved herself—no baby."

"Easy to say. Girls are human."

"Yeah," said Arky. "You can get yourself in a hell of a lot of trouble just being human."

6

Pay night. Zand drove the car in behind the Club Imperial and took the usual stall; Leon's chartreuse convertible was parked near by, polished and waxed and shining like a big curved mirror; the usual colored boy in the gold jumpers came round the corner, took a look at Zand's car, then went away again.

Arky got out. "I may be a little longer than usual, Zand," he said. "That is, if I've got it figured right. Don't get nervous."

"Okay," said Zand, then as Arky disappeared he got out and went over to study the convertible. It fascinated him. He made up his mind that one day, when he had enough moo to leave the big town, he'd have a hack like that, only maybe pink with cream-colored upholstery. This kind of green was all right— but for clothes, not automobiles.

When Arky entered Leon's outer office, the Indifferent One glanced up quickly at him. This time her eyes showed some emotion, but what it was Arky couldn't make out.

"Hello, ball of fire," said Arky.

Robbie smiled slightly. "Hello, country boy."

"Oh, a tumble."

"Yeah. I didn't realize what an important guy you were before. I like important guys."

Arky hesitated. Whatever this was, he didn't like it. Had Leon been talking? "I tried to tell you I was a big stockholder," he said.

"Must be pretty big," said Robbie, "the hell I got from Leon. Say, Elmer, what's the idea giving Leon the run? You know you called me up and tried to fix a call!"

"Maybe you got your days mixed up or your men." Arky smiled slightly. Apparently Leon had *not* talked; only in general, that is.

"All right, all right," said Robbie. "Play games. But you got me one masterpiece of a bawling out. Don't I even get an orchid, or something?"

Arky decided that it might not be a bad idea to have an "in" with Robbie. Could come in handy. He slipped a bill out of his fob pocket and palmed it.

"Sorry, girl; I don't carry orchids around with me. But you're a good kid. Shake."

Robbie stared at him blankly but shook hands. When she felt the bill in her palm, she drew back. "I don't take money from men," she said. "It's one thing my mother always warned me about." Then she glanced down at the bill Arky was now displaying between his fingers. "Unless, of course, it is in very large denominations." She daintily extracted the bill with her pointed fingertips. "Thanks, Elmer."

Just as Arky started for the inner office, the door burst open and Leon came charging out, his face red with annoyance.

"Say, where in hell...!" he began, then he noticed Arky. "Oh, hello, Arky. I saw you drive up the alley and I just wondered— Come on in."

Arky winked at Robbie and followed Leon into his private office, looking about him with veiled disappointment. He had expected Leon to have a visitor. Maybe Leon was smarter than he'd thought, and was going to play his cards very close to his vest.

Leon seemed nervous and kept running his hands through his hair. "Let's get our business over quick, Arky," he said. "There's a couple of guys waiting to see you. I had a hell of a time getting them to stick around for a day or so. They're big guys, used to having their own way. They don't wait for anybody."

Arky smiled to himself. He'd been right after all.

Leon took the thick, sealed, manila envelope out of his desk and tossed it to Arky, who caught it and put it carelessly into his coat pocket.

"Twelve G's short," said Leon.

"It figures, I guess. Anything else?"

Leon lit a cigarette, combed his hair nervously with his fingers, then shook his head. "No. Think not."

Wasn't he going to mention the Bandbox? Arky wondered.

"Sure there's nothing else?"

Their eyes met. After a moment, Leon lowered his gaze uneasily. "They went over my head, Ark," he said. "The sonsabitches—after all I've done for them...."

"I thought Augie was a particular friend of yours."

"I thought so, too. And here he puts me behind the eight-ball with you, with the Mover—with everybody. Swear to God, I didn't know a thing about it till I read the papers and talked to you. The guys who bought in were on the square, too. You'll talk to 'em in a minute. Augie lied to them like he lied to me. Told 'em it was okay with the Front Office."

"Augie leave town by any chance?"

"Took a plane out. He's gone, and with a load of dough. Even jumped his bond. That costs us, too. What do we do about Augie?"

"I'll have to ask the Mover. Look, Leon. If you can't control these guys better...."

"I know. I know," said Leon, nervously. "It's always a guy's friends that eventually get him in a corner. He trusts them."

"I didn't know you trusted anybody, Leon."

Leon threw his cigarette away, paced back and forth. "For instance, Ark," he said, "I trust *you*." Now he glanced at Arky to get his reaction, but Arky's face was blank. There was a short silence. Then Leon spoke again. "All right. Let's talk to these guys. Okay?"

Arky nodded, crossed his legs comfortably, and lit a cigarette. Leon went out through an alcove at the back which led to some small business offices and to a little apartment where Leon often spent the night when he'd been held late at the club. In a moment two strangers entered the room through the alcove, followed by Leon, who seemed to be showing exaggerated deference.

Leon introduced them to Arky, who got up, nodded, shook hands solemnly. The short, fat one was Mr. Riebe: he was about fifty and had a pink, chubby, almost blank face. His glasses gave off sharp reflections under the lights. He was wearing a curled blond toupee and it gave him a too-young, rather unnatural look, like an actor made up for a character part. An enormous blue-white diamond flashed from a ring on his right hand: otherwise he was dressed drably and correctly, and could pass among any crowd of businessmen.

The other one was introduced as Mr. Kelly, but it was obvious that that was not his name. He was a little above medium height, slender, wiry-looking, and as conventionally dressed as Mr. Riebe, except that he wore his businessman's uniform with a certain strange air, as if the clothes did not quite belong to him and had been rented for the occasion. He was very dark and his face was not unlike Zand's, except that the features were larger and coarser; he could be a Syrian, an Armenian, an Arab, or even a Sicilian.

He said nothing and sat in the background. Nevertheless, it was obvious to Arky after a moment that Mr. Kelly was the boss. Leon and Riebe gave it away by the looks they cast in his direction and by an indefinable something in their attitudes. In fact, gradually, as time passed, Arky got the impression that Mr. Kelly was a very big boy indeed. Sure of himself, contemptuous, even slightly amused.

Arky did not once catch Mr. Kelly looking at him, but he knew that he was being observed, pigeonholed if possible, carefully weighed.

With Riebe it was a different matter. He seemed to be trying to give the impression that he was a rather befuddled and cheerful soul, which of course, obviously, he was not, or he wouldn't have been the spokesman for a hundred-million-dollar mob.

"...You may ask," Riebe was saying, "why we even want to come in? Sounds silly, doesn't it?" He chuckled good-naturedly. "Here we are, you'll say to yourself, with a city of three million people and yet we would like to move into a town, co-operating, of course, with the locals—*co-operation*—I want to emphasize that... now where was I? Lord, I don't even seem to know what I'm talking about. Oh, yes! Why should we be interested in a town of nine hundred thousand souls when we are already operating in a town of three million? First, let me say that expansion is a very normal phenomenon. You know that, Mr. Uh... yes, you know that well. But that's not all. We have a population of three million—yes; but two million of them are, shall we say, peanut-eaters?" He chuckled again. "I'm sure you know what I mean. At the dog-tracks, they eat peanuts and bring the family. They don't bet. At the horse-tracks it's the same. Every place the same. Here it's different. This is one of the biggest gambling towns per capita in the whole United States; a real field for the operation of a smooth-running corporation like our own, a corporation which I don't like to boast, being a member of it—but a corporation with statewide influence; I might even say nationwide...."

"Why not international?" Mr. Kelly asked with a straight face. "Don't undersell yourself, Chub." Kelly's voice was soft and flat, almost inaudible.

Arky looked at him, then at Riebe, who was flushing. The little fat man had just been rebuked and showed some nervousness. Arky glanced at Leon, who seemed pale and remote, and overawed by the presence of Mr. Kelly.

"Mr. Kelly thinks I am overdoing it," said Riebe with a chuckle. "A very modest man, Mr. Kelly. As I am myself ordinarily, but... well, where was I...?"

"Maybe I don't understand what you're talking about," said Arky, cutting in. "But I don't get all this about you operating here. We're operating here right now—and doing all right...."

"You'll pardon me," said Riebe, "I don't mean to offend, but you are not even scratching the surface, Mr. Uh.... Not even scratching the surface. Besides, and Mr. Kelly will bear me out, and also Mr. Sollas, I believe, you will not be able to operate at all—not on any citywide scale, I mean—if something isn't done here, and done fast."

"You mean the Commissioner?"

"Yes. Naturally. Also several members of the city government are now taking heart due to the way Commissioner Stark is being backed up by a large section of the community.... Pretty soon you'll have that 'clean town' business. A reform administration will be voted in and then you will have real trouble on your hands. A reform administration is very hard to deal with; we know, having weathered several. Am I right, Mr. Kelly?" he demanded, turning deferentially.

Mr. Kelly did not even nod. He folded his hands on his knee, and stared in what seemed like profound boredom at the carpet.

Riebe cleared his throat and went on. "No, Mr. Uh... you haven't even scratched the surface. If we come in and co-operate with you, no matter what we take out of the town, your share will be larger, much larger, than it is at present. Doesn't that interest you?"

"I'm here to listen," said Arky. "I got no authority to say aye, yes or no. I'm—you might say—kind of an errand-boy."

Mr. Kelly looked up and glanced at Leon as if to say: "What does that make *you?*" Leon winced faintly, though Mr. Kelly said nothing at all and went back at once to his contemplation of the carpet.

"I'm sure you are too modest," said Riebe. "Now the Commissioner. Your problem is to get him kicked upstairs. That we can guarantee."

"Guarantee? You don't know the Commissioner. He don't want nothing but a clean town."

"Not even a seat on the Supreme Bench?"

Arky started slightly. The Mover had broached the same subject. "Maybe, maybe," he said.

"A simple matter. Politically, it would be considered a fine appointment—and from every angle: not a single objection in the state. Our governor would be a hero. Everybody would be happy, including ourselves. We can guarantee that, Mr. Uh...."

"You might be able to guarantee the appointment. But you can't guarantee he'd take it—especially if anything got around."

"How would anything get around?"

Arky hesitated, then he rose. "Tell you what, I'll talk to the Mover. Then I'll call Leon. One question. What's George Cline got to do with all this?"

Riebe smiled blandly. "Who, may I ask, is George Cline?"

But Mr. Kelly cut in harshly. "He made a few suggestions. We pay him off. He don't come in here. Satisfied?"

Arky looked around him. Very pale, Leon avoided his eyes. Fat Mr. Riebe was cringing at the brutal way Mr. Kelly had taken the play away from him and made a liar out of him. Mr. Kelly returned Arky's gaze calmly, his black eyes narrowed, opaque, as inhumane as those of a wolf.

"It's not up to me to be satisfied or not," said Arky. "I'll talk to the Mover."

Arky went out. Robbie looked up from her magazine.

"'Night, honey-chile," she said. "Home to your sorghum and corn-pone."

"How long the boys been around, baby girl?" asked Arky.

Robbie hesitated, glanced at Leon's door, then said in a low voice: "Moonface has been here about three weeks. He's a garter-snapper. The other one just got in—by plane. He's the kind you run from—girls, I mean. Not you, you big, strong, silent man!"

Arky winked at her and went out.

In Leon's office, Mr. Riebe was fuming. "Sending a big farmer like that to talk business with *us!* It's... it's an insult! A rank insult!"

"Don't underestimate him," said Mr. Kelly, quietly.

About ten o'clock Arky called Robbie and told her he wanted to speak to Leon.

"Big party on in the banquet room, Ozark," she said. "Leon's throwing a spread for our visitors. Dancing girls coming out of pies and things—so I hear.

Traffic's pretty heavy. If I go in there, I'll get trampled—or worse. That Mr. Riebe's an octopus. If you hold two of his hands, he still seems to have six or seven more."

"Ain't there a phone in there?"

"Just a house phone. And nobody would have the nerve to call Leon to it. The waiters like their jobs too well at the Imperial."

"Looks like you're elected, honey. Sorry, but it's important."

"All right, Ozark, if it's *that* important. My last words are as follows: 'She put up a gallant fight but what could one small girl do alone in this big city?' I'm now putting on my suit of mail."

"What's that?"

"M-a-i-l! What's the matter, don't you ever see any of those movies where they write with feathers?"

Arky had quite a long wait. Finally Leon came on. He sounded nervous and eager.

"No tricks this time, eh?" he said, with a forced laugh. "It's really you, Ark."

"Yeah. I'm with the Paymaster. We just talked to the Mover over the phone."

"Yeah?" said Leon eagerly. "Well... what did he say?"

"Leon, he said for you to tell your friends to get out of town and stay out. And that means stay out, period! We don't want 'em around here. The Mover's keeping pretty good tabs and if they buy in again there will be real trouble, not just a raid. We need no help of any kind, nothing. The Mover's got a real big deal on the fire, and if it cooks, we're in clover."

"My God, Arky, I can't tell these guys things like that. They're big. They're the biggest. They...." Leon broke off as if unable to continue. Arky could hear him panting with concern.

"Oh, yes," said Arky calmly, "another thing. The Mover says to tell Mr. Kelly he knows who he is and that all he can say is that things must not be going so good in the Big City or Mr. Kelly wouldn't be trying to cut in in the sticks. Make it strong. As strong as you like. Give it to 'em hard, Leon."

"Arky, my God!—I *can't*. You want the shooting to start?"

"Okay," said Arky. "Hold the fort. I'll be right down. *I'll* tell 'em."

"No! No!" cried Leon, hastily. "I... I'll tell 'em. Don't worry. I... I'll make it strong. Just as the Mover says, Arky. He's the boss. He calls the turn."

"Don't forget now. Make it strong. The Mover don't want 'em to misunderstand and keep trying. Somebody will get hurt that way, and it might be you, Leon. After all, you're out in front. You get the publicity. You're the newspaper Big Man."

"All right, Arky. I'll do my best. But, Arky—just a minute. Something mighty puzzling to me. These guys got a wonderful angle. The Commissioner. If he moves up, things will go back to normal. What am I saying? They'll double, triple. But if he don't... well, you can see how things are going with our take off 12 G's this week."

"Look Leon, just follow orders. Other people got angles too. Remember that; and be a good boy, Leon, be a good boy."

Arky grinned to himself as he heard a faint groan at the other end, then he hung up. Leon was slowly working himself out on a limb, and if he wasn't careful somebody, maybe even one of his out-of-town friends, might saw it off. Arky waited for a while, then he rang Leon's office again. Robbie answered.

"Did you make it, ball of fire?"

"In a photo finish," said Robbie. "He almost had me at the door, but a big blond just happened to be going in the other direction so I shook him off."

"Nice going. Thanks."

"Leon didn't even get sore. Au 'voir, as we say at the Club Imperial."

"Skip the gutter," said Arky, laughing, as he hung up. Then to himself: "That's a right cute kid. And no bunk about her. She's on the make and she don't care who knows it."

Zand almost went to sleep driving home, so Arky took the wheel in spite of Zand's yelps of protest. After a few miles of grabbing the door and almost putting his feet through the floorboards, Zand said:

"Arky, why don't you go back to the horse and buggy? An automobile's too much for you."

"Relax, will you? What's the matter, yellow? I was a chauffeur for over five years."

"Chauffeur!" cried Zand. "It must have been for a lunatic."

Arky laughed to himself, remembering his old boss, the Mover, and how he used to sit rigid in the back of the car, too proud to tell Arky to slow down and take it easy. That was the Mover, all right. You'd never get a show of fear out of that fellow. He'd face down Old Horny, himself.

Arky, laughing, told Zand about his former boss, not mentioning that it was the Mover, of course. Zand tried to appear interested as they burst through an intersection like something shot out of a gun, not quite beating a red light. Trying to keep his voice from trembling he asked:

"And who the hell is Old Horny? Sounds like my Uncle Alexander who used to chase his own daughters around."

"Old Horny is the devil," said Arky, then with disgust: "Where was you brought up?"

"Not in a cotton patch, anyway," said Zand, feeling irritable because he was afraid for his life. "You mean to tell me you believe in the devil?"

"I don't know," said Arky. "Some of the things I've seen in this world, I'm not so sure there *ain't* one, or something like it."

"You believe in God then, too, eh, Arky?"

"Sure," said Arky. "Don't everybody?"

"Well, slow down then, will you?" cried Zand. "Let's don't meet Him tonight."

When Arky got up to his apartment, Anna had just finished feeding the baby and, wearing a Chinese kimono, was sitting at the dining-room table drinking a bottle of beer.

"I don't know what we're going to do with her," she said before he could speak.

Arky grimaced as he sat down at the table. "The animal again? What now?"

"If she don't hear from Chuck pretty soon... well, we're going to find her lying down there on that pavement some morning."

"Well, I'm not her father. She's just got to work it out. Other people have troubles, too, don't they?"

"You got any?" asked Anna.

"No. At the moment, I haven't. But I've had plenty in my time."

"Not since I've known you."

"That's a fact. I been eating pretty high up on the hog for a long time."

Anna made a face. "Such talk! Didn't you ever go to school?"

"What's the matter with my talk? That's just an expression. Means living good."

"Well, say so. Sometimes you turn my stomach with them hick remarks. Want some beer?"

"No," said Arky, sulkily. "Hick remarks! At least they're in English."

Anna glanced at Arky, then burst out laughing. "I'm only kidding—like you kid me." She leaned over and kissed him. "Let me get you a bottle of beer. I had Zand send up a couple of cases this afternoon. It's the only thing I can get Milli interested in. She won't eat. So I remembered beer's a food. At least she won't starve herself to death."

"Are you kidding? She's fat as a pig now."

"She's lost ten pounds already."

"She can stand it. She's got a keister like the rear end of a Pier Avenue Bus."

"Just because you've got no rear at all...."

"I'm sitting down, ain't I?"

Laughing, Anna went to the kitchen and got him a bottle of beer. When she came back, he looked up at her quickly, remembering something.

"How's the kid? How's Orv?" he asked.

Anna suppressed a smile. She poured his beer for him, then kissed him again.

"Orv's fine," she said. "Sleeping like a little lamb."

"Good beer," said Arky, smacking his lips. "Nice and cold. Hits the spot."

7

Reisman heard the news just as he was leaving the hospital. He was at the desk, arguing about his bill and trying to get some of the more ambiguous items explained to him, when Sarah hurried over, followed by his three daughters, and told him excitedly that he was being paged, and that the *Journal* was trying to get in touch with him.

"All right, so I'm late with my column," said Reisman, impatiently; then he turned to the girl at the desk. "What happens when you operate on a guy and then he don't pay his bill? Do you put it back?"

"Put *what* back?" asked the girl in bewilderment, wondering if Mr. Reisman was in the right kind of hospital.

"What you took out?"

"Ben, for God's sake," said Sarah, grabbing his arm. "Pay the girl, pay the girl; and stop this... this...."

"Daddy," shrieked Ruth who was fourteen, "it's the *Journal!* They're *paging* you!"

They all seemed very much impressed with the fact that Reisman was being paged by the employer he'd worked for for over twenty years. Females were funny, from nine-year-old Selma, to Mama herself! Why all the excitement?

They finally managed to drag Reisman to a phone in the foyer and Sarah took over paying the bill, apologizing to the girl for her husband's attitude.

"You see, miss," she said, "he writes that 'Day In, Day Out' column for the *Journal,* and he thinks everybody knows it and he thinks he has to be funny all the time or people will think somebody else writes his stuff. I have plenty trouble with him at home."

"I can just imagine," said the girl, looking at Sarah with deep sympathy, infuriating her; in a moment, Sarah began to argue about some of the items.

It was Downy on the phone, and he was so eager to impart information that he could hardly talk.

"Did you hear it over the radio, Ben? I just thought maybe you might be too busy to listen or something so I—"

"I didn't hear anything," said Ben. "For two hours I've been trying to get out of this joint, with no luck. I'm going to ask the governor for a pardon."

"Then you didn't hear...?"

"What? What? *What?*" screamed Reisman.

"Leon Sollas has disappeared. They found his car parked at the Transco Airport, but he didn't take a plane from there."

Reisman was calm now, his sad, dark eyes showing deep interest. "How do they know that? Couldn't he leave under an assumed name?"

"No one answering his description—"

"Oh, bunk! You can't trust most people to pick their own mothers out at a show-up. Don't give me that 'answering his description' stuff...."

"Anyway, it's red-hot. Just thought you'd like to know. Mush Head's got all the bird dogs on it. Headline stuff. *You* know. The ten-thousand-dollar green convertible. I understand the *Examiner's* getting ready to run Leon's life story."

"That I want to see. Even the police don't know where he came from or why."

"Just thought you'd like to know, Ben...."

Reisman changed his tone, realizing that he was not being very gracious to Downy, who was only trying to do him a favor. "Thanks. Thanks, kid. Mighty nice of you."

"How you feeling, Ben?"

"The Swede nurse was beginning to look good to me so I realized it was time to go home to Sarah. Blood pressure's up twenty points. Guess I'll see another Christmas. Say—any more on the Commissioner and that Supreme Bench deal?"

"He won't comment, Ben," said Downy. "You know him. I was talking to Ed Lord. The Commissioner had Ed ejected from his office for asking questions out of turn. He's a character."

Reisman chuckled to himself. Good old Commissioner Stark. Used to handling the average politicos, who would do a handstand on Blackhawk Boulevard at high noon to get their names in the papers, the boys from Newspaper Row hadn't the faintest idea how to manage the Commissioner. Nothing seemed to work with him!

"How you coming with the sports page?" asked Reisman.

Downy laughed uncomfortably. "Last night I covered a girl's softball game. You know, the Newspaper League."

"Lucky fellow. Those kids are a lot cuter than the oafs at the ball park. Be patient, son. We've all been through stuff like that. You're not going to be a Bill Corum overnight. Thanks again. 'Bye."

Reisman wandered back toward the desk, lost in thought. Here was the big story again; and like a schnook he'd backed away from it. "What's the matter with me?" Reisman demanded of himself. "One bad lead and I blow it. I used to run down fifty bad ones. I must've been sick." He worried about himself for a few seconds, then he began to think of ways and means. Column or no column, he wanted a piece of this one, even if it did turn out ultimately to be a mistake, a bust, or a hoax. Worth a try. If Leon was finally found with his toes turned up—what a story! Might set off a chain of explosions that would blow the city sky high.

Was there any use to say anything to Mush Head? He'd merely look pained and begin to talk about all the money they were paying Reisman, and why didn't he relax, write his column, a big feature now, and leave the slugging to the younger men. Did he think the *Journal* was short of talent? Did he think that he was the only grade-A sleuth on the Row? Et cetera. Still, it would be better to have his help.

Reisman winced at the thought of all the objections.

Sarah woke him from his preoccupation.

"Good thing we had that disability insurance," she said out of the blue. "Or we wouldn't be taking any vacations this year."

"I just *had* mine," said Reisman. "You and the kids can pack for the Lakes any time. I got to stay here."

Sarah did not argue. The *Journal* had just called Ben. Probably something important. Business was business.

It was about six o'clock when Reisman wandered into the bar of the Regent Hotel and ran his eyes indifferently over the crowd. The Regent was a big, antiquated place on the northern edge of the Front, and for fifty years its bar had been a hangout for newspapermen, touring actors, horsemen, gamblers of all descriptions, and gentlemanly upper-crust hoodlums. The atmosphere was quiet and friendly. A loudmouth was quickly eased out unless he happened to be one of the regulars; then he was moved into a private room. The walls, paneled in the original dark wood, were covered with autographed pictures of ball players and other sporting figures, even golfers. The place had a mellow, well-aged, permanent air (it had even survived Prohibition) and smelled of good draught beer.

Reisman ordered black coffee and a corned-beef sandwich on Russian rye. The Regent bar had the best plain male food in town.

He nodded here and there to a few men whose faces were familiar to him; then, in a moment, he spotted Harry Radabaugh, who was talking to a couple of plain citizens at the end of the bar. As he ate his sandwich, Reisman kept glancing about him, but masking his interest by a bored look. Not a single hoodlum in sight. Not even a fringe-character. At least none that Reisman had ever seen before. Had the boys gone underground till the Leon business was cleared up?

He ate leisurely, waiting for Harry to complete his conversation. Finally Harry nodded to the others, paid his score and started out, moving past Reisman without seeing him.

"Harry!" called Ben.

Radabaugh smiled, but it was more than a little forced. "Hi, Ben. Thought you were still in the hospital."

"I'm out on parole. Drink?"

"Up to here. Got a date. See you."

"Wait a minute, Harry," said Reisman. "I been behind walls. Thought you might bring me up to date."

"I don't know a thing, Ben. Any more than you or anybody else does. All I know is, the boys were all mighty happy for a day or so and now they're all sad."

Reisman glanced about him ironically. "How can you tell? Looks to me like they all followed Leon."

"It figures. It's a nice time to stay home."

"What were they so happy about?"

"Your guess is as good as mine. But I'd be happy if I was one of them."

"As if you're not," thought Reisman, but asked: "Why?"

"With Commissioner Stark moving up to the State Capitol! Come now, Ben."

"Is he?"

"You think he can resist it? A local judge? He's human."

Something stabbed at Reisman and it wasn't the ulcer. "Nice for the boys, eh?"

"It looked like it. Now I don't know," said Harry. "All supposition on my part, of course. I don't get the Leon business at all." He glanced at his wrist watch. "See you, Ben. Can't keep this doll waiting. It's a first. Later, she can wait." Harry laughed and went out.

"Hm," said Reisman, as he finished his sandwich. A break for the boys, all right. But an accidental one. Had to be. Nobody was big enough to swing a thing like that. But why did this whatever-it-was keep stabbing at him? "No, no, Ben," he admonished himself, "it's a hangover from all that junk that was shot into you at the hospital."

All the same....

Commissioner Stark's secretary was not pleased to see Reisman. He was a huge harness-bull named Balch and his white-blond hair was cut in a butch.

"Not tonight, Reisman," he said. "You should have called. No chance tonight."

"I was just passing by. What's so special about tonight?"

"Don't you read your own paper?"

"Only my column."

"Well, Judge Greet's giving a reception—kind of a party, a get-together, for Commissioner Stark. I guess the Judge figures the Commissioner won't be with us much longer."

"How do you feel about that, Balch?"

"He ought to be governor, I think," said the harness-bull. "Or even president."

"Oh, he's a bigger man than *that*," said Reisman.

Balch glared at him. "All right. Make jokes. Here I am trying to talk serious. You asked me a question, didn't you? The hell with you, Reisman. Go home."

"Now, now," said Reisman. "Don't I mention your name every chance I get?"

"Twice!" cried Balch.

"That's every chance I got. But, Balch... won't things be easier here for all of you? The Commissioner... he's quite a driver, if you know what I mean."

Balch flushed angrily. "I know perfectly what you mean. At first we didn't like it. Thought he was too rough and tough. Now we like it. It's going to seem mighty funny without him... if he goes, that is. And why wouldn't he? A Supreme Court Justice is a pretty big man."

"Yeah, good salary, and no work."

"Go home, Reisman," said Balch, really outraged and trying not to show it.

Reisman lit a cigarette and considered. If he had any sense he *would* go home. The old City Building was like an oven and smelled of mustiness, dust, and disinfectant. But he did not have any sense, he decided.

"Couldn't you just buzz him? Is he busy? Got somebody in there with him? He sent me flowers when I was in the hospital. I'd like to thank him."

"I know he did, and then you talk the way you do. You ought to be ashamed, Reisman."

The buzzer sounded and Balch grabbed up the intercom immediately. It was amazing to Reisman the way the Commissioner had these big cops jumping around for him.

"Yes sir?" Balch snapped out, like a top sergeant talking to a colonel. "A bow-tie, sir? No, sir, I'm afraid that I... maybe one of the girl secretaries...."

"What's the matter?" asked Reisman.

"He's getting dressed in there for the party. Can't tie his bow tie...."

"I can tie one."

"Mr. Reisman's here, sir," said Balch. "Says he can tie one...." A curt harsh laugh came through the wire, then a few harsh-sounding words. "All right, Reisman," said Balch, hanging up. "Go ahead in."

Reisman opened the door. Commissioner Stark was standing in front of a minute wall-mirror with his lean face screwed up, trying to knot a black evening tie. He was wearing a rusty-looking, old-fashioned Tuxedo and his hair was standing up angrily all over his narrow skull. Reisman closed the door quietly.

"With a simple twist of the wrist, Commissioner," he said, "I can solve your problems."

The Commissioner said nothing. He merely turned around, came over, and stood in front of Reisman, who knotted the tie deftly, patted it into place and said:

"That's what comes of going to so many banquets. I can tie one in my sleep. In fact, I have—in a drunken stupor."

The Commissioner went back to the mirror, glanced at the tie briefly, then he took out a small ivory pocket-comb and whipped it carelessly through his hair. "Thanks," he said. "All my wife's idea. I haven't had a Tux on for ten or eleven years. You want something, Reisman?"

"No. I was just passing by. Thought I'd drop in and thank you for the flowers."

"Don't mention it. You're all right now, I understand."

"I'm fine. Are you really moving up to the State Capitol, Commissioner? I haven't seen any confirmation."

"To tell you the truth, I haven't made up my mind yet. But I suppose it is inevitable. My wife's all for it, naturally. She was always against me coming in as commissioner, thinks I'm working myself to death. Says it is a thankless job. But thanks are not what I want."

"What *do* you want, Commissioner?"

"A clean city. That's impossible, I know. Let's put it this way: as clean a city as humanity allows. And I'm not trying to disparage humanity. Don't misunderstand me. We've all got plenty of the Old Adam, and a man must admit it to himself frankly or he's not fit to be a dog-catcher, let alone a high public official. A self-righteous man can be very dangerous in a high position. He's a man with a warped mind, and will insist on the impossible. I only insist on the possible, but my idea of the possible does not seem to agree with anybody else's. Wouldn't you say so, Reisman?" The Commissioner laughed curtly.

"It agrees more or less with mine."

"Yes, I know that," said the Commissioner. "And you've been a big help to me. By the way, what about this Leon Sollas business? Do you think he was murdered?"

"Could be. But I'm inclined to doubt it. The boys have their little squabbles. And sometimes it's better politics, and safer, for them to disappear till the atmosphere clears."

"Know any reason why somebody should kill him, aside from the fact that he's a rather sad specimen of the human race?"

"Oh, he has his enemies, I suppose, considering the business he's in, but the boys don't seem to kill each other any more, Commissioner. It's a politer age; in the underworld, that is, though not with us, apparently. Maybe we'll gradually learn from them."

The Commissioner seemed to think this over for a moment, then a frown passed over his lean face, and he said: "Reisman, give me your honest opinion. Do you think I'll be able to get by at Judge Greet's in this suit? My wife insisted I have a new one made. But I wouldn't hear of it. Too expensive."

"Oh, I think so," said Reisman, hesitantly, rather appalled at the thought of the Commissioner appearing at such a disadvantage among the swells of Riverview. The Greet mansion was one of the showplaces of the city. Judge Greet had married a Byron, *crème de la crème*, and though he seemed like rather a nice man himself, Reisman, in the long course of his city career, had seen enough of the Byrons to hate them thoroughly. The Judge's only son, Byron Greet, was a real Byron: a supercilious intellectual and social snob, now an English professor at City College. Once Reisman had spoken on journalism and kindred subjects at the college in front of a sophomore English class, and Byron Greet had heckled him—young son of a bitch!

"Well, it doesn't matter," said the Commissioner. "I'm no Beau Brummel. Everybody knows it. However, the Judge has gone to a lot of trouble to honor me. Maybe I ought to go home and put on my good blue suit."

"May I say something?" asked Reisman.

"Yes. Certainly."

"I think the blue suit is a very good idea."

The Commissioner looked down at himself. "Hm! That bad, eh? My wife tried to tell me.... All right. I'll do it."

"I'll drive you home, Commissioner. Right on my way."

"All right, Reisman. First, I've got to use the phone."

"Want me to go outside?"

The Commissioner merely shook his head, then he sat down and called his wife to tell her about the change of plan. Apparently he got quite an argument. Reisman looked away, tried not to hear.

"...All right, all right," the Commissioner was saying, "I *know* you told me—but it can't be helped now. I'll be right home. Won't take me ten minutes to change—save you driving down here to pick me up. All right, all right. Anyway, I understand it's fashionable to be late. I don't care what all the others will wear. What's that? What difference does it make what *I* wear? *You* wear what you please." The Commissioner shook his head impatiently from side to side. "Stop splitting hairs. I'll be right home. We'll talk about it then. Good-bye." The Commissioner hung up, then he sat smiling at the desk for a moment. "Reisman," he said finally, "do you know anything about women?"

"No," said Reisman bluntly. "I've only been married fifteen years."

"Well," said the Commissioner, "you wouldn't believe what this party means to my wife. New dress, nervous as a girl. And yet she always says it's a waste of time to go to parties, and things like that."

"It's so they can get you going and coming, Commissioner," said Reisman. "If you want to go to a party, they can say it's a waste of time. If you want to stay home, they can say you never take them any place. It's a kind of feminine game. A little hard for a man to understand. Like poker to most women."

They drove along in silence for some time. It was a very hot night and there was hardly a breath of air stirring. The pavements were still hot from the day's glare and the huge town had a dusty, stale smell, somewhat like a long-closed attic room.

Finally Reisman spoke. "If you go north, Commissioner, this town just won't be the same."

"It's getting along without Theo. Hardy. It can certainly get along without me. I won't be around forever, in any case. I'm not growing any younger. Still... I don't know."

"Oh, it will get along all right. No doubt about that. But it will be so much easier for the boys to operate."

"I'm not so sure. There's a new temper in the town. It's been coming. I guess I'm just a reflection of it."

Reisman glanced at the Commissioner, but said nothing. Did he mean it? Was he an incurable optimist? Did he really think that aside from Hardy, now out of the picture, there was another public servant in the city of the selflessness, the determined honesty and decency of himself? Plenty of good men, of course. But all flawed—by ambition, or laziness, or a bad marriage, or an ineradicable weakness, like drink, or by ideological confusion, or by dangerous tie-ups.... The Commissioner was at the moment, literally one man in a million, or seemed so to Reisman, who had been around for a long time and had watched the public servants come and go, like actors striding for a brief space on a stage they couldn't hold.

"Well," said Reisman, "all I know is, the boys are mighty happy at the news that you're going north."

The Commissioner glanced at Reisman. "Is that a fact?"

"A cold fact."

8

About eight o'clock that night a long-distance call came through for Arky. He was lying on his bed, smoking a cigar and talking to Anna, who had young Ory in her arms, bouncing him, trying to get him to go to sleep; he'd been wakeful since his six o'clock feed. Arky motioned Anna out of the room, and finally, after a long wait, Leon came on.

"Leon? What did you ditch the car for?" asked Arky without preamble.

"Didn't Rudy pick it up?"

"No. Haven't you seen the papers? Lot of people think you're dead."

"I'm close. You are too. Keep your head down, Arky. That goes for everybody."

"The Mover, too?"

"Yes. They know who he is, and I swear to God they didn't get it from me. I told Kelly the Mover knew who he was, like you told me to. Kelly laughed. He says: 'I got news for you. It's mutual. I've known about your pal for two years.' That's the straight truth, Arky."

"When you coming back?"

"Never."

"What's that?"

"You heard me. Rudy's all ready to take over for me, if it's okay. But I don't know why he didn't pick up that car."

"Are you crazy? It will all blow over, Leon."

"No. Not this time. The Big City boys think the Mover pulled the dirtiest double-cross of all time on them."

"What was it?"

"Getting the Commissioner moved up, after Kelly was just starting to work on it. Kelly figures he gave you the idea and you and the Mover beat him to the draw. This means war, Arky. With the Commissioner out, anybody with enough drag and money can operate, not just us."

"Oh, I don't know. Besides, Kelly didn't give us the idea. Me and the Mover had already talked about it. What makes Kelly think anybody could work that fast?"

"I'm only giving you the facts. And another thing. Kelly's got a lot of friends in town. He's already got a partial fix running."

There was a brief pause, then Arky said: "Well, you finally outfoxed yourself, didn't you, Leon?"

"What do you mean?"

"Horsing with the Big City boys. Now you're out in the cold."

"I'm just happy I'm alive. But naturally they'd come to me first. I wasn't horsing."

"Stop kidding. We know all about the Bandbox deal."

"All right. I'm not arguing with you, Arky, I'm just trying to tip you off. Keep your head down. You're playing in the big league now. Good-bye...."

"Wait a minute. Where can I call you?"

"No place. But I may call *you* later." He hung up abruptly.

Arky was deeply puzzled and sat lost in thought for a long time. What was Leon's game? He knew Leon well enough to feel pretty certain that he hadn't just called up to warn them. If Leon was out for good, what did he care! Maybe there *was* going to be trouble; maybe Leon was certain of it and had taken a runout and was sweet-talking both sides; then after the smoke cleared, he'd have an "in" no matter who won. Sounded likely.

The more Arky thought about the situation the less he liked it. As it was an odd hour and an odd day, he felt that he should not bother the Mover, so he put in a call for the Paymaster.

"You caught me just in time," said King. "I was leaving. What's all this nonsense about Leon?"

Arky explained at some length, then he said: "I'd sure like to talk to the Mover, but it might not be convenient for him."

"It definitely wouldn't be," said King. "But I can get him. I'll call him right away. Stand by, Arky. Call you back."

"Make it strong, now. I know there's no way in the world to scare the Mover or make him cautious. But put it on strong. This might be serious, damn serious."

Arky hung up and waited, pacing back and forth nervously. In a few minutes Anna put her head in the door.

"Are you busy? Can I ask you something?"

Arky glanced at her in irritation. "All right. What?"

"Suppose, just for instance," said Anna, slowly, "that Milli didn't come back...."

Arky stared blankly. "What the hell are you talking about? Don't bother me with that nonsense now."

"Well, she's been gone three hours, and she never stays away over half an hour—scared to be out."

"She probably got lost a block from here and we'll have to send out a rescue squad."

"Ark, I think she got a letter today. You know how she always grabs the mail—waits for it downstairs?"

"I don't know nothing about it."

"Well, I'm telling you. She's so crazy, if that sap, Chuck, wrote to her, told her where he was, she might run off and leave the baby. Suppose she does?"

The phone rang. Arky motioned for Anna to go away but Anna persisted. "Suppose she does, Arky?"

Arky reached for the phone. "Then you're stuck with him. Beat it."

Anna rushed over to Arky, kissed and hugged him, knocking him off balance, then she turned and hurried out, slamming the door, laughing and crying at the same time.

Arky shook his head slowly from side to side as he picked up the receiver. "Yeah?"

"I talked to him, Arky," said the Paymaster. "No use. Just wasting my breath. He's got nothing but contempt for the boys—thinks they are all yellow cowards...."

"Yeah, but a yellow coward can shoot you in the back."

"You don't have to sell me, Arky. But take my advice—don't call the Mover. He was even annoyed with me. By the way, Rudy Solano's the Front Man till further notice—which won't be long in coming, I hope. Rudy means well, but that's all. Leon's a genius compared to him. You keep the same schedule. Rudy's running the Club Imperial. And by the way, in case you don't know it, due to a newspaper story in the *Examiner* the boys have got Rudy down at headquarters sweating him over Leon's disappearance.... Rudy's going to get a big build-up now. The new underworld boss—same old newspaper stuff."

"You got any idea why Rudy didn't pick up Leon's car at the airport?"

"Yes. A couple of dicks from downtown were hanging around the airport all day for some reason or another. And a fellow from the D.A.'s office—named Radabaugh."

"Hm! You think they saw Leon blow?"

"I don't know how they could miss him."

"What was Rudy worried about then?"

"He didn't like the set-up; anyway, it doesn't matter. Just makes more noise, more stories in the newspapers about Rudy and Leon. And that's what they get paid for, more or less."

Arky considered for a moment. "You sure there's no way to make the Mover see that there might be real trouble?"

"Take my advice—do nothing. Don't bother him, except about routine business. It's just no use, Arky. I've known him for years. He doesn't know what the word fear means. He just laughs, or gets irritated."

After he hung up, Arky sat smoking thoughtfully for a long time, looking out at the dark river and all the lights clustered along its banks; finally he made up his mind what to do. If the Mover found out later, well, then he himself would have to take the consequences, whatever they were. It was up to him to protect the Mover whether he liked it or not.

He put on his hat, went out into the hallway, opened the door and started down the stairs. When he was halfway down, he met Milli coming up. She was flushed and panting as if she'd run a mile uphill. With a gasp, she flattened herself against the wall to let him pass. Her obvious fear of him always irritated Arky. What had he ever done to the damn-fool girl but feed her and give her a place to stay?

"Where you been?" he demanded.

"I go... movie," gasped Milli. "So late!"

"Anna's looking for you."

Milli stared at him in open fear for a moment, then she tore past him, took the stairs in a couple of bounds, and tried frantically to open the apartment door— but it was locked. Swearing quietly to himself, Arky went back and unlocked the door for her. Milli gave a hurried bob of her head and a sort of stumbling curtsy, then she disappeared.

"I don't know," said Arky, starting down the stairs again. "Maybe it would be better if she *did* run away. Looks to me like Anna's going to be kind of disappointed to see her." He laughed to himself.

Big Brannigan was on the desk at the Pier 7 Station House when Arky entered, and several police reporters were playing hearts at a table just below his desk. They all looked up and stared at Arky, who smiled at them in easy friendliness and nodded.

"Well, Arky," said Brannigan, "finally decided to give yourself up, eh?" The big Irishman laughed and hit the desk with his hamlike fist.

"Yep," said Arky. "It's been worrying me for years. Can't sleep nights. Captain here?"

"Yeah, he's here."

"I got a complaint to make and I want to talk to the Captain."

The reporters began to prick up their ears. Joe Pavlik came over.

"Say, let us in on this, Arky."

"All right," said Arky. "No secret about it. Them young hoodlums—got so we can't handle 'em any longer. We just had a bad fight down at the place. I want it on record just so maybe if Zand knocks somebody's head off, the Captain will know the reason."

Pavlik's interest faded. "Yeah," he said. "I had a run-in with a couple of 'em myself last night. I caught 'em fooling with my car."

"You better talk quiet. They always gang you. You haven't got a chance."

Brannigan got the Captain on the inter-com, told him about Arky's complaint, then he turned to Arky. "Captain says come right in. He'll see you. But he's only got a minute."

Arky thanked Brannigan, then turned and went down a dark hallway to the Captain's office. The reporters resumed their game, sighing. Hoodlums, hoodlums, young hoodlums! The papers had been full of them for weeks. Everybody had a bellyful of them, from editors to subscribers.

The Captain, in uniform, was sitting at his desk, smoking a cigar and drinking coffee from a paper carton. He needed a haircut and his big head had a savage, shaggy look to it. He showed no expression at all and did not even speak until Arky had closed the door.

"You're taking a big chance coming here, Ark," the Captain said finally.

"It's important. Didn't want to talk on the phone. Relax. I put 'em all to sleep out front."

"You even had me wondering for a minute. Well?"

"We got to protect the Mover."

"That bad?"

"Could be. Might be. And if anything happens to him it'll be our fault."

"Take it easy, Ark."

"You heard me. Our fault. He won't look after himself—never would. I don't have to tell you that. I guess you've known him longer than anybody."

Dysen ran his big, fat, powerful hand wearily over his face, and sighed, sounding like a hippopotamus in distress. "I guess that's right, Ark. All right. How do we do it?"

"That's up to you. You're a copper. Protecting people is your business."

"Sure, but we got problems. The Mover lives to hell and gone from my precinct. I can't send prowl-cars; they're bound to bump into the ones that belong there... then we got questions from headquarters. Foot patrol... worse. The only thing I can see is plainclothesmen, and we still got problems."

"Well, let's solve 'em fast," said Arky, impatiently. "Time's passing."

"Why don't you get Rudy to dig up some boys? Wouldn't that be easier?"

"No," said Arky emphatically. "First place, them boys are no good. They'd take your money and then soldier on the job. Second place, might tip off the Mover to a wrong one."

"That's right," said the Captain. "Let me think. I could give some of my best boys an open fugitive-warrant—in case they ran into some boys from headquarters. That'd explain what they were doing in a faraway precinct. But even so... round the clock, day and night, it's going to look bad...."

"Don't worry about daytime," said Arky. "Just from sunset to sunrise. And they don't have to stand guard, for God's sake. It's a quiet neighborhood.

Damn few strangers go there. Can't they comb 'em?"

"Sounds all right."

"Besides, there are special police in the neighborhood, hired by the people who live there. Retired coppers—old guys, you know. Not much use against real rough boys, but they can keep their eyes open, can't they? Why don't one of your boys contact 'em, give 'em any cock and bull story you like about suspicious characters in the neighborhood? Use the fugitive gag. This may all blow over in a few days."

"All right, Arky," said the Captain, sighing again. "I'll do the best I can."

There was a short silence, then Arky spoke. "I don't really think the fellows have got guts enough to try to take care of the Mover. All the same there is one pretty big boy mixed up in this and he don't impress me as the kind of boy who would let much of anything stop him."

Arky got up and walked to the door. "I'm counting on you, Captain."

Dysen nodded wearily as Arky went out.

Commissioner Stark was glad he had not worn his rusty old Tuxedo, and he kept reminding himself that he must thank Reisman at the first opportunity. The columnist had saved him from considerable embarrassment. In his good dark-blue serge suit he felt more or less at ease, even though he was the only man at the reception not in evening clothes.

A steady stream of elegantly dressed people were introduced to him and he stood sipping his punch, nodding and smiling, and wearing himself out conscientiously shaking hands. Not being a practiced politician, he had never learned the trick of pressing an outstretched hand and then getting away before his own hand was pressed or squeezed or pumped. It was amazing to him how many men seemed to enjoy holding on to his hand as they talked. His right shoulder began to feel numb, his hand ached, and now his feet were beginning to hurt.

Why did nobody sit down?

He glanced at his wife. In her new black evening gown—a little low in the neck, wasn't it?—she was having the time of her life, bowing, talking, laughing.

And to crown it all, Judge Greet himself took her away to the conservatory, where, through the glass doors, the Commissioner could see them whirling round and round while the string band played an old-fashioned waltz. Was it *Blue Danube*? Perhaps. The Commissioner had no ear for music and could hardly distinguish one tune from another. And yet he felt pretty sure it was *Blue Danube*. He'd always liked waltzes and had at one time been quite a waltzer at the big dances given by the Knights of Pythias in his home town.

Time went on interminably. The Commissioner shifted from one foot to the other. A colored servant replenished his punch. He began to sweat and dab at his forehead with a handkerchief. Gracious, it was a hot night! A scorcher. No wind at all even out here on the upper river among the trees and open country, far away from the heated asphalt of the city.

From time to time he glanced about him at the sumptuousness of his surroundings. But he did not envy the Judge his beautiful house with its beautiful furniture. Possessions meant nothing to the Commissioner. He considered them merely a source of worry. Not that the Judge seemed worried about anything.

At fifty-five the Judge looked about the same as he'd looked ten years earlier— no heavier, not a touch of gray in his abundant dark hair, which he kept pasted down to hide the curl, no sign of aging in his broad face; a big, robust, sometimes arrogant, but almost always genial man, who had hundreds of friends and well-wishers, was considered an ornament to the community, an unsurpassed toastmaster and political speaker, a first-class citizen who was always ready to give time and money to any worthy civic venture.

He had been called "judge" for a long time, but actually he was an ex-judge, and had only been on the bench for a few years in his thirties. Since then he'd made a fortune out of various businesses, including real estate; he'd been one of the original developers of Riverview, and besides, he was the senior member of the firm of Greet, Judson, Braithwaite and Judson, corporation lawyers who handled some of the biggest accounts in the city. The Judge seldom appeared at the office, and paid little attention to the handling of cases. He merely lent his name and prestige to the firm.

Although he had never run for an elective office, he had been in politics for years: City Party Chairman, State Party Chairman, National Committeeman, and other offices so numerous as to be lost in the mists of the past. He had a sure hand in such matters and his advice was eagerly sought and almost always taken. He had been responsible for the election of Charles Marley as mayor—not a very good choice as it had turned out—and it was said that his influence extended even to the State Capitol.

On top of all this, he had married money. His wife was reputed to have a million or so in her own right. She was fifty, but hardly looked forty. She was slim and blond and nervous, and rushed about like a young girl. It was hard for the Commissioner to believe that Mrs. Greet was the same age as his wife.

Later, he danced with her, feeling very awkward and at sea due to her strong perfume, her semi-nudity, her quick graceful movements, and her chatter. She talked incessantly, looking about her with a bored air.

The Commissioner sighed with relief when the dance was over, and he was once more back in the huge living-room with a glass of punch in his hand.

Commissioner Stark sat smoking a cigar in the Judge's book-lined study. Through the open French doors the music drifted back from the big glassed-in conservatory, sounding remote, sad, and nostalgically sweet. There was bright moonlight and from where he sat the Commissioner could see the tall old trees, big elms and oaks, casting sharp black shadows across the bluish-white lawn. A cool, damp breeze was blowing in from the direction of the river now, dispersing the heat, and the Commissioner, sweaty, tired, and aching, began to feel a certain relief, and sighed.

"Nice breeze," he commented.

Smoking, the Judge nodded. "Yes," he said, "if there is a breeze going, I get it in this room. Spend most of my time here. Not so active as I used to be. Been doing a lot of reading and thinking."

The Commissioner smiled slightly. "Well, I wouldn't say you'd exactly re-tired, Judge."

The Judge smiled. "No, not exactly, but I'm moving toward it. The men of my family begin dying off about my age. My father was fifty-six. My Uncle Tom was fifty-four. My grandfather about sixty. But the women live forever. You know what they say about women on a pension." The Judge laughed. "Not that our womenfolks were ever exactly on pensions. But it amounts to the same thing. They always end up with all the money. That's the secret of woman's power in America; they outlive all the men."

"They do at that," said the Commissioner. "Never thought of it before, though."

"Well," said the Judge after a moment, "if there is anything to heredity—and nobody seems to think that there is any more, except horse breeders—then I might as well slow down my activities a little, and prepare myself. I've always tried to be realistic about things, not emotional." The Judge sat turning some-thing over in his mind for a moment, then he went on. "However, realistic thinking can lead a man into strange paths. Maybe idealistic thinking is best af-ter all. Take my son now—Byron. Strictly idealistic. At times, talks like a jack-ass, for my money. Fooled around with communism for a while. Then it was socialism. Now it's... well, God knows. But at least he's looking for something... a faith. I never seemed to need a faith. I just took the world as it was—a dirty place, so make the most of it!" The Judge laughed again and glanced at the Com-missioner. "I don't know why I'm boring you with this silly talk...."

"You're not boring me at all," said the Commissioner, quickly. "I find it very interesting. In fact, I've done considerable thinking myself along those lines. Most people consider me a sort of wild-eyed idealist—a jackass, as you say—but I'm not. At least I don't *think* I am. All I'm after is a reasonably clean city, for reasonably clean people, including myself. As long as men want to gamble, there will be gambling an army couldn't stop. As long as men want women for a night, there will be prostitution. The best that any man can do is to try to con-trol it. The greatest danger is the corruption of officials. As you know, Judge, I have no sympathy for the corrupt official. If I had my way he'd be dealt with to the limit of the law. There is no excuse for malfeasance. None at all. Some-times a professional thief, even a murderer, has my sympathy—a corrupt of-ficial, never."

"Those are harsh words, Commissioner," said the Judge, laughing slightly.

"I'm sure you've raised yourself a nice crop of enemies in the city. I've heard many officials talk that way, but nobody thought they meant it—and they didn't. Everybody *knows* you mean it. It's made you a big man, Commissioner—and it's the reason for the appointment that's being offered you."

"That appointment worries me," said the Commissioner.

"In what way?"

"Well, Judge, I never was more than an average lawyer and an average judge, and I've been growing more and more rusty of late. The thought of the Supreme Bench... well, frightens me. I'll be frank. Am I up to it?"

The Judge looked down at the carpet and composed his face. What a man! Remembering some of the party hacks and worn-out slobs who had been railroaded to the Supreme Bench in order to get them out of everybody's way, the Judge could just barely restrain his laughter.

"Oh, you're too modest, Commissioner," he said. "You have a good enough grounding in the law, and you're a man of marked conscientiousness. Nobody owns you. You're a free man. Any decision you hand down will be a true decision—uninfluenced, unbiased, honest. Can the taxpayers ask for any more?"

The Commissioner thought for a moment. "To tell you the truth, Judge, if it wasn't for my wife, I'd stay right here. I've been a part of this community all my life. I'm no longer young and I'd like to finish out my life here. Besides, I'm worried about what might happen here if I left. Don't misunderstand me. I don't think I'm indispensable. If Commissioner Hardy wasn't, nobody can be. But I've got a movement started now and I'd like to keep it rolling."

"Times are changing, Commissioner," said the Judge, easily. "More and more people want a clean town, and are talking about it: civic groups of all kinds. Your work will carry on here, Commissioner. Don't worry about that." There was a brief pause, then the Judge went on. "For myself, I would prefer to have you stay—for selfish reasons. I admire your work, and I appreciate your friendship. But I don't think I ought to look at it that way. You are too valuable a man to spend the rest of your life as a police official. Good men are scarce."

The Commissioner sighed. "It's a hard decision for me, Judge. Very hard. I was ready to give my word this evening... and then I talked to a certain newspaperman and he unsettled me...."

"A newspaperman?" exclaimed the Judge, raising his eyebrows. "I'm surprised one could have so much influence on you. I stopped paying any attention to them years ago."

"Well, he's been with me almost from the first. He's got behind everything I've tried to do. He told me this evening that the underworld would feel very happy if I left the city—it would make it so much easier for them to operate. When I say underworld—a silly, meaningless word the way it is generally used—I mean the men who control the gambling and the vice. Not the professional thieves—that's a precinct matter."

"Well," said the Judge thoughtfully, "he is probably right, in a sense. The men you refer to will no doubt feel very happy—at first. But your leaving will not make it any easier for them to operate. You've started the ball rolling, Commissioner, and I assure you it is not going to stop. As you know, I was to some extent responsible for the election of Marley. And in a sense, he's answerable to me. I'll keep a close eye on him, Commissioner. You have my word."

The Commissioner sighed heavily, then a smile broke over his rather solemn face. "You don't know how you've relieved my mind, Judge. Naturally, the idea of being on the Supreme Bench is very attractive to me. So attractive that I've tried to resist—being a Puritan at heart, I suppose, and afraid of all temptation. I couldn't quite make up my mind which way my duty lay. You've convinced me, Judge."

"Well, now I feel highly flattered," said the Judge, "that I've been able to influence a man like yourself. As you know, the Party will be delighted—we need some favorable publicity for a change...." The Judge laughed heartily. "It will be a very important announcement for the newspapers. How would you like to have it announced? Will you handle it at a conference? Or will you leave it up to the Party?"

"Either way," said the Commissioner, "but I would like to give my newspaper friend a little head-start with it. He deserves the favor."

"Oh, certainly, certainly," said the Judge quickly. "I'm sure he won't divulge the source. Shall I handle it otherwise?"

"Maybe that is best," said the Commissioner.

Later that night the Commissioner called Reisman at his home and explained the whole business to him.

"I have Judge Greet's word on the matter," he said when Reisman seemed inclined to question the wisdom of the decision. "And his word should be good."

"It's been good for many years," said Reisman. "The only thing I've got against the Judge is Marley. On the other hand, good men are hard to find. Well, congratulations, Justice Stark. I suppose I'm the first."

"Except for the Judge and Mrs. Stark. Good night, Reisman."

"One of these days I'll come up to the Capitol."

"You'll always be welcome."

"Thanks, Commissioner."

As soon as the Commissioner rang off, Reisman phoned the *Journal* and asked for Pee Wee. Pee Wee came on at once and Reisman gave him the story.

"Whoops!" cried Pee Wee. "Now the boys can go back to their marbles again."

"Even Pee Wee knows it," mused Reisman, shaking his head as he hung up.

He sat lost in thought for a long time, then he went out to the icebox to get himself a snack, moving as quietly as possible, but in a few minutes Sarah appeared in her bathrobe and slippers, then just as Reisman was yelling irritably that he only wanted to fortify himself, as he intended to write a column before he hit the hay if it took him 'till dawn, the three girls peeked into the open kitchen door, giggling, and Ruth said:

"Mom, we're hungry."

Reisman blew up. But in a little while they were all sitting around the kitchen table eating cold fried chicken and drinking milk. The girls wanted to know who had called, so Reisman told them about the Commissioner at considerable length, being as boring as possible. They tried to escape but he wouldn't let them. Fixing them with a stern eye, he began to elaborate on the operations of the police department. At first Sarah didn't grasp what was going on and listened with some interest; presently, she got the idea and it amused her; but finally she grew as bored as her three daughters.

"All right, all right, Ben," she cried. "That's enough."

"Oh, I'm just getting warmed up," said Reisman.

But finally he allowed the girls to file off to bed.

"You ought to be ashamed of yourself," said Sarah.

"I'll teach 'em to get up in the middle of the night and ask me questions!"

Later, he shut himself up in his workroom and wrote a column devoted entirely to the career, character, and achievements of the new Supreme Court Justice, Thos. W. Stark. It was a deadly serious column, which was unusual for Reisman, though it had sardonic overtones and ironically sharp comments about the Administration, and Mush Head shook his head over it, said it would offend a lot of bigwigs, but ran it just the same.

9

It was mid July and the weather in the big town had been almost unbearably hot since the 4th. Otherwise things were pretty much as usual.

Commissioner Stark had left for the Capitol and a party hack by the name of Creeden, a former chief of police, had been appointed by Mayor Marley to fill out the Commissioner's unexpired term. The appointment was received in silence by the press, except for a few mild jeers from the *Journal.*

The disappearance of Leon Sollas was still an unsolved mystery and his Life Story, hastily whipped up by a bored police reporter, was still running in the *Examiner.* Rudy Solano was now the target for editorial blasts from several papers and his activities were highly publicized and "viewed with alarm."

Here and there a few bookies were arrested, a few prostitutes jailed, a few poker and dice parlors knocked over in the remote suburbs. But the Front was flourishing as convention after convention hit the big town like a plague of locusts.

Things were so quiet that Arky felt uneasy. Captain Dysen had phoned him three times, wanting to call a halt to the guarding of the Mover. "It'll get us in trouble yet, Ark," said the Captain. "And I don't think it's necessary. Such a thing as being too cautious." But Arky wouldn't listen.

If Leon had called again, if the Big City boys had made new overtures or even threats, if there had been the slightest hint of another effort to work in on the Front, Arky would have felt better. But the weeks passed... and... *nothing!* He picked up the take from Rudy, who looked fat and happy; kidded with Robbie, who seemed to like Rudy as well as she had liked Leon, or as little; Zand drove him to the Paymaster's; and at long intervals he talked to the Mover on the phone. The Mover now always seemed in a good humor and made many jokes, convulsing Arky at times, although the Mover accused him of overdoing it and trying to get in good by being an easy audience.

Under Creeden, things moved smoothly. It wasn't that Creeden knew anything about what was going on; he didn't. Nor did he care. After a rather protracted siege of "retirement" he was in office again, and basking. He had a big tough copper drive him about the city in a limousine both Hardy and Stark had disdained to use, siren going. He never missed a station on the banquet circuit, and made long boring speeches interspersed with tired jokes, prefaced by: "And that reminds me of a hilarious incident that...." Judge Greet was called to the phone time after time when Creeden rose to speak. He always apologized at length later to Creeden for "missing your amusing talk," flattering Creeden so that he went around boring people by bragging about his friendship with "our eminent fellow-citizen, Judge Greet," and beginning many of his remarks by the statement: "As Judge Greet was saying to me just the other day...."

Yes, things were very smooth, but Arky was worried in spite of the fact that the take rose steadily week by week, bookie arrests fell sharply, and the big madams, with the exception of Mrs. Lansing, who was still in clink, operated unmolested.

Money passed from hand to hand. Big smiles broke out all over the city, from the suburbs to the slums.

Creeden was a success, and the only sour note heard was an occasional faint rumble from the newspapers.

Arky, in his shirtsleeves, sat in the deserted bookie-room, smoking a cigar and from time to time wiping his face with a limp handkerchief. This was the worst yet! That day at noon the thermometer had registered a hundred degrees of heat. A young hoodlum in the pool hall had told Arky that he'd tried to take a swim in the river and the water had been so warm it had made him sweat. Ambulance sirens had been going all day as people collapsed in the streets.

Zand came in, mopping his face, and sat down beside Arky in gloomy silence. Arky glanced at him finally. "What's the matter, Zand—the heat?"

"That, too," said Zand. "But Lola, mostly."

"What now?"

"She's gone baby-crazy. It's all I hear day and night. Say, couldn't we work out a trade for that little Polack you got upstairs?"

Arky glanced at Zand resentfully. "Don't start on me. You want a poke in the nose?"

"What did *I* say? He *is* a Polack, ain't he? That's the last report I heard, but after talking to Milli, or trying to talk to her, I ain't sure she knows."

"Go 'way," said Arky. "It's too hot to talk even." There was a long silence, then Zand spoke. "Will you please tell me what women see in babies? All they do is eat, cry, and fill their pants. What's so cunning about that?"

Arky turned to stare at him. "What's so *what?*"

"Cunning," said Zand. "She says it all the time. Lola, I mean. Thaddeus is so 'cunning.'"

"His name's Orv. Never mind that Thaddeus stuff."

"Why don't you go all the way and call him Orval Wanty? You can't call him Orval Sienkiewicz."

"Why don't you mind your own goddamn business?"

There was a pause and Zand sat sighing. Finally he spoke. "I still say 'cunning' don't mean cute. We been arguing about it all day. It means... well, *cunning*. Like a guy is... well, he's shrewd or conniving. Ain't that right, Arky?"

"I don't know. Come to think of it, seems to me when I was a boy I used to hear my old lady refer to a baby as 'cunning' or maybe even a little pig sometimes."

"My God!" cried Zand, hastily. "Don't tell Lola that or I'll never hear the last of it."

"I don't tell Lola nothing," said Arky disdainfully.

There was a long silence and both men wiped their faces repeatedly. Zand spoke at last. "Lola says you're going to get the kid baptized. Is that on the square?"

"Anna wants to; but I figure it's too complicated. I don't know what you have to go through—records and stuff, I mean. Some day I'll ask the Officer. He's got six or seven kids."

"Eight, I think," said Zand. "But he's got a television set now so maybe he'll slack off."

Arky laughed curtly then threw his cigar away. "How was business today?"

"'Way up, like every place. I don't know where these cheap jerks around here get all the money they bet. They can't steal *that* much."

"Money's loose right now. At least for gambling. The Front's roaring. The take was up ten G's last week."

"All them conventions, brother! I hear they had to get a traffic cop to route the girls in the lobby of the Regent Hotel. They were trampling the guests."

Arky laughed again, then he got up. "Might take a walk. I don't know. This heat...."

"Look," said Zand, seriously. "Don't take no walks. If you want to go some place I'll drive you." Arky turned and stared at him. "Well, it figures, don't it? You got cops guarding the Mover. If there was trouble, you'd be the first guy shot. Ain't you got sense enough to know that?"

Arky considered then sat down again. "Yeah. If they'd happen to blast me, the Mover'd be in a hell of a spot."

"The *Mover?* How about yourself?"

Arky took out another cigar, bit off the end, and lit up. "I don't worry about myself."

"Only crazy people don't worry about themselves."

"I mean," said Arky, "I figure it's my job to look after him. He looked after me once, and how! Straightened me out when I needed it."

Zand smothered a question and veiled a quick eager look of curiosity. He'd often wondered about Arky and the Mover. No use to ask, however. If Arky wanted to tell him, he would: if not, a third degree wouldn't help. "Yeah," he said, "a guy feels like looking after *them* that look after *him.* Like us."

Arky glanced at Zand. "How do you mean?"

"You know how I mean. I was in with a bad bunch when I went to work for you—and practically starving to boot. I was a cinch for the Walls. Now look. I'm doing fine, thanks to you."

"I didn't do nothing," said Arky uncomfortably. "You went to work for me and you made good. I could turn this joint over to you tomorrow and blow. And nobody'd know the difference."

"Did anybody ask you to cut me in? But you did."

"You had it coming. Now shut up."

There was a pause. "All the same," said Zand. "Don't go taking any walks. You look after the Mover and I'll look after you."

Arky sat smoking in silence for a long time, staring off into space, and then finally he began to talk, not looking at Zand or even seeming to acknowledge his presence. "You figure a young fellow, maybe about twenty. He's had a bellyful of farm and fighting with his brothers about whose turn it is to do what. Also he's had a touch of gambling and cheap dames, running away with a carnival once when he was sixteen. So with maybe twenty bucks in his pocket, he hits for the big town. Don't know a soul. The way he talks makes everybody laugh, and they kid him. That's okay but it can get mighty tiresome. What can he work at? You don't pitch manure on the Front. But you can swing a pick in a ditch. So that's what he does for a while. Then he gets to playing the horses and the numbers, and hanging around with a lot of cheap tramps, male and female. Maybe the guy's just no good. That may be the explanation. I wouldn't argue with you about it.

"Anyway, one night he gets into one of them things in a bar. A bunch of guys been kidding him about going back to the Ozarks. That's okay. But a couple of 'em are telling him to go back to the Ozarks in broken English. That ain't so okay, and it begins to make him sore. He drinks too much; so does everybody, and pretty soon the swinging starts. Three guys jump him. He has one down, then two: but he can't keep 'em all down long enough to do him any good. Finally he goes down himself and somebody kicks him in the face and breaks his nose. After that he don't remember much.... All the same one guy's dead, and everybody's saying the young guy used a chair on him. More than likely he did.

"Well, this young guy's got no money and no friends. They throw him in the can and get him a lawyer for free, a jerk who's so dumb he'd get a man sent up for a year for double parking. He tells the young guy to plead guilty to manslaughter, waive trial, and throw himself on the mercy of the court. The young guy don't know it, but he could have been sent up for ten years with the wrong judge. But the young guy's luck has finally turned. He gets the right judge. And he don't serve a day. Looking over the case, the judge won't accept the plea, and declares that the lawyer is incompetent and should be subjected to re-examination by the Bar Association. Turns out he's a stinking lush. Later, the case was dismissed."

Arky turned and looked at Zand. "Understand what I'm talking about?"

"I think so," said Zand solemnly.

Arky nodded, then relapsed into silence.

It was almost midnight. Arky and Zand had all the windows open in the bookie room, a cool breeze was beginning to blow up from the river, and the mercury had started to fall. They were playing gin rummy for small stakes and complaining about the heat. But now, feeling the breeze, they looked up at each other and grinned.

"Ah!" sighed Arky. "That's something like it! May be able to sleep tonight after all."

Zand nodded slowly, then he studied his hand for a moment and went down with ten, but lost. Just as Arky was dealing the cards the screaming started. They both jumped up, appalled. It seemed to be coming from Arky's apartment upstairs.

Arky jerked a gun out of the desk, banged back the door, and took the stairs at three bounds, followed by Zand, who had also grabbed up a gun.

The apartment door was locked; Arky tried to kick it open but it was too stout for him; and he was forced to unlock it as the screaming and yelling continued.

He ran back through the dark hallway, followed by Zand. The noise seemed to be coming from the spare bedroom. Arky slammed back the door, then stopped stock-still and stared. Zand, behind him, dropped his gun with a clatter.

Anna was beating Milli with her fists, and the girl was screaming, pleading, terrified, trying to get away. Arky looked on for a moment a little appalled by Anna's violence, and her red, contorted face. Finally he stepped in and broke it up, shoving Anna so hard that she fell backward across the bed. Milli tried to duck out the door, but Zand got in her path and pushed her back, then shut the door behind him.

"What the hell is all this?" shouted Arky. "You want the cops to come?"

"That little sly bitch," cried Anna. "No wonder Thad beat her. He didn't beat her enough."

Anna was sitting up now, glaring at Milli, who cringed away and stood looking about her helplessly, as if she felt that now finally the end had come.

"What did she do?" Arky demanded impatiently.

"She tried to run off with Orv. I was taking a nap and by the grace of God I woke up in time. And besides—she had stole money out of my purse, after all I've done for her."

"I need money... for... to... to get there," wailed the girl. "Anna... she give me lots money. I didn't think... wrong."

"You didn't think wrong!" screamed Anna. "No, you didn't think wrong, trying to take Orv with you when it says in that letter right there if you brought the baby he'd give it to an orphanage to raise."

Milli screamed out a long explanation in Polish.

Arky yelled for silence, and when he didn't get it he picked up a newspaper from the table, calmly folded it, and slapped Milli across the face with it, then Anna. There was a sudden dead appalled silence.

"I'm tired of this goddamn screaming," said Arky. "Now talk quiet or I'll take care of both of you."

"She's been getting letters from that meathead she's married to," said Anna, after a pause. "Now he's got some kind of a piddling job and he wants her to come back to him. You should read the letters. He'd spell cat with a k."

"How *do* you spell it?" asked Zand.

Arky began to snicker, but Anna burst into tears and, turning sideways, fell over and buried her face in the coverlet. Milli began to wail in sympathy, big tears running down her fat, babyish face.

"Oh, Jesus," said Arky in disgust, then he went over to Anna and shook her gently. "Look, Anna. Sit up now. Behave yourself. Don't act like that silly kid. After all she's only sixteen, she can't talk good—maybe you don't know what's going on in her mind."

Anna sat up and looked at Milli indignantly. "I know what's going on in her mind all right. The same thing that got her in all this trouble in the first place."

"That's natural," said Arky. "That's the way girls are. She didn't invent it."

"That's right," cried Anna, "stick up for her!"

"You better shut up, Arky," said Zand in a low voice.

"Anyway, that's not what I'm talking about," cried Anna. "She can sleep with who she pleases when she pleases, but she's not going to take that baby away."

"It's hers, Anna," said Arky. "She's its mother."

"She couldn't be a mother to a litter of puppies," cried Anna. "Look at her— the silly fool. Chuck's going to put the baby in an orphanage, and she's all for it."

"Please... no," said Milli. "I don't like... budder."

Anna stared at Milli in surprise, then she asked her a question in Polish. Milli went into a long explanation, also in Polish. Arky looked on in irritation. Finally, Anna gave a loud cry, got up from the bed, rushed across the room, took Milli in her arms and began to kiss her; then they both burst into tears.

Arky and Zand looked at each other in stunned silence.

"She just didn't want to bother us with the baby, the poor little dear," cried Anna. "We can have him, Arky. We can have him. Oh, God, Milli, I'm so sorry, dear."

Milli grinned rather weakly and looked timidly from Zand to Arky.

"Well," said Arky, "seems to me you could have settled that in the first place without all this screaming and carrying on."

"I did... not... understand," said Milli, smiling shyly at Arky.

Anna hurried over, struck by a sudden thought, and grabbed Arky's arm. "It's all right, isn't it, Ark? I mean, he can stay. You don't mind, do you?"

"Will it keep you quiet for a while?" asked Arky.

"Yes," said Anna. "I'll be quiet. You won't hear a sound out of me from now on."

Slowly things got back to normal. Anna took down one of her own suitcases and helped Milli repack her things. Arky gave Milli fifty dollars so she would have some money of her own, and Zand insisted on driving Milli clear across town to Steelton, better known as Polish-town, where Chuck Sienkiewicz had found a job and a room.

"It's getting late," said Zand. "No sixteen-year-old girl ought to be out running to hell and gone at this time of night." At a look from Arky, he added: "I'll take Lola along. She's always yacking she never gets out of the district."

Two a.m. Tugs moaning on the river, towing coal-barges downstream toward the faraway Mississippi. Juke boxes playing in the bars along Pier Street, four or five different tunes fighting with each other in the stillness of the night. Faint wail of police sirens beyond the river.

The city going about its night business as usual. Three hours till dawn at least: plenty of time for love, thievery, another couple of drinks, or even murder.

But in Arky's apartment two a.m. only meant one thing now: Orv's feeding time. He was a greedy baby, a heavy eater, and although he was nearly three months old, he showed no signs yet of skipping the dead-hour feed.

Anna, looking remarkably plump, blond, and happy in her blue bathrobe, had Orv on her lap, feeding him. Arky sat with his legs crossed, looking on.

"Sure is fat and sassy," said Arky.

"Sure is," said Anna, imitating Arky's accent, then laughing lightly. There was a pause, then Anna went on. "I'm certainly glad to have Milli out of this house. She was beginning to get on my nerves. I hope I wasn't such an empty-headed fool when I was sixteen, but I'm afraid I was."

"I *know* I was," said Arky. "I run off with a carnival, got mixed up with a belly-dancer old enough to be my mother, and got a package. Wasn't easy to cure in those days."

"You ought to be ashamed to talk like that in front of Orv."

"Oh, I don't know. Probably be running off himself when he's sixteen. A guy's got to learn."

Anna thought this over for a minute, then she said: "In sixteen years I'll be fifty-one. Not so old I can't look after him."

"I'll be fifty-six," said Arky. "Pretty old. However, we're a tough lot. Had a grandfather could do a good day's work when he was eighty. Got married again when he was seventy-five."

"What for?" cried Anna, laughing loudly.

"You don't know us Wantys," said Arky.

10

Downy, sitting comfortably in a booth at the Regent rathskeller, eating Polish sausage and hot potato-salad and drinking beer, wanted to have a quiet literary discussion with Reisman, who apparently had found time during his somewhat busy life to read practically everything, but Reisman seemed morose and preoccupied as he ate his potato soup and glared enviously at the highly spiced, aromatic sausage on Downy's plate.

Finally he sighed and said: "Want to make an advantageous swap? Your stomach for my brains and experience."

"I'd do it in a minute if it were possible," said Downy.

"That's what you think *now*. But you'll learn." Reisman pushed the soup away and took out a cigarette. "What about Dorsey? Is he okay—or the silly schnook he seems like?"

"I don't think he's very bright," said Downy. "But nobody wants that 17th Ward beat, and he put in for it."

"How would you like to go back for a couple of months?"

Downy choked on his food. "Look, Ben. I'm just getting a foothold in sports. The boss is even beginning to notice that I'm in the department. If I went back now...."

"I'll fix it. You won't lose a thing by it. I already talked to Mush Head, who tried to get me to go to his psychiatrist, but finally gave in. If you yell at him long enough he usually gives in just to get some peace of mind."

Downy tried not to show his disappointment, but he shuddered inwardly at the thought of going back to the 17th with those appalling young girls who tried to pull you up alleys, those crop-headed, insolent young hoodlums—the dirt, the stench, the hopeless wrecks of humanity begging with trembling hands for "just a dime, son. Look at me shake! I need one bad, son. You got a kind face, son. You don't want me to go on shaking like this, do you?" The dirty old women at the curb markets, pawing over the food; the poor filthy devils of kids, running around with nobody to look after them. What was the sense of it? Why did these people go on? What did it mean?

Young Downy, one of the fortunate ones, had always lived well. His father, a business executive, had sent him to a military school and later to the state university, though Downy had wanted to go to Princeton, outraging his father, a graduate of State. The fraternities had competed hotly for Downy: he was considered a catch. After some indecision, he went Beta, again outraging his father, who was a Deke. His father always referred to the Betas as cake-eaters, dating himself, and making his son feel a little sorry for him. Nevertheless, the Betas had the highest rating in the university, socially at least, and were considered the *crème de la crème* and therefore hated and envied.

In other words, Downy, though he considered himself an average American, had been top-rung all his life, sheltered, looked after, pampered. And even after he graduated from the College of Journalism, the process went on. He wasn't forced to go running around, looking for a job. His father spoke to somebody, the somebody spoke to the son of the *Journal's* owner, the son spoke to Mush Head, and Downy was in.

Mush Head was very much taken with Downy, and introduced him to his daughter. Unfortunately, Mush Head's daughter was an intellectual who wore glasses and made fun of the handsome and correct young reporter. Mush Head moaned about it and told his wife: "Joan will marry some goddamn silly writer or one of those painters, who needs a bath—I can actually *smell* them—that she's always dragging to the house. Commies to a man!"

In spite of his daughter's disapproval of Downy, Mush Head kept an eye on the boy for the future. He came of a good family, he was a damned decent kid, and he tried hard. Too many bums in the newspaper business. Mush Head was always thinking and talking about "building for the future." In fact some of the office cynics called him Old Building-for-the-Future Hanneman. Downy was tapped—as usual.

Then Reisman took him up. Tapped again. Always the same.

Downy's first contacts with the real world floored him. At twenty-five he was still in a state of confusion, and his stint in the 17th Ward had unsettled him further. He hated the thought of going back to it.

"...Well, maybe you can suggest somebody," said Reisman, eying the boy shrewdly.

Downy came out of his haze at once. "No, Ben. I'll go back if you want me to. Perfectly willing if I can help."

"All right. It's on the q.t. Dorsey moves into sports where you flopped, understand?"

Downy stared. "Flopped? Oh, yes. I see."

"It's just a reason for you going back. That Pavlik's a shrewd character. Give him the narcotics routine again. Take him aside. You know. Confide in him." Reisman laughed. "Tell the rest of 'em nothing. Make 'em think you're deeply hurt."

Downy was beginning to show eagerness now. "What do I look for?"

"I don't know. But here's a couple of tips. Keep tabs on Dysen. The Front couldn't run without him. Keep tabs on Arky. Only lead I got."

Downy nodded slowly, then went on eating. "The town's roaring, I hear," he said, "since Stark left. It's common talk."

"Yeah," said Reisman; then he turned to a waiter and ordered some Polish sausage. "If I suffer, I suffer," he said to Downy, who was laughing.

At Dysen's insistence, Arky had Zand drive him out to Locust Grove to talk to the Captain face to face. The Captain was getting nervous about talking over the phone, and Arky did not want to put in another appearance at the station house—might cause comment. They were to meet at a filling-station on the outskirts of Locust Grove. The station had closed for the night and was deserted. A faint bluish-white light burned inside. Beyond, the highway curved off over a hill into open country. A gentle breeze stirred the tall trees; the moon was up over the fields, showing them dimly; crickets chirped on all sides. At a farm beyond the low hill a dog barked from time to time.

Waiting for the Captain, Arky sat listening to the night sounds. "Almost like home," he said to Zand. "Ought to get out in the country more, away from them hot bricks."

"I'll take the hot bricks, you take the country," said Zand. "It makes me nervous. Too damn quiet."

"Noisiest place in the world, a farm," said Arky. "Damn roosters start crowing at midnight. City people think they crow at dawn. Some kind of noise all night long."

"I'll take streetcars and buses and taxicabs," said Zand. "And I'll take carbon monoxide to manure."

"Well... it's all in what you like," said Arky, mildly. Sometimes Arky irritated Zand so that the little Syrian had an almost irresistible impulse to get into a fight with him. Always the country. Always Arkansas. Always the city stunk. But here he was just the same, and had been for maybe twenty years. "If you're so set up about the country," said Zand, "why don't you go back? What's holding you?"

"Never had guts enough to work a farm," said Arky. "Wanted it easy. Do nothing. Lie in bed. All the rest of the family had the guts."

"That's silly talk. You got more guts than any guy I ever met."

"No," said Arky. "I only got the easy kind. I ain't got the kind it takes to keep slugging no matter what happens. Tough, raising crops. One bad year and you can get wiped out. You're bucking the weather, and what can you do about the weather? People always making fun of farmers. Why? I never been able to figure out. Takes guts, hard work. Wasn't for the farmers, these goddamn silly jerks here in this big town wouldn't eat. Wouldn't even drink, for that matter. Takes crops of some kind to make liquor and beer."

"Yeah," said Zand, his mood changing, "never thought about it that way before."

"Suppose all the farmers said the hell with it. It's too tough and a low-profit business to boot. Suppose they said we're tired; from now on we just raise enough for our own use. Good-bye, boys. Everybody but them starves to death. Money wouldn't mean a thing. Here's a guy with a million bucks in the bank, a house in Riverview, six servants, and a Cadillac car... but no food... what's he going to do?

"Look at it this way. Some lucky character invents some jerky thing that don't amount to nothing. People would get along okay without it. But it's a novelty. So what happens? This character gets rich—he's a millionaire. All right. He was smart. He put something on the market that wasn't there before. But it don't matter one way or another whether it is or not, nobody'll die for it. Now take the farmer. If you haven't got food, you haven't got nothing. You're dead. Ever hear of a farmer making a million dollars? Rock-bottom essential and yet ninety per cent of 'em just barely make the grade. And people in cities think they're funny. Is that cockeyed, or ain't it?

"All this crap about the laboring man—all of 'em overpaid now and pampered. Strikes all over the place. Suppose the farmers went on strike. Talk about a nationwide tie-up, brother. Would make a national railroad strike look like a picnic. They'd be begging them on their knees before they were through...."

"Jesus, Arky," said Zand, amazed. "You ought to run for Congress."

Arky restrained himself with some difficulty from going on; finally he laughed and said: "Yeah, sound like a Philadelphia lawyer. But sometimes I get goddamned fed up with all the bunk I got to listen to here from people who don't know what the hell they're talking about."

The Captain looked very weary, his big face sagging more than usual. He had driven out by himself in a little Ford coupé and he had to squeeze out of it as if taking off a glove. He loomed huge in the dim light from the filling-station.

"I got to call a halt, Arky," he said. "Too many people are getting in on it."

"How do you mean, Captain?"

"Well... we contacted the hired police out there. They're co-operating, though they don't know what it's all about. We've picked up quite a few suspicious characters, nothing to do with our problems, just nuts, Peeping Toms, you know— but the hired police are beginning to ask too many questions. A guy from headquarters buzzed us, but one of the boys happened to know him well and told him to keep still. I just don't like it, Arky. Things are quiet. You know that."

"Yeah," said Arky, "maybe too quiet. But I don't like putting you on the spot any longer, and no use to talk to the Mover." He thought for a moment, then went on. "Tell you what, Captain. Let's finish out the week. Okay?"

"All right, Arky," said the Captain, then he gave a long sigh. "It'll sure be a relief to me to get this over with, especially when I think you're barking up the wrong tree. Nobody would have nerve enough to tackle the Mover."

"Maybe not, maybe not," said Arky. "Okay. We'll finish out the week."

The Captain nodded, waved good-night, squeezed painfully back into the Ford, and drove off toward the twinkling lights of the little suburb, Locust Grove.

"Pretty good guy, the Officer," said Arky thoughtfully. "The thing is, he knows the Mover personally. If a guy knows the Mover personally, he's for him a hundred per cent. Would have been better if Leon and the Mover had got acquainted; then Leon wouldn't have been so anxious to play horse. Let's go home, Zand."

They drove in silence for a long time toward the far-away smoky-red glow of the city lights. Finally Zand asked:

"How's the kid coming? How's Orv? I ain't seen him for a week."

"Swell," said Arky. "Beginning to notice things—looks you right in the eye. Makes me feel kinda uneasy."

11

It was one a.m., a dry west wind was blowing, and the reaches of Paxton Square and the 17th Ward, both on the west bank of the river, were like an oven. The sidewalks, streets, and buildings were still warm to the touch. Dust, dry as powder, blew along the gutters and rose in tiny whirlwinds; stray newspapers scraped over the asphalt with a sound as of dead leaves. In the brick tenements all the windows were wide open, and dirty curtains were bellying out and flapping.

Downy left the hothouse atmosphere of the station and stood out in front talking to a couple of fat, tired, shirt-sleeved coppers. Downy wanted to take a walk along the river and try to get a breath of fresh air, but he decided it was not a very good idea. Only the night before a drunk had been beaten to death and robbed at the foot of Pier Street, less than three blocks from the police station. Downy shuddered at the memory of the bloody, contorted, scarecrow-like figure lying on the pavement with all his pockets turned inside out. "Must've got a quick buck fifty out of him," a big copper had said sadly, shaking his head over the wickedness of this world, of which in fifteen years on the force he had seen plenty.

Downy took off his coat and folded it carefully over his arm; then he got out his cigarettes and he and the cops lit up.

Far off down the street, on the edge of Paxton Square, the clock at the fire house struck one solemnly.

Downy sighed and puffed on his cigarette. The graveyard watch now. Reisman's idea. Joe Pavlik was on it too, now. Had he been told to keep an eye on Downy? Downy laughed. Joe was snoring in a tipped-back chair by the sergeant's desk.

For crime, the district couldn't be matched in the city; and it all happened at night. But it was dull, sordid, penny-ante—worth no more than a line or two. Of course the Front was near by, where a big story might break at any time—but it never seemed to. Downy sighed again, then flipped his cigarette out into the street.

The cops talked baseball, ignoring the antediluvian world about them. Downy chimed in from time to time. After all, hadn't he been on the sports desk?

Arky couldn't sleep. Lying on his back in the darkness, he'd gone through every batting order in both major leagues, growing more and more wakeful as he worked, in a descending curve of interest, from the New York Yankees to the St. Louis Browns. It was no use. This was going to be one of the bad nights.

The apartment was very quiet. Anna had been in bed for some time and for a moment he considered going back to her bedroom, waking her up, and making her talk to him. He had the jimmies and kept fidgeting about, unable to relax. If he could talk for half an hour or so the tension might leave him. But on second thought he changed his mind. Anna had looked sort of tired tonight, which was unusual for her. No wonder she looked tired, though; lugging that fat baby around all the time, bathing him, feeding him, giving him a sunbath, rocking him to sleep. "Why, hell," Arky told himself, "he gets more care than a millionaire. Life of Riley for *that* baby." At least he'd got so now that he missed his two o'clock feed, which meant that Anna could sleep straight through for six hours or so.

"Let her sleep," said Arky. "Hell, I don't do nothing all day but watch chumps lose their money."

Finally, swearing quietly to himself, he got up, switched on a bridge lamp, sat down at a little table and laid out a game of solitaire. The room was hot and stuffy in spite of the blowing curtains, and Arky sat sweating under the light. Little by little he became preoccupied with his game. Time passed. The wind died and it grew a little cooler. Arky found himself yawning.

"I'll finish this one, then try the hay again," he mumbled.

But suddenly he jerked to attention. He'd heard something. But what? The stealthy slide of a foot on the roof just outside his window? The roof was covered with sanded tarpaper and a bird could hardly move about on it without making a noise. Arky listened intently, a slight chill going up and down his spine. Then finally he laughed to himself and mussed up his layout. He really had the jimmies, the fantods! The place for him was bed, sleep or no sleep.

Just as he started to rise he heard the sound again. This time there was no mistake about it. With one swift movement Arky dove for the floor, taking the lamp with him. A sharp metallic click sounded outside his window, then a bullet whined through the room, and slammed into the hall door with a shrill, tearing sound.

The light-bulb in the bridge-lamp had shattered on the floor and the room was in utter darkness. Arky lay waiting for another movement. Smart guy, using a silencer two blocks from the police station. Somebody had planned this out in pretty good shape. Leon? Could be. Though of course Leon would be sitting in a supper-club some place with a doll and a magnum of champagne, smiling at everybody, seen by everybody.

Arky raised his head cautiously, but the window was almost as dark as the room and he could see nothing. Damn fool, sitting around with the windows open and the lights on with a roof just outside for somebody to crawl up on.

Arky had an automatic in the night-table, but the night-table seemed a long way off at the moment. He waited. In the distance he could hear sirens, and a tug moaned on the river. But around him it was so quiet that it was almost as if he were walled in. Little by little a faint throbbing came to his ears, a throbbing which went on and on, and finally he knew what it was. A car in the side street with the motor running. The guy outside the window had friends. But they were really taking chances. If a prowl went past, the coppers would comb them sure, as it was a cinch they were strangers to the neighborhood.

Groping about, Arky's hand came in contact with a book of matches. Raising up on one elbow with painful care and slowness, Arky tossed the matches toward the window. The book lit with a little plop, and Arky heard the quick shifting of a foot on the tarpaper roof, then... nothing.

Covered from below, this guy was patient.

Arky decided to wait him out. The longer it went on the better chance Arky had to get the upper hand. A prowl might show up; anything might happen. But if Arky couldn't restrain his impatience, if, in other words, he couldn't keep his nerves steady, he was as good as on a slab.

Arky groped cautiously about him for something else to throw and in a moment he found a few pieces of paper-thin glass from the broken light-bulb. Moving very slowly, he tossed the glass through the window. It was so still that he could hear a faint tinkle. But nothing happened. Not a sound.

This guy was a professional, no humpty-dumpty: he had steady nerves.

Arky lay still for a long time, then inch by inch, with long waits between each movement, he worked himself on his belly toward the night-table. It wasn't that he thought he could open the drawer and get the gun out without being shot. That was too much to expect. All he wanted to do was to get close to the gun so he could get to it in a hurry, if there was a break of any kind. The minutes passed slowly. The wind rose fitfully from time to time, tossing the curtains. Arky was within six inches of the night-table when the phone began to ring.

It rang and rang and rang, with a senseless persistence, startlingly loud in the unnatural stillness. Arky froze and lay cursing the phone to himself for a moment, then it occurred to him that the sudden ringing of the phone might have slightly unsettled the man outside the window, and he decided to take a chance on trying to ease the automatic out of the night-table. He slid his hand up for it inch by inch, and his fingertips were just touching the drawer when he heard the quick thump of footsteps in the hallway—Anna, no doubt, awakened by the phone and hurrying to his room in her bare feet. Flattening himself on the floor, he shouted:

"Anna! Anna! Don't come in!"

There was a sharp click, then the tearing whistle of a high-caliber bullet, which buried itself in the floor near Arky, splintering the wood.

The bedroom door was flung back and Anna stood silhouetted against the dim night-light in the hallway.

"Arky!" she screamed. "What...?"

The man outside fired three more shots, the bullets whistling and shrieking as they tore through the room, one of them ricocheting from some metal object with a sharp ringing and a high-pitched wail as of the damned.

Arky felt something rip through his scalp, then, blind with fury, he jumped to his feet, grabbed the automatic out of the drawer, knocking over the night-table, and rushed to the window. A dark figure was just disappearing over the edge of the roof. Gritting his teeth, Arky fired repeatedly at a shoulder, then an arm, then a slowly disappearing hand.

Below, there was the loud clatter of some heavy metal object falling. Then groans and cries, and somebody grunted: "Throw him in the back. Hurry—*Jesus!*"

Arky jumped through the window, falling to his knees on the tarpaper roof, then, recovering, he rushed to the edge, but the car had already shot off like a projectile and was making for the intersection. Arky fired a futile shot after it, then he dropped his empty gun to the roof and fell to his knees, overcome by a sudden rush of nausea and dizziness.

"What the hell's that?" one fat shirtsleeved copper cried. "The Battle of the Marne?"

Downy and the other copper stared, open-mouthed, then without a word they turned quickly and began to run toward the sound. The other copper went back inside, yelled something to the sergeant, then came out again carrying his gun-belt and revolver, and puffed up the hill after the others, who had a big head-start on him.

Lights were appearing all over Arky's place now. Doors were banging; Lola screamed as she ran up the stairway in her nightgown, followed by Zand, who, gun in hand, was struggling to button his trousers on over his pajamas.

The hall door was locked. Zand used his latchkey, cursing his awkwardness. Lola rushed in ahead of him, crying: "Anna! Anna!" Then she stopped stock-still and turned greenish.

Zand came in, bewildered, and stood staring down in blank unbelief at Anna's body lying in the dim-lit hallway.

Inside, the phone went on ringing. But Zand was so badly shaken he could not bring himself to answer it. Moving cautiously into the dark bedroom, he switched on the overhead lights. Then he started violently. Arky, with blood on his face, was just climbing shakily back through the window.

In the side street below, the siren of a prowl-car wailed to a stop. Cops' voices rose on the night.

Downy stood with a white face, looking on. Grier, one of the fat cops, was trying to question Arky, who sat staring off across the bedroom in a daze.

"But why did you do it, Ark?" Grier insisted. "I thought you and Anna was...."

"I told her not to come in," said Arky. "I yelled at her. Look, Tubby. I got clipped. I ain't thinking straight...."

Grier looked about him helplessly. In a moment there were heavy footsteps on the stairs and a couple of boys from the prowl-car came into the hallway, glanced down at Anna's body, then entered the bedroom. One of them was carrying an odd-looking carbine-like gun with a hooded silencer on it.

"Somebody try to blast you, Ark?" asked the one carrying the gun.

"Yeah," said Arky. Then he lifted a shaking hand toward the hallway. "They got... they hit... Anna. I got clipped, too."

"Where the hell's that doctor?" cried Grier, more bewildered than ever now and trying to hide it.

Wild with excitement, Downy turned, ran down the stairs, stumbling and almost falling, and hurried to an all-night drugstore to call Reisman, then the *Journal.*

In the bedroom, the phone began to ring again. Coming to himself, Arky answered it; then his face turned from white to greenish as he listened to the usually calm Paymaster's excited voice.

"They tried to kill the Mover tonight, Arky. He was sitting reading in his study with the windows wide open. He's got a bad arm and shoulder wound. But somebody shot at the killer—nobody seems to know who, and a prowl-car from the Pier 7 Station was wrecked chasing the getaway car. There is going to be a terrible mess. He should have listened to you."

"Yeah," said Arky, keeping his voice calm. "I had an inquiry here, too."

"Are you all right?" the Paymaster asked anxiously.

Arky glanced about him at the policemen, who were all trying to appear as if they weren't listening.

"Oh, sure," he said. "Business as usual. You know. Track odds." He hung up.

"I can't figure why that doctor don't get here," said Grier, peevishly.

After a moment, Arky got shakily to his feet and went out into the hallway to take a look at Anna. Somebody had covered her face with a handkerchief. There was dust on the bottom of her bare feet—dust she'd picked up hurrying to Arky's bedroom to see why he didn't answer the phone.

Lola, who had been revived, stood with her arms around Zand and her head on his shoulder, crying quietly.

"Poor Anna," she sobbed. "Oh, God! Poor Anna. She was such a wonderful woman."

In the back bedroom the baby began to cry, wailing persistently in the silence that followed Lola's remarks.

"Go look after him, will you?" cried Arky, harshly, turning to Lola.

Lola started violently. "Oh, God! The poor kid! What'll become of him now?"

"Go look after him," shouted Arky. "Never mind the Goddamn carrying-on."

"She'll look after him, Ark," said Zand. "Take it easy. This has been rough."

Lola moved back from Zand and went down the hallway as if in a daze; the spare-bedroom door closed quietly. In a moment, the crying ceased.

Arky stood staring down blankly at Anna. "I told her not to come in. I yelled at her," he said at last. "But that's the way she always was—wouldn't listen." After a moment, he went on in a low voice: "I guess she figured something must be wrong with me—that's why she wouldn't listen. She didn't know what fear was, that woman!"

A few moments later the doctor arrived. After a brief examination, he said to Arky: "I can't do anything for her. But I can patch you up good as new. What a lucky man you are! Half an inch more and you'd be lying there with her. This is the kind of crease you read about, but seldom see."

Grier came over and looked on, then he asked Arky: "Got any leads for us, Ark? Got any idea who might be gunning for you?"

"No," said Arky; then he shouted: "*Take it easy, Doc—for God's sake!*" Returning to his normal voice he spoke again to Grier. "Lots of guys lose a little money and they get sore. You know how it is, Tubby."

"Yeah," said Grier. "But you don't expect some 17th Ward slob to come shooting with a gun like that—silencer and all."

"I wouldn't know," said Arky.

Downy was frantic. He couldn't locate Reisman. He couldn't even raise anybody at Reisman's house, which was very strange, considering the hour: after one o'clock.

Not certain just what to do, Downy finally called Pee Wee at the *Journal* and gave him the story about the attempt on Arky's life and the accidental death of his girl friend, Anna.

"What do you expect me to do with *this?*" cried Pee Wee irritably. "I'll bet the girl friend wasn't even a blond beauty. Or even a blond."

"Yes," said Downy. "She was a blond. Kinda fat though and maybe thirty-five."

"You said *twenty-five*, didn't you? That's what I thought. And a blond beauty? Good. Love Nest Murder. But no matter what I do with it, brother... it will be mild stuff tomorrow. Hear about Judge Greet?"

"No," said Downy indifferently. Judge Greet was a dull figure to him. A civic leader, for God's sake! "What about him?"

"Somebody tried to *kill* him, that's all! So get off the wire, will you?—with this 17th Ward stuff. I'm standing by. Get off, Downy." Pee Wee banged up the receiver at the other end and Downy winced.

Who would want to kill Judge Greet? Downy shook his head in bewilderment, recalling the several times he'd met the Judge, a big, genial, rather pompous man, who made surprisingly brief and witty speeches on the banquet circuit. Some lunatic, no doubt. Who else?

Downy had worked his way downtown from the 17th Ward now and went into an all-night sandwich-shop for a snack. There was a cute redheaded kid with a glib tongue behind the counter and Downy sat eating a Denver sandwich and chinning with her.

"Aren't you even going to ask me when I get off?" she inquired.

"I've been thinking about it," said Downy.

"I can see you're the shy type. Well, I get off at six in the a.m. Does that discourage you?"

"It certainly does. What an hour for a date!"

"You said it, curly. Romance at six a.m. My husband's just getting up to go to work. Six feet tall, weighs two hundred."

"The same size as my wife," said Downy and the girl giggled appreciatively, looking at Downy with even more interest than before.

Suddenly Downy came to himself and almost fell off his stool. Turning, he took the thirty feet to the phone booth at a run. The redheaded girl stared after him in amazement.

"I hope he's not going in the wrong direction," she said as he shut the door of the booth.

Reisman answered at once. He sounded violently irritated.

"I been trying to call you for—" Downy began, but Reisman cut him off.

"I've still got my hat on. All this is what comes of living in the sticks where they haven't got a first-run house. We drove into the Bijou. Double bill, both features; newsreel; comedy; Community Chest short; two intermissions so the yokels can buy peanuts, popcorn, and candy, which is the real purpose of showing movies now. All around me people were crackling paper and chomping. I missed a lot of the dialogue so Selma began to explain the plots to me. Very interesting. On the way home, I blew a tire. Nobody is speaking to me after what I said."

"Listen, Ben. They tried to kill Arky tonight. He—"

"What! What!" cried Reisman. "Give it to me, and give it to me slow."

Downy explained at some length, and then as Reisman said nothing, he added: "I phoned it in to Pee Wee, but he says it will get nothing, nothing at all on account of—"

"Good," Reisman interrupted, "the less the better."

Downy persisted. "... on account of the Judge Greet business."

"The what?"

"Judge Greet. Somebody tried to kill him tonight."

"You *sure?*" Reisman's voice sounded almost hysterical.

"Yeah. Call Pee Wee."

"Okay. Hang up."

"Wait, Ben. What do I do now?"

"Go back to the 17th if you want to. Go home to bed. I don't care." Reisman broke the connection abruptly.

Downy returned to the counter. A tough-looking taxi-driver was kidding the redhead now but she wasn't paying much attention to him, and in a moment she walked back to Downy.

"Was she home?" she asked, jerking a thumb toward the phone.

"A man answered so I hung up."

"Another cup of coffee, wise guy?"

"Yes," said Downy.

When the girl returned with the coffee, she said: "Are you really married?"

"No," said Downy. "Are you?"

"No."

They looked at each other in silence for a long time, then the taxi-driver began to tap irritably on his water-glass with a knife.

"You want something else?" she called.

"Yeah," said the taxi-driver, glaring at Downy. "A little service, sister, if you don't mind. Another glass of water. Another cup of coffee. And a piece of apple pie."

The girl served the taxi-driver in silence, then she came back to Downy.

"I must've done something to annoy him," she said, giggling.

"I got to go clear across town on business," said Downy. "I might be driving back around six."

"Yeah? Funny hours. What business you in?"

"Police reporter."

The girl's face lit up. "Yeah? Murders and stuff? Some fun."

"What's your name?" asked Downy.

"Eunice Kubelik."

"Mine's Downy. Will I be seeing you?"

"Maybe," said Eunice.

Downy went out whistling. All memory of the dead Anna lying on the floor of that dingy hallway had temporarily left his mind. The world was actually a delightful place, when, by the merest accident, a guy could make a connection with a redheaded doll like Eunice Kubelik. A wonderful place!

12

At downtown and the Pier 7 Station House, the two main police department clearing-houses of the big town, things were in an uproar. Yammering reporters were chased from room to room by the police, who kept falling over them. The attempted assassination of Judge Greet was the biggest crime story in a decade. Phones rang, and kept ringing. Girls on the switchboards looked haggard and spent, and cops kept bringing them coffee.

Legmen, hanging around the Judge's house, and getting shooed away from time to time, kept calling one station or the other, trying to get some news.

At about three in the morning, Captain Dysen, looking grimmer and more formidable than usual, showed up at the station house, refused to talk to anyone, pushed reporters out of his way, and shut himself up in his office. Snooping, some of the boys heard him talking on the phone at intervals in a low voice; but they could not make out a word he was saying.

As time passed, Downy kept looking at his watch, the hands of which seemed to be stuck. Wouldn't it ever get to be six o'clock? The hell with Judge Greet. He himself had more pressing business.

It was very quiet in Arky's apartment. Lola was sleeping in the spare bedroom so she could look after the baby. Arky was lying full-length on his bed, staring up at the ceiling, his bandaged head propped up on three pillows.

Zand was sitting near by, smoking nervously, and from time to time glancing at the open window. He looked pale and shrunken in his loose, violently striped pajama top. He had a .45 revolver jammed down into his waistband, but the cold barrel against his bare skin began to bother him, so he took it out and put it on the table beside him. Arky winced at the sound and turned to look at him.

"Don't bang things around, will you, Zand? I got a head like a drunken bear."

"Like a what?"

Arky grimaced and didn't speak for a moment. "I got a headache, for Christ's sake. Feels like the top's coming off."

There was a long silence, then Zand spoke. "What do we do now, Arky?"

"We don't do nothing. We wait to hear from the Mover. Why don't you go lay down some place and get some sleep?"

"Not tonight," said Zand. "I'm going to sit and wait for that friendly sun to come up. Them guys might come back."

Arky laughed mockingly. "They won't be back. Not *them* guys. Never. They bungled it and they're going to hear about it at their end. This was a big try. Bigger than you think. Anyway, I got the guy that was on the roof. I think I hit him twice. Once in the hand, and once in the shoulder. At that range, a .45 slug ain't going to help him any. I give it to him worse than he give it to me." He paused, then spoke in a low voice: "Except for Anna."

"Son of a bitch ought to be cut up in small pieces," said Zand.

"I did my best," said Arky. There was a long silence. In spite of himself, Zand began to nod and jerked his head up with a start when Arky spoke again. "I should've married her, Zand. I'll never find another one like her—I ain't even going to look. That's my last woman. Permanent woman, I mean. No more."

"Why *didn't* you marry her, Ark?" asked Zand. "I used to wonder. You two were always just like married people. I used to keep reminding myself you wasn't."

Arky sighed and rubbed his hand gingerly across his forehead. "Some crazy idea I had, I guess. You got to be pretty well satisfied to stay with a woman nearly ten years. I mean satisfied every way. It's not just sex. That ain't so important as most people seem to think it is. If that's all a guy wants, he can get it and forget it, once a day, once a week, once a month—whatever his system calls for. Easiest thing in the world to get if you ain't too particular. Never went over a week myself since I'm sixteen. No... it was just that Anna was... well, Anna was a gentleman...."

At another time, Zand would have laughed. Now he nodded solemnly. Arky had a funny way of expressing himself: you had to get the hang of him: but Zand knew what he meant, all right.

"She was a hundred per cent," said Arky. "Square. She put up with a lot from me at first. I was always seeing some cutie, and taking a stab. But that wore off, swear to God. I been like an honest married man for quite a while now, though I did see one lately was beginning to interest me. Right now she interests me about as much as you do, Zand."

Zand repressed a quip and stared at the floor. "Yeah," Arky went on, "I should have married her. She always wanted to; then she could have had some kids. I didn't want kids. After all... the business I'm in, well.... But if I'd've been back home where kids could grow up right it'd been different. Not in this place. Besides, I always disliked kids... till Orv showed up. Now I don't dislike 'em any more. The reason Anna took such a shine to Orv was she wanted kids of her own...."

"What are you going to do about the kid, Arky?" asked Zand.

"We got to get him back to his parents. Remember where you took that girl?"

"Yeah," said Zand. "I can find it."

"All right," said Arky. "Tomorrow early you and Lola take the kid and all that stuff Anna bought—cost me two hundred...." Arky laughed sadly. "You take it—find them Polish kids and give 'em back their baby. If they want to put Orv in an orphanage that's their business. He's their kid. Besides, a kid's better off in an orphanage than in a dirty, filthy, stinking place like this. You see 'em on the street every day, Zand, poor snotty-nosed little bastards...."

"Yeah," said Zand thoughtfully. "I think you got something there. Only thing is, Lola's going to raise a howl. She wants him."

"That's stupid," said Arky.

"Yeah," said Zand. "It sure is."

There was a long silence. Arky closed his eyes and lay thinking about Anna. Half dozing, he saw her coming toward him, laughing, her plump cheeks dimpled, her pale blond hair shining—big, healthy-looking, strong—a whole lot of woman, Anna: a whole lot of woman!

...The coroner's man had removed Anna's body in a basket. There was to be an autopsy. The ballistic experts would check with the bore of the carbine the bullets removed from her body. It was merely routine. Nobody suspected Arky.

At Downtown there was an argument going on. Red Seaver cried: "I'd like to talk this over with Ben Reisman. He used to be the best. But I can't locate the son of a bitch. He took a powder. I called Downy at Pier 7 but he don't know where he is. Now where do you suppose Ben's got to this time of the night?"

"Could it be women?"

"No. I think he's past that. At least he hinted to me he was."

"Liquor?"

"With that famous ulcer?"

"I've seen him tight—and not so long ago."

"Not late at night."

"You got me there. Gambling?"

"Gambling! Reisman! With all *he* knows? Oh, please now."

"Well, there's only one other answer. He's on to something."

"He's a *columnist.* Jesus, you're no help at all." Red turned to a young blond fellow standing near by. "Rooster—go try Reisman's house again."

"Okay, Red," said Rooster, pleased that the great Mr. Seaver was even aware of his presence, then he dashed off.

"Now you were saying..." somebody called to Red.

"I was saying," said Red, "that my hair's not carrot color if there isn't a cover-up going on in the police department. Now mind you, I don't know what kind or why I can't get the ends together—but ain't it a little funny, a prowl-car from Pier 7 getting smashed up in Riverview? You all got the same information. *Do* something with it."

"What? Our man at Pier 7 said the boys had an open fugitive-warrant, looking for a suspect. They chased a car that wouldn't stop. They went *boom*, or even *powie*. It can happen. It's happened to me. I just smashed my heap up last week and I wasn't even chasing anybody."

"Did you have an open fugitive-warrant?"

"Don't be bitter, Red."

"All the same, it's funny."

A phone in the hallway began to ring. They all made a grab for it; Red got it; but it was some silly citizen trying to find the humane society.

"At this time of night?"

"Yes," said an agitated voice. "There's an enormous bat flying around in my bedroom."

"What do you expect, flamingos?" asked Red. He was on the point of hanging up when Casey appeared, puffing. "Here, Case," said Seaver. "This is for you. Very important."

The fat desk-sergeant, who was just going off duty, gave Red a suspicious look then picked up the phone.

"Yes? Sergeant Casey speaking." An infuriated voice began to yammer at him over the line. "But, mister," Casey protested, looking at Red Seaver in disgust, "I didn't say.... Now wait a minute. Sure, I'm a public servant but... look, mister, the humane society closes at five thirty—unless there is an emergency. That's no emergency. Get a broom and chase him away. What? I can't help it how nervous you are. I'm nervous, too, and my feet hurt and I want to go home to bed. Mister, you shouldn't talk like that...." A loud slam came over the wire and Casey grimaced sadly, then hung up.

He looked at Red for a long time then he took him by the suspenders and shook him gently. "Red," he said, "do you know what you are?"

"Yes," said Red, "I'm the most brilliant newspaperman in the city, bar Reisman, and I only say that to show my modesty."

"Red," said Casey, "I don't like to speak to you in this tone of voice, but you are the nearest thing to a horse's ass I ever saw in clothes."

"Now isn't that a coincidence!" cried Red.

"I won't even ask 'what?'" said Casey, going out hurriedly.

"He's learning," said Red.

The Rooster came in out of breath. "Can't find him anyplace, Red," he panted. "Had the girls on the switchboard downstairs half-crazy. Can't be found."

"He's out looking," said somebody.

"For what?" Red demanded. Then he turned to Len Seyter of the *Examiner*. "Why do you think Judge Greet was shot?"

Seyter shrugged. "He was a Criminal Courts Judge at one time. He sent a lot of guys up. Might be."

"That's very conventional thinking," said Red. "But the truth is almost always conventional, so you are probably right."

"What are you hoping for—a fourteen-year-old baby-sitter that he deflow-ered one night while they were watching the wrestling matches on television?"

"Those matches give guys ideas. Not bad. Anybody else?"

"I think he was shot by mistake," said somebody. "By a deer-hunter, no doubt," said Red.

"Well, people are shot by mistake."

Red groaned and sank down into his chair. "Rooster," he said, "go keep try-ing, will you?"

"That I will, Red," said the Rooster, running out eagerly.

13

It was ten a.m., weak sunshine showed in the cluttered streets of the 17th Ward, and there was a faint haze over the river.

Like a lost soul, Arky wandered about the big apartment, which seemed as empty now as an abandoned barn. Lola had put all of Anna's clothes away and Anna's bedroom looked as cold, as uninviting, as devoid of any personality, as a sample-room at a hotel. It was as if Anna had never been. And now Orv was gone, too, and all his small furniture had been removed from the spare bedroom; the padded-silk basket, the crib, all the bottles and clothes, all the odds and ends of a baby's little life.

Arky looked in one room after the other. He felt a piercing sense of loneliness. At the moment he would even have been glad to hear the animal, Milli, stum-bling up the stairs, out of breath, afraid of getting hell from somebody.

He heaved a long sigh of relief and made a dash for his bedroom when the phone rang. It was young Mr. Black of Dighton and Black. The firm would han-dle Arky's interests at the coroner's inquest. Young Mr. Black, who seemed to consider himself a ball of fire, assured Arky that there would be no difficulties of any kind and that he should rest easy and not worry. Arky assured young Mr. Black that he was not worrying.

When the conversation was at an end, Arky hung up absent-mindedly and sat looking off down the hill toward the river. It was a funny thing how a man never knew when he was well off. Yeah, a funny thing. A man never seemed to get any satisfaction out of the present minute; it was always tomorrow that he was going to be happy, always tomorrow.

Arky got up and started to pace the floor. A couple of tough, quarrelsome lit-tle sparrows began to hop about the window-sill, and Arky stood idly watch-ing them. They were a hardy breed; the only birds that stayed north the year around. He'd often seen them hopping about in the snow on a cold winter day, searching for food.

The phone rang again. It was the Paymaster and he sounded agitated.

"How's the Mover?" asked Arky.

"Not so good, but he thinks he's fine. He wants you to stand by—all day if necessary. The lineman's working on the telephone now—fixing the private line so he can talk in the bedroom. Arky, I want you to know the truth. The Mover's in a bad way. I had a long talk with the doctor. We're not saying anything to the Mover's wife or the rest of the family, but I think you ought to know. It's not the wound so much: of course that's not helping matters any; but the Mover's blood pressure is very high and the doctor's afraid of a heart attack or apoplexy. All the Mover's family go that way and at just about his age. The Mover even makes jokes about it. A couple of months ago he made a new will, and he told me over a month ago that everything was in order in case he popped off. That's exactly what he said: popped off. Never saw such a man, Arky. Guess I don't have to tell you."

"No," said Arky, feeling lonelier than ever. Anna, Orv, Milli, now maybe the Mover. "Looks like I'm running out of people," he thought.

"Among other things," the Paymaster went on, "the Mover said he'd like to see you and talk to you, but I made him understand the impossibility of that. Reporters all over the place: men from headquarters, and even the district attorney's office. What about Harry Radabaugh, Arky?"

"He's a rat—cheap friend of Leon's. Keep him away from the Mover. If you have any trouble with him, call me. I'll settle his hash."

"All right. Now stand by."

"I'll be right here, day and night."

The Paymaster got into his little coupé and drove back to the Judge's house. Mrs. Greet was in the study, taking care of some chores with the help of Miss Waite, her social secretary. Byron Greet, tall, slim, bespectacled—nothing like the Judge—was pacing in the hallway, nervously smoking a cigarette.

"Did you talk to him yet, Byron?" asked the Paymaster.

"Yes," said Byron. "Briefly. But we seem to have nothing to say to each other, which is not surprising. We haven't had since I was sixteen or seventeen. You know he hates my guts."

"Now, now, Byron; nothing of the kind. Nonsense."

"Don't try to soothe me, Gord, or kid me. I'm a Byron, not a Greet, and he's never forgiven me for it. He wanted me to be an athlete like himself, and a... well, God! I don't have to go through the catalogue for you! He thinks a scholar is the next thing to a preacher—and you know what he thinks of preachers. I don't see why he and Mother didn't have a few more children...."

"They lost two."

"I know. But couldn't they have kept on trying?"

"Your mother's health wouldn't stand it."

"Oh, she's fifty, and she can still dance all night and run around to all hours. It's more than I can do."

The Paymaster glanced at Byron, then lowered his eyes. From the Judge's viewpoint, Byron was a weakling and the Judge did not have any sympathy for weaklings. It was unfortunate and unjust and unfatherly. But how could you put the Judge right about it? You could not put the Judge right about anything. You accepted him, or left him. No other alternative. At times the Paymaster had the suspicion that the Judge thought more of Arky than he did of his own son, which was grotesque! But the Judge was a strange man, very strange; none like him.

"Byron," said the Paymaster, "why don't you go back to town? No use getting yourself in a state. If there's anything you can do, I'll call you."

"There won't be anything I can do," said Byron. "There never has been."

Without another word, he picked up his hat, nodded to the Paymaster, and went out. The Paymaster stood watching him go, feeling very sorry for him. Byron, with all his advantages, was a very unhappy young man. He had always wanted his father's approval—he'd even tried to play football in high school, weedy and thin-chested as he'd been, and his failure, against odds, had only made his father more contemptuous. Then Byron had revolted from his father's authority, still hoping, some day, to gain his approval. He'd never succeeded.

The Judge turned his head on his propped-up pillows when the door opened and the Paymaster came in. A colored male nurse bowed to the Paymaster, then went out.

"Where's the lineman?" asked the Paymaster.

"Working around outside the house someplace," said the Judge. "I can talk to Arky shortly. Terrible thing with poor Arky, losing his woman. Somebody will die for it eventually. Mark my word." The Judge seemed to speak with a certain satisfaction, and the Paymaster glanced at him in surprise.

"I hope this shooting won't go on and on," he said.

"No more shooting," said the Judge. "I'll do my best to prevent it. But I won't be around forever."

"There you go again."

The Judge laughed. "The penalty of a realistic view of life. In fact, my whole career—certainly from a conventional standpoint—has been ruined by a realistic viewpoint. Or maybe opportunist, is the word. What do you think, Gord?"

"I've got far beyond theory, Judge."

The Judge laughed again. "And you're quite right. Amazing how we all drifted into this. Amazing!"

"It crept up on me."

"Oh, I dragged you in, Gord. I needed somebody I could trust besides Arky. He's trustworthy, God knows, but not very presentable with that pinched Arkansas face and that accent. Yes, I'm afraid I dragged you in."

The Paymaster made no comment, but sighed, sat down, and lit a cigar.

"At least," said the Judge, "life hasn't been dull and I can't stand dullness. A man's got to make a choice. He can't have it every way at once, although my son seems to think so. However, he's young...."

"I was talking to him downstairs. He didn't seem very happy, Judge."

"Did you ever see him when he did? When I die he'll inherit close to a million dollars in his own right. Give him some responsibility, some practical worries. May take him out of the cloister. May, and may not." The Judge turned to his night-table for a cigarette, lit it, and puffed on it with little evidence of satisfaction. "Doctor's idea," he said. "Bars the cigars. It'll be cubebs next. Oh, well. I shouldn't have allowed myself to get shot. Damned careless of me." The Judge glanced down at the thick bandage on his arm, and the sling. "Yes, damned careless. I should have listened to Arky. When you live to fifty-five, you begin thinking you're immortal, or at least that you won't die by accident. Well...."

There was a long silence and the two men sat in the huge shadowy bedroom, smoking and staring into space. Finally the Judge spoke.

"I got to thinking this afternoon about how I drifted into this thing. Funny. Corruption breeds corruption. First, we're collecting campaign money; and having quite a hard time getting any, with the local party showing definite signs of falling apart. Then the picture changes. We begin winning elections again. All over the city men start running to us with money: we have so much now we don't know what to do with it." The Judge laughed, then considered. "I just said 'corruption breeds corruption.' Maybe I should have said '*success* breeds corruption.' We were a huge success, and we soon found ways to spend our money. This always happens. The more you spend the more in the habit of spending you get, and finally the business pyramids into an insanity. Pretty soon we were combing the town for money again. No matter how fast it poured in we never had enough. We took the gambling-house proprietors in, gave them service; then the bookmakers, and finally the panderers. Not very pretty, is it? But you have to be a moralist to separate, in this day and age, clean money, from dirty. How do you draw the line?"

The Judge paused and puffed on his cigarette, made a face, finally, and then stamped the cigarette out in an ashtray. "Tastes like the dry grape-leaves I used to smoke behind the carriage-house when I was seven years old. Whew! Well, Gord, how do you like my story?"

"Fine," said the Paymaster. "It sounds so harmless the way you tell it. But how will it end?"

"End? It will never end, Gord. Never. To win elections you've got to raise money. To raise money you've got to do more than promise, you've got to perform. Men do not give you money because they love you, but in order to make more money. A candidate has only one choice—choice of masters."

"I'm glad you don't speak this way in public."

The Judge laughed. "I've been tempted. Many times, Gordon. Many times."

There was a tap at the window and a young lineman, grinning, looked in.

"Okay now, Judge," he said. "It's all yours."

"Thanks, young fellow," said the Judge, smiling; then he turned to the Paymaster. "Get him a bottle of the Johnny Walker out of the cabinet over there."

"Aw, now Judge," said the lineman, grinning eagerly, "you don't have to do that."

But when the Paymaster handed him the bottle he took it quickly and patted it. "Black Label," he said. "Brother, that goes in the basement where I keep my fishing tackle, and none of my thirsty relatives can find it. Thank you, Judge, and long life and health to you, sir."

The Judge nodded and smiled.

The Mover's voice sounded about as usual, strong, healthy, pleasant, and Arky felt heartened.

"How you feeling, sir?"

"Fine, fine. The bullet just ripped through my arm and shoulder. Didn't touch the bone. I guess I'm tough. Sorry to hear about... well, you know."

"Thank you, sir. Damn shame."

"More than that; a senseless, inexcusable thing, but don't let it unsettle you. Don't do anything foolish because of it."

"I'm waiting for orders."

"Why, business as usual. Collect at the usual time. Rudy's still functioning as far as I know."

Arky laughed shortly. "No changes, eh?"

"No. But, Arky—might be a good idea to take a man in with you just on the remote possibility there might be trouble. Not that I'm expecting any—the boys misfired and it will take them some time to recover. However, it's not a bad idea to have a man behind you. We don't want any accidents."

"Okay. Say, one time you told me you knew who this Mr. Kelly was. If you want him looked up, I'll be glad to accommodate you—teach him a lesson."

The Mover laughed quietly. "A very intriguing idea, Arky; intriguing, but futile. Like trying to cut Russia down by shooting Stalin. Just means another Stalin right away and another Mr. Kelly. That's a big organization. Not like us, Arky. We are strictly whistle-stop."

"All the same they want to cut in."

"An organization like that has got to expand. It's inevitable. Besides, George Cline and Leon gave them the idea. They were practically asked in, and by now must be a little bewildered, if not deeply hurt." The Judge chuckled.

"What about Leon and George?"

"Well, George will no doubt go back to Las Vegas or Reno or wherever he came from; and Leon will keep his head down. Or, maybe, Leon will try to come back in."

"Let him try."

"Now wait a minute, Arky. Leon's useful. We could do worse. Rudy's a rather shaky citizen and who else is there? This has been my major problem for years. Maybe Leon has learned his lesson."

"He fingered us both and in my opinion he ought to join Anna in the cemetery."

"He didn't finger us, Arky. Leon is a double-crosser but he's a little squeamish about murder. No. We were fingered, all right, by somebody who knew, but I'm sure it wasn't Leon. I think Leon left town so he wouldn't have to finger us."

"Well, I'm damned."

"And you know it wasn't Rudy."

"That you can bet on. What about George Cline?"

"I doubt if he could have given them the necessary information. These boys knew what they were doing. They were just unlucky, shall we say?"

"You got me going round in a circle."

"Well, it's no great matter. Collect as usual, Arky—taking the suggested precautions, and don't do anything rash. Things are booming, as you know. Good-bye, Arky." The Mover hung up abruptly, as he often did, leaving Arky dangling.

Arky replaced the receiver, then he sat staring out the window. It was late afternoon, the sun was setting beyond Italian Hill, and the slow-moving river, looking almost as still as a lagoon, showed faint tints of pink and mother-of-pearl, with greenish shadows where the big bridges arched across to the far shore. A squat, powerful, dirty-white tug moved slowly upstream, trailing a long plume of iron-gray smoke that was faintly touched with rose. Arky saw a man reach out and jerk the whistle-cord and a moaning blast drifted up to him, then another.

He felt again that piercing sense of loneliness. Night would soon fall: the big apartment would be like a tomb without Anna and Orv. He even considered the possibility of moving into a hotel, but rejected the idea at once as fantastic. What about the calls from the Mover? The set-up was perfect now. What was the matter with him? Was he getting childish?

He started slightly at the sound of a footstep on the stairs. Opening the night-table, he took out the automatic and shoved it into his pocket; then he opened the bedroom door cautiously and listened.

A voice spoke intensely in the outer hall: "Oh, God, Zand, I hate this. He'll...." Lola!

"It's not our fault, damn it! We couldn't..." came Zand's voice.

Arky sighed with relief, crossed the hall in one stride, and opened the front door of the apartment; then he took a step back and stared in astonishment. Lola had Orv in her arms, and Zand was carrying his basket.

Lola talked and cried at the same time. "I know what you'll think, Arky. But... but we just couldn't help it. Wasn't anything to do but bring him back. We...."

Zand cut in, showing weak defiance. "We been to hell and gone, Arky, try-

ing to find them kids, but nobody knows where they went. They moved out of
that first place right away. Honest to God, Arky, we're both worn out chasing
all over Polishtown. Lola's about to drop."

"Well," said Arky, mildly, "if you couldn't find 'em, you couldn't find 'em.
Come on in."

Lola turned and stared at Zand in blank bewilderment, then she turned
back to Arky. "You mean you're not sore?"

"No," said Arky. "I'm not sore. What is there to be sore about?"

Lola began to cry. "Oh, we were so worried. Zand said you'd think we did-
n't try to find the kids because you knew I wanted the baby so."

"Never mind. Never mind, Lola," said Arky. "Bring him in. Put him back
in the bedroom. I guess you and Zand better move in here with me if you're going to look after him. Okay, Zand?"

Zand stared open-mouthed, then he began to look about him at Arky's
"swell" apartment. "Sure, sure, Arky, if you say so. Sure. How about all this
stuff of the baby's, the crib and all? I got a carful."

"I'll help you bring it in," said Arky.

He and Zand went down the stairs. Lola stood staring after them, jiggling Orv,
who was tired and peevish and beginning to whimper. "Well, I'm damned,"
said Lola. "Men are all crazy. Here we been worrying ourselves gray and...."
Orv gave a loud yell, startling her. "All right, little man," she cooed. "All right,
doll-dear. You been an angel all day. I guess you're entitled to give out now.
Come with Aunt Lola. Aunt Lola change oo, then oo feel better!"

Zand and Arky lounged around in the spare bedroom while Lola gave Orv
his midnight feed. Zand smoked a cigarette, and with his legs crossed took his
ease, looking about him with deep satisfaction at the big, beautifully furnished
bedroom. He and Lola had been pigging it downstairs before: this was the life!

Arky was not at ease, however. Lola made him nervous, the way she handled
Orv, and he could hardly keep from cutting in; but what the hell did he know
about babies? With Anna everything always went smoothly and Orv had always seemed calm and happy. But Lola did not even seem to know how to hold
him, and kept jiggling him about and once almost dropped the bottle. Arky got
up and began to pace the floor. In a moment Orv drew back from his bottle
abruptly and threw up some of his milk.

"Oh, God!" cried Lola, almost letting Ory slip from her hands. "Look—he's
sick. What's the matter, honey-bunch? Don't like your nice milk?"

"Give him a chance, give him a chance," cried Arky. "If somebody stuffed a
bottle in my kisser like that I'd throw up, too."

"What did I do wrong?" asked Lola.

"Don't stick it in his mouth so far," cried Arky. "Anna never did. Let *him* do
it. Just put it out there for him."

Finally Arky got up and went out. Zand followed him.

"No place for us, anyway," said Zand. "Babies give me the creeps."

"How about some gin rummy?" asked Arky.

"Okay. Okay," said Zand. "But I'm going to hit the hay pretty soon. All that chasing around wore me out."

They sat down at the table in Arky's bedroom and began to play, arguing mildly.

"Give Lola a chance, will you, Ark?" said Zand finally. "She may not be no Anna with kids, but she'll learn."

"Okay. Okay," said Arky.

In the spare bedroom Orv began to howl at the top of his lungs. "Well," said Arky to himself, "at least I'm not lonesome."

14

Pay Day, again. For the first time, Zand strapped on a shoulder holster and took his big .45 with him; before, he had always carried a small .38 in his inside coat-pocket. Arky waited impatiently while Zand got into his coat. The bookie room was deserted but all the lights were still on; the floor was littered with newspapers and Racing Forms, and bluish tobacco-smoke hung in thick strands in the heavy air. Almost time for the roustabouts to appear with their brooms.

"Come on, Zand," said Arky. "I want to be there on the dot."

"This thing binds me," said Zand, trying to get the holster-strap into a comfortable position. "Not used to it."

"You think this Turkey kid is okay?"

"Sure," said Zand. "Toughest boy in the neighborhood—kicks these young hoods around like they were dogs. I give him a twenty and I thought he was going to kiss me."

"Okay," said Arky. "Come on, will you? A guy would think you were getting dressed for a party."

"Maybe I am," said Zand. "Maybe my last one."

"Want to stay home?"

"Christ Almighty, where's your sense of humor?" cried Zand, flaring up. "I got as much guts as you have—maybe more."

"Stop bragging—and let's go."

As they went out the alley door, Arky cuffed the little jockey-sized Syrian and they both laughed.

Turkey was at the wheel of the Ford, waiting for them. He had a tough, square face, a corrugated brow, and a small round head covered with short, stubbly blond hair. He was wearing a checked shirt and a pair of dirty corduroy pants. He was about eighteen years old and occasionally fought a club fight for five bucks and a couple of tickets. He was a very rough young man, and seemed like a cinch for the Walls later in his life, but he was very much in awe of Zand and Arky. Zand weighed a hundred pounds but he carried a spring-blade knife in his pocket at all times and would gizzard you if necessary. Arky was a smiling, polite fellow, never raised his voice to anybody, but he was Zand's boss, so...!

"You know where we're going?" asked Arky as they got in.

"Yes sir," said Turkey.

"Know all about how to get there—park?"

"I told him everything," said Zand impatiently. Arky leaned across and handed Turkey a short-barreled revolver of high caliber, known as a belly-gun. "Don't let nobody take the car away from you."

Turkey took the gun with a proud look. "Don't worry, sir. I won't."

Almost eight o'clock; everything as usual—the Front jammed with people going to the theater in taxis, private cars, and buses. The air was still and damp, and there was a heavy mist from the river, wetting the pavements and turning them into mirrors that sharply reflected the street lights, the car headlights, and the flashing neon signs above. The wheels of the Ford passed over a distorted, upside-down version of the Front, a surrealist image more striking than the thing itself.

A prowl-car whipped past them, then went on, siren going, tires skidding and slithering on the wet car-tracks. Arky glanced at Turkey. The kid drove with set face, giving no indication that he'd seen or heard the prowl-car. Maybe he was okay. They had nothing to fear from a Pier 7 prowl-car, but how would the kid know that?

Arky began to wonder just exactly what was going through the kid's head. Zand had said that he'd told him everything; but he'd only meant everything about getting there and parking. Turkey was absolutely in the dark about what Arky's real intentions were. For all he knew, it might be a stick-up. Didn't seem to bother him. But why make it tougher on him?

"Kid," said Arky, "this is nothing. We got a date with a guy, that's all. Some guys would just as lief we didn't keep this date, see? So we want the car in the parking-lot when we come out."

"It'll be there," said Turkey, keeping his eyes on the street.

Overhead the big golden sign of the Club Imperial flashed on and off as usual. Eight o'clock struck someplace, the strokes of the bell vibrating and giving off overtones in the heavy air.

The parking-lot was deserted. Turkey eased the Ford into the right stall, and Zand leaned out to stare.

"Look, Arky."

"As I live," said Arky. "The goosy-green convertible."

"You figure Leon's back?"

"I doubt it. The coppers had the car impounded, but maybe Rudy managed to talk 'em out of it."

As they got out, the colored boy in the gold jumpers came round the corner of the alley, took a look at them, and went away again.

"We won't be long," said Arky, and the kid at the wheel nodded, his face set.

Arky went through the padded door, followed by Zand, who had dressed quietly but elegantly for the occasion in a black broadcloth double-breasted suit, a pink shirt with a black tie, black patent-leather shoes and a black snap-brim hat. He was more than a foot shorter than Arky, and seemed about half as wide, his smallness accentuated by the dark clothes.

The back corridor was filled as usual by cooking smells from the vast kitchens: the front corridor was deserted, but at the end of it a piano tinkled in the bar and a girl with a husky voice was singing a blues. Arky wondered absent-mindedly if it was the same girl who had sounded so sexy to him weeks back. Very doubtful. The turnover at the Imperial was fast: the girls went in and out like the moving ducks at a shooting-gallery; you could hardly tell the difference, anyway, and nobody cared; they all dressed alike, made up alike, and sang alike; some were redheads, some blonds, some brunettes—but this was a superficial difference and might have been merely a change of wigs. All chesty contraltos. A soprano would have been thrown out in the alley. Why? Arky could never figure that one out.

He pushed open the door and entered the outer office, followed by Zand.

Robbie looked up, gave a start. She seemed prettier than ever, but at the moment Arky felt nothing at all in regard to her.

"What's that behind you, Ozark?" cried Robbie. "Your shadow?"

But Arky was in no mood for quips: he felt cold and sullen. Without a change of expression, he jerked his thumb toward the inner office.

Robbie studied his face, then her smile faded. "Yeah," she said. "Go ahead. Say, you been neglecting me. What is this?"

Zand was staring at her openly, running his eyes over her. "Some kid," he said.

"Take it easy, shorty," said Robbie. "Pull the lenses down over those eyes, will you? You make me self-conscious."

"Some kid," Zand repeated, beginning to grin.

"Things must be tough at the race-track," said Robbie, looking to Arky for encouragement, then back at Zand. "What's the matter, buddy-boy, couldn't you get a mount?"

Zand laughed with delight. "She kills me, like Lola used to, only prettier and funnier."

"Shut up," said Arky, moving toward the door of the inner office.

"What's the matter with *you?*" called Robbie. "Did you meet one you liked better?"

"Not a chance, baby," said Zand. "Not a chance, unless he's got mighty funny taste."

"You doll," said Robbie. "Jump up on the desk and kiss me."

"Don't encourage him," said Arky.

"I see what you mean," said Robbie, drawing back in mock fright, her hands raised as if to ward off a monster.

At a look from Arky, Zand finally sobered, though he kept glancing at Robbie out of the corner of his eye. Arky opened the door and went in, followed by Zand. Rudy, plump and red-cheeked, was sitting behind his desk. He had a fixed grin, showing strong white teeth. Rudy was half Italian and half German, but looked like an Irishman. He had dark brown hair and light blue eyes. He was smoothly handsome, but much too fat. He ate spaghetti by the yard, cheese by the pound, and drank red wine all day long. Everybody who knew him well considered him a "good joe," and some of the stuff that appeared in the papers about him convulsed his friends. He had once been referred to as "Rapacious Rudolph" by an overheated police reporter on a tabloid. Another paper had called him "that sinister figure of our nether-world." Some people even insisted that Rudy had murdered Leon and disposed of his body, so he could "muscle in."

Rudy had started out as a saloon-keeper on Italian Hill, taking over from his father who had died. A gambler friend suggested opening a game in the back of the place. Rudy agreed; he always agreed—with everybody, complicating matters a little at times. The game prospered to such an extent that the police knocked it over. This made Rudy very sad. Who was he bothering? It was unjust. Somebody told him to get in touch with Leon. It took him eighteen months, but he finally made it. Leon took a liking to him and gave him money to open a bigger place in a better neighborhood. Rudy prospered; he served good food, good liquor, and his game was a hundred per cent straight. "Why not?" Rudy would always ask. "I don't have to cheat nobody to get along. The percentages do the cheating." In a little while he was Leon's closest friend and running unimportant errands. Leon felt like a very big man indeed in Rudy's company. Rudy was slavishly devoted.

So now, here he was, rattling around in Leon's chair, running Leon's big night-club, and getting headlines, which at times frightened him.

Although Rudy's fixed grin remained, he quailed visibly in Arky's presence. Zand studied him with contempt.

"Everything okay, Arky?" he asked in his high-pitched, comical voice.

Arky took off his hat. "I'm parting my hair different now."

"Yeah. I heard about it," said Rudy. "Terrible! Awful!"

"Leon around?"

Rudy jumped eagerly in his chair. "*Leon!* Something I don't know?"

"We saw his car outside."

Rudy seemed to sag, like a slowly deflating balloon. "Oh! The coppers turned it back to me—after they give it a going-over for bloodstains, all that scientific stuff. They never catch nobody with it—but I guess it gives them something to do."

"You know where Leon is?"

"No," said Rudy. "I wish I did. He used to phone in—told me he phoned you, too. But he's gone dead on me—I mean like a telephone wire. I don't like it. That's why I kinda took it big when you asked me. Where the hell *could* he be?"

"He'll turn up," said Arky.

Rudy took out a handkerchief and mopped his brow. "I wish to hell he would. This is getting me."

"What about the take?"

Rudy looked blank. "The... take? Jesus, I forgot this was the day. Just a minute, Arky. Everything's okay. I got the dough right here someplace. Now lemme think—did I put it all in the safe, or did I...?"

Arky and Zand exchanged a disgusted look. Rudy buzzed the inter-com. Robbie's voice answered sweetly over the wire, and Zand perked up and smiled. "My right arm up to here," Zand told himself.

"Honey," said Rudy, "did I put all that stuff in the safe with the ledger, or did I...? Oh, sure, sure. That's right. Come on in, honey."

"Jesus, Rudy," Arky complained, "you mean this kid knows—"

He broke off as the door opened and Robbie came in, patting her hair self-consciously and throwing a quick, veiled look at Arky.

"It's in the safe, Rudy," she said. "I'll open it for you. What a safecracker Rudy would make," she added, crossing over in front of Arky, brushing him. "Even with the combination, he can't open the thing."

As the three men looked on, Robbie stooped down, deftly opened the safe, took out a large thick manila envelope, shut the safe door, spun the combination, then rose slowly, showing considerable leg, walked across the room, and handed the envelope to Arky.

"This is yours, I believe."

Arky took the envelope without a word, avoiding her eyes.

"Thanks, baby," said Rudy.

Robbie shrugged, raised her eyebrows at Zand as she passed him, then went out, closing the door softly.

Zand whistled sadly. "Some kid!"

Arky turned to Rudy. "You damn idiot—when Leon was here she didn't know the time of day. Now she runs the joint."

"Take it easy, Arky," said Rudy, drawing back a little. "She don't know anything. She thinks you own this place, that's all. I had to tell her something because I needed help, brother. I got this wished on me. I didn't want it. And if anybody else wants it, he's welcome."

Owned the place, eh? Arky smiled to himself. No wonder he was getting such a big play from Robbie. On the make, strictly on the make, and why not? It was a rough world unless you had dough in your pocket and a place to light.

"She's a sharp cookie," said Arky. "So watch it, Rudy. Don't tell her anything you don't have to. Collections okay?"

Now Rudy beamed. "Forgot to tell you. Up about ten G's from last week and last week was high. Since the Commissioner left, it's been hand over fist. If Leon would only come back, things would be perfect."

"Yeah," said Arky; then he slipped the manila envelope into his pocket, turned and started out, followed by Zand.

"Good-bye, Arky," Rudy called. "You got to excuse me; I been kinda befuddled today. Next week it'll be different."

"What's the matter, Rudy—wasn't you expecting me?"

Rudy stammered for a moment. "Well... I read in the papers you got shot pretty bad. I didn't know... and so I was kinda befuddled when...."

Arky went out. Zand gave Rudy a searching look, then closed the door.

In the outer office Robbie was making coffee on a little electric burner.

Zand leaned on her desk and gnashed his teeth at her. "Some kid," he said.

"Ozark," called Robbie, "make Dracula let me alone, will you? How about a spot of coffee—as we say in Dee-troit?"

"I'm in a hurry. Come on, Zand."

"I'll be back," said Zand grinning.

"You ain't kidding," said Robbie. "No use to lock the door. You could crawl under it. I wish I knew why Ozark is so cold to me today. I thought it was one of my *good* days."

"I may give you a ring," said Arky. "And I may not." Wanting Anna back was one thing. Going without a woman was another. He might feel different in a few days. If he did, him for Robbie!

Robbie scribbled something hastily on a pad, tore off a sheet and handed it to Arky. "Home phone, too; and you're the only man who has got it."

"The only tall slim guy named Ozark," said Arky, and went out laughing.

"Oh, well," said Zand to Robbie, "I tried."

"Don't give up," said Robbie. "You never know. And half a man is better than none."

Zand went out roaring. But in the hallway he sobered, jerked his thumb over his shoulder and asked Arky: "Is that Rudy slippery or stupid?"

"Stupid," said Arky. "The Mover better get a new man."

They found Turkey waiting for them calmly. As they got in he said: "Guy with a badge buzzed me. Tall guy."

"What did he want to know?" Arky demanded.

"What I was doing here."

"What did you tell him?"

"Told him I was driving for a guy inside. The colored boy came and tried to chase him away. He got pretty tough with the colored boy. Then a prowl went down the alley and he beat it."

Arky and Zand exchanged a quick look then Arky said: "All right, Turk. Let's go home."

As they turned into the alley, a prowl-car, lights out, slid up beside them and cut them off. Turkey had to stop to avoid a collision.

"Arky?" called one of the cops.

"Yeah?"

"It's me—Lon Bucher."

The big cop, Bucher, was one of Arky's customers at the bookie room. "Yeah, Lon?"

"A bastard from the D.A.'s office was buzzing your boy while you were inside."

"Yeah. The kid told me. Know him?"

"Yeah. Pal of Harry Radabaugh's—kind of a bird-dog for him. We don't like them D.A. jerks horsing around on the Front so we run him off. Did you hear about Harry?"

"No. What?"

"He got into some kind of a thing with the D.A. and the D.A. kicked him out. Harry's running out of law-enforcement bodies to work for. Crooked bastard—they always catch up with him. Guess he'll end up as a private dick. Them kind usually do."

"Oh, he'll light someplace. Much obliged, Lon."

"It's okay. Get moving."

Turkey drove off. His face was set as before but his eyes were big and uncomprehending. Coppers for friends. What next?

While newspapermen ran round in circles, and a twenty-four hour watch was kept at the Judge's house, and daily bulletins dealing with the Judge's condition were front-page stuff, the coroner's inquest into the death of one Anna Hunchuk, 35, went practically unnoticed.

It took place in a dingy corner of the old Criminal Courts Building in the 17th Ward. Two policemen from the Pier 7 Station House testified with professional aplomb; then Zand (identified as Alexander Aydeb) and Lola (identified as Rosalka Novotny) gave their versions of what had happened, according to their knowledge; then the doctor testified, and the coroner's man, and the report of a police ballistic expert was read; finally Arky (identified as Orval Smith Wanty) told his story in a low-pitched, flat-sounding voice, staring at the floor. He gave his occupation as "pool-hall owner, cigar store on the side," and his place of birth as Dry River, Arkansas.

There was hardly anything at all to the inquest: the evidence was so cut-and-dried, so obvious, and a verdict was reached without difficulty: death at the hands of a person, or persons, unknown—murder—full exoneration for Arky.

Downy sat in, wondering what it was all about, and why Reisman was so interested in Arky, a mighty dull fellow in Downy's opinion. When it was over he hurried out, made a routine report to the paper, then called Eunice, who was just getting up. She had crazy hours: went to work at ten in the evening and quit at six in the morning. But things were panning out. Eunice was no pushover, but a clever, teasing little girl, always holding out a promise, never fulfilling it—till maybe next time. Would next time ever come? Downy felt that it would; meanwhile, he was in no hurry—the exploratory phase was far from unpleasant with a doll like Eunice.

15

Nobody could find Reisman, although it was reliably reported that he'd been seen here and there in the City Building and even in the morgue at the *Journal*. No matter where anybody called him, he never seemed to be in. Red Seaver finally got into a rage about it and made up his mind he'd find him or else. First he sweated Downy; but Downy, usually docile enough, couldn't—or wouldn't—help; then he began to call Reisman's house at all hours until Mrs. Reisman finally told him that if he didn't stop calling she'd complain to the police; at last he drove out to Lakeside Village and camped outside Reisman's door. Nothing happened that day.

The next day, however, Red had just taken up his stand when Reisman slipped out the back door and into the alley where a taxi was waiting for him. Smiling grimly, Red trailed him to the airport and accosted him at the barrier.

"Why hello, Red," said Reisman. "Where have you been lately?"

"Look, Ben. This is no time for gags. I work on the *Journal*, too. I'm a co-worker, a fellow employee, and also a friend of yours. What is all this?"

"All what? I been sick. I'm flying up to Cleveland to see Dr. Grunwald, the stomach specialist."

"Dr. Grunwald's in Europe. Don't you read the papers?"

"Dr. Grunwald is crossing the Atlantic at this moment, out of Lisbon."

"Just to look at your stomach, I suppose."

"It's pretty. But I checked with his office. Nothing to do with my stomach."

"Ben—man and boy we've known each other for many years. I hate to say this to you. You are a goddamned, double-crossing liar."

"Please, Red. The children."

Red looked about him wildly, immediately contrite; then his face hardened as he turned once again to Reisman. "What am I doing—playing straight man? I'm beginning to act like Casey. So you won't break down."

Reisman's plane was called. "You know something, Red," said Reisman; "I've been going stale on my reading lately—nothing satisfies me. So I decided to take a shot at Shakespeare. Haven't read him for some time. I picked up one of the volumes at random and began to read the first play I came to: *The Two Gentlemen of Verona*—never read it before...."

"Listen, Ben...."

"Well, it's a masterpiece: beautiful. I almost fell out of bed laughing. Funny thing, Red; but I wouldn't give Launce and his dog, Crab, for *War and Peace*, or even the works of T. S. Eliot—all of them."

"Wait a minute, Ben. All right; you're a cultured guy, I'm a yahoo—but I'm also a reporter. I work for Mush Head... we...."

"Do me a favor, Red," said Reisman putting his hand on the big fellow's shoulder, "read *The Two Gentlemen of Verona*. You'll like it."

Turning, Reisman made a dash down the runway for his plane. Red called after him futilely, then subsided in disgust.

"Well, after all," said Red philosophically, as he went back toward his car, "he *has* got that stomach ulcer—and that column must be one hell of a chore."

Red headed out from the airport and made for a country tavern he liked where they had good beer, a plump barmaid who leaned over the counter in a low blouse, and a quarter machine that sometimes paid off.

Although Reisman had taken a sedative, and his nerves felt fairly steady, he turned green on the take-off and longed to be home. He detested flying.

In a moment the plane was up and leveled off. Reisman looked about him morosely at all the happy, careless people, hating them, and also hating the little chic brunette stewardess with her uniform cap cocked over one eye. Invincible, she looked: immune to the terrors of the sky.

"The trouble with me is," Reisman told himself, "that I'm a neolithic man at heart. Left to myself—on a desert island, say—in ten years I couldn't think up an improvement on a flint arrowhead. If I killed anybody it would be with the same old artifact. I'm just a slob, one of the million. Look at the march of civilization: flint, copper, bronze, iron; gunpowder, dynamite, TNT, atom bomb, hydrogen bomb. The field is unlimited. But, look at you—Reisman: still throwing rocks!"

Although Reisman had bought a through ticket to Cleveland, when the plane landed at the State Capitol airport he disappeared into the bar, took a stiff drink, went out the back way, and caught a taxi for town. With him was a small brief-case containing a change of underwear, a toothbrush and toothpaste, an electric razor, a suit of pajamas, and a few documents: he might not have to stay overnight but on the other hand he might, and he liked to have his own things with him. New things irritated him.

Justice Stark was staggered. Reisman sat watching him as he paced up and down the big sitting-room of his suite. He and Mrs. Stark were staying at the eighty-year-old River House, where the rooms were enormous, the ceilings high, and the food and service wonderful, even if the plumbing was somewhat primitive and the old cage-elevator often stalled.

The Justice went to one of the tall old windows which reached to the floor, and stood looking out. Before him lay the sylvan expanse of the Capitol Square with its ancient trees, stone benches, scampering gray squirrels, and its many monuments. Beyond, the huge old Capitol, with its stained and weathered Doric columns and its huge three-story-high porches, seemed to sleep among the greenery, as if dreaming of another age.

In 1865 the then governor had received the high officers of the victoriously returning Union Army in the front reception-room, the windows of which Stark could see as he looked out from the hotel. Early in 1919, other officers had been received in this same reception room by another governor; and again in 1945. The tides of history had rolled steadily over the Capitol for more than a hundred years: it had watched, unchanged, age after age, administration after administration, wars, rebellions, depressions, all the hopes, fears and insanities of men; but it had never seen anything to equal the present, and stood now as a silent reproach, a reproach, however, that went unheeded.

Nobody had any love for the old Capitol any more. It was to be torn down in 1951 to make room for a modern office-building. More and more floor-space was needed for more and more bureaus, necessitating more and more taxes, which of course meant more and more employees to collect and handle the taxes, which meant more officeholders, more Party voting strength, more campaign money, more of everything. This was progress, and the old Capitol had no place in it.

The Justice sighed and turned away from the window. "I don't know what to say, Reisman. I am dumbfounded. Surely there must be some mistake. Some...."

"That's why I came to you, Commissioner." Reisman grimaced to himself. He just couldn't think of Stark as anything but "the Commissioner." "Do I call you Mr. Justice, or Judge... what?"

"I don't care what you call me, Reisman. Let's go over this again."

"All right. First, Arky. His name is Orval Wanty. He killed a man in a saloon brawl in 1930. Clear case of self-defense. I've got the whole record. At that time Judge Greet was on the bench in the Criminal Court. Wanty's lawyer was incompetent and later disbarred. Judge Greet refused to accept the plea and maybe saved our friend Arky a few years in the Walls. Apparently the Judge took a liking to this Arkansas boy, because he acted as the Judge's chauffeur and factotum for over five years."

"All right. Nothing incriminating so far."

"No. For a few years I can't find any record of Wanty; then he turns up again." Reisman shuffled his papers. "Assault with a deadly weapon: no disposition—in fact, some of the records are missing. Arrested on bookmaking charges twice: dismissed, both times. No fingerprints in the files. I was told that they must have been mislaid. Things certainly get mislaid a lot, Commissioner...."

Stark flushed slightly. "I'm afraid you are right. Go on, Reisman."

"It is obvious, Commissioner, that this man is being protected—and by high authorities. Right?"

"Right."

"Now let's come to the attempt on Judge Greet's life. There's a lot more in between—you can read the documents. But this is the nub. The Judge and Arky were shot about the same hour of the same day. All right. Maybe it was a coincidence, you'll say. Maybe it was. But this is no coincidence. For weeks the Judge's house had been watched by prowl-cars from the Pier 7 Station House—Arky's stamping ground. I've got affidavits here from a Riverview special policeman. I scared him and he talked. Not only that. Some unknown person, probably a police officer, saved the Judge's life by shooting at the assassin after he had fired only one shot. Something else. A Pier 7 prowl chased the getaway car and was smashed up taking a curve at a high rate of speed. There is a definite police cover-up going on. Dysen won't talk; and apparently no one is powerful enough to *make* him. Chief of Police Frick is in bed with a virus condition, or maybe with a nurse—excuse me, Commissioner—but he can't be reached...."

"And what do you deduce from all this, Reisman?—just between ourselves."

"Leon Sollas was a cheap front. The same goes for Rudy Solano. Our Arkansas friend is a very big man indeed, and very smart to be able to seem so obscure. Leon runs the vice and collects. Arky is his boss. Arky is apparently Captain Dysen's boss, too, and has the run of the police department, at least in the 17th Ward. This would be impossible without the strongest pressure from above. So who is Arky's boss?"

Stark was staggered as before. "Incredible! Simply unbelievable. Why, I've known Judge Greet... and his father the Old Judge, for... well, I can't recall how many years. One of the ablest families in the whole county. Why, I...." Stark broke off and sat down heavily.

There was a long silence. Finally Reisman spoke. "For a long time, Commissioner, there has been talk of George Cline coming in—but that was just talk. George is too small to make a dent now. But the Big City boys have had their eyes on us for a long time, and now with you out of the way.... In other words, the Judge finally outfoxed himself."

"How do you mean, Reisman?" asked Stark, glancing up quickly.

Reisman hesitated and took a deep breath. "Well, Commissioner, if you speak the word, I'll leave quietly—but this I've got to say. Judge Greet was largely responsible for your appointment to the Supreme Bench."

Stark turned pale at once, glanced blankly at Reisman, then sat staring for a long time at the carpet. Finally he spoke, as if to himself. "Incredible! Simply beyond belief." He rose now and walked back to the window. "There must be some other explanation. There *must* be."

"I hope there is," said Reisman, moved to see the Commissioner so shaken. "I could be wrong. It wouldn't be the first time."

The Commissioner turned. "Would you mind leaving all the documents here? I'd like to study them carefully before I make up my mind to anything. Could you stay overnight, Reisman? I'll call you early tomorrow morning."

"I'll stay as long as you say. You understand, Commissioner, that this is the biggest newspaper story in fifty years, and that I'm not going to print a word of it, even a hint, without your permission."

"I understand," said Stark. "And I want to tell you how much I appreciate your co-operation. Too bad there aren't more like you."

"That's a horrible thought, Commissioner. But I'm learning. In the twenties, I'd have splashed this all over the paper, and screamed for a bonus."

"Well," said Stark, "if we don't improve with age and experience we should be shot. Will you stay here at the River House?"

"Yeah," said Reisman. "I'll get a room right away." Now he opened his brief-case and added a stack of documents to the ones already on the desk, dropping a striped pajama coat and a toothbrush in the process.

Stark watched him absent-mindedly, his face puckered with thought. The phone rang and Stark answered it.

"Yes? Yes, Justice Stark. I'll hold on." He turned to Reisman. "It's Marley. Something must have happened in town."

There was a long wait. Reisman picked up the pajama coat and the toothbrush and stuffed them back into the brief-case.

"Yes? I'm holding on," said Stark. "Charles? Yes, it's me. I can't hear you. Lower your voice—stop shouting. What! When? Well, I'm certainly sorry to hear it. Yes. That's the way we all feel. Yes. Yes...." Stark covered the transmitter and spoke in a low voice to Reisman. "The Judge just died."

Reisman did not hear any more of Stark's phone conversation. The brief-case slipped from his hand and fell to the floor and Reisman sank down into a chair. After a moment Stark hung up.

"Well," said Stark, "at least this gives me an excuse to go back to town. I'll fly back tonight."

"I'll take the bus," said Reisman. "Red Seaver's on my trail as it is."

"Will you leave these documents with me?"

"Yes. Do what you like with them. I'm afraid the big story is out the window now."

"Time will tell," said Stark shortly, then: "In your opinion, Reisman, what will happen now?"

"I think the big boys will walk in—that is, with the present set-up in the city. Creeden's a joke, and you know it, Commissioner."

Stark nodded, turned away and moved to the window. After a moment, Reisman went out, closing the door softly, and hurried down to the bar. The thought of that bus-ride back was making his stomach crawl: squalling babies, smelly people, oafs with their feet in the aisle, the guy who always wanted to talk to you and started by saying: "What's your racket, brother?"; old ladies, far from home, clutching their purses and looking at you suspiciously; insolent brats who wandered up and down the aisle blowing bubble-gum which eventually ended up on the seat of your pants.... Reisman pulled himself up short. "Quit kidding," he told himself. "You're tickled to death. No take-offs."

He stood in a dark corner of the bar and ordered a double bourbon with water. The thing to do was get out of the River House bar fast. It was a hangout for political reporters, and some of them had sharp noses—not many, but some. He thought about Red, and laughed.

"No, Arky," said the Captain stubbornly, "I'm through—all through."

A dark cloudless night. Arky and Zand had driven to the closed filling-station out beyond Locust Grove to meet Dysen.

"Now listen, Captain," said Arky quietly, "it's up to us to run it. Run it, or get out. And I ain't getting out. They killed him, Captain. Murdered him. And if they want me out of here they got to kill me, too."

Dysen groaned. "When he was in, all right. But now that he's gone, I got no belly for it, Arky. No belly at all. I'm going to quit—retire. I'm done. Done!"

"They run you out, eh? Listen, without you they can't operate, Captain. As fast as they open you can knock them over. You'll be a big hero in the newspapers—maybe Chief of Police."

"I don't want to be Chief of Police, Arky," said Dysen with one of his hippopotamus-like groans. "I don't want anything. I'm tired. I just want to rest. When he passed on, I lost my starch. All my starch, Arky. You're just wasting your breath."

"You and the Paymaster! Jellyfish—the only thing holding you up was the Mover."

"The Paymaster's a mighty sick man, I understand. Nurses day and night. He collapsed—just like that. Heart—I don't know. But he collapsed, Arky—and let's look at it fairly: all our asses are out with the Mover dead, and the Paymaster on his back in the hospital."

"Mine's not. They killed the Mover and they killed Anna, and they tried to kill me. They are now in bad trouble. I want the finger man. As soon as I figure out who he is, he's dead."

"Don't talk to me like that, Arky. I'm still a police officer, you know."

"Oh, come on, Captain. Cut it out, will you? Your wits leaving you?"

Dysen took his big head in his hands and groaned. "Yes, I think they are. I haven't been myself for a long time—worry, worry; something hanging over my head ready to drop...."

Zand stared at the big police captain with astonishment, Arky with contempt. "Snap out of it, Dysen, will you?"

The Captain lowered his hands and peered sadly at Arky, whose face was marble-pale and marble-hard in the bluish glow of the filling-station night-light.

"I just don't know what to do, Arky. I've come to a pass like that."

"You just do what I tell you," said Arky, harshly. "We'll run these guys out if we bust up the whole damn town doing it."

"Why? For what?"

"*For what!*" Arky shouted, grabbing the Captain's lapels and shaking him. "For the Judge, Goddamn it! He was a man if *you* ain't—and *I* ain't. He's dead. They killed him. Don't you understand?"

There was a long pause and the Captain stood breathing heavily in the semi-darkness. Finally he spoke in a low voice. "All right, Arky. All right. We'll go ahead."

"Good. Give you a ring."

Dysen squeezed his huge bulk back into his little coupé and drove off toward the lights of Locust Grove.

"I wouldn't give you a nickel for him," said Zand. "He's got the shakeroos. He's a lost cause."

"Just so he holds together for a while," said Arky, "then he can fold if he likes."

Arky tried to get into the driver's seat, but Zand pushed him determinedly aside. "Not the way you're feeling, brother. There's enough guys in the hospital now."

Arky did not argue, but got into the other seat. Zand drove back toward town.

"Never saw anything blow like this before," said Zand quietly.

"Things are like that," said Arky. "Sometimes one guy holds 'em together."

Getting toward midnight; tugs moaning on the river; and the clamor from the Front—taxi horns, ringing traffic-signals, bus air-brakes, clanging surface-cars—drifted back faintly between the tenement buildings of the Ward in a steady medley of sound. Clouds low over the big buildings across the river, and an intermittent damp wind blowing, with a just-noticeable touch of fall in it.

Arky paced back and forth nervously in his bedroom, smoking one cigarette after another. He was so keyed up that he could not even force himself to sit down and try to distract his mind with a game of solitaire. He hadn't had four straight hours of sleep for nearly a week.

Below him in the darkened bookie room Turkey sat to one side of an open window with a sawed-off shotgun across his knees. Turkey was happy, living in clover. Plenty to eat; plenty spending money; nothing to do but keep his eyes open, and that was easy. Big doings—and he was in on it. This Arky—a great guy: none better. Just let somebody turn up. "I'll halve the son of a bitch," Turkey told himself grimly.

He thought about his former life with distaste: the crowded dirty flat with his mom and pop and six little brothers and sisters—Turkey was the oldest. Hair-raising stinks coming up the ventilator chute; family fights all around, yelling and screaming; dirty kids with no one to look after them; drunken bums falling down the sagging stairs; garbage in the gutter; little kids getting raped on the roof; police; inquiries; the can, with nobody worrying much whether you're in or out, guilty or innocent.

"One thing about me," Turkey told himself proudly; "never touched a girl under fifteen. Them guys must be crazy."

Course there was always the club fights. It wasn't the five bucks so much—not that that didn't come in handy—but it was the fighting itself; fun, kicks; that's why a guy was given strength and guts by the Lord, or whatever give it to him; and anyway in the 17th you had to be a fighter—you got nothing but the rind and abuse otherwise. Like this Arky; plenty tough boy, and rolling in dough. Always had a bankroll would choke a mule. Try and take it away from him!

Turkey chuckled to himself. Yeah, *try!* That's the way you had to be.

He paused for a moment in his reflections and leaned forward to listen. A car was slowing down just outside in a rather suspicious manner; but in a second it picked up speed again and squeaked across the intersection just beyond. "That's right," said Turkey. "Keep moving, boys. It's healthier."

In the spare bedroom, Lola was face-down on the bed, crying loudly. And Zand was walking the floor, waving his arms and cursing. The baby had been crying off and on for almost four hours; nothing seemed to pacify him. Lola had tried everything: jiggling him, singing to him, rocking him in his basket, pacing the floor with him; giving him water, formula, orange juice; massaging him with baby oil; and even bathing him in his bathinette. No matter what she did, after a moment he started howling again.

"I'm telling you," cried Zand, "pretty soon you got to make a choice, you hear what I'm saying? Ain't the baby enough without you joining in? Be quiet. What the hell kind of a life is this, anyway? I'm sick and tired of it, you hear me? All right. It's nice living in this swell apartment—or it would be, if that damned Polack brat would shut up for two minutes so I could hear myself think!" Zand clutched his head. "Oh, God! There he goes again, hitting them high notes."

Lola turned over, lay sobbing. "I don't know what to do. What will we do, Zand?"

"Give him to somebody. Arky ain't going to keep him. You know that—he just got stuck with him, that's all. Arky's got his own life to lead and so have I—and so have you, I hope."

"You mean you want to say something about it to Arky? You mean you...?"

"Yes," said Zand. "Things are rough enough without this."

Lola turned over on her face and began to cry again. "Oh, the poor little thing—the way he's been passed around. It's awful."

"All right, all right, but you can't handle him, Lola. You know that. No use kidding yourself, and it's wearing you out. You've aged ten years."

Lola sat up abruptly and stared at Zand in dismay, then she rose, hurried to the bathroom and studied her face in the medicine-cabinet mirror.

In a moment she began to sob again. "Oh, I look awful! I didn't realize...."

The baby drowned her out with piercing howls and Zand clutched his head again. At that moment the door was banged back and Arky came in.

"What the hell is going on back here?" he shouted.

Zand started but made no comment, a little worried by the look in Arky's eyes, but Lola said hurriedly: "It's Orv. He's been crying for four hours. I don't know what to do, Arky—I'm half crazy with worry."

Arky walked over and stood looking down at the fat blond baby, whose face was puckered up and purple in color. Ear-splitting howls were coming out of his little mouth, and he was sawing the air with his small fists. Arky poked him gently with a long forefinger. Making a blind grab, the baby caught the finger in his right hand and hung onto it. He stopped crying immediately, his face resumed its usual smooth fat placid look, and he stared up at Arky with blank round blue eyes.

"Little bastard," said Arky, grinning. "Look at him hanging on to my finger. Say—he's got quite a grip—this kid."

Zand and Lola exchanged a quick look behind Arky's back, and Lola shook her head warningly, but Zand spoke up anyway. "Ark," he said, "this is getting too rough—for Lola I mean. It's wearing her out. She worries all the time and she don't get half enough sleep. Look at her. Hardly looks like the same girl."

Arky turned and studied both of them. "I thought you were so set up about having this kid, Lola."

"I was—I *am*," Lola stammered. "But... I don't know. I guess I'm just not up to...."

"Well, hell, who's going to look after him?" Arky demanded. The baby began to howl again, and Arky stared down at him in dismay, then poked him again with his forefinger, but this time the baby ignored the finger and began to kick wildly, throwing off half his covers.

Lola hurried over to him, cooing, and tried to work his blankets back into place, but he kept kicking them off.

"Maybe he's sick," said Arky. "Maybe he's caught a disease or something. I ain't got enough to worry about—now I got to worry about him, too... got any gin up here, Zand?"

The abrupt change of tone and sense startled Zand for a moment and he stared; then he came to himself and said: "Yeah. I got a pint. Want it?"

"Yeah."

"Arky," cried Lola, "you're not going to give that baby gin!"

"No! No!" exclaimed Arky in disgust. "It's for me. Sometimes when I take a shot or two of gin it relaxes me and I can get some sleep."

Zand brought him the bottle of gin and he slipped it into his coat pocket. The baby was crying loudly.

"Tell you what," Arky went on, "you better call Doc Fiaschetti, Zand. Have him come take a look at this baby. If he's sick, we ought to know about it. If you ain't going to look after him, Lola, I'll have to get a nurse or something."

"You mean you're dead set on keeping him?" asked Zand.

"What do you want me to do—throw him out in the gutter?"

"No, but... look, we run all over hell and gone trying to get rid of him for you."

"That wasn't getting rid of him. That was giving him back to his father and mother."

"But you told me yourself he'd be better off in an orphanage."

"Than with most people around here. He *would* be."

"I don't get it," said Zand. "But if you want to keep him, Lola'll look after him till she drops or I blow my topper."

"All right. We'll figure it out. Go call the Doc."

Zand went out, shaking his head.

"I'll be only too glad to look after him, Arky," said Lola, "but... it's sure wearing me down."

Arky studied Lola for a moment; she certainly seemed washed out and sagging. But wasn't it a woman's business to take care of a baby? Back home they looked after them, and did all the housework; and not just one kid, maybe six. Lola just wasn't cut out for it; or maybe she'd lost her woman's touch after years of lying around the big town, drinking and staying out to all hours, and trying to live like a man.

"I'll hire you a girl, Lola," he said at last, then: "Pick him up, why don't you? Jounce him around a little. That's the way they do back home."

Lola said nothing. No use to explain to Arky that she'd done everything under the sun. She picked the baby up, rocked him gently in her arms, and sang to him in what was left of her voice. The baby stopped crying immediately and went to sleep, and even gave off thin little wheezing snores.

"You see?" said Arky, then he turned and went out.

Lola could not trust herself to speak, or hardly to think.

Arky woke with a start and looked about him in bewilderment. He was sitting in the armchair beside his bed and all the lights were on. The Racing Form he'd been reading had fallen to the floor. The gin had relaxed him and done the trick, but he felt a little uneasy; sleep seldom crept up on him like that, and this was a bad time to be dropping off without meaning to.

Zand, looking very tired and drawn, was in the doorway.

"The Doc just left, Arky. You were snoring when he got here, so I let you snore."

Arky cleared his throat and got himself together. "Doc? Yeah. How's the baby?"

"Hell, he's fine," said Zand wearily. "And Doc ought to know. He's got eight of 'em himself. Doc says Orv's as husky a kid as he's seen in a long time; most of 'em round here are pretty weedy. Doc says he ought to get more sun-baths, though, and take vitamins. He left a prescription. You just drop the stuff in his milk, like a mickey."

Arky laughed shortly, then said: "Okay. But why does he cry and yell so much?"

"Doc says the healthier they are the more they yell, and the louder. Great, eh? We got to end up with the healthiest baby in the Ward. Look, Ark. We got to do something about this. Doc put Lola to bed. She's got a temperature— maybe virus, or something. Doc says maybe it's only exhaustion, but is that good? I know you got your troubles and all, Ark, and this is a hell of a time for Lola to blow up on you, but she's just human—if she can't, she can't."

"Okay. Okay. I'll get her a girl. Good God! Back where I come from a woman has a baby one day and scrubs the floor the next."

"I can't help that," said Zand. "Besides," he added bitterly, "I just got no more home life than a rabbit."

Arky studied Zand for a moment. "What you mean is, you wish the baby was to hell and out of here, is that right?"

"Well," said Zand, "where's the percentage? You ain't even married or any-thing, Arky. Why don't you think it over? What in hell are you going to do with him?"

Arky waved his hands impatiently. "Look, I'll think about that some other time. You tell Lola I'll get her a girl—maybe right away; then all she'll have to do is tell the girl what to do." Arky got up, yawning and stretching. "I'll go down and talk to Turkey. He knows every girl in the Ward. If it don't work out, we can get a nurse. But I don't want some smart nosy dame around here if I can help it. One from the neighborhood's better."

"I don't get it," said Zand, then he turned and went back down the hallway to the spare bedroom.

Arky wasn't sure he "got it" either. Why was he being so stubborn? The last thing in the world anybody would think he'd want would be a baby. Maybe it was because Orv now seemed like a part of Anna—all that was left.

Arky shook his head, puzzled; then he put on his coat and went down the stairs toward the bookie room. As he was a few steps from the bottom, the door opened below, and Arky caught a foreshortened glimpse in the dim night-light of Turkey, whose head, seen from above, looked like a muskmelon.

Turkey glanced up. He had the shotgun gripped tightly in his right hand.

"Mister," he said, "there's a guy asking for you—a boog."

"Where is he?"

"Alley door, waiting. Seems like a nice polite fellow."

Arky shrugged and followed Turkey back through the bookie room, which was dark except for the dim glow of a street-light just outside.

"Where did he come from, do you know?" asked Arky.

"I heard him pull into the alley," said Turkey, "so I took a quick look—big car. Think maybe there's a couple other people in it."

Turkey unlocked the alley door and opened it a few inches. An arc-light in the alley gave off a feeble, whitish illumination, and against it a tall man in dark clothes was silhouetted.

"Yeah?" said Arky, stepping up to him.

The colored man was about forty, with a lean face and a self-assured manner.

"Mr. Ark? There's a man in the car up the alley would like to talk to you. You come along with me."

"Look, fellow," said Arky, "if he wants to talk to me tell him to come here to the door."

"I don't know. I'm just doing what he said. He's a pretty important man, Mr. Ark, and he's sick."

"He can walk, can't he?"

The colored man gave Arky a rather contemptuous look. "I'll see what he's got to say," he said, then he turned and went back up the alley.

There was a long wait. At a gesture from Arky, the Turk went back to his place by the side-street window, and sat hardly moving with the shotgun across his knees. Big Stuff! Big doings!

Arky lit a cigarette and leaned against the wall beside the doorway, smoking. He had the belly-gun in his coat pocket just in case, but actually he wasn't worried by this visit. Nobody would be stupid enough to step out into an alley to get shot. That wasn't the pitch. It was something far different, he was sure. But what?

In a moment he heard rapid light footsteps coming down the alley toward him: a car door slammed. High heels? Arky started slightly. A dame? Funnier and funnier.

A tall slender form appeared in the doorway. Arky caught an aroma of expensive perfume. Then a soft agitated voice demanded: "Ozark! That you?"

Arky gasped and stood away from the wall abruptly. "Robbie! What the hell...?"

She reached out and grasped his arm. "Oh, God, I'm glad you're here. I'm half crazy... no kidding, really... I'm about to scream and kick...." She began to sob in such a wracked and hopeless way that Arky reached out and took her in his arms. She was so soft and delicate, smelled so sweet, that he could hardly stand it.

"I didn't know what to do with him, Ozark. I've had him on my hands in that little apartment of mine for nearly a week. He's all to pieces—jumps if the telephone rings. Cries sometimes at night. I can't stand a man crying; it drives me crazy...."

"Slow down, baby," said Arky, shaking her gently, then holding her at arm's length. "Take it easy. Easy. Everything's going to be all right. Rudy's a slob. Everybody knows that."

"It's Leon," she cried. "Not Rudy...."

"What?" Arky was so surprised he released Robbie and took a step backward.

"Look. I don't know what's going on. I don't want to know. But Leon keeps saying they're going to kill him. But when I tell him to get out of town, he says he's been out of town and they been keeping tabs on him—he just can't get away.

And when I told him to go to California he said they'd never let him get that far. I think he's off his head myself. People get funny ideas like that, don't they? Think somebody's trying to kill them?"

"Sure, sure," said Arky. "That's probably it. Sometimes Leon has to deal with some pretty rough boys. Maybe that gave him the idea."

"Of course they always used to be writing Leon up in the papers about what a criminal he was and also Rudy—but that's a lot of... you know what I mean. The police even came and got Rudy and said he was suspected of killing Leon. Which is so ridiculous you can hardly laugh at it. Maybe Leon reads the papers too much. I don't know. I don't want to know. I just want to get somebody to help me with Leon. I can't take it another night. Arky, you've got to help me."

She grasped his arm again. Arky slipped his arms around her and kissed her on the cheek. She smelled like a flower and she seemed so soft and warm and alive as he held her.

"What a time for love!" said Robbie bitterly; then, much to Arky's surprise, she pushed him roughly away. "Let me alone. I never want to see another man as long as I live." She sounded a little hysterical.

"All right, all right," said Arky, trying to hide his anger. "What do you want me to do with Leon?"

"Keep him here. Hide him. Maybe he'll get over this—this, whatever it is— with you around." Robbie seemed to come to herself and glanced about her, puzzled, at the dingy alley and the shadowy, barnlike bookie room. "Say, Ozark, what are you doing in a place like this?"

"Don't ask questions. Go tell Leon to come in. See what I can do for him."

Robbie hesitated then reached out and touched his arm. "Sore?"

"No," said Arky.

"There are times and times," said Robbie. "If I don't get relaxed I'm going to pop. I'll be imagining things worse than Leon."

"Go on. Get him," said Arky, harshly.

Robbie glanced at him quickly in the half light, then she turned and went back up the alley, her high heels clicking as before.

Arky tried to calm his growing anger. The briefest gesture of rejection by a woman when he had made an unambiguous move always infuriated him. Who the hell did she think *she* was? Little by little, he quieted himself, re-membering after a moment what Robbie had told him about Leon. A crying man! Awful! She'd really been through it.

In a little while he heard them coming down the alley, all three of them, at a slow pace. He waited, wondering. Finally they appeared: the colored man was on one side of Leon, helping him, Robbie on the other. Leon started slightly when he saw Arky in the doorway. Leon was carrying a cane and wearing dark glasses. He'd raised a mustache. All the same, nobody who knew him would ever mistake him for anybody but Leon Sollas, even in the half light—with his big shoulders, his sharply cut clothes, the jaunty angle of his snap-brim hat, his general handsomeness.

"You going to take me in, Ark?" he gasped.

"Sure," said Arky with a short laugh. "But it's not much of a place—and *everybody* seems to know where I live."

"Robbie said you would," Leon went on, half crying. "Smart girl, Robbie. She knows everything. I don't know what I'd do if...."

"Stop it, Leon," said Robbie shortly.

"I'll go back now, Mr. Sollas," said the colored man. "You be all right. I give the young lady the keys. I'll grab a taxi on the Front."

"Thanks, Mo. Thanks, thanks," cried Leon effusively.

The colored man went out.

"Who's he?" asked Arky. "Is he okay?"

"He's the only friend I've got left," said Leon, "except you and Robbie. That's Mo Camp. I set him up in business and he's never forgotten it."

Arky whistled faintly. Mo Camp was the Big Boy in the Black Belt, practically owned it, and was fawned on by all the colored politicians.

"Say, wait a minute," said Arky. "I don't want that hack left out in the alley—that circus-wagon...."

"It's not the convertible," said Leon. "You think I'm crazy?"

"Whatever it is, I don't want it out there." He turned to Robbie. "Give me the keys." She handed them to him without a word. "Turk," called Arky.

The big crop-headed kid came over to them, carrying the shotgun. Leon moved back away from him behind Robbie, who stared at the gun, then at Arky, but Arky ignored both of them and explained to Turk about the car.

"Okay, sir," said Turk.

"If the garage is closed, honk your horn till that Greek wakes up. He'll be in the back some place. And leave that gun here."

Turkey handed Arky the gun, gave Robbie a quick, up-and-down, insolent look, then went out.

"Say, wait a minute," cried Robbie, "what about me?"

"You?" demanded Leon. "You're going to stay right here. What do you think?"

"Now listen, Leon, I told you that when...." She paused and glanced at Arky. "Oh, never mind. But, Ozark—do me a favor. Put that blunderbuss away. It makes me nervous."

Arky gave Leon Anna's bedroom. After he was settled Arky told Robbie to go in the living-room and wait for him, then he shut the door behind her.

"I told you, you'd play tag once too often," said Arky. "Now look at you."

"I was only trying to do what I thought was best for everybody, Ark. You know that."

"You were horsing. What is all this, Leon—are *you* on the list, too?"

Leon nodded, swallowing.

"Rudy?"

Leon shook his head. "Nobody worries about Rudy. He just nods and smiles and agrees with everybody. He might even be useful to them. But we're dead, done for, Arky."

"*You* may be."

"Oh, I know you're a fighter, Ark. But you can't fight the wind, or shadows. The big boys just give a couple of the plumbers your address and that's it. If the first set of plumbers don't fix the leak, they send another set."

"One of the plumbers got a leak himself maybe it was tough to fix."

"Futile, Arky. They just keep coming."

"You wouldn't finger for 'em, is that right, Leon?"

Leon gave a jump, began to shake, then calmed himself with an effort. "What kind of talk is that?" he asked in a weak voice.

"Straight talk. Why don't you tell me the truth, Leon? It's in your favor. You might be riding high if you'd fingered us."

"It's a thing I wouldn't do to my worst enemy," said Leon with quiet conviction. "And as for my friends...."

Arky got up, walked over to Leon, and patted him on the shoulder. "Goddamn it, Leon; you may be a little on the jumpy side, but you're all right." He patted him hard.

Leon burst into tears. Arky started slightly and withdrew his hand; then he sat down again.

"Look at me!" cried Leon. "This is awful." Reaching into his pocket, he took out a couple of pills and gulped them down, then he lit a cigarette with shaking hands, and gradually grew quieter.

Arky leaned forward and tapped him on the knee. "All I want's the finger. That will satisfy me. I might even die happy, like the fellow says. When you get up nerve enough, Leon, you tell me. Meanwhile, you relax. I'll look after you. You're safe here, no way to get to you in this room; no porches, nothing. The kid downstairs would shoot his old man if necessary. He's a real rough boy and is going to be heard from some day. So you relax. In order to get to you, they got to get Turk, Zand, and me."

Leon began to smile a little, then he looked about him for the first time. "You got this place pretty well fixed up, Arky. A guy wouldn't expect anything like this from the downstairs."

"Anna did it all," said Arky. "Fought with me all the time to get the money out of me." He laughed sadly. "So you see, Leon, I'd like to know the finger. Anna was a right nice woman. And the Judge... well, he was a right nice man."

Leon sighed and stared at the carpet for a long time. "How would I know about the finger?" he asked.

"Well, you either know or you don't know," said Arky; then he rose. "If you do, tell me. Okay. See you tomorrow. Hit the hay, and relax. You're as safe as a baby in his basket."

"Wait a minute. Where's Robbie?"

"In the living-room."

"She's a great kid. Tell her I want her."

"She's worn out, Leon. You give her a rough time. Go to bed. Don't worry about Robbie."

Leon studied Arky's face for a moment, but said nothing. Arky went out.

Robbie was asleep on the big davenport in the living-room. She was on her side with her knees drawn up and her camel's hair topcoat thrown over her. Her face looked pale, her cheeks hollow in the dim light from a small table-lamp in the corner.

Arky tiptoed in and stood looking down at her. "God," he said to himself, "I never saw such long eyelashes in my born days."

Robbie woke with a start, then sat up quickly and drew back from Arky, staring.

"You want to go to bed?" asked Arky.

Robbie blinked a couple of times, then recovered. "Arky, I hate to say this to you, but I just don't like the subtle approach."

"I don't mean that," cried Arky. "Like you say, there are times and times. Look. There's a good bed in that front bedroom. Go on in. Undress. Relax. Turn the key in the lock."

"No trapdoors? No sliding walls?"

Arky laughed shortly. "What do you think this is—a panel joint?"

"What is a panel joint? I'm just a young girl, remember, and I haven't been around much, so if it's too awful... be sure and tell me."

"Well," said Arky, sitting down opposite her on a chair, "a panel joint is a fast shuffling clip. The girl brings the sucker in. A bedroom, see? They undress. She puts the sucker's pants over a chair for him. While they're in bed, a panel in the wall opens, and a guy reaches in and frisks the sucker's pants. When the sucker looks for his money to pay the girl, the money's gone. And the girl raises a big commotion about what a cheap-john this sucker is, trying to get out without paying. The sucker forgets all about his money. All he wants to do now is to get away from this yelling dame."

"That's a panel joint, is it? Ozark, you must know some charming people."

"Oh, I been here and there. Why don't you go to bed? You look tired, honey."

"I am—dead. But it relaxes me to talk. Especially about literary topics. Got a cig?"

Arky took out his pack, lit a cigarette and handed it to her; then he lit one for himself. They sat smoking and looking at each other for a long time.

"Arky," she said at last, "Leon's a lot more handsome than you are. You're ugly."

"Leon's a very handsome fellow. The dames take one look at him and say that's for me!"

"He makes me ill. His eyelashes are almost as long as mine, and his hands are softer."

"I was noticing your eyelashes. They look real."

"They are. Honest. Arky, you're one of the ugliest guys I've ever seen in my life. Where did you get that face?"

There was a pause, then Arky asked: "What's your name?"

"Robbie. It's *me*—remember?"

"Is that all the name you got?"

"Is Ozark or Arky all the name *you* got? Or maybe Johnson?"

"My name's Orval Wanty."

"Oh, *no!*" cried Robbie, laughing. "I wasn't so far off with Elmer, was I?"

"Got a brother named Elmer."

"You want all my name?"

"Yes."

"Well, my name, believe it or not, is Rosa Maria Venuti."

"You don't look like no Italian."

"What does an Italian look like?"

"I've seen thousands of them on the Hill. You got blue eyes, fair complexion; you're tall and slim; and you got a build like a model."

"All right, take me to court. But that's my name."

"I thought your name was Roberta."

"I took it. Roberta Osborn. Nice meaningless name, but classy—like the Front. Rosa would get laughs on the Front."

"So does Orval. Not that I give a damn."

"You don't really give a damn about much of anything, including women, do you, Arky?"

"Somebody's been stringing you. If there's anything in the world I like, it's women."

"In their place."

"Something wrong with that? The man does his part; the woman does hers. That's simple."

"You know something, Arky? You're not very far from a jerk. You look like you ought to be in the show with Lum and Abner. But I'm kind of nuts about you. Why?"

"Well, maybe you figure I'm an important guy, and loaded. It always helps."

Robbie lowered her eyes slowly and stared at the floor. Arky noticed again how long her eyelashes were and how they made faint bluish shadows on her cheeks. "Yeah," she said finally, "it always helps."

There was a long, rather awkward and embarrassing silence. Finally Arky asked: "Where you from, Robbie?"

"Little town outside Detroit. Wonderful little town with trees all along the streets, and a big lake where you can swim."

"Why didn't you stay there?"

"And waste myself on the yokels? Me—the big glamor girl? Miss American Legion of 1948?" Robbie laughed ironically.

"You sound like you got a gripe. You been doing all right. Miss This-and-Thats are a dime a dozen on the Front. Why didn't you try Detroit—close to home?"

"I did. Give me another cig?"

Arky lit one and handed it to her. "How about the Big City over the border?"

"Photographer's model. *Brother bar the door!* I decided to learn Judo. By the time I learned it, it was too late."

"Well—what do you *want* to be—a nun?"

"It has its points. Arky, is there a cup of coffee in the house? I need a slight stimulant, although I must say your conversation has helped some. I've been living a crazy life for a week. Even you seem normal by comparison."

Arky flushed slightly. "Listen, sister, if there's anything in the world I am, it's normal."

Robbie laughed lightly and got up. "I believe you, Orval. Never had the slightest doubt. I was only trying to make a very feeble quip."

Arky rose. "Kitchen's back here. Can you make good coffee?"

Robbie glanced at him as they walked side by side down the narrow hallway. "I think so. Been doing it for years."

"Not many years. How old are you?"

"Young enough to tell you. Twenty-one."

They passed the door of Leon's bedroom. Arky jerked his thumb at it. "Leon said he wanted you. He's in there. I told him to relax and get some sleep."

"Oh, he's harmless," said Robbie. "But very very boring. I hope he's not too good a friend of yours."

"He's just a guy I know."

Arky switched on the light in the kitchen and showed Robbie where the things were, then he sat down and watched her as she moved gracefully about. Her legs were long and slim, her feet small and narrow. Her black hair was cut almost like a boy's but still looked thick and luxuriant.

"You were a sucker to cut your hair," said Arky. "I'll bet it was something."

"Don't you like it this way?"

"I like lots of hair."

"Like that blond in the front room? I saw her picture."

"Yes," said Arky, flushing slightly. "Like that."

"Is that your girl friend, Arky?"

"She was."

All of a sudden, Robbie turned and flashed a strange look at Arky. "Orval Wanty!" she cried. "I read it in the paper. You... she...!" Robbie dropped the coffeepot and water spilled all over the kitchen.

"Yeah," said Arky.

"Got a mop?" cried Robbie.

"I don't know. Look in that broom closet."

Robbie found the mop and worked in silence for a long time.

"Why did they do it?" asked Robbie in a low voice.

"Somebody gunning for me."

"Oh, that's awful." She stopped mopping and turned to stare at Arky. "Maybe Leon's not as crazy as I thought he was. Am I right?"

"Leon's not crazy."

"What have I got myself into?" Robbie demanded.

"Better off if you don't know. *You're* okay. Don't worry."

"I don't know what I was thinking about. I guess I was out on my feet when we got here. That tough-looking kid with the shotgun; all the hocus-pocus. That strange colored-man. I've got eyes. I can see. The thing was, I'd heard so much raving from Leon, that...."

She broke off. Finished with her mopping, she filled the coffeepot again and put it on the stove; then she sat down and studied Arky's face.

"You don't seem like a criminal or anything, Arky."

He laughed shortly. "I'm not, baby, I'm not. Never been more than a young guy trying to get along without much education and practically no ambition. Not so young even any more."

The conversation lapsed. When the coffee was ready, Arky showed her where the dishes were; she put out the cups and saucers, then poured the coffee.

"You never had much training around the house, did you, Arky?" she said as they sat sipping their black coffee.

"How do you mean?"

"Well, you just point, like a man who's used to being waited on."

Arky thought this over for a moment. She was right. Anna had spoiled him, waiting on him hand and foot for nearly ten years. "Yeah," said Arky, "I just sit down and expect the grits to be on the table."

"The what?"

"The food, the food!"

There was a long silence as they sipped the coffee. Arky began to study Robbie's face, noting that she was very pale and seemed nervous and worried.

"Look, honey," he said finally, "want me to get that heap of Leon's and take you home?"

"No," said Robbie.

"Well, seems to me like you've got the jumps. Maybe you'd feel better at home."

"No," said Robbie. "I'm never going back there—not even to get my clothes."

"Don't talk silly. I'll bet you got lots of nice things."

Robbie sighed. "Yes, Ozark, I've got lots of nice things. But they can stay there. Leon kept trying to tell me those men were watching the apartment. But I thought he was imagining things...."

"They might have been, but I doubt it. Leon's got plenty on his mind, all right—plenty to worry about—but he may be building it up a little too. See what I mean?"

"You're wasting your breath, Ozark. This little girl's not going back."

Arky shrugged, and smiled slightly. "That suits me fine. I'll send Turk after your things tomorrow. They may get back here in a mess, but they'll get back."

"But, Ozark—I can't stay here. This is just as bad. Worse."

"I'll figure something out," said Arky, carelessly. "You stay here tonight and I'll tell you what I told Leon. To get to you, anybody's got to take care of the Turk, myself, and another guy. Rough going."

Robbie sighed, and the color slowly began to come back into her cheeks. She started to pour herself another cup of coffee. Arky tapped her sharply on the forearm.

"Hey! What about me?"

Robbie looked at him blankly, then understood, and poured his cup full. "I'm sorry, Ozark," she said. "You first, is that right? Always you first. I'm not much good at being a squaw, but maybe I'll learn. Back home the women eat at the second table. Right?"

Arky laughed. "They used to."

There was a long silence, then Robbie turned her head slightly and seemed to be listening. After a moment, she said: "Sounds to me like a baby crying in the house. You wouldn't by any chance have—among other things—a baby around here, would you, Ozark?"

Arky looked at Robbie for a long time before he asked: "How do you feel about babies?"

"Ozark, that *is* a baby crying! How do I *feel* about them? That's a silly question. I *love* 'em."

"You're kidding."

"Why should I be kidding? I was a baby once myself."

"Anything for a laugh," said Arky in disgust.

"My goodness! What lungs that baby's got!"

"He's a strong little bastard all right," said Arky and there was a touch of pride in his voice which made Robbie study him with surprise.

"Is he *your* baby, Ozark?"

"Sure is," said Arky.

Robbie stared at him, speechless, her pretty lips parted, showing even, white, fanatically cared-for teeth, seeming almost artificial in their perfection.

A door banged someplace; then Leon's voice called: "Arky! Ark!"

"His Highness is being disturbed," said Robbie with a certain satisfaction in her voice.

Arky got up and went out into the hall. Leon was in the doorway of Anna's bedroom, staring. His thick dark hair was standing up all over his head in oily curls. He was in his underwear: a monogrammed silk undershirt and silk shorts, both lavender. He looked soft and out of shape minus the sharply styled façade of his outer clothing.

"Something wrong with me, Ark," he said. "I keep hearing a baby crying in the next room. There! Don't you hear that?"

"Sure I hear it. It's a baby all right. Go back to bed."

"What the hell is a baby doing in your apartment, Arky?" Leon demanded peevishly.

"Shall I drown him?"

Leon noted a certain spark in Arky's triangular eyes, and recoiled slightly.

"No. No," said Leon. "Only kidding."

He went back in and shut the door. Arky could hear him mumbling to himself, then Arky returned to the kitchen. Robbie was laughing.

"What's the matter with *you?*"

"And some people smoke the weed for kicks," said Robbie.

Just as Arky sat down, a door was banged back loudly, the baby-howling rose to a new high, and someone could be heard tramping barefoot down the hallway.

Zand suddenly appeared in the kitchen doorway. He was wearing purple and orange striped pajamas about three sizes too big for him. His black eyes were flashing with indignation. He raised his right hand menacingly and pointed the index finger at Arky.

In a loud voice, trembling with emotion, he began: "Ark, I'm telling you, if you don't...!" Then he saw Robbie and a look of blank bewilderment crossed his lean, aquiline face. He stood stiff as a clothing-dummy, unable to continue, but with his hand still raised. Finally he recovered, as the two sat staring at him in silence. "What in Christ's name is *she* doing here?"

"I got her to look after the baby," said Arky.

Zand leaned against the door-jamb and laughed hysterically, then he said: "This is good! Wait till Lola sees the new nurse."

"She knows all about babies, don't you, Robbie?" said Arky, glancing ironically at her.

"I certainly do," said Robbie mildly. "I raised three of them."

"You *what?*" cried Arky, getting up so suddenly that he almost upset his chair.

"I was the oldest," said Robbie. "My mother was only sixteen when I was born and she just kept having them. In fact she's got one two years old right now."

"Well, I'm damned," said Arky.

Down the hallway, the baby-howls rose louder and louder.

"Listen at that," cried Zand. "We got to do something. Lola's so sick she can't hold her head up and I...."

Robbie rose. "You really want me to help?"

"Will you?" asked Arky.

"I'd like nothing better."

"It's a funny world," said Zand.

Lola, pale and haggard, raised up on one elbow as they all entered the spare bedroom. In the basket, Orv was yelling at the top of his lungs and kicking wildly with his sturdy little legs. Lola stared in unbelief at the tall, elegant girl bending over the basket. Then she began to stammer.

"You mean she... that girl... she's going to...? *Where* did Turk find *her?*"

"Never mind now," said Zand, soothingly. "Just relax. Lie back. Take it easy. Your troubles are over."

Robbie picked the baby up and cuddled him. "Oh, you little love," she said. "Arky—my God!—what a beautiful child."

Arky began to grin and shift about, and Zand stared at him with a mixture of irritation and envy.

As dawn showed weakly among the brick tenements and sagging frame boarding-houses of the 17th Ward, Leon, wakened by the daylight, and feeling much refreshed by a few hours of sleep, put on his shirt and pants and went looking for Arky. He wanted to talk.

After a cautious search, he found Arky lying asleep fully dressed on the davenport in the living-room. At the sound of guarded footsteps, Arky woke at once and with one swift movement his hand went behind him and came up with a short-barreled, ugly-looking revolver. Leon recoiled, seemed about to run.

"Hello, Leon," said Arky, putting the gun away and sitting up. "What the hell time is it?"

"Sun's just coming up," said Leon, sitting down opposite Arky. "I had a pretty good sleep, thanks to you. Funny what a little decent sleep will do for a guy. I'm going to make another run for it."

"Where?"

"I figure I'll drive to the Capitol and take a plane for New York. It's an easy place to disappear in. Then I'll get a boat to Rio. Quite a town, I understand."

"If you're fixed."

Leon looked at Arky steadily. "I'm fixed, loaded. Don't know why I've been taking these knocks so long."

"Gets to be a habit. Well, Leon?"

"Well... what?"

"You're feeling better now. Give me an earful."

Leon started slightly and grew a little pale; then he looked about him, stalling. "Where the hell *is* everybody? What you doing, sleeping in here?"

"I run out of rooms. Robbie's in my bedroom with the baby."

"She's *what?*" Leon shook with laughter, then calmed himself at a look from Arky. "Okay. Okay. But that's sure a yuk. Robbie with a baby!"

"What's so funny about it?"

"Robbie and babies don't go together, like me and church. That's a smart little girl—Robbie. Always got her eye on the main chance. Watch it, Arky—or she'll take you for the roll. They talk about dames being sophisticated. Most of 'em are about as sophisticated as my old Aunt Marie up in Quebec—it's all talk, paint, and hair-do. Not with Robbie."

"All right, all right," said Arky. "The hell with Robbie. Let's talk."

Leon stared uncomfortably at the floor, then he searched himself nervously and futilely for a cigarette. Arky handed him one in silence and lit it for him.

"Well," said Leon, burning up half an inch of tobacco with every puff, "to make it brief, we're dead. When the Mover kicked off, that was it. But even before that, we were in trouble. The boys are already operating with a strong fix in the Paxton Square district—I think they got to Captain Megher, must have. He was scared to death of the Mover and also the Commissioner, but now with both of them out of the way...." Leon nervously waved his cigarette in the air and left his sentence unfinished.

"Okay," said Arky impatiently. "Who's running the show?"

"Why, the Big City boys, naturally. Riebe's still here, I think."

"I don't mean them."

"Well, Stub Baxter's the front. You know Stub."

"Sure I know him. A nothing."

"He'll be hitting the headlines soon. He's getting paid big for taking the heat."

"All right, all right," cried Arky. "What I want to know is, who's *really* running the show for Kelly? Who's the in-between, the *me* of this outfit?"

Leon swallowed and almost dropped his cigarette, then he sat for a long time staring off at the open window. A couple of noisy sparrows were hopping about on the sill, greeting the new day.

"You know him well," said Leon. "He's been horsing around here for a long time, trying to get a real foothold, and a boost into the real money."

"Well...?"

Leon flipped his cigarette butt at the sparrows; it passed harmlessly over them and they ignored it. "Harry Radabaugh."

Arky got slowly to his feet. His face was hard as flint and his blue eyes seemed to give off electric sparks for a moment.

"The finger!" he said quietly.

Leon fussed around in his chair. "Well, now, Ark; I wouldn't know about that.... I wouldn't really be able to say that he...."

Arky came over to Leon and patted him on the shoulder. "Okay, Leon. Thanks. I know you couldn't say positively. Forget it, forget it. Just get out of town."

Leon, pale, glanced up at Arky as if expecting a blow, but Arky was smiling at him somewhat indulgently.

A few hours later, Turk and Leon set off for the Capitol in Leon's black Cadillac limousine. Leon liked Turk's looks and felt safe with the crop-headed, tight-lipped kid. Before they left, Leon said to Arky:

"Tell you what. You been a life-saver to me. I'm going to make you a little present. Rudy's got the convertible—he's in love with it. But this Cadillac's yours. Okay?"

Arky merely nodded, but Turk's eyes popped, though he kept his face emotionless. What kind of guys were these—handing Cadillacs around like they were cigarettes? Turning to Arky he said:

"Don't worry, mister. I'll be back before dark. With this hack, it's a breeze."

Later, Arky chased Robbie out of the bedroom and settled down to make a few phone calls. From time to time, he glanced over at the basket where Orv was sleeping with his tiny fists raised above his head.

"What a promoter that Robbie is," he said with a smile. "A guy would think she was really *nuts* about that kid."

First he called the Dighton and Black law firm and had a long talk about various matters with the senior partner, who was so agitated that he could hardly keep his voice from trembling. He slavishly agreed to all of Arky's requests and kept saying: "I know he'll be delighted to co-operate in every way. In fact, it isn't really necessary to bother him. I can assure you of his cooperation."

"How is he, by the way?" asked Arky.

"Very low. Very low. He may be hospitalized for months. A general collapse. Too bad, too bad. But he'll be glad to co-operate."

Then Arky called Rudy, who began to scream at him right away.

"Don't come here, Ark—for God's sake. They'll be laying for you if you do. Take my word for it. Things have gone to hell. I don't know whether I'm coming or going. Even Robbie has disappeared. I don't know where anything is.... I don't know where—"

"What about the take?" Arky broke in, harshly.

Rudy laughed sadly and derisively. "What take? All the boys are talking poor. Business is falling off, you know. Some of them are even saying 'try and collect.'"

"All right," said Arky grimly. "Sit tight. They'll change their tunes before they're through. Just ignore them, Rudy. Don't call them. Nothing. If they call you, don't talk to them. Just be busy. We'll sweat 'em. Then later, we'll see."

"Just as you say, Ark. But it's terrible—I lost five pounds this week."

"You can stand it," said Arky, laughing, as he hung up.

Later, he managed to run Captain Dysen down. The Captain's hippopotamus-like groans sounded more dismal than usual over the wire.

"Hopeless, Arky. Hopeless. If the rumors are true...."

"Never mind the rumors. Get a pencil and paper. I got a list for you."

The Captain patiently wrote down on his pad the list of business addresses Arky gave him, and when Arky had concluded he said:

"I got 'em. Now what?"

"You knock 'em over. All of them. Sneak raids. Knock 'em over good. We'll teach these guys to switch."

"But, good Christ, Arky! At a time like this... listen a minute. Listen! Stop shouting. I want to tell you about the rumors that are flying around. We hear that the Commissioner did not go back to the Capitol after the funeral, but is hiding out."

"Why would he be hiding out? He's not the kind of man that hides."

"Lot of talk about it."

"Well, suppose it's true? It will make you look pretty big right now, won't it? Knocking over all these gambling joints? Go to it, Cap. Like I told you, you may end up Chief of Police."

A deep bass groan like an organ-note came over the wire. Arky hung up.

As a "big" man now, Reisman had an office of his own in the Journal Building, an office that he used merely as a place of refuge when things became too irksome and irritating at home, or when his co-workers, acquaintances, and friends bored him to the point of homicide.

The room resembled a rather large and neglected clothes-closet more than it did an office, and it was somewhat of a surprise to find not only a window in it, but a desk and a chair.

In the past it had been used by the "literary department," which consisted, under the old dispensation, of Professor Crews, his old-maid sister, and an office-boy who had run errands for half a dozen of the other offices and had also written fifty per cent of the book reviews. But now fuzzy-minded old Professor Crews, who had spent much of his time quoting Longfellow, W. D. Howells, and William Cullen Bryant, and viewing with alarm such revolutionary writers as H. L. Mencken and Eugene O'Neill, was dead, his sister on a pension, and the office-boy a reporter on another paper. The department had been streamlined and moved to new quarters, but an office-boy still wrote half of the reviews.

Reisman's refuge was covered with dust and stank of aging, mildewed books. Nobody had ever thought to clean it out, least of all Reisman. He was always running across "sensational" novels of the thirties by authors who had long since gone back to whatever they had been doing before they fell on their heads and wrote a book. It was a melancholy experience and, sighing, Reisman would sit at the window reading an impassioned blurb of a book which had had a life of maybe three weeks and an impassioned thumbnail sketch of an author nobody had ever heard of. The author was usually pictured with his hair mussed, his shirt open at the neck, and a pipe in his mouth.

Reisman would tell himself that maybe after all it was a good thing that he'd stayed on a newspaper and not written those excessively clever novels and plays everybody had expected him to write. They were in his head. Let them stay there and not come out to clutter dusty corners or lay unwanted on out-of-the-way remainder counters.

Today, however, he was enjoying himself in the quietude of his dingy, dusty, melancholy retreat, abode of stillborn masterpieces and dead authors. He was reading a good book, a new one; in fact, he'd just finished it, and he sat looking through the dirty window-pane at the crowded Boulevard, feeling somewhat uplifted, lost in rather pleasant thoughts.

The door was violently banged back, and Reisman gave a wild jump, almost upsetting his ancient, creaking swivel-chair.

Red Seaver stood in the doorway, staring at Reisman in almost comical surprise. His eyes were bloodshot, his face pale, his freckles prominent. "Jesus! I found you!" he yelled, then he came in, slamming the door and knocking a few masterpieces down from a shelf.

"You uncircumcised dog!" cried Reisman, waving his arms. "Do you realize that you almost made me fall over backwards and break my neck? *Me!*"

Red uttered with feeling a four-letter word and pulled up a chair.

"Listen, Ben..." he began, but Reisman waved him to silence.

"I've just gone through a great experience."

"Yeah?" cried Red, eagerly.

"Yes. An experience I haven't had for a long time. I've just read an intelligent new novel."

"Christ, Ben," cried Red. "Will you please...?"

"I repeat. An intelligent new novel. The author is not selling anything, not even himself; not even one of the smelly little orthodoxies that are now contending for our souls. Don't look at me like that, Red. I didn't make up that wonderful phrase: smelly little orthodoxies. It was George Orwell—God rest his soul!"

"Orwell, eh?" said Red, trying to restrain himself and enter into the conversation. "I heard of him."

"Your wife belongs to the Book-of-the-Month Club probably."

"Yeah, she's a great reader."

"Well, tell her about this book. It's called the *Barkeep of Blémont*, and I think Maupassant, or maybe Anatole France, wrote it under an assumed name."

"You're crazy. They're dead."

"Really?" said Reisman, sadly.

"You didn't even know they were sick. You bastard!" said Red. "Look, if you give me any more of this literary gab when I'm trying to talk to you I'm going to forget you're a friend of mine and—"

"Here's the book. Take it home to your wife, Red." Red grabbed the book and flung it against the wall, knocking down a few more volumes.

"Ben, listen to me—please! I work on the same paper, remember? I can't scoop you—nothing like that. It's all in the family...."

"You're bringing tears to these old eyes...."

"A punch in the nose will bring 'em quicker. Ben—why did you fly to the Capitol?"

"I'm lobbying for better working conditions for the glamor-girls on the Front."

"All right. You flew to the Capitol. That much I know. Now I'll tell *you* something. The Commissioner's right here in town at this minute."

"Naturally. He came back for Judge Greet's funeral—dope!"

"Okay. Why did he stay? I hear he's in hiding."

"My goodness—these politicians! What do you suppose *he* did?"

Red took his head between his hands and sat staring for a long time at the top of the desk.

"I'm assigned," he said finally. "Understand? Mush Head assigned me personally. Where is Leon Sollas? Nobody knows. Who shot Judge Greet so efficiently he died of it? Nobody knows."

"You mean there is a connection?" asked Reisman innocently.

"Of course not!" screamed Red. "I'm just trying to tell you... what's the use! But there's a big story knocking around all the same—and there's a cover-up in the police department. Did you ever hear of Herman Frick being sick before—that big bull!"

"Only when convenient."

"That's what I mean."

"But a cover-up in the police department is an old story, not a new one."

"Maybe, maybe. But things are cooking in the so-called, frigging underworld. There's a lot of talk about Harry Radabaugh I don't understand. The other night a drunken bookie told me the new motto was: See Harry. And why did Harry get canned by the D.A.?"

"I wouldn't know. All I know about Harry is that he slugged me one night, and you slugged him."

"I wish to God I'd let him slug you a couple more times now," said Red vehemently. "He's in the Regent bar every night. Won't talk to me. Won't look at me. Got hoods around him. Guys who smoke cigars and try to look interesting—you know. Why has he got hoods around him? And why does the bartender almost kiss him now? You know—Emil. Never used to."

Reisman yawned and began to clean his fingernails with a desk-knife. There was a brief silence, then Reisman said: "Look, Red. All right. I've been clowning. Now I'll tell you the truth since it doesn't matter any more. Judge Greet and the Commissioner were friends. The Commissioner was deeply shocked about the Judge's death, and not trusting the police department, at least some sections of it, he wanted to know what was being done to run down the guy who killed him. So he called me. I hopped around as best I could to see what I could find out, then I flew to the Capitol to talk to the Commissioner. To tell you the truth, I found out practically nothing. There you are, Red. Now ain't you ashamed of yourself for hounding me?"

Red sat nodding sadly to himself, and patting a huge freckled paw on the desk; then he sighed and got up. "All right, Ben. Sounds reasonable. What a life! You think maybe I could learn to write sports?"

"Well, you played enough of 'em."

"Don't seem to help. I been knocking at Gushy for years. He won't even give me tickets to things. Now he's boss in sports, he'll hardly speak to me."

"Trouble is," said Reisman, "Gushy's a polo, tennis, badminton, aquacade man; you're a lowbrow who knows nothing but baseball, football, and horse-racing."

"Yeah, but those three are the most important."

"Red," said Reisman, "the trouble with you is, you have got too much common sense. You think things are done in this world according to reason, when they are actually done only according to emotion and prejudice. It's an irrational world, Red. So just because you know baseball backwards is no reason why Gushy is going to ask you to write about it. On the contrary."

"Well, you ought to do all right then," said Red after a moment. "Because you're more than half crazy."

"If I was all crazy I'd do better. But thanks at least for the small compliment."

Red hesitated, then he bent over and picked up the book he'd flung against the wall.

"I think I'll take this to my wife at that," he said. "She's always beefing I never bring her anything."

When Red had gone, Reisman hesitated for a long time, thinking he might pop back in; then, reassured, Reisman called Commissioner Stark and gave him the information about Harry Radabaugh. The Commissioner, sounding harassed, thanked him and hung up abruptly.

Reisman sighed and turned to stare out the window. In a moment an office-boy burst in yelling:

"Mr. Reisman—hear the news?"

"No. What?"

"Big battle with the Reds in Korea. Full scale! The works!"

"Sure?"

"Just came in."

"Okay, son. Thanks." He picked up a book at random and, without looking at it, tossed it to the boy. "Here, son. A present for you."

"Gee, thanks," said the kid.

The book was called *The Well of Loneliness*. The boy clutched it and went out.

Reisman was staring out the window when the door was banged back violently again. He turned and glanced mildly at Red, who was regarding him with fury.

"Ben!" cried Red. "The Judge wasn't dead yet when you flew to the Capitol. He died later that same day."

"I know," said Reisman. "But I've got a special news-service, like those Washington news-letters. I always know about it before it happens."

Red sat down, took off his hat, propped up his feet and lit a cigar.

"Better call your wife and tell her not to expect you for supper, Ben."

"Did you know there was a full-scale battle with the Reds going on?"

"There is? Goodness me! More special-service stuff, eh?"

"No. It's true."

"You're not going to get me out of here that way."

"I'll bet you a new hat it's on the wires right now."

"All right. You got a bet. Give me the phone."

They were driving north through the city in Leon's big black Cadillac, on the way to the upper river. It was a warm day; the streets were bright with sunshine, and yet there was a thin, vague haze over everything: fall seemed close at hand.

The Turk was driving. He hardly looked like the same kid. Arky had bought him a lot of new clothes, including a good blue-serge suit that he was now wearing with a white shirt, a dark tie, and black shoes. Arky had even told him to let his hair grow longer. "Then," said Arky, "you won't look so much like you just graduated from reform school." The Turk seemed to notice his butchered hair for the first time and, becoming self-conscious about it, had doused it in oil, hoping it would grow faster.

Arky sat beside Turk. Robbie was in the back seat with the baby, who was chortling in his basket and waving his little fists.

"He's beginning to notice things," said Robbie. "He's watching that street-car. What a love he is!"

Arky made no comment. In spite of himself, though, Robbie's attitude toward the baby pleased him. Okay, so maybe she was putting it on—promoting; all the same it sounded fine.

After a moment he turned to the kid. "How did you ever happen to get the name of Turkey?"

The kid glanced at him sideways. "One time I'm fifteen, mister; it's Christmas, and I win myself three raffles, and there I am with three frigging big turkeys. We et turkey till it come out of our ears—me, and the rest of the family. So I been Turkey ever since."

"What's your real name?"

"Joe Batz."

"All right, you're Joe from now on." He turned to Robbie. "The kid's name is Joe. We'll call him that. I don't like this Turkey routine."

"Me neither," said the kid, "but I got tired beating guys up over it, skinning my knuckles all the time. And I don't like hitting guys with tire-irons and stuff. That's for panty-waists."

Robbie shook with laughter in the back seat. Arky glanced at her in annoyance, but made no comment. Silence fell. They rode for miles without speaking through the jammed streets of the big town. The kid had a sure hand with the wheel and after a while Arky stopped paying any attention to his driving, and sat lost in thought.

In a way it was a kind of wrench leaving Zand and the Ward where he'd spent so many years. Zand had been flabbergasted and kept stammering.

"But you'll be back!" he cried.

"Maybe, maybe not," said Arky. "The place is all yours. I'm turning it over to you lock, stock, and barrel. Like I said one day, makes no difference any more whether I'm here or not. You know how to handle it. However, better get a good guy or two to spell you. Like maybe Cherry Nose Ryan. He won't drink on the job; only in off-hours. He's a pretty honest guy and knows horses and percentages."

"But, Jesus, Arky, you'll be back."

"Whether I come back or not, the place is yours. The profits are yours. Now here's the thing. I want you to do something for me. Spread it around I've left the city. You're kinda disappointed in me because it looks like I been run out. Know what I mean?"

"No," cried Zand, "I'm not going to give out talk like that. I'll be damned if I will. What do you take me for?"

"It's important, Zand. Don't be a chucklehead."

"A what?"

"Never mind. Listen now: this is the story. Anna got killed here, see? And I got hit in the head. Maybe it changed me. Anyway, I'm scared, like. I took a powder. But you don't give it out straight. You ease it out. Maybe to a couple of coppers from the Pier, and four or five young hoods. They'll tell everybody in the Ward. Understand?"

"No," said Zand. "Nothing doing."

Arky wagged his head from side to side. "All right. Be a mule. Then maybe you can come down to the morgue and see me and say don't he look natural."

Zand stared in unbelief. "You mean you're really running?"

"No. I'm just disappearing for a little while till I can string my bow...."

"I wish, for Christ's sake," yelled Zand, heatedly, "that you'd talk English. Chocolate-head... stringing the bow... what kind of language is that?"

"There's a certain guy I want to run down. If it wasn't for him the Mover would still be flourishing, and Anna'd still be bouncing Orvie on her knee. But I want to do it my way. I want to make him look like the yellow jerk he is before they pat him with a spade."

"All right, Arky," said Zand. "It'll kill me to do it, but I'll do it."

Zand hated to see him go, and kept detaining him. Lola got very tearful over the baby, irritating Arky so that he had to move away from her to keep from telling her what he thought. She had had her chance with Orv, hadn't she? And folded?

At last they got away.

Downy, frantically telephoning every place, finally, much to his surprise, reached Reisman at his office at the Journal Building. Reisman, reversing himself for a reason he could not put his finger on, was sitting at his battered typewriter, which spaced erratically and occasionally stuck altogether, trying to write a short story about his youngest daughter, Selma, who asked questions that would have baffled Einstein and then was too impatient to wait for the answers and passed on immediately to something else.

"Ben? Downy."

"Well, wherefore art thou Romeo? Couldn't thou be Mercutio? Or even the noble County Paris? I don't like guys working for me who mess around wit' dames."

"Only in off-hours, Ben. She's a real cutie, like I told you, and lives alone."

"I always preferred to jump out windows myself. It's more fun; that is, if the girl lives on the first floor."

"I've got nothing to jump for yet. But I'm hopeful. Ben, there's a rumor going around the Ward. May be true, and it may not. But they say Arky's gone."

"Gone? Where?"

"Nobody knows. They say he hasn't been the same since that woman got killed and he got hit; they say he lost his nerve, figuring they'll make a good job of it next time. But big Grier—a copper down here—you know him—he says it's all lies. Arky's around some place."

"Okay. Keep plugging."

Reisman hung up, then he sat looking sadly at the mass of words in front of him. It seemed so futile to be sitting pecking at a typewriter with life swirling around him on the Boulevard, the town seething and ready for an explosion, guys getting shot at, running for their lives...! Who cared about Selma and her unconsciously funny antics? Who cared about *any* characters in *any* books?

Maybe he'd made the right choice after all. A newspaper mirrored life as it was lived from day to day—at least that was the general intention. News had *some* value, even garbled, slanted, or butchered news; value for the moment, at least. But not one book, story, or play in a hundred thousand had any value at all, either momentary or permanent.

Reisman jerked the page out of his typewriter, read a few phrases with a wan smile, then tore it up. Finally he called the Commissioner and gave him the rumors about Arky.

Robbie was delighted with the cottage on the upper river, could in fact hardly get over it. While Arky talked interminably on the phone, she settled Orv into his new quarters, a beautiful little alcove with pale-blue wallpaper covered with silver stars; then she went from room to room—the place being much larger than it seemed from the outside—and examined the wallpaper, all imported, the drapes, the furniture, the cabinets and knickknacks, and lastly the many modern paintings scattered about. She had known quite a few art students in Detroit and Chicago, and was familiar with this type of picture. She tried to connect Arky with the elegant cottage but could not. It was obvious that he'd had nothing to do with furnishing it. She was very curious about the whole thing, but decided to ask no questions.

She spent a long time hanging up her clothes, taking a bath, and loafing about in the beautiful bedroom, just off Orv's alcove, that Arky had assigned to her. Strange guy, this Arky. He made her feel like a governess for the kid. What was cooking in his narrow, impenetrable skull?

At six o'clock Orv began to howl like a banshee and kick his sturdy legs. He was hungry as a little wolf. As Robbie changed him and he lay grunting and swinging at the air with his fat little fists, she talked to him in a low voice:

"If you're Mountain Music's son, little man, you surely must have had a beautiful mother. Look at you! Prettiest baby I ever saw in my life—and I've seen quite a few. The huskiest, the strongest! And look at that so-called old man of yours. Lean as a rake and with a face cut out of wood." A sudden thought struck her and she studied the baby carefully. "Yeah," she said. "Of course. That big blond *has* to be his mother. He looks like her, as a matter of fact. Take fifteen pounds off of her and she wouldn't have been bad at that. The Big Mamma type, of course—but I never saw any of them starving to death. Some men like a lot for their money, or, as Leon once said, plenty for all!"

Shortly after she'd got Orv fed and back to sleep, Arky came out of the study, looking for her.

"How do you like the joint, Robbie?"

"It's beautiful."

"Belongs to a friend of mine. He's sick in a hospital so he said I could use it. If we stay here very long, though, I'm going to go nuts if we don't take down them pictures."

"They're good pictures, Arky."

"Good for what? Who wants to sit around, trying to relax, and then look up and see something like that? Looks like they were painted in a bug-house."

"I used to know a lot of painters. They all painted like that. Except some of them painted fairly realistic nudes to sell. I posed for a lot of them."

"In your birthday suit?"

"Sure. Why not? It's a business like any business."

"I guess it's all right as long as they had a stove in the room."

Robbie laughed and sat down. Arky lit a cigarette and gave it to her, then lit one for himself.

"You fracture me, Elmer," she said. "To look at you, a person would think you just came in with a carload of cattle, except for the clothes. But here we are, in the nicest little house I've ever seen in my life. You call people on the phone and order them around. Leon's scared to death of you and, whether you know it or not, admires you very much. Cadillacs, a Barrymore wardrobe, French cuffs and beautiful cuff-links; clean fingernails, even; and the prettiest baby I ever saw. What's with you, Elmer?"

"Just forget the baby," said Arky. "But aside from that, all this you're talking about is just because once in my life I met an A-number-one man. It's got nothing to do with me. I might still be swinging a pick, or back in Dry River trying to make a living with cotton on ground hardly worth farming."

"Well, all I can say is, it's fun," said Robbie. "I don't even want to know what's coming next. I can wait and see."

As she talked, the Cadillac drove up, then a caterer's truck. Arky rose to look out the window and Robbie came over beside him. He put his arm around her.

"Here's supper," he said. "They got good country sausage at this joint—Langenbeck's. The Mover—I mean, a friend of mine told me about it. And as for what's coming next—after supper I got a pretty good idea."

Robbie felt a faint flutter of excitement. "You don't say. Just like that. Well, all I can say is, I hope you didn't order country sausage for me."

"No," said Arky. "Chicken à la king. Dames like it."

"Next time maybe it might be a good idea if I ordered my own dinner. Is that possible?"

"Sure," said Arky, looking at her in surprise. "And mine, too. This was a special occasion, sort of. You don't think I'm going to have Langenbeck's every night, do you? It's your business to look after the meals. I like ham and ham gravy with mush; I like country sausage, and T-bone steaks. I don't like hash or meat loaf or croquettes."

"You want me to write all this down?" asked Robbie innocently.

"No," said Arky. "You can remember it, can't you?"

It was ten p.m. Turkey was snoring in the small but beautifully furnished three-room suite that had formerly been occupied by Gordon King's old colored servant, Ambrose.

In the main part of the cottage, Orv was sleeping in his alcove, cooing a little and occasionally pulling at his thick, silky blond hair; Arky was in the study, wearing a maroon silk dressing-gown and watching the late innings of the baseball game on television; and Robbie was in her large, pink-tiled bathroom, taking a bubble-bath in the sunken tub.

She felt shaken, disoriented. As a general thing, she could take men or leave them. In two short years of intimacy with the opposite sex she had grown almost apathetic, and had begun to say to herself: "Surely there must be something more to it than this. Such a hullabaloo about so little!" Now she wasn't so sure. Either Arky was unique, or she hadn't met the right people. Arky was rough, direct, almost brutal. No softness about him, even in love; and maybe that was the way a man should be. "I don't know," Robbie reflected as she stretched lazily in the tub, "but maybe there's something to be said for Arkansas after all."

Sensitive to her own reactions, she realized that her feelings toward Arky had changed radically. Very strange. It had never happened to her before, even with Charley Cousins—the boy she'd had such a crush on in Chicago—the Lake

Forest snob who dressed like a bum, let his hair grow, and tried to pretend he was suffering for Art in a Rush Street studio that was hardly more than a brothel. She'd gone around in a fog all right; but she realized now that it had been mostly pretense. With Arky there was no pretense. At the moment she really felt as if she belonged to him, like a dog, or a daughter, or maybe even a wife.

Thinking about the over-handsome Charley Cousins, with his little childish white teeth, his pretty blue eyes with dark lashes, and his girlish complexion, she laughed out loud and kicked around exuberantly in the tub. "I'd like to hear his comments on Arky," she mused. "Why, Charley would think I'd lost my mind." She remembered the autographed picture Charley had given her one Christmas: an "art" photo of himself posing on the beach, and signed: "To my beloved beautiful one, to my adored one, to my confrere in the Arts." Robbie began to giggle uncontrollably, and finally had to call a halt when she realized she was getting hysterical.

But really it was too funny. Charley and Arky!

16

Arky woke about seven. Sunshine was flooding the master bedroom where he lay alone in a huge, low bed. Faint cooking odors drifted in through the open windows, and Arky got up at once, washed, combed his hair, brushed his teeth, put on his maroon silk dressing-gown and hurried toward the dining-room. He'd had a fine sleep and he was very hungry. Pretty nice of Robbie, getting up this early to cook breakfast. And then he remembered Orvie. "Hell," he said, "she feeds him at six. No wonder she's up."

But there were no signs of life in the dining-room, the table wasn't set, the curtains were still drawn, so Arky went on through the swinging door into the kitchen. The kid Joe Batz, wearing an apron over his new pajamas, was at the stove, frying eggs; coffee was percolating on another burner and the electric toaster was buzzing.

"I woke up, mister," said the kid, "so I went out to get the paper. Baby woke me up. Sure was yelling like hell."

"Deal me in," said Arky, gesturing at the stove, then he walked over to the kitchen table where the paper was opened at the sports page.

"That ball team!" muttered the kid, shaking his head; then: "How many eggs, mister?"

"Three," said Arky. "Turn 'em over." He sat down and began absent-mindedly to read the sports news.

Bustling about, the kid said: "They sure knocked 'em over on the Front last night."

Arky glanced up at the kid quickly, then without a word turned back to the first page. A headline read:

POLICE ATTACK FRONT IN GIANT RAID

Smiling grimly to himself, Arky glanced indifferently through the account of the raid.

> ... fifteen gambling-houses raided, some of them very plush places... patrons not arrested but herded out, told to go home... gambling equipment estimated at a hundred thousand dollars destroyed... flying squads led by Lieut. John Motley of the Pier 7 Station... largest raid in over ten years... does the new Commissioner, James Creeden, mean business...?

"Yeah," said Arky at last, "they sure did knock 'em over."

"What's the idea?" asked the kid. "Same places been running for a long time."

"New orders from above, I guess," said Arky, innocently.

"I don't get it. A guy puts his capital in a place, they let him open, they let him run—then one night they knock him over and bust up his stuff. Is that justice?"

"You looking for justice?" asked Arky. "Well, stop looking."

The phone rang and the kid went to answer it. In a moment he came back, smiling slightly. "It's Zand," he said. "Kinda upset, sounds like."

He was right. Zand was definitely upset. He began to shout at Arky over the wire. "They been calling for you since four o'clock. Twenty calls an hour. We're going nuts here. I just keep telling 'em you left. Maybe you're in Arkansas by now. But, look here, Arky...."

"Keep telling 'em," said Arky. "Anybody who should get to me has got my number. Just keep telling 'em."

"How about Rudy? He's about to cut his fat throat."

"Tell him the same as everybody else."

"What a hassle!"

"Some people have to be taught the hard way."

"Okay, Arky. Okay. How does it feel to be living up there with the plutocrats?"

"Smells a little better. Beds are softer."

"How's the nurse?"

"She's sleeping, and so is Orv—at least I don't hear him yelling, so he must be asleep. Lola okay?"

"No. She's crying because the baby left. Can you beat it? The older I get, the less I know about women. The kid was killing her, now she wants him back."

"Don't make much sense, does it? Okay, Zand. Tell 'em nothing. I'll be here all day if you want me."

Just as he was hanging up, Robbie came into the study, looking beautiful in a Chinese banker's coat and Chinese slippers. Arky studied her with open admiration.

"Well, look at you," he said. "Pretty as a guinea hen on a fence."

"I thought I smelled food. I'm starved. Orv just finished his bottle—in fact, he took over eight ounces. Who's doing the cooking? Not *you?*"

"Are you kidding? Joe's out there struggling with the eggs. Give him a hand."

"Why, okay, master. Okay," said Robbie. "Sorry to be dilatory about my duties. Kin I eat at the first table, pa, huh?"

They were walking up and down in the trim little garden just outside the French windows of the living-room. It was a warm night and a cloudy yellow moon showed vaguely through the trees.

Inside, beyond the open French doors, a little clock on the mantel softly chimed seven.

They'd already eaten dinner. Feeling expansive, Arky had had it sent in again from Langenbeck's. He'd let Robbie do the ordering and had eaten pizza, spaghetti, and Italian-style veal without a murmur.

Now he turned to Robbie. "A guy would just never think you were an Italian to look at you. But you sure liked that food, didn't you?"

"I get hungry for it."

"Raised on it, hunh?"

"Yeah."

"Like me with ham and mush and stuff. All in what you're raised on. Say, how big is that home town of yours?"

"About twenty thousand."

"Too small."

"How big is Dry River?"

"Five hundred. But what's that got to do with it? I guess Detroit's the place for me."

Robbie stopped and turned to look at him. "What do you mean, Arky?"

"I figure to be pulling out of here soon. Might try Detroit. Sounds all right."

"What about me and Orv?"

"Well, what do you think?"

"You mean we're all going?"

"Sure. Why not? We can't live in this joint forever. Besides, it don't belong to me. The guy that owns it may get well and want it back."

Robbie looked about her quickly with a certain amount of regret. This was the nicest place she'd ever found in her whole life. However....

"You're the boss, Ozark," she said. "Whatever you say."

They walked up and down in silence for a little while. Finally Robbie stopped and looked up at the moon. "Swell night," she said. "In the city somehow you never notice that there's a moon or a sky." As Arky made no comment, she gave an embarrassed laugh. "So there's a moon and a sky!"

"Yeah," said Arky, as if coming to himself. "Down home you see the moon rise every night, or at least when it's rising early enough. And as for the sky— hell, down there it's all you think about. Will it rain? Damn it, if it don't rain we're ruined." Arky laughed.

Just as Robbie started to say something, the kid put his head out of one of the French doors. "Mister—phone."

Arky walked away from Robbie without a word. She called after him. "Two bits it's Sam."

He paused, then came back. "What do you know about Sam?"

"What do I know about Sam!" laughed Robbie. "You talk pretty loud on the phone sometimes, Ozark. It's Sam this, and okay, Sam, and don't let me down, Sam. Et cetera. Et cetera. I'm expecting you to come out any time and say to me: 'That was Sam.'"

"Aw, you're just too smart for your britches," said Arky. "You're so smart you'll probably outsmart *yourself* some day."

"What do you mean—*some* day?"

Arky went in the house, laughing. A few minutes later he came back. He was no longer laughing. His face had a tense harsh look that was not habitual, and although he tried to keep his eyes veiled, Robbie noted the flash.

"I got to go to town," he said. "Joe'll drive me. You'll be okay."

"Of course I will."

"Listen, Robbie. Get everything packed. We're blowing tonight. I ought to be back in a couple of hours."

"Tonight?" cried Robbie.

"Yeah. A little deal came up all of a sudden."

"Something wrong?"

Arky patted her awkwardly. "No, no. Don't worry. Everything's going to be all right."

"Okay, if you say so."

Arky forced a smile, then he disappeared into the house. After a moment, Robbie heard a door slam; then she heard the Cadillac drive off. She felt uneasy, worried, disoriented. To pick up and run just when...? But such thinking was futile, and she brushed it aside and in a moment went into the house and started to pack. In his crib, Orv was sleeping with a crooked smile on his fat face and his tiny fists raised.

Robbie bustled about, trying not to think. Finally she told herself: "If there's a man around who knows what he's doing, it's Ozark."

The kid pulled into a dark, one-way side-street, half a block from the Regent Hotel, and parked.

"You know where the old Metropole Hotel is?" asked Arky. The kid nodded. "Know the newsstand just beyond it?" The kid nodded again. "Okay. Wait for me there."

"But that's eight blocks from here, mister."

"Never mind that. Wait for me there. Give me an hour and maybe fifteen minutes. If I don't show up in that time, go home, load up the car, and wait. You'll hear from me, one way or another."

"Okay, mister."

Arky stood back and waited for the kid to drive off. When the car had disappeared a short, fattish, stocky little man stepped out from a dark doorway and came over to Arky, who turned and studied him in the half-light. The man, about forty-five years old, was nondescript in every respect; it would be a cinch for him to lose himself in a crowd. Nobody would possibly pay the slightest attention to him.

"You the pitcher Sam sent me?"

The man nodded. "That I am."

"How about the taxi?"

"Waiting on the next street. You just walk out of the side entrance and there it is. The hackie's a hundred per cent okay. In fact, he's my brother."

"All right," said Arky. "Any change in what's going on in the bar?"

"Hardly think so. But the hackie will know. He'll office me if we lost."

"Go ahead then."

The pitcher nodded and went back to the through-street, then turned toward the Regent Hotel. He waddled slightly as he walked. It was the only thing about him, Arky decided, that anybody would notice.

Arky followed leisurely. At the far corner, the pitcher hesitated and lit a cigarette. When Arky paused at the entrance to the Regent, the pitcher nodded slightly. Arky went in.

The lobby was packed and bellboys and porters were falling over each other. A bus for the airport was parked outside and air passengers were checking out at the desk, all of them wanting to be looked after first.

Arky picked his way carefully through the thronged lobby, calmly smoking a cigar. Hardly anyone gave him a second glance. As he reached the far end of the lobby, he could hear the noise from the bar. It was jammed to the rails, and hummed like a hive of bees. Emil, the head bartender, had five helpers tonight.

It was a big night. The baseball team was in town; three new shows had opened during the week, including a huge musical; the Plainfield Race Track opened Saturday for its fall meet; and the night before, the Front had been given a knockout raid, and many gamblers and hangers-on had no place else to go.

A sort of nervous and unnatural gaiety rolled over the big, old-fashioned bar in intermittent waves.

Arky paused in the doorway. Men were four and five deep at the bar. Drinks were being passed back overhead, and there were a few accidents, but everybody laughed. Arky did not look over his shoulder for the pitcher. He knew that he would be along in a minute.

Nobody noticed Arky, everybody being too intent on yackety-yacking and trying to find footholds and elbow room. This gave Arky plenty of time to look around, and finally he located the man he'd come to find.

The man was about halfway down the bar where several servile gents with cigars in their mouths were trying hard to keep a place for him and at the same time catch every word he said so they could laugh in the right places. His big shoulders bulged out his plaid sportcoat. He was talking and laughing and looking about him as if he owned the place; and from Emil's attitude an outsider might have thought he did.

Yep, Harry had really got up in the world. No more penny-ante jobs with the police department or the D.A.'s office for him. He was a big man now.

Arky slowly elbowed his way into a far corner of the bar and ordered a drink. Turning now, he saw the pitcher standing outside the row of phone booths beyond the bar, leisurely leafing through a tattered phone-book on a stand. A professional, as he'd expected, knowing Sam!

After a long wait, Arky got his drink and the bartender stood with his hand out, waiting for the money. "I may want another one," said Arky.

"With a crowd like this, sir," said the bartender, "we collect on serving—from strangers."

"Okay, partner," said Arky, exaggerating his accent. "I'm a stranger here all right."

After another long wait, the bartender returned with the change. Arky shoved it back at him just to see the look on his face, then he laughed. The bartender flushed slightly, knowing he was being ribbed but able to stand it at the price.

"You drink whatever you like," he said, "and pay whenever you like."

"Thank you, partner," said Arky.

Down the bar, a glass fell and shattered, and little by little the yackety-yacking began to die down.

Harry Radabaugh had seen Arky and was staring at him with shocked surprise through the thin haze of tobacco smoke hanging in the heavy air. Instinctively, Harry looked about him for a fast way out; but he was surrounded by his husky, blue-chinned, cigar-smoking stooges. Besides, the place was packed with other people he knew, people who some time back had started to fawn on him, after ignoring him for so many years. His face hardened slightly, and he tossed down a full drink with one motion of his arm.

Anyway, what the hell could the farmer pull in a place like this? Outside, it was another matter. Only thing to do was stick—face him out. However, it still wouldn't be a bad idea to take precautions. Turning, he looked meaningly at a tall young man behind him, who was drinking in the third tier. The young man followed Harry's gaze and started slightly; then he nodded.

The young man's name was Watrus and he was a special investigator for the D.A.'s office, a budding Harry Radabaugh that the harried D.A. hadn't caught up with yet—the same fellow who had buzzed Turkey in the parking-lot behind the Club Imperial.

He worked his way through the crowd as unobtrusively as possible, and finally managed to squeeze in behind Arky, who had watched his progress out of the corner of his eye.

"Hello, sir," said Watrus, putting his hand on Arky's back and running it up and down, feeling for the shoulder strap of his holster. "How are you?"

"How's the D.A.?" asked Arky.

"Nice old gentlemen. How's tricks?" Watrus continued to paw him.

"Pretty good. We got beat a little on the Front last night. But it'll pass, I hope. I'll hold still for a frisk, son."

"Oh, no," laughed Watrus. "Nothing like that. Just glad to see you."

Arky turned all the way around and looked at Watrus. His blue eyes were hard as glass and menacing. "I said I'd hold still for a frisk. You better frisk me. Might save trouble later."

"Okay. Okay," said Watrus, hurriedly. "If you look at it that way, we'll frisk." With the hands of an expert, he quickly patted Arky all over, laughing at the same time as if it was all in fun. "Well, I'll give you a clean bill of health. What an idea!"

"It was Harry's, not mine," said Arky. "How about a drink?"

"Thanks just the same," said Watrus. "I got friends waiting for me."

"It's like this," said Arky. "I just dropped in for a quiet drink to settle my nerves. Haven't been sleeping so good lately."

"Is that a fact?" said Watrus, looking at Arky curiously.

"Yeah. Lots of worries."

"Sorry to hear it," said Watrus, still studying Arky, wondering if maybe the talk floating around might not be true at that: Arky was losing his grip. All the same it was mighty strange for him to be showing up in the Regent, of all places.

Watrus worked his way back through the crowd slowly, and took up his third-tier spot behind Harry, who turned and brought him a drink.

"Well?"

"He's clean. Says he just came in to get a drink to quiet his nerves."

"They might be jumpy at that," said Harry. "Well, well."

The clamor of loud conversation, which had died down to some extent, rose again; there was much laughter as Front scandal was passed and gags repeated, but some of the gamblers and hangers-on, knowing Arky's reputation, scented trouble, and in spite of Harry's apparent indifference, began, one by one, to drift down to the far end of the bar, and then out into the street or through an archway into the thronged lobby. Little by little, although the place was still very crowded, pressure was eased along the line of the bar.

Newcomers arrived and pressed forward, unconscious of the slight tension. A nationally known radio comic, on tour, showed up with his writers and a few other stooges, and a place was made for him. Laughing, expansive, he got off half a dozen carefully rehearsed ad libs and had the people round him roaring at his cleverness while his writers glanced at each other with sardonic amusement.

Time passed. Arky had his fourth drink, and settled his bill. The radio comic went out, waving to his public like a touring president, followed at a little distance by his glum-looking entourage. Meanwhile, a dark sweat-stain had appeared on the back of Harry Radabaugh's coat.

Arky nodded to the bartender, who was very friendly now, lit a cigar, puffed on it briefly, then started out of the bar, toward the side entrance. His way took him past Harry, who turned to watch his progress. Arky paused and smiled at him.

"Hello, Harry. How's tricks?"

"Fine. With you?"

"Tolerable."

Arky stood smoking for a moment; then he moved through three tiers of drinkers and took a place at the bar beside Harry.

"How about a drink?" he asked.

"All right," said Harry.

Arky ordered, then he said: "Sure is warm in here tonight. Too bad a man can't take his coat off. Emil!" he called. "Mighty hot in here. How about me taking my coat off?"

The stiff-faced German bartender turned and glanced at Arky contemptuously. He hadn't the faintest idea who the man was. "No rule against it," said Emil. "But we just don't do it."

"You mean I'll get tossed out?"

"No," said Emil. "But maybe *looked* out."

Laughing, Arky took off his coat and hung it over his arm. Harry turned and glanced at him, feeling a great relief; in spite of the frisk he'd still had a few nagging doubts; but now it was obvious that Arky was naked—no heater; and little by little Harry's relief turned to irritation then to anger. No use trying to kid himself: he was afraid of Arky, and for over half an hour had been sweating with fear. Harry began to look Arky over surreptitiously: a tough-looking boy with a reputation for not backing up, but too slender, too long-legged; the kind of guy you could easily get off balance and upset. Harry was a dirty saloon fighter and knew all the holds, tricks, and blows.

After all, he was taking over. The Big Boys were in for good now, and it was only a question of time until Arky would be completely out in the cold, if he wasn't already. Why not do it up to perfection before a large and appreciative audience?

Arky was standing with his hands loosely on the bar, the coat over his left arm. Harry waited, steeling himself. In a moment, Emil put the drinks down before them and Arky dropped a bill on the bar.

"Well," said Arky, "here we go." He picked up his glass.

But Harry pushed his own glass away from him with such a violent gesture that it overturned and spilled. Emil grabbed up the bar-rag without a word.

"I changed my mind," said Harry. "I don't see any reason why I should drink with you."

"No?" said Arky, showing mild surprise. "Something wrong?"

Beyond them, men were nudging each other and pressing forward to listen, tense with anticipation and excitement.

"Why don't you put your coat back on?" asked Harry. "You look like a farmer in for the State Fair. Gives the place a bad name. Emil don't like it. Do you, Emil?"

"No," said Emil, mopping the bar.

"Just because a man's a little hot..." Arky began mildly.

But Harry cut in. "We all heard you'd gone back to Arkansas, didn't like the city ways any more. It's a good idea, Arky. Why don't you get... *going?*" As he snapped out the word "going," Harry turned with the ease of a boxer and gave Arky a hard shove in the chest.

Arky staggered back, knocking into a few men, who immediately and sharply drew aside, causing a pressure jam beyond. There was much shoving and loud talking. And then... the roof seemed to fall in. Three loud explosions shook the bar, and heavy blue smoke rolled upward. Emil stood transfixed, staring at Harry Radabaugh, who tried to say something to him, but coughed blood.

And then, all of a sudden, Harry fell to the floor as if somebody had pulled a rug out from under him. Men drew back from him in a semicircle, then froze. Watrus, shaken with horror and fear, tried to keep his wits about him, and turned to look for Arky. But much to his surprise, Arky was standing there in his shirtsleeves, his coat over his arm, his hands on his hips, looking down at the body of Harry Radabaugh. As Watrus watched him, Arky turned and searched the crowd behind him with his eyes.

"Well, that was a fast one," he said.

Completely baffled, Watrus ran for the phone booths. A fattish little man got in his way before the booths and apologized.

"What happened, chum?" he asked. "I was trying to find a number when...."

Watrus brushed him aside, flung himself into one of the booths and dialed a number, then screamed into the receiver: "Emergency! Casey! Downtown!"

The fattish little man shrugged and, turning, went out into the lobby.

Several of Harry's blue-chinned, cigar-smoking friends, their faces the color of parchment, were now bending over him. Arky put on his coat and walked slowly back toward the side entrance. Nobody seemed to be paying any attention to him except one man, who moved along the bar with him parallel to his course.

Smirking, he came up to Arky as they neared the entrance.

"Somebody was trying to hang one on you, Ark," he said, "and missed."

"Is that a fact?" asked Arky.

"Yeah," said the fellow with a wise look. "I'm tipping you. That was a pitcher and catcher routine. Somebody pitched somebody a gun."

"How do you like that?" said Arky.

"Yeah," said the fellow. "And between ourselves, it couldn't happen to a nicer guy."

The fellow winked and melted back into the crowd. Arky went out the side entrance. The taxi was waiting for him, he got in, and the hackie drove off without a word. When they had turned the corner, Arky said:

"Metropole."

Arky saw the big black Cadillac waiting for him in front of the newsstand. The taxi drew in behind it. Arky leaned forward in his seat and offered the taxi-driver a bill.

"I'm took care of," said the driver.

"This is extra," said Arky.

The driver took the bill, starting slightly when he saw its denomination. "Okay, mister. Thanks a million."

Arky got out and walked toward the Cadillac, past the brilliantly lighted newsstand. The biggest and blackest headline he'd ever seen in his life hit his eye, and he stopped to buy a paper.

The kid leaned out. "I got one, mister."

Arky got into the front seat, took the proffered paper, and the kid drove off toward the dim, faraway lights of Riverview to the north.

The headline read: COMMISSIONER STARK BACK

Staring blankly, unable to understand how the Commissioner could possibly be back, Arky switched on the overhead light and started to glance through the long, two-column article. It was a tremendous scoop for the *Journal*, but Arky knew nothing about that.

The article read in part:

> ...Commissioner Stark is back in our midst. Appalled by the death of his old friend Judge Greet and by the brazen activities of the underworld, recently appointed Justice Stark has asked for and obtained temporary leave of absence from his duties at the Capitol. His appointment as Director of Public Safety is momentarily expected... the boys are running for cover as the inevitable shake-up has already started. Police Captain Megher of the Paxton Square District has been removed and suspended. Police Captain Dysen, of Pier 7 Station House, and the most powerful police figure in the city with the exception of Chief of Police Herman Frick, has been removed, suspended, and allegedly put under arrest. No confirmation of these moves has been forthcoming from Chief of Police Frick, who is at Greet Memorial Hospital suffering from a virus condition... it says here. But Mayor Charles Marley has given us the confirmation...."

Arky sighed and turned off the light.

"What's it all about?" asked the kid.

"Church is out, son, that's all," said Arky, then he laughed. "Now the Big Boys will have to tuck their tails between their legs and git back home where they are appreciated. My hunch to get out was sure right."

Arky laughed grimly, then they rode in silence for a long time. They had passed over the Dearborn Street Bridge and through the business district long ago, and now were moving through a close-in suburb with a large shopping-center and cars parked all over the place. It was a little after nine and a warm night. There were crowds at all the corners and people were pouring into a big movie theater for the last show.

They finally cleared the shopping-center, where the going was slow, and turned off into a wide boulevard that passed through a pleasant middle-class residential section. Here the lights were dim, the traffic not very heavy.

After a moment, Arky turned to the kid and said: "We got a tail on us. Where's the gun?"

The kid reached under the seat between his knees and came up with a heavy .45 revolver. Arky took it from him and put it in his lap. "Slow down little by little," he said. "We'll see what these guys are after."

The kid obeyed, and the car behind them followed suit.

"They're either tailing me to see where I'm staying," said Arky, "or they're looking for a dark place to knock me off. Speed up a little."

The kid speeded up and as before the car behind them followed suit. Arky studied the car in the rear-view mirror for a long time, then finally he said: "Pull into the curb just beyond the next intersection and park."

The kid glanced at Arky in surprise.

"It's prowl," said Arky. "Probably from Downtown. This is no good. We'll have to see what they want."

"How about the gun?"

"I got a permit for this one." He opened the glove compartment and shoved the gun in.

The kid drew into the curb and parked. In a moment the prowl-car swished past, and turned the corner up ahead of them. They sat waiting. In a few moments the prowl came round the corner behind them and parked.

A uniformed copper got out and came toward them cautiously. Arky leaned out.

"You want something, officer? I notice you been following me."

The copper came up to him. He was young, big, and tough, looking like a professional football player. Arky noticed the new uniform and the word "Special" stitched into his shirt.

"Where do you live?" asked the copper.

Arky told him, giving him his old address in the 17th Ward.

"What's your occupation?"

Arky told him, adding: "Used to run a book, too, till things got too rough."

The cop merely stared. "Get out," he said.

Shrugging, Arky obeyed, and stood still while the copper frisked him. "Okay," said the cop.

"I got a gun in the car," said Arky. "A permit gun."

"Get it out."

Arky unlocked the glove compartment, removed the gun, then carefully handed it to the cop, butt forward. The cop took it gingerly, smelled it, then broke it open and shook out the shells. Putting the shells in his pocket after examining them, he handed the gun back to Arky, who tossed it into the car.

"Let's see the permit."

Arky gave it to him. The cop studied it with his flashlight, then he turned and called: "Okay, Ed. This is the guy we want."

The other cop got out, came over and took a look at Arky.

"Were you in the Regent Bar a while back?"

"Yeah," said Arky.

"Anything happen?"

"Yeah. A guy got shot."

"Know him?"

"Yeah."

"Friend of yours?"

"I wouldn't say that. I know him."

"What did you shoot him for?"

Arky laughed slightly. "Who said I shot him? Somebody must be crazy. I was standing there with my coat off and my hands on the bar. What would I shoot him with?"

"He pushed you, didn't he?"

"Yeah. We had a couple of words. Nothing serious. Say, you boys work fast."

"We got a tip."

"Did the guy who handed you the tip tell you he frisked me and gave me a clean bill of health? Now don't you young fellows get yourselves in trouble taking me in. They'll just let me go again."

"Don't get tough, chum."

"I'm not getting tough," said Arky. "I'll go in with you if you want me to. Just trying to save you a little trouble."

A call began to come in on the car radio and the second cop hurried back to see what it was. In a moment he returned, looking a little surprised.

"Everybody seems to want this guy," he said. "You're Orval Wanty, right?"

"That's me."

"You're wanted in the Commissioner's office. General bulletin just came over."

The two cops started to look at Arky with different eyes now, in spite of themselves, but Arky was shaken and began to wet his lips. Finally he took out a cigar and chewed on it, unlit.

"Don't know what the Commissioner wants with me," he said, "but...."

"Let's go, fellow," said the first cop.

"All right," said Arky; then: "I guess I'll just send the boy on with the car. Okay? You don't want him, do you?"

The cops hesitated.

"Hell, he's just a punk kid drives for me," said Arky. "Ain't even eighteen years old."

The first cop glanced into the car at the kid, then finally said: "I guess it's all right, eh, Ed?"

"Sure. Why not?"

"All right, Joe," said Arky. "You know what to do with the car."

Tight-lipped, the kid nodded.

17

Commissioner Stark was sitting at the desk in his old office in the dingy, antiquated City Hall. It was very hot downtown, the big buildings cutting off any breeze, and all the windows were open, admitting the clamor of the thronged streets below.

The Commissioner was smoking one of his cheap stogies, the smoke polluting the heavy air. Seated opposite him, Charles Marley the Mayor, looking pale about the gills anyway, drew back from the smoke and finally coughed.

The Commissioner watched the Mayor with a certain amount of irony, and some sympathy. There had been a revolution in the Mayor's small world and the thought of it was plaguing him, giving him no rest. Marley was a politician of moderate ability, who all his life long had used but one method of procedure: talk a lot but do nothing—let the other fellow make the mistakes—if you do nothing yourself there is no danger of you making the mistakes. But now the fat was in the fire. As Mayor, he had allowed himself, through political coercion and shaming, to be committed to a policy of drastic and violent action, and there would be repercussions—there always were!

Megher suspended, and home sulking! Captain Dysen, of all people, held in detention in a little room down the corridor, with two men watching him to prevent him from committing suicide, as he'd threatened several times to do. And, worst of all, there on the Commissioner's desk was Herman Frick's resignation as Chief of Police.

What next? And did this mean the end of power for the Party, or the beginning of a new era? At least the newspapers were unanimously reassuring. But was much attention paid to them? In order to win an election the Party had to carry the Paxton Square District and the 17th Ward. Dysen and Megher had handled these two sections with masterful ease for years under the expert tutelage of Herm Frick, an old 17th Ward man himself.

While the Judge was alive—God rest his soul!—these things simply did not happen. But with the Commissioner... well...!

"You look tired, Charles," said the Commissioner. "Why don't you go home? Better still, run up to the Lakes for a rest as soon as you can get away. I'd suggest a city hospital but too many friends of ours are hiding in them at the moment."

The Mayor smiled wanly. "Wouldn't mind doing a little fishing at that. But I think I'd better stay on the job with things the way they are."

"Oh, they're going to be much worse," said the Commissioner with a certain amount of satisfaction, "before they get any better. There will be raids every night next week. We intend to flatten the Paxton Square district. We are going to try to run every bookie out of town, every gambling-house operator. Of course, they'll drift back and gradually the whole business will start all over again, in a sense. But once I get them disorganized, it will be a little hard for them to work themselves together again. However, my main object is to run the men from out of town away. We don't want them. We've got trouble enough of our own. As long as they are trying to move in, there will be gambling wars and murders on our streets. The local boys seem more polite in their methods."

There was a sharp knock at the door, and big Balch put his head in. "Excuse me, sir. Very important. A former D.A. investigator was murdered at the Regent bar a little while ago. Can Lieutenant Morgan see you about it?"

The Commissioner nodded. "In a few minutes. Just have him wait."

The Mayor groaned slightly and stood up. "I'll go out through the back. Lester's waiting for me in the hall. He'll drive me home. Shall I announce your appointment tomorrow?"

"It's the only thing to do, I suppose," said the Commissioner. "On the understanding that it is temporary. I could go back to my old job but I'm afraid poor Creeden would never survive the shock. He likes to ride around in that big car with the siren going. Take that from him, and he might pine away."

The Mayor flushed slightly. As a matter of fact, he wasn't above using the siren on his own car; to be frank about it, he enjoyed it very much. Stark was such a... well, what was the word? A kill-joy! Didn't he have any human juices in him at all? "I think you're right. It's simpler. Mason's been wanting to retire as Director of Public Safety for nearly a year. Getting old. Sick man. Well...."

The Mayor turned and walked to the door, but paused at a sudden thought. "Something I want to ask you. It's about Dysen. He conducted the biggest series of raids on the Front we've ever had. Right away you remove him from office. This I find very puzzling."

The Commissioner smiled slightly. "Charles, go home and go to bed. You've got a thousand other things to worry about without worrying yourself with police matters. But take my word for it, Dysen has been abusing his authority, and if I'm not mistaken, will spend quite some time in the Walls."

The Mayor recoiled. "As bad as that?"

"It's very bad," said the Commissioner. "Worse than you could ever imagine. So go home, Charles. Get a good night's sleep. You've got to preside at that meeting of the City Planning Commission tomorrow and make up your mind about a ten-million-dollar project. You leave small things like crime to me."

The Mayor brightened. "That's right, by God! I forgot about that. And when that's over, maybe I *will* go fishing." He started out again.

"Charles," the Commissioner called. "If you hear from Frick refer him to me. I've got his resignation here to hold over his head. He's not a bad man, generally speaking. But he sometimes shows an unfortunate tendency to protect old friends, even crooked old friends. At the moment, I hardly think I'll accept his resignation. However, everything depends on how he conducts himself from now on."

"All right. Good night. Might be a good idea for you to get some sleep yourself."

The Mayor went out the back door, then Stark buzzed the inter-com, and in a moment Lieutenant Morgan came in. He was a big, red-faced, heavy-set man in his late thirties. He was dressed in a rather shiny old blue-serge suit and the knot of his tie was crooked. His face was square and rather hard-looking, his complexion swarthy, his eyes dark but far from soft. His father, a Welshman from Cardiff, had worked in the coal mines in the southern part of the state, and the lieutenant had taken a fling at the mines himself as a boy, but decided they were not for him. He had got his education the hard way. He did everything the hard way, but he did it thoroughly and the Commissioner had had his eyes on the Welshman for some time now, considering him loyal and trustworthy, though perhaps far from brilliant.

"Sit down, lieutenant," said the Commissioner. "What's this about a murder at the Regent?"

"A rat by the name of Harry Radabaugh was killed right in the middle of the evening rush." Morgan perched on the edge of his chair, a little awed in the presence of the Commissioner, but spoke in a strong, assured voice. The Commissioner liked his moral simplicity. When he said rat, he meant rat, with no qualifications or extenuations. Speaking carefully, the lieutenant gave the Commissioner a quick rundown on Radabaugh, explaining that there had been rumors for some time that the ex-D.A.'s man was fronting for the Big City corporation that was trying to take over the gambling. In fact, word of it had got to the D.A. and the D.A. had braced Radabaugh about it. Getting no satisfactory answers, the D.A. had thrown Radabaugh out of his job.

Giving no indication that these facts were not news to him, the Commissioner showed marked interest. "And who killed Radabaugh?" he asked. "Do you know?"

"No," said Morgan. "But the rumor flying round is that he was shot by a small-time bookmaker known as Arky."

"I see," said the Commissioner, his eyes now flashing behind his glasses. "Do you know this Arky?"

"No, I don't, Commissioner. Never heard of him before. Understand he has a place in the 17th Ward, right near the Pier 7 Station House. Operates openly, so he must have a fix down there."

"Obviously," said the Commissioner, veiling his irony.

"Well," Morgan went on, "I've talked to nearly a dozen what you might call eyewitnesses and none of them saw a thing. And it's not a cover-up. But one thing all of them do say is that Arky couldn't have done it. He was standing right beside Radabaugh. He was in his shirtsleeves with his coat over his arm. He got into some kind of an argument with Radabaugh, and Radabaugh pushed him. Just as he pushed him, somebody shot Radabaugh three times."

"Isn't there a possibility this Arky might have done it?" asked the Commissioner.

"No, I don't think so," said Morgan. "I'll tell you why, sir. Arky was frisked for a gun before the trouble started."

"Why?"

"I'm not sure. But a boy from the D.A.'s office, named Watrus, frisked Arky and said he was clean."

"I still want to know why Arky was searched," said the Commissioner sharply.

"I'm sorry about that, sir. I neglected that."

"First thing tomorrow morning you take this up with the D.A. personally. If the D.A. is smart, and he is, he'll want a word with that man of his. Too much connivance between certain enforcement officers and lawbreakers. How do you know that Arky wasn't deliberately given a clean bill of health?"

Morgan flushed slightly. "I don't, sir."

"Well, make it your business to find out about that. All right. Anything else?"

"Yes sir. Quite a few men think that somebody was trying to kill Arky and killed Radabaugh by accident."

"Why should anybody want to kill Arky?"

"There is something funny there, sir. No one seems to have any theories about that."

"In other words, they are sure that somebody wanted to kill Arky for no reason at all."

Morgan flushed again. "That's about the size of it, sir."

"Has Arky been picked up?"

"Not that I know of. The word's out for him, though."

"Check with Downtown. And stay outside. I may need you."

"Yes sir," said Morgan, and went out crestfallen.

The Commissioner puffed meditatively on his stogie for a few moments, then tossed it into a spittoon beside his desk. This Arky was a strange man, very astute, very dangerous, and yet there was nothing in his record to indicate anything above the mediocre. One way or another, he must be taken out of circulation. The Commissioner, with his inside knowledge of the background of the business, felt reasonably sure that Arky had killed Radabaugh. But proving it was another matter—at least judging from Morgan's sketchy report.

Strange coincidence! The Commissioner had had a general pick-up bulletin sent out on Arky, apparently almost simultaneously with the killing of Radabaugh. He had intended to question him secretly about his relations with the late Judge Greet, also to observe him and to catch him out, if possible. But the killing of Radabaugh had put a different complexion on the matter. Now Arky, if picked up, was in his hands—could be held as the Commissioner saw fit. Of course, there would be lawyers, and demands that Arky be charged; and then, inevitably, the writ of habeas corpus presented by a smiling young man from Dighton and Black or from some other law firm specializing in the perfectly legal, but sometimes unethical, protection of lawbreakers.

The Commissioner saw the whole process in a flash. Nothing new; same old gambits. Sighing, he rose and went to look out the window at the hot busy streets of the night city. Neon advertising-signs flashed all along the rim of the circumscribed brick-and-stone horizon. A beer sign, featuring a flowing waterfall, made the Commissioner thirsty and he went to the water-cooler for a drink.

Behind him, the back door opened and he turned with paper cup poised. It was Markland, one of the best detectives in the city, now assigned to the Commissioner personally as a special investigator.

"Well?" snapped the Commissioner.

"The Lutheran minister's here, sir. Is it all right to take him in to see Captain Dysen?"

"Yes. How's Dysen?"

"Bad. I don't like the look of him. His face is gray. He don't do anything but groan."

"You think he'll sign that statement? I could use it to very good purpose."

Markland nodded. "I think he will, sir, after he talks to the minister. No fight in him at all. Makes me awful sad to see a man like Captain Dysen in that kind of shape."

"It's not your business to feel sad, Markland," snapped the Commissioner, his eyes glinting behind his old-fashioned spectacles. "Too many people feeling sad about crooks, lawbreakers, corrupt officials. Not enough people feeling sad about the victims."

"Yes sir," said Markland, flushing. "The only thing is, sir—I've known Carl Dysen for fifteen years."

"We all have. Does knowing a man excuse his guilt?"

"No sir," said Markland.

"I must say I'm disappointed in you," said the Commissioner. "All right. Go

ahead. Take the minister in to visit him. Then see if Dysen will sign that statement. If he does, bring it in to me at once."

"Yes sir," said Markland; then he hesitated as the Commissioner turned
back to the water-cooler. "I want to say something, Commissioner."

"Say it," called Stark without turning.

"Makes no difference how I feel—all men got feelings—I do my duty."

"If I didn't think you did, you wouldn't be here. All right, Markland."

Still unsatisfied, Markland sighed and went out.

The Commissioner smiled slightly to himself. He had plans for Markland,
so he felt that he might as well start giving him a few lessons. Later on he intended to advance Markland to a captaincy, in spite of civil service and police
politics, and perhaps in a little while put him in charge of the Paxton Square district. Megher, though a good man in many ways, had under the general laxity
grown more and more corrupt, and anyway he had kinged it long enough. His
suspension might teach him a lesson. If so, the Commissioner intended to send
him to River Station, which included Riverview and the Upper River. There
he could look after the rich, bask in their smiles, and at the same time be removed from the temptations of seething Paxton Square.

Megher had allowed himself to be corrupted, but in a minor sense. His case
was nothing like Dysen's. The captain from the 17th was a hoodlum in uniform
and had used the men assigned to his station as a personal police force, shock
troops for certain hoodlum interests. This was anarchy, and Dysen would have
to pay for it.

The ordinary policemen themselves could hardly be blamed. Like soldiers,
they carried out orders. Not too-well paid, they had families to worry about, and
retirement pensions and the future, always problematical. Why should they be
expected to defy their captain? You could not expect the impossible from human nature.

The Commissioner did not worry too much about the rank and file. With
honest men in authority, the rank and file would be honest. No system, no matter how idealistically devised, is, or can be, any better than the men adminis-
trating it. The security of a city, of a country, or of the world, for that matter,
could not be guaranteed by law and statute, but was dependent ultimately on
the decency, good will, and ability of a handful of men.

The Commissioner always found this thought staggering and generally shied
away from formulating it. Finally brushing it aside, he lit another stogie, and
sat at his desk, contemplating with single-minded concentration the matter in
hand. Speculation was futile: that was for philosophers and university profes-
sors.

There was a quick knock at the back door and Markland put his head in.

"Well?"

"The minister did the trick, sir," said Markland. "Captain Dysen wants to
get the whole business off his chest. Says he won't sign the prepared statement,

though, even if he did give it to you word for word. Says it is true, but does not go deep enough...."

"Ah!" cried the Commissioner, jumping up. Then he paused, and grew thoughtful. Finally he spoke. "This statement will be dynamite, Markland. You take it yourself. No stenographer. I don't care how long you spend at it."

"My shorthand's fair, Commissioner."

"And Markland—prepare yourself for a shock."

"Yes, sir."

The detective went out, his face eager, and the Commissioner returned to his place by the window. Again the beer ad made him thirsty.

Both of the young cops rode up in the elevator with Arky. An old colored man was running it and joked amiably with them, paying no attention to Arky.

"What does he do, Pap," one of the cops finally asked, "work round the clock?"

"The Boss? Yes sir," said the old colored man. "Sometimes round the clock. Sends me out for coffee and them cheap stogies he smokes. Them stogies hard to find. Nobody can stand 'em but him."

The cops laughed. Arky felt completely shut out, but in his present state of mind it was not an unpleasant feeling. The excitement of the evening had entirely worn off, and he was at peace with the world: so much so, that it was almost as if his real life had come to an end and now all that remained was a brief and unimportant epilogue. Anna and the Judge could be tranquil now, wherever they were; and that they were *someplace* Arky never for a moment doubted.

Both Balch and Morgan looked up curiously when the two cops brought Arky into the Commissioner's anteroom.

"General bulletin," said one of the cops. "This is Orval Wanty, known as Arky."

Morgan got up at once, almost overturning his chair. "General bulletin!" he snapped. "This man is wanted as a suspect in the Harry Radabaugh business at the Regent."

"That, too," said the cop, mildly. "In fact he seems to be a badly wanted boy."

"Sit down," said Balch to Arky; then he turned to the cops. "All right, boys. You delivered him."

One of the cops shoved a form across the desk for Balch to sign, then they went out.

"What's the general bulletin on him?" asked Morgan.

"Special priority," said Balch. "Commissioner sent it out."

Morgan showed amazement, but made no comment, and turned to study the tall lean farmerish-looking fellow who sat staring tranquilly at the floor. Farmerish and yet not farmerish. Here was a man who didn't seem to hang together at all. He had a rough, weather-beaten face like a cowboy or a farmer, and the build, apparently, of a clothing model. Morgan wanted to hear him talk. Would his talk fit the face or the clothes?

Balch interrupted him by buzzing the inter-com. "Orval Wanty's here, sir," he said.

In spite of himself, Arky felt a slight tightening of his stomach muscles.

"All right, sir," said Balch. "You buzz me when." Balch clicked the inter-com, then picked up a magazine, ignoring Arky, who sighed and crossed his legs.

"Can I smoke?" he asked.

"I guess so," said Balch. "Go ahead."

Arky took out a morocco cigar-case and offered it to the others.

"You fellows join me?"

Balch glanced at the expensive cigars, then took one. "I'll smoke it later," he said.

Morgan did likewise, running the cigar under his nose, then putting it carefully in his coat pocket.

Arky bit off the end of his cigar and lit it with a gold lighter. Morgan leaned forward.

"Can I see that?"

Arky handed him the lighter. "Friend of mine sent me that one Christmas," he explained. "He's dead now."

"Never saw one like it," said Morgan, noting Arky's country accent. "Nice job." He handed it back.

"This friend of mine," Arky went on, "he picked it up one time he was in Paris, France."

"Your friends seem to get around," said Morgan.

"Only friend I ever had who traveled in foreign countries for pleasure. Course I knew a lot of fellows who were across the water fighting, in one war or the other."

"Were you in?"

"No," said Arky. "I was in a defense plant for a while but some bastard dropped a sledge-hammer on my foot and broke four toes. I was on crutches for a long time." Every once in a while Arky would refer to the period when he'd worked in a defense plant. But he'd only done it as a blind and to keep out of unnecessary beefs during the war. At first he hadn't even taken the trouble to cash his paychecks, but just stuffed them into a drawer. Anna found them one day by accident and appropriated them. After that, he gave them to her for pin-money.

The conversation lapsed. Morgan was baffled by this strange man, and kept glancing at him surreptitiously; finally he took Balch aside and asked:

"You think I ought to question him now, or wait?"

"You better wait," said Balch. "The Commissioner sent the special out for him, and I can't bother the Commissioner about this now. He's busy."

Morgan sat down again.

Time passed slowly in the stuffy office.

Arky smoked lazily, with a controlled face, but inwardly he was struggling to snap himself out of the worst feeling of slackness he'd ever experienced in his life. He wanted to lie down someplace and go to sleep, and the hell with it! Nothing seemed to matter now at all.

Morgan studied him out of the corner of his eye. Sensing the dick's covert scrutiny, Arky put his cigar on the edge of the desk, took off his hat, got out a comb and ran it through his hair; then he picked up his cigar and puffed on it slowly.

"Any idea what the Commissioner wants with me?" he asked, smiling.

"No," said Morgan.

Inside, the Commissioner, with a stiff face, was reading the newly written statement that Captain Dysen had signed. Markland sat near by, looking on, with a sort of horror still showing in his eyes. He was so badly shaken that his face was as grayish as the face of Captain Dysen himself. A whole world had fallen down about him. Judge Greet? Gordon King? Impossible! Fantastic! Nightmare stuff!

But the Commissioner read on and on without a change of expression, and finally at the last page nodded, as if the whole wild, unbelievable thing merely confirmed a preconception.

He glanced up, noticed Markland's discomposure. "I warned you, didn't I?"

Markland nodded and wet his dry lips with his tongue.

"How's Dysen?"

"The doctor's with him now. He looks to me like a very sick man."

The Commissioner sighed. "The Judge dead. Gordon King not expected to live. And now Dysen. Shall we talk to Orval Wanty?"

Markland's eyes showed a flash of life and the color began to come back into his face. "Yes," he said. "There's a man I'm curious about."

"Why—particularly?"

"Because he was able to operate the way he did and still stay in the background."

"A dangerous man, you'd say?"

"I would."

"That's also my opinion," said the Commissioner, then he turned and buzzed the inter-com. "Send Wanty in. Morgan still there? Have him wait. He can book Wanty at Downtown later." The Commissioner glanced at Markland. "How's your shorthand coming along?"

"Not bad. I did pretty well with Captain Dysen."

"I'll go slow with Wanty. Get it all down. This man is going to be questioned a lot, in regard to the Radabaugh business at least, and I want to keep a check."

Although Arky felt a slight nervous tremor when Balch told him he was wanted inside, also a certain curiosity, he could not shake off the basic feeling of indifference, of apathy even, that had been possessing him ever since he'd been picked up by the two young cops. "I played my hand out and won," he told himself, "and it's like it was time to cash in my checks now and go home to bed."

But his attitude changed almost at once when he stepped into the Commissioner's office and saw Stark and the big dick, Markland, waiting for him. His hackles began to rise, his nerves tensed up, and his normal feeling of wariness, of going armed against the world, came back on him so suddenly that his eyes flashed before he could veil them, and his face set into grim lines. He saw the Commissioner's quick, inclusive, weighing glance; he noted Markland's curious, unwinking appraisal; then he brought his feelings and his face into control, smiled easily, indicated his cigar and said:

"Excuse me, Commissioner. I didn't realize this thing was in my hand."

The Commissioner smiled slightly. He had noticed the quick transition from grim, resentful wariness to amiability, and he was interested and ironically amused. "That's all right, Wanty," he said. "You can smoke. Sit down."

Arky picked out a straight chair near the Commissioner's desk, sat down, and took a puff or two on his cigar. His curiosity grew as the seconds ticked past, and the big dick put a notebook on the table in front of him and toyed with a pencil, and the Commissioner walked to the water-cooler and got himself a drink. What did the man want with him? The general bulletin had been sent out, he was almost certain, before the Commissioner had had any knowledge of the Radabaugh business. The Commissioner was a big man, almost as big as the Judge had been: he didn't fool around with penny-ante stuff. Could Dysen have talked? Arky felt a definite tightening in his chest at the thought. Dysen had been in bad shape the last time he'd spoken with him. All the same, he'd ordered the raids! Unlikely he'd talk. Arky crossed his legs and tried to appear at ease.

Nobody said anything. The Commissioner went to his desk, sat down, and began to shuffle some papers about. The clamor of the city came in the open windows.

Were they trying to make him uneasy? Sweating him? Arky smiled inwardly. He was a pretty good man at that little trick himself.

"Wanty," said the Commissioner finally, "I've got quite a few questions I'd like to ask you. But first, let's have your version of the Radabaugh business."

"Yes sir," said Arky; then he glanced over at Markland. "I see he's going to take it all down, and by rights, I shouldn't answer no questions at all without talking to a lawyer. I don't know nothing about legal stuff and I might put my foot in it, one way or another. I don't mean because I'm guilty of anything serious. But I've sure seen a lot of fellows get tangled up in the law because they didn't know any better. I did myself once." He spoke in a low, reasonable voice, exaggerating his accent. "However, Commissioner, I've heard you're a man that can be trusted, so I'll waive all that about a lawyer and dive in."

"Go ahead," snapped the Commissioner, not liking Arky's attitude of doing the police a favor, or his flattery. "I assure you, your rights will be protected."

"I figured so," said Arky; then he calmly gave his version of the Radabaugh business in as few words as possible, stopping once to relight his cigar with the gold cigar-lighter the Judge had brought him from Paris. The Commissioner, who never paid any attention to irrelevant trifles and was immune to gadget-love, ignored the lighter, somewhat to Arky's surprise and disappointment—it almost always caused favorable comment, and was useful, for that reason, as a distracter. Finally he stopped talking. He had given nothing but facts, and had made no attempt to generalize or give a resume.

The Commissioner considered it a model of testimony. "I see," he said finally. "You have nothing to add?"

"No sir," said Arky. "Nothing I can think of at the moment."

"All right. Now I'd like to ask you a question or two."

"I'll do my best to answer."

"Were you a regular customer at the Regent?"

"No."

"Why did you go there to get a drink, then?"

"I was driving past. I needed a drink. I saw the sign. So I went in."

"Ever been there before?"

"Yeah. But not for a few years. I suppose I been there six or seven times in ten years."

"Why did you *need* a drink?"

Arky hesitated, then smiled slightly. "Didn't you ever need a drink, Commissioner?"

Markland coughed uncomfortably behind his hand.

The Commissioner showed a flash of anger. "Just answer the questions, Wanty. What I need or don't need has nothing to do with this."

Arky showed a sober face. "Sorry, sir," he said. "Now as to that question: I think, sir, that I should refuse to answer it as the answer might tend to incriminate me."

"In regard to the murder of Radabaugh?"

"No sir."

"Well, that's the matter in hand. Anything else is irrelevant, and will be treated as such, so answer the question."

"Well, you see, Commissioner, I'm a bookmaker. Things are getting rough. The police are knocking the boys over one by one lately. I was figuring I might be next, so I needed a drink."

The Commissioner nodded to himself. Shrewder and shrewder! "I see. All right, Wanty. I guess that answer is sufficient. Now—why did Watrus search you for a gun?"

"I'm not sure, sir. But I think it must have been Harry's idea. Harry was a jumpy kind of fellow."

"But why *you*? Did he have anything to fear from you?"

"No. But maybe he *thought* he did."

"Why?"

Arky hesitated. "It's a long story, Commissioner, and it's one I don't think I ought to tell. Informing's not my business."

"Clearing yourself is."

"In this case, I'm clear, sir. You can't hang a shooting on a man who didn't have a gun. However, I'll say this much. The story has to do with the gambling set-up in this town. And in a way, Harry was on one side and me on the other. Of course, Harry was a big man and I'm nothing but a small bookmaker. But I was one of the bookies getting crowded by Harry and his bosses, so he might have figured I came in to get him. He always hangs out there. Everybody knows it."

The Commissioner glanced at Markland, who was writing busily, and paused to give him time to catch up. His respect for Arky's cunning was growing.

"All right," he said, finally. "Another question. You say Radabaugh quarreled with you and refused to drink with you because you took your coat off. That's a little thin, Wanty."

"Sometimes the truth is kinda thin," said Arky. "However, you can check all that, sir. Plenty of witnesses. He told me I looked like a hick who'd just come in for the State Fair, then he pushed me and told me to get going. Then he got it. Somebody right behind me. I could feel the heat."

"I see. All right. Why didn't you stay there, then? Why did you run away?"

"I figured it might be a good idea. First, I'm searched for a gun by one of Harry's friends. Then Harry gets killed. I got no friends in the place. Harry's got fifty. I was figuring I might get one in the back. Could happen."

"All right. Then what?"

"How do you mean, sir?"

"Where did you go afterwards?"

Arky hesitated for a split second. "I went out the side entrance and grabbed a taxi...."

"Just a minute," said the Commissioner. "Same taxi? Did it wait for you?"

"Same taxi? I didn't drive up in no taxi."

"Well, where was your car then? Why take a taxi?"

"This is getting more and more complicated, Commissioner. But, okay. I have a boy drives my car for me. I'm a lousy driver and people have kept telling me for so long I'd kill myself that I don't drive much any more. Well, Commissioner, I sent this boy on to the newsstand at the Metropole to pick up a lot of newspapers and magazines for me. Told him to wait, I'd come along in a taxi in a few minutes...."

"I don't understand all this, Wanty. Elaborate."

Arky laughed quietly. "I'm telling you it's getting complicated. I wanted him to pick up these papers and magazines because I was figuring on taking a long trip...."

"Where?"

"Chicago."

"Why?"

"I was taking it on the lam, Commissioner."

"Why?"

"I figured the gambling game was played out. I turned my place over to my partner. That's why I was feeling low and went in for a drink."

"When the police picked you up you were where?"

"I was in my car going to Chicago."

"I see. And the boy? Wasn't he picked up, too?"

Arky looked at the floor to veil the triumph in his eyes. "No sir. He wasn't."

The Commissioner hit the ceiling. Markland jumped up, almost upsetting his table, and ran out into the anteroom, leaving the door open. Arky could hear three voices going at once, then he heard Balch calling Downtown and giving the switchboards a blanket call for a certain special radio-car. The young cops were really going to get hell.

"Excuse me, sir," said Arky, "but I think maybe I can help you. I told the kid to take the car to the garage till he heard from me, so...."

"Wait till Markland comes back," shouted the Commissioner, his eyes blazing; then he took out a stogie and gnawed on it.

In a moment Markland returned and Arky gave him the address of the Greek's garage in the 17th Ward, then he added: "The kid ought to be there by now unless he's picked up his girl and took her out for a ride. Though I don't know what you want with this poor kid."

"What's the license number?" asked Markland.

"That I don't know," said Arky. "I got no head for remembering figures."

"Where's your driver's license?"

"I haven't got any."

"With you, everything is illegal—right?" snapped the Commissioner.

"I wouldn't say that," said Arky. "I told you I don't drive much any more. That's why I got the kid."

"How's that car registered?" asked the Commissioner.

Arky hesitated. He felt a strong and growing antagonism for Stark. Anger nagged at him, but he controlled it. Right now was a good time for a guy to keep his head. "I refuse to answer," he said, shortly.

The Commissioner turned his back and went to the water-cooler.

"You better co-operate," said Markland, showing a flash of anger.

"I been co-operating. If I ain't careful, I'll end up in jail co-operating over stuff that's got nothing to do with what we're talking about. A guy gets killed standing next to me. I'm in my shirtsleeves; I got no gun. And what happens? Now I got to prove who my car's registered to. I answer no more questions about this till I talk to my lawyer."

Turning, ignoring Arky, the Commissioner called: "Sit down, Markland. Start a new section. I'm through questioning him about Radabaugh. We'll now take up another little matter."

Arky felt that tightening in his chest again. This was *it*, the real thing! They would now get down to cases. He decided to play along with the Commissioner—at least until he could get some insight into the reason for his being hauled in by the Commissioner's special police.

"Commissioner," he said, "you got to excuse me. I guess I lost my temper."

Not fooled at all by Arky's sudden docility, the Commissioner merely nodded, glanced at Markland to see if he was ready, then turning to Arky asked bluntly:

"Do you know Police Captain Carl Dysen?"

Arky's face did not show a quiver. "Yes, sir."

"How well?"

"To say hello to. I been within hollering distance of him for maybe ten years."

"He's not a friend of yours?"

"No, Commissioner," said Arky with a straight face. "I got no policemen friends. You see, I'm a bookie."

This was insolence, but hard to pin down, so the Commissioner let it pass. "Without policemen friends, how can you operate?"

"I'm pretty small. Just a little book. Not much take. I'm what is known as a weak tap."

"You look prosperous enough."

"Well, I been operating a long time, and I'm careful with my money."

"What kind of car was that you were driving to Chicago... I mean, your *chauffeur* was driving?"

Arky laughed. "Oh, he's no chauffeur. Like I said, he's just a kid drives for me to keep me from killing myself. I feed him, that's all."

"What kind of car?"

"A Cadillac. But I've only had it about a week. Bought it cheap, second-hand."

"I see. Well, as that Cadillac is a part of the Radabaugh case we'll leave it for the moment. You say, then, that Captain Dysen is a mere acquaintance."

"Very mere, sir. In fact I doubt if he'd remember me. Maybe he would. I been around the 17th long enough."

The Commissioner rose and went to the water-cooler, but came back without getting a drink, realizing suddenly how much water he'd been pouring down, and fearing that if he didn't stop it he'd be up all night. He glanced at Markland, who seemed to be doing very well; then, fooling with some papers on his desk, not looking at Arky, he said:

"There are a couple of what for want of a better word I must refer to as public figures I want to ask you about. Leon Sollas and Rudy Solano. Do you know them?"

Arky spoke without hesitation. "Rudy I don't know, only what I read in the paper. Leon I know."

"How do you know Leon?"

"He set me up in business, Commissioner. He was a big man around town."

"You think he was murdered?"

"I wouldn't know, sir."

There was a brief silence. Markland studied Arky covertly. The Commissioner sighed, turned away and paced the floor; finally in a quiet voice he asked: "Do you know Gordon King?"

Arky gave a start, but controlled himself and answered at once: "Yes, sir."

"How do you happen to know Gordon King?"

Arky thought this over for a moment, then he said: "Well, sir, I've managed to get myself in a little trouble here and there—never convicted of anything, though—and about ten years or so ago somebody, maybe it was Leon, recommended Dighton and Black to handle things for me. Well, Mr. King—a very fine gentleman, by the way—was the boss at Dighton and Black then, and that's how I happen to know him."

There was a long silence. The Commissioner sat drumming on his desk. Markland waited, studying Arky out of the corner of his eye. Although Arky showed no nervousness, and his face was blankly calm, cold sweat was beginning to trickle down between his shoulder blades. This was bad, very bad. Little by little the Commissioner was linking up the chain. Had Dysen really spilled the beans? Or was the Commissioner, knowing little but suspecting much, out on a fishing expedition? Would he get as far as the Judge? Very unlikely; and if he did not, none of the rest mattered very much.

The Commissioner woke him out of his thoughts by demanding explosively: "Did you know Judge Greet?"

Arky paled visibly and both Markland and the Commissioner noticed it. "Yes sir," said Arky, after having some difficulty clearing his throat.

"Will you tell me how you happened to know him?"

Arky explained at length about how the Judge had saved him from prison and befriended him and how he'd worked five years for the Judge as a chauffeur. "Finest man that ever lived," Arky concluded warmly. "Salt of the earth."

For a moment the Commissioner said nothing and narrowly studied Arky. There seemed to be little doubt of Arky's sincere regard for the Judge. Was there, then, something in this strange man besides hardness and duplicity? Almost in spite of himself, the Commissioner began slowly to revise his initial opinion of Arky. Finally he asked: "Why did you leave the Judge's employ?"

Arky smiled slightly. "By request."

"You mean you were discharged?"

"Well, more or less. The Judge put up with my driving as long as he could. He had iron nerves, sir, but I shook 'em. We parted friends, however."

"Did you see him regularly?"

"Haven't seen him for over ten years. Talked to him on the phone a few times."

There was a long silence and the Commissioner sat lost in thought. Finally he said: "To sum up—you admit knowing the following men: Carl Dysen, Leon Sollas, Gordon King, and Judge Greet. Now, Wanty; I want you to do something for me."

"All right, Commissioner."

Stark took a document from the top of his desk and handed it to Arky. "Read this. Then give me your opinion. Take your time. No rush."

The document was the final statement that Captain Dysen had signed. Arky tried to keep his hands from shaking as he read it. There was dead silence in the Commissioner's office; and little by little the roar of the big town below seemed to grow louder and louder. Finally Arky handed the document back after examining the signature.

"You have any comments to make?"

"Yes sir. Dysen is crazy, and you better have him locked up in a padded cell."

"For your own part, you deny everything in there, is that right?"

"Yes sir."

"You deny that you bossed the vice and gambling of the town?"

"That's plumb ridiculous."

"You deny you practically bossed the police of the 17th Ward?"

"I can hardly keep from laughing."

"You deny that you sent police from the 17th to protect the Judge and that one of them shot or shot at the assassin?"

"I tell you the man's crazy."

"What motive would Captain Dysen have for telling such a story if it weren't true?"

"If he's crazy, he don't need no motive. Look, Commissioner, you can't ruin the reputation of a man like Judge Greet just on this big lobster's say-so."

"Why are you worrying about the Judge's reputation, Wanty? You'd better worry about your own hide." The Commissioner spoke with unnecessary sharpness and heat because Arky was touching on a sore and vital point. The naming of Judge Greet in this affair was going to cause an appalling scandal. Politically, it would shock the whole community. And after all, what good purpose did it serve? The ring was broken up. It could never operate in this form again.... The Commissioner lost himself in vague and fruitless speculation, but Arky brought him up short.

He was shouting at the Commissioner with sudden animosity: "My hide ain't on the barn door yet, mister. And neither is the Judge's. I'll give Dysen the lie to every word he says—and in court, too."

The Commissioner flew into a temper, only partially feigned, and jumped to his feet, confronting Arky, who had also risen. "Fine!" shouted Stark. "Lie under oath and we'll also have you for perjury." He turned to Markland. "Explain to Morgan that this man is to be held as follows: for questioning in the killing of Radabaugh and as a material witness, for questioning in the disappearance of Leon Sollas, also for bribery and corruption of police officials, maybe a hundred counts, also for running a gambling establishment in defiance of the laws of the city... and if there is anything else I can think of I'll call Casey."

"I sure got my rights protected, all right," said Arky.

"You are innocent until proven guilty. I will shortly leave your fate to the D.A. and to the grand jury. All right, Markland. Turn him over to Morgan."

But Arky held back. "Look here, Commissioner," he said mildly, "you mean to tell me you're going to let a thing like this about the Judge get out? Why, he was a friend of yours, wasn't he?"

"Yes," said the Commissioner. "But that is irrelevant. I'm afraid he's going to have to take the consequences of his acts."

"But he's dead."

The Commissioner winced slightly and shifted. Turning, he noticed that Markland was studying him curiously and suddenly he remembered the "lesson" he'd given the big detective not so long ago. "Does knowing a man excuse his guilt?" he'd said. Now the big detective was watching *him*, wondering. "There are still consequences," said the Commissioner. "Dying doesn't settle everything."

"That's a hell of a note," said Arky. "What about his family?"

"You might have asked the Judge that some time back."

Arky swallowed, then took the plunge. "Supposing he's guilty—which he ain't—it's not their fault."

"Are you leading up to something, Wanty?"

"Yes, sir. A deal."

"I don't make deals."

"All right," said Arky. "But it's like this. Dysen's already confessed. Mr. King's about dead, I hear. But I'm still alive and kicking. Wouldn't it be enough to send me and Dysen up? Dysen—he could be the Big Boy."

"What about you?"

"Well... I might hold still for this, but it makes me laugh."

"You still deny everything?"

"I sure do."

"Then why do you want to do this?"

"On account of the Judge. Finest man I ever knew in all my life."

The Commissioner looked at Arky for a long time. Loyalty was a great virtue, and a rare one, misguided or not.

Arky waited, glancing at the Commissioner. Markland folded his arms and stood with his back to the wall. The Commissioner paced up and down for a few moments, then he went to his desk and lit one of his stogies. The smoke from it made Markland cough. "Wanty," said the Commissioner at last, "I don't make deals. I'm against them on principle. They are always unfair. Goats and favorites. See what I mean? It's not just."

"Maybe by law it's not," said Arky. "But I'm not talking about law."

"Anyway you look at it, it's not, law or no law. And in this case, it would be particularly unjust. The Judge was without a doubt the ablest man I've ever come across. He made other men seem pretty tame and flabby and conventional. He had the makings of a great leader, and God knows we need them. But, Wanty, he evaded his social responsibilities; he turned against the very people he should have helped...."

"I don't know anything about all this," said Arky impatiently.

"Yes, you do," said the Commissioner. "You just won't listen. Loyalty is one thing; blind loyalty another...." Arky broke in. "All I know is, I never met a man in my whole life that I liked as well as the Judge."

"I liked him, too," said the Commissioner. "But that is beside the point, Wanty. The point is, that deals are unjust, and in this case particularly so. The way we live is a matter of choice. We have to go one way or another. No one can have it both ways. The choice is often a hard one. But for the Judge it should have been easy. He had everything: health, looks, brains, ability, education, and money. He deliberately took the wrong way. In other words, there is no excuse for him, so why should he be protected at the expense of others?"

With his lips compressed, Arky shifted, took a step toward the door. "No deal?"

"Listen, Wanty; you knew the Judge intimately. Wouldn't you say that he was a man who knew perfectly well what he was doing at all times?"

"Yes sir, I would."

"All right. Then the Judge knew that at any moment there might be a crash. It was inevitable. He gambled and he lost. If he was alive, do you think he'd let you make a deal for him and go to prison to save his reputation?" Arky swallowed but said nothing. "He'd take his medicine, wouldn't he?"

In a low voice Arky said: "Yes sir, he would."

"All right, Wanty," said the Commissioner. "Think that over."

Arky turned and went out into the anteroom, followed by Markland. The Commissioner took out a handkerchief and mopped his brow, then he went to the water-cooler and drank two cups before he remembered and flung a third cup to the floor in exasperation.

He felt very tired now, but easier in mind; he'd clarified his thinking in regard to Judge Greet by talking about him to Arky. No matter how hard he tried he could not conceal from himself the fact that for one brief moment he'd been tempted to make a deal. Why? Did charm extend from beyond the grave? The Commissioner smiled grimly and uncomfortably.

18

The police car was moving slowly along at the edge of a dingy city park. Beyond the trees of the park, the garish lights of the Front flared, spreading a purplish glow over the low-hanging clouds.

A young policeman was driving. Morgan and Arky were in the back. The traffic was very heavy, and the driver kept cursing the taxis, which were darting in and out all along the boulevard, grazing his fenders from time to time.

"Sonsabitches," cried the young cop. "Ought to be a law."

Morgan laughed sardonically, then glanced at his prisoner, who was leaning forward with his elbows on his knees, staring apathetically at the floor. Arky hadn't said a word or even looked at Morgan since they'd left the Commissioner's anteroom. He seemed completely sunk, Morgan thought, and he had a right to be! It was obvious that the Commissioner, for reasons of his own, intended to see to it that the book was thrown at this fellow, who seemed, to Morgan, singularly inoffensive. Not a loudmouth, nor a braggart, nor one of those irritating but pathetic I'll-get-you-for-this boys! In fact, he was a strange type to Morgan. Not the kind of man you'd expect to see in the hands of the law at all.

"Sure is a warm, close night," said Arky, finally. "I keep sweating. You mind if I take my coat off?"

"No," said Morgan. "Help yourself."

Arky removed his coat and held it across his lap, then he leaned forward again and sat with his elbows on his knees, his hands dangling.

"Sure feel low," he said in a melancholy voice. "I can understand it," said Morgan.

"That little Commissioner," Arky went on, "he means well, but he can sure be rough and tough on a fellow. He just wouldn't listen to me at all. He just kept talking...."

"He knows his business," said Morgan shortly.

Arky sighed. "I guess he does. He sure sounds like it. But a fellow can't make no headway with him. He just won't pay no attention...." Arky went on and on in his sad, monotonous voice, complaining mildly, making few charges of any kind against anybody, seeming to be interested only in lamenting his fate.

The young cop at the wheel was still cursing the taxis. Morgan, lulled by Arky's voice, sat contemplating the crowded boulevard. Suddenly Arky acted. With his right hand, he flung his coat in Morgan's face, then he reached forward and with his left hand jerked the wheel sharply to the right, and there was a shuddering crash as the police car banged into a taxi, and at once there was a general shrieking of brakes and many collisions all along the line of traffic; tires whined as they skidded on the asphalt, and there was the crash and tinkle of breaking glass.

Arky leaped out the car door into the middle of the traffic jam and ran across the boulevard, darting here and there among the cars, heartened by the shouting, the blasting horns, the utter confusion; and in a moment he disappeared into the shrubbery of the city park.

The taxi-driver, a shrewd-looking, middle-aged little man, pulled up in front of the Paymaster's house. "This it, mister?"

Arky got out. "Yeah," he said, "this is it." Then he laughed. "Just went out for a walk, ran into a friend of mine in the Village, and ended up downtown. Didn't even put my coat on." He gave the driver a five-dollar tip.

"Thank you, sir," said the driver, smiling and touching his cap.

Arky called good-night, and crossed the pathway through the shrubbery. Dim lights were showing in the cottage and Arky saw the Cadillac parked at the far end of the drive, beyond the garage. As he stepped across the narrow porch, the front door was opened from within and Robbie looked out.

"Ozark!" she said in a rather unnatural-sounding voice. "Where's your coat? I was getting worried about you."

Joe was just beyond her. "I kept telling her not to worry," he called.

"Hi," said Arky. "Never mind the coat." Then he hugged Robbie and stepped into the cottage.

Robbie closed the door, then she and Joe stood looking at Arky, waiting for him to say something, to explain, to tell them what to do.

"You all ready to blow?" asked Arky.

They nodded, then Robbie said: "We've been ready for a long time."

"Okay," said Arky. "But I kind of changed my plans a little. Sit down. I'll be with you in a minute. I got to call Zand."

He went into the study and shut the door. Robbie started to sit down on one of the straight chairs in the hallway but sudden baby-howls rose in the back of the house and she hurried off to see what was the matter with Orv. Joe lit a cigarette, sat down, and began to hum to himself. "Like I said," he told himself, "you don't have to worry about that guy. If he says he'll show, he'll show."

Arky sat in the study impatiently chewing on a cigar. It was some time before Zand answered the phone. "Arky!" came Zand's rather agitated voice. "Where the hell are you?"

Arky told him, then asked: "What's up?"

"Cops been here twice, looking for you. They also combed the Greek's garage for the Cadillac. The Greek came and told me about it. He just left. What *is* all this?"

"Never mind about that. Now listen carefully, Zand. First thing, don't open the bookie joint tomorrow. Lock it up and keep it locked until things quiet down. Save you a lot of trouble."

"Yeah, I saw in the paper... the Commissioner...."

"That's right. This town's going to be hotter than a July 4th picnic for a good long while. Just keep your head down. Okay. Another thing. Do you remember the street number of Anna's old lady's house? She lives on Kosciusko Street, near the bridge, but what's the number?"

There was silence at the other end for a moment, then Zand said: "Anna's old lady's house? Wait a minute. I'll ask Lola."

A long pause, and Arky chewed impatiently on his cigar. Finally Lola came on the phone. "Arky? We sure miss you down here—you and Orv. Place seems empty...."

"How about that address?" snapped Arky.

"I got it wrote down here. 2371 Kosciusko Street, near Parkway."

Arky made a note of it on the telephone pad. "Okay. Thanks, Lola. Put Zand back on."

"What's all this about Anna's old lady?" Zand demanded after a brief pause.

"Don't ask questions. Just listen. If you don't hear from me in a week I want you to start sending Anna's old lady a couple of hundred a month. Understand?"

"Yeah," said Zand. "But...."

"No 'buts.' When I get around to it, I'll make some kind of arrangement with Dighton and Black. The thing is, I don't want to hand them Polacks a whole hunk of dough at once. They might go wild and blow it."

"Okay, Arky," said Zand, wearily. "Maybe you know what you're doing."

"One more thing. Get a car out here to me as fast as you can. I'm lamming. Read your paper carefully tomorrow and you'll know why."

"It ain't going to be easy, Arky. The Greek's out on account they got coppers hanging around. I can't bring the Ford; they'll tail me. But I'll see what I can figure out. Call you back when I get a chance. Coppers been coming in and out.... Arky—they're downstairs again. I can hear them big feet. Sit tight." Zand hung up abruptly.

When Arky came back into the hallway, Robbie was sitting near the door, holding Orv on her lap. The baby was looking about him sleepily and from time to time he waved his little fists vaguely in the air. Joe was standing leaning against the wall, smoking.

Arky handed him a slip of paper. "There's an address on there. That's where I want you and Robbie to go...."

Joe glanced at the slip of paper, then looked up blankly at Arky. "Polishtown?"

"Yeah. Deliver this kid to Mrs. Hunchuk. She's a big fat good-natured dame about sixty. You can hear her laugh two blocks away."

"Deliver... the... kid...?" Joe stammered.

Robbie was staring in unbelief. "What are you talking about, Arky? I thought we were all going to Detroit. I thought...."

"We are," said Arky. "All but the kid. He's going to stay where he belongs—

with Anna's people. No sense us dragging him all over hell and back. For what?"

"For *what?*" cried Robbie. "You want him to grow up in the slums? Polish-town!"

"Anna grew up there, and she was a hundred per cent okay. Now I ain't going to argue about this. I was talking tonight with a guy who knows what he's talking about. This kid deserves a chance. Slums don't matter. When he grows up, he can figure out himself what he wants to do. You kidding yourself about us being the right people to raise him?"

"Why not?" cried Robbie, defiantly.

Arky looked at her for a long time. She slowly lowered her eyes and studied Orv, who was nodding on her lap.

"Now listen," said Arky, "you and Joe deliver the kid. Here's a hundred bucks. Give it to the old lady—tell her there'll be two hundred coming in every month and that she's to look after the kid. Tell her a friend of mine's gonna check on it every once in a while. And take your time with her—be patient. She don't understand English so good. See what I mean?"

Robbie began to cry.

"What the hell's wrong with you?" Arky demanded, violently irritated.

"Nothing, nothing," said Robbie.

There was a long silence. Joe tossed his cigarette away and stood waiting. He felt depressed and bewildered; things weren't working out the way he'd hoped they would.

"What's a good little hotel in Detroit?" Arky asked Robbie. "Not one of the swell ones."

Robbie thought for a moment, then said: "The Randall. Nice place."

"Randall, eh? All right. I'll meet you there."

"Aren't you going with us?" Robbie demanded.

"I can't," said Arky. "I'm hot. Nice mess if they'd happen to run up on me with you and Orv and Joe in the car. Damn fine mess. No. I got to go by myself."

"In what?" asked Joe.

"Zand's getting me a car. Okay, Joe. You wait outside."

Joe shrugged and went out. They heard a car door slam.

"I wish I knew what this was all about," said Robbie, jiggling Orv who was whimpering.

Arky wagged his head impatiently, then he went to a small table, unlocked the drawer with a key he took from his wallet, and extracted a thick manila envelope from which he counted out a stack of bills.

"Here's five G's, Robbie," he said. "Put 'em in your purse. You might need 'em."

Robbie sobered at the sight of the money; she glanced up at Arky, searching his face, then she delicately took the bills from him with her long, pointed fingers. And Arky remembered how she'd taken that large bill from him in the same manner that day in Leon's outer office. Robbie was an all-right kid; and she really liked the baby; but with her, money talked—and loud!

She rose, holding Orv.

"All right, Arky," she said. "Whatever you say."

"You and Joe deliver the kid, then keep right on going. It's on your way. Come on."

Arky opened the front door, then took Robbie by the arm and led her across the porch and down the pathway through the shrubbery to the parked Cadillac. Joe got out and opened the rear door. Robbie leaned in and put Orv in his basket. He was sound asleep now.

A fleeting picture crossed Arky's mind: Anna in her blue kimono, plump, blond, amiable, and pretty, bouncing Orv on her knee and laughing as he waved his arms and chortled....

"Well, good-bye," said Robbie, looking at Arky strangely. "Be seeing you soon in *Dee*-troit."

Robbie was like she used to be now. Arky grinned.

"Okay, ball of fire."

"Okay, Elmer."

He kissed her perfunctorily. A curtain seemed to drop between them. They looked at each other uneasily, and laughed; then he helped her into the back seat.

"Just keep moving, Joe," said Arky, then he handed the kid a few bills. "Spending-money."

"Thanks, mister," said Joe, his face stiff.

Arky stood watching the Cadillac drive off; then he turned and started back to the cottage.

After Arky returned to the cottage he paced the floor for a moment, then went back through the house, turning off the lights. He took a small revolver from a dresser drawer, and returned to the living-room. Putting out all the lights there but one, he lay down on the big davenport, slipped the gun in between the cushions, settled himself, and tried to relax.

Things were rough now and maybe Zand wouldn't be able to deliver. It didn't matter too much, however. For the moment, he was safe. If he didn't hear from Zand by morning, he'd go to the Village, grab a taxi, give the driver some cock-and-bull story, and have him drive to the nearest town where Arky could catch a train for Detroit. Much safer lamming by taxi in the daytime. Might make the driver suspicious if he tried it at night.

Arky sighed and lay staring at the ceiling. He felt nervous but tired, and little by little a not altogether pleasant lassitude began to steal over him; a sudden letdown after all the excitement, he told himself.

Finally he dozed. Vague scenes began to pass before his eyes. Anna when he'd first met her: wearing a tight pale-blue dress, her yellow-blond hair to her shoulders. She had made several shocking remarks, which convulsed him, and later she'd smoked a cigar. Big Anna—nobody like her: good-hearted, amiable, human; a fiery temper, but no meanness—she seemed to be looking at him through a pale haze, smiling at him. Then she had Orv in her arms but she was calling him "Thaddeus"! Now she was gone... somehow; and he could see Robbie holding Orv and weeping. What the devil was the silly fool woman weeping about? She had that fine big kid in her arms, didn't she...?

...Orv seemed to have grown up. He was quite large now, although his face looked the same, fat and babyish, and his hair was soft and silky. He was walking along hand in hand with a very pretty girl who seemed no older than himself. "Why, I didn't know she was that young," Arky mused. "She don't look a day over sixteen, so how could she have been around the Front with Leon and all them other bums all that time?"

...Robbie in a white dress—her thick black hair long and hanging down her back. But almost at once she seemed to thicken and grow fat, her hair turned blond, she shortened; and then, finally, she was gone... and there was the animal Milli, and Orv was a baby again. "What the hell is going on here?" asked Arky.

He woke with a start, sweating, sat up, and glanced at his watch. What a doze! He had been out for over an hour and a half. His head ached and he had such a heavy, lethargic feeling all through him that he could hardly force himself to get to his feet and walk to the kitchen. But it was no good lying there with silly, unsettling dreams running through his head.

He made himself some coffee and, as he sat at the kitchen table drinking it, he remembered Robbie and that night in his apartment in the 17th. An all-right kid, Robbie, but no Anna. Nobody could ever take Anna's place; just as nobody could ever take the Judge's place, no matter what the Commissioner thought of him.

Arky gradually realized that he was now looking out on a different world, and was greatly surprised that such a familiar, taken-for-granted place could change so radically. Was that all there was to it—people? Didn't a man in himself mean anything at all?

Arky tried not to think about the future, but visions of it kept rising in his mind in spite of himself, visions without savor. A new life? What kind? Arky had plenty of money; too much, if anything. Most of it free of taxes, it had accumulated like corn in a bin over the years. But he was not much for spending money. Sucker gambling bored him. The thought of traveling left him cold; and as for leisure, loafing, all he knew of it was an armchair or bed, four walls, some cigars, maybe a fifth of gin, and a few newspapers, and magazines like the *Racing Form* and the *Sporting News*—took no money for that. And as for women— well, women were damned interesting and necessary, but they didn't fill your life... couldn't be your whole future. Couldn't be *his*, anyway. Maybe with Leon it was different.

Arky sighed heavily, finished the last of his coffee, then rose and went back to the living-room.

"Damn it," he said to himself, "I feel like a watch with a broken main-spring."

He searched the living-room, then the study, for a deck of cards but couldn't find any; finally he went back and sat on the davenport, stared at the floor, and waited for the phone to ring. Two clocks ticked in staggered time, lulling him. At last he lay down, put his hands under his head, and studied the ceiling, following the various patterns of light with his eyes. Once or twice he sighed heavily, then his eyes closed and he fell asleep.

This time he did not dream.

...He woke with a start. Dawn was showing grayly at all the windows. A big man was standing over him with a gun in his hand. The man had a set, determined look in his eyes. Arky's right hand fumbled sleepily among the pillows.

"Go ahead," said the big man. "Reach for it. Give me an excuse."

Arky blinked rapidly and came fully awake. Lieutenant Morgan was standing over him with a police revolver in his hand.

"Hello, lieutenant," said Arky, smiling slightly. "This is sure a surprise."

"What do you take us for—idiots?" snapped Morgan. Then he pulled a pair of handcuffs out of his pocket. "I want to see you get out of these."

"Well," said Arky, rising slowly, "looks like the hounds treed the coon after all. I guess that's nature. The coon ain't got a chance."

Morgan made no reply. He was all business now. He'd had a bellyful of Arky and his disarming, homely talk. It had almost got him busted by the Commissioner after all his hard work and application, his years of effort. He clicked on the heavy cuffs with a feeling of deep satisfaction and jerked Arky toward the door with unnecessary roughness.

What he would never know was that as they moved across the dewy grass through the lavender-gray twilight of early morning his prisoner was experiencing a swiftly growing sense of relief.

A carrier-boy rode past on his bicycle and tossed a newspaper up onto the porch of Gordon King's house. "That's a copy I'll never get to read," said Arky.

Morgan made no comment.

Reisman was back in the hospital again. They had decided to operate. He had made his will and had been very heroic about it, he thought; and Sarah had even cried over him, with his three daughters looking on, round-eyed. Yes, outwardly he had been very heroic, joking with everybody; inwardly, he was petrified. Was this it? Could be, could be. Although it was a hard thing to admit to himself, he knew that he was no more immortal than anybody else. People died every day. Why not him?

He had visitors. Red Seaver, diffusing a strong odor of bourbon, was sitting with his feet propped up, smoking a cigar. Across the bed from him was young Downy, also diffusing an odor of bourbon. In fact, they were both mildly drunk.

Occasionally Red reached down, picked up a newspaper from the floor, and stared at it with a bemused expression.

"You sure had me fooled for a while, Ben, you old bastard, you! I was thinking many unkind thoughts about you—yes I was. Don't shake your head at me. But I might have known you'd come through. I might have known." Red smiled happily and slapped the paper where it read:

> ...Commissioner Stark acknowledges the help given him by the *Journal* in tracking down the Greet Ring, the greatest source of corruption our city ever saw in its long history.... Commissioner Stark, now Director of Public Safety as well as Justice of the Supreme Court, and a future Governor, we hope, goes further than a mere acknowledgement; he names names: and we, with the Commissioner, want to cite the following trio for their services as public servants as well as crack newspapermen: Ben Reisman, well-known columnist and former police reporter; Langley "Red" Seaver, and Francis Downy III....

Red and Downy were glowing with triumph; they had been taking bows all afternoon, and allowing people to buy them drinks. But Reisman felt only a kind of mild sadness. By the grace of God, he'd run the thing down. Luck, hunch, and random information had done the trick. Actually, there was nothing to it at all, and in a few days it would be forgotten. Or maybe by tomorrow. Compared to the trouble in Korea this was all very small potatoes!

Reisman groaned faintly and surreptitiously slid his hand under the covers to massage his stomach. In spite of the dope, the pain was nagging at him faintly—the enemy within! Pain was a very mysterious thing and very demoralizing. There you were, enjoying a good meal, or a good book, or merely a good doze, when all of a sudden... whap!... and the world was a different place. A man with a toothache thinks that everyone who hasn't got a toothache is happy. And as for stoicism... the silent and patient bearing of pain: well, it sounded pretty to read about in tranquillity. But philosophy was always great for past ills, or future ones: never for present ills. "I'd like to see Epictetus with a boil on his ass," Reisman told himself, groaning slightly.

Red glanced at him in irritation. Damn it all! Ben was spoiling their triumph. Couldn't he smile a little, for God's sake? This was terrific, unheard of! Why, Red was even a hero to his wife at the moment. Of course that wouldn't last very long... maybe until he spilled cigar ashes again on the new living-room rug.

As for Downy, he was woozy with happiness. Eunice Kubelik... now *this!* He was so woozy with happiness, in fact, that he didn't even notice Ben's long face or hear his rather apologetic groans.

"Come on, Ben," cried Red. "Perk up! Perk up! You're the biggest man in town. You can write your own ticket. You are also a gentleman and a scholar. The whole Seaver family loves you. Mush Head might even give me a raise now, though I doubt it. Come on, Ben. Let's see a smile."

Turning his head on the pillow, Reisman spoke to Red for a moment in uncouth monosyllables, making impossible suggestions as to what he should do; then in an altered voice he went on: "Why, let the stricken deer go weep, the hart ungalled play; for some must watch, while some must sleep: thus runs the world away."

Red grimaced and got up. Nuts to this: he wanted action, good cheer! But Downy, smiling brightly, asked: "Hamlet?"

Reisman nodded. "Hamlet."

THE END

Vanity Row
by W. R. Burnett

For Butch, Jimmie and Whitney

1

The newspapers all said that heavy thunderstorms were general over the whole Midwest, from the Great Lakes on the north to the Ohio River on the south, and from the Pennsylvania border on the east to the Kansas steppes on the west. But so far no storm had appeared over the big city by the wide, slow-moving river. Yet there was storminess in the air, a feeling of oppression and unquietness, the night sky was low and black, reflecting the sullen red glow of the city lights, and a fine rain, hardly more than a mist, was blowing in waves between the wet, shining façades of the big buildings downtown.

The Civic Center clock struck one—eleven-thirty—the sound of the chime vibrating in the heavy, damp air; then the huge minute hand on the big illuminated dial took up its labored journey toward midnight. It was a Monday. The city was almost deserted. The river flowed southward, black and silent, under its mammoth, many-arched bridges, empty of traffic.

Rosey, the little Italian newsboy, wearing a black rubber poncho and cursing the weather, was trying to make up his mind to go home and the hell with it! But he had his regular customers to think about. Guys who ducked out of side-street hotels every night to get the late editions of the morning papers: complete race results, baseball scores. Some of them were gamblers, careless with money, and would often hand him a quarter or even four-bits and say: "Keep it, bud." Rosey had a good corner, protection, everything. Right down the street from him burned the green lights of the Downtown Police Station, and all the big, beefy coppers knew Rosey, and liked him. Rosey was a tough little kid, and would fight at the drop of a hat. He was fourteen, small for his age, but wiry and strong. Some of the cops liked to needle him just to see him flare up. He'd fight a cop even, if necessary.

Rosey lit a stogie somebody had given him and stood in the huge, arched doorway of the Farmers and Drovers Bank, puffing slowly and staring out at the empty street and blowing mist with melancholy eyes, dark as ripe olives. He had stacked his newspapers in the doorway to keep them dry, and after a moment he sat down on one of the stacks and waited for customers. Monday night was usually murder downtown, anyway—and now with this frigging weather…!

A huge truck towing a trailer as long as itself pulled up at the traffic-light, backfiring loudly in the dampness. The driver leaned out of the window and called to Rosey. He was as high up as the engineer of a locomotive. Rosey grabbed an armful of papers, ran out to the truck, and stood looking up with a sort of awe. Jeez, what must it be like to drive a monster like that all through the night!

"*Racing Form*, kid," called the tough-faced driver, "and a *World*. Did the

Yanks win?"

Rosey handed up the papers, standing on tiptoes, and the driver tossed down the money. "Yeah," said Rosey. "DiMag hit a homerun in the seventh."

"Hell," said the driver. "Them Yanks! I got a big bet on Cleveland to win the pennant. Nice odds, too. Why don't them Yanks drop dead!"

"What you got in that truck?"

"Groceries, for Christ's sake. Tons of 'em. Why?"

"You driving all night?"

"Yeah. Toledo. Highway 81. It'll be a rough go tonight. Why?"

"I don't know," said Rosey. "I was just thinking—I'd like to drive one of them things all night."

The light changed with a sad, off-key clanging.

"Go get your head examined, boy," cried the truck-driver as he drove off, the truck backfiring with startling explosiveness.

The mist was turning to real rain now, a soft rain which fell straight down soundlessly, blurring the boulevard lights and turning the wide, plaza-like streets of this part of town to lakes of black patent-leather.

Rosey hurried back to the doorway, thinking about the tough-looking truck driver wheeling that gigantic crate northward through the night. Nice to think about. Rosey liked the night. He liked to stay up till the sun peeped over the roofs. Broad day bored him. As he turned to push his stacks of newspapers back further into the doorway away from the rain, he could still hear the truck far down the empty boulevard, backfiring heavily, the sound gradually diminishing with distance. And then suddenly the backfiring sounded loud again: once, twice, three times; almost as if it was just across the plaza, and Rosey turned in surprise. How could that be?

A dark sedan had turned the corner far across the plaza and was roaring off into the darkness of a side-street. Rosey saw a man standing on the corner. Where in hell had *he* come from? Rosey stared. Suddenly the man seemed to be overcome by a seizure of some kind; he reeled about, grabbing his chest, then he took several steps out into the street, and finally fell heavily on his face.

"Jesus!" cried Rosey, looking about him in bewilderment. What *went* here!

Rosey was a great little guy for minding his own business. It paid. But this was too much. He couldn't let that poor bastard lay out there in the street. A car might turn the corner suddenly and....

"Wow!" cried Rosey, starting to run across the shining plaza, snapping his fingers as his thoughts cleared. "That wasn't no backfiring—that last. Somebody blasted this poor guy."

Rosey couldn't understand all the excitement at Downtown. Guys got killed practically every day. But all the big cops—his pals—were acting hysterical, almost like girls, for God's sake!

"Look, Coonan," he said to a big Irish plainclothes man. "I told you all I seen."

My papers are down there at the corner. I'll get robbed."

"Don't bother me, midget," said Coonan, and although he was one of the biggest kidders on the force, this time, Rosey could see he wasn't kidding.

"What's the idea keeping me here?" Rosey shouted, waving his arms. "Did I do something wrong? A favor's all I done. *Now* look!"

Nobody paid any attention to him. Phones rang all over the place. What an uproar! Rosey had an idea and looked about him for Mike Antonnelli, the wop dick. A good Sicilian, maybe he'd be a pal to another good Sicilian. He found him at last in a corner of the big room, sitting with his chair tipped back, holding a receiver to his ear with his neck and shoulder while he unwrapped a package of gum.

"Mike," Rosey began, but the dick waved him away and talked into the phone. "All right. All right. Goddamn it, keep trying. I don't know. I don't know. What are you supposed to be getting paid for?" He banged up the receiver.

"Mike, listen. My papers...."

Mike looked at him wearily, hardly seeing him. "Rosey, go pick yourself out a chair and plant your ass in it. Stop bothering everybody."

Rosey bit his thumb at Mike. "I shoulda let the son of a bitch lay there. He was dead. But no—I gotta be a big hero."

Mike studied him sadly. Mike was chewing gum now and his jaws moved slowly sideways like a cow with a cud.

"I was figuring *you* might give me a break," mumbled Rosey, fighting mad. "But no—you gotta act like an Irishman!"

Mike ignored him, picked up the phone and began to dial a number, but he stopped dialling suddenly, slammed down the receiver, and stood up as a big grayhaired man in business clothes entered hurriedly, his hat wet from the rain. It was Captain Shellenbarger, the boss of Downtown.

There was loud conversation and then a wave of excitement passed over the room. Rosey felt nervous as the crowd of dicks parted and he saw the big, hard-faced captain looking at him. His hand shaking slightly, Rosey relit his stogie, stuck it into his mouth, and stood staring defiantly at the captain.

"Mike," called Shellenbarger, "take the kid over to the City Building. Captain Hargis's office. Wait there."

There were faint whistles of concern and amazement.

"Yes sir," said Mike; then he turned to Rosey. "Come on, Gyp-the-Blood."

But Rosey got mulish and tried to make a complaint to the captain, who said nothing, but merely stared grimly, and in a moment reached out, took the stogie from Rosey's lips, and threw it on the floor.

Rosey flared up at once. "What's the idea, you big bastard!"

Someone laughed inadvertently, then there was a deep silence as the captain threw an irritated look about the room.

Cursing under his breath, Mike took Rosey by the arm and hustled him out through the door.

"This is going to cost somebody," Rosey cried over his shoulder. "I'm gonna sue the city."

The door closed. The captain looked about him mildly, then sat down and took out a cigar. Four dicks sprang forward: two with lighters, two with matches. The captain let one of them light his cigar, then he puffed on it slowly, sighing.

"Well, boys," he said, "you can all relax. Go back to your gin rummy, or canasta. The Administration took this one away from us. It is now Hargis's baby."

"The hangman," said Coonan.

"Yeah," said Delahanty. "You fellows know that fat guy, Wesson—the political reporter down at the Hall? He wrote a song about Hargis called 'The Hangman Has No Friends.'"

There was a short, curt laugh, then one of the dicks said: "Well, this is a big one. I guess they want to grab the credit."

The captain looked about him, smiling slightly. "Maybe, maybe," he said, and though he spoke rather noncommittally, there was a note in his voice giving his men a clue that it was perhaps not a mere question of credit-grabbing but something more serious.

The dicks glanced at each other eagerly. As soon as the captain left they intended to talk this one out. They'd had many cases pulled away from them by the Hall and handed to Hargis, but heretofore, it had always been done after they'd flopped—according to the Hall. This case was hardly half an hour old!

The captain got up slowly and put on his hat. "I'll be home if you want me, Coonan. But I don't know what you'd want me for."

The captain went out, Delahanty holding the door for him.

"It's a rough deal," said Coonan, shaking his head sympathetically.

2

It was misting rain at Half Moon Beach, too, and things looked pretty dismal. Of course, things always looked pretty dismal at a summer resort after the first of September. The season was over, most of the cottages were empty, many of the concessionaires had shut up shop, but a few reluctant souls always tried to preserve summer by staying on, and at the big dance-hall on the pier a bored and listless orchestra was playing a waltz for twenty or thirty couples, the vast hall echoing like an empty train-shed.

Joe Boley, born Joseph Boleslayski, Captain Hargis's driver and righthand man, was sitting in a rocking-chair on the screened-in porch of the cottage looking sadly off across the lake and listening to the dance music which had a blurred and plaintive sound. Everything looked or sounded blurred in the misty, heavy air. Snake-like reflections from the dance-hall lights seemed to swim toward him over the black water. And the boulevard lights along the pier looked like giant dandelions, and appeared to sway. It was a sad, desolate night and Boley felt like hanging himself. And for what reason? *No* reason. He was in good health, had a little money, and a fair job. No reason at all.

But he was not too worried about his state of mind. He knew that he would not hang himself and that the feeling would pass. He lit a cigarette and sat thinking about how different he was from his boss, Roy Hargis. Smiling wanly, he tried to picture himself saying to Hargis: "Look, Roy. The music sounds sad across the water and the lights are all fuzzy, and I feel like hanging myself." He knew the look he'd get: one of mild contempt from narrow gray eyes without human warmth.

Roy had everything all figured out. It was just a game and he knew how to beat it. He never seemed to feel sad, silly, happy, or anything else; not even sore. Annoyed, yes; and once in a while contemptuous or irritated. But were these true emotions at all? Boley didn't know.

Yes, Roy had it all figured out. He was close-fisted to an extreme degree and had quite a lot of money in the bank for a guy in his position. Yet he was not naturally close-fisted: it was a system. And then he never paid for anything, except maybe his rent (he lived in one room in a cheap hotel), and his clothes; and even that was doubtful. Boley knew of three suits Sam Brod had made for him and given him.... And like tonight. He was having himself a ball, and all for free. A fifty-dollar girl from the Front, and somebody else's cottage: an alderman's to be exact. One of the big percentage boys on the Front had no doubt provided the girl, and she was a beaut, too, and young and playful.

Boley groaned to himself. After all, he had Myrt. But he was forced to admit that this party-girl of Roy's made Myrt look like something left over.

The girls were a system, too! You had one every so often, then you forgot about sex. Women had no power over you. They couldn't browbeat you, get you in a jam, marry you. It was quite a system. "Yeah," Boley said to himself, "quite a system. But how do I get to playing it? I couldn't afford the five-buck ones once a week and as for dolls like that Kit in there—wow!"

There had been a lot of talking and laughing earlier, but things had been quiet for quite a while. Boley rose and began to walk up and down the porch. It was really raining now; he could hear it hissing against the screen. The orchestra had stopped playing and far across the water, one by one, the lights of the dance-hall went out. He saw the headlights of cars swinging round as they left the pier.

Yeah. System! System! But it took a tough-willed, coldhearted guy like Roy to play one. No use for him. "No use for you, Boley, old kid," he told himself. "You're a real hit-or-miss guy. And then you've got a heart."

"Have I?" he wondered a moment later. "Or maybe I'm just mistaking not too much guts for a heart. Like Myrt. She irritates me. Why don't I give her the brush? Is it heart? Or am I scared of what Myrt might do?"

Just as he shrugged, bewildered, the phone rang inside. Cursing, Boley bolted through the doorway into the Hawaiian living-room and grabbed up the receiver. It *had* to be Lackey—he never sleeps day or night, Lackey, he never sleeps! But why would *he* call? Maybe some damned friend of the alderman's.

"Hello. Hello."

"Boley? It's me. Emmett. Sorry. Got to talk to Roy."

"Take it easy, Lackey. Roy's busy."

"I know, I know. But the City Hall's on fire, or almost. You know I wouldn't call if I didn't...."

"Sure, sure."

Emmett Lackey, Hargis's special investigator and stand-in, knew Hargis's habits as well as Boley did. One night a week Roy disappeared—to Half Moon Beach; to the Reservoir, or to the big town in the next county. Lackey never bothered him, though he envied him plenty. Poor old fumbling Lackey, six foot five and afraid of girls! Poor old silly, fumbling, bumbling Lackey.

"Wait a minute," said Boley, then he put down the receiver and started back to the bedroom, but the bedroom door opened and Roy looked out.

"Lackey—for God's sake?"

"Yeah, Roy. Wants to talk to you."

Roy stepped out into the Hawaiian living-room. He had on trousers and socks but no shirt. Although he was tall, slightly stooped and of linear build, he looked hard as iron in the half light; his narrow chest was not puny in the least and he had powerful biceps, thick strong wrists, and big hands.

He hurried to the phone. Boley turned to listen, but just then the doll put her head around the doorjamb.

"What's up, buster?" she called in a husky, low voice that sent a chill down Boley's spine.

"Phone," Boley stammered. "For Roy... he...."

The girl's long, thick blond hair was all tousled and she seemed to have nothing on. Boley turned his back on her.

"We go in now?" called the doll.

"Maybe. I don't know," said Boley, keeping his back turned.

At least he had enough self-possession to notice that Roy had banged up the receiver.

"We got to go in. Right now," said Roy, "and fast as we can get there."

"Bad night for stepping on it, but..." said Boley.

"I'm insured," said Roy with a curt laugh; then he called: "Kit—you insured?"

The tousled blond head was thrust round the doorjamb again.

"You must be kidding, slim. You think I want somebody waiting for me to die?"

"Smart girl," said Roy, then he pushed her back into the bedroom. "Throw 'em on fast, honey. I'll give you two minutes—then we go, ready or not."

The drive back slowly turned into a nightmare as the impending thunder-storm finally broke over them. Kit was in the back seat alone holding onto the strap in fear, as Roy kept urging Boley to step on it. Heavy rain crashed into the windshield as if somebody was throwing buckets of water at them. Thunder rumbled across overhead with a sound of doom; blue-white lightning, low in the sky, danced, dazzled, and threw two-pronged forks at the earth.

"What's the matter with me?" cried Kit in anguish. "I got leprosy?" Her face looked chalk-white as the lightning flashed again and again.

"Chrissake, can't she sit up here?" cried Boley in distress.

"Keep driving," said Roy curtly.

"But good God," Kit wailed, "I'm rolling around back here. And I'm scared to hell of lightning. I had a brother got hit once. He was pitching baseball."

"If the car gets hit, we'll all get it," said Roy.

"Please, please," cried Kit.

Boley's hands seemed to waver on the wheel. Roy glanced at him, then turned. "Okay, honey. Climb up. Come over the seat. We're not stopping."

With a cry of relief, Kit came scrambling over the seat. Her tight black dress went up to her hips. The car skidded, tires whining and slithering, and for a moment they moved down the road sideways, splashing water. Then, just as a terrific clap of thunder broke loose and Kit buried her face in Roy's shoulder, Boley got the car straight and back on the right side of the road.

"Pull down your dress, will you, for God's sake?" cried Roy. "You want to get us killed?"

"I jogged him when I came over, I think," said Kit.

"You sure did. Some jog, eh, Boley?"

But Boley said nothing. He kept his eyes on what he could see of the road. The white line rushed at him interminably through the rain and soupy mist. They all fell silent. Then thunder rolled far off, harmlessly.

"Say," said Kit, "what is thunder anyway?"

"What now? A quiz program?" asked Roy.

"No, I mean it. I always wondered because I'm scared of lightning—and they go together: thunder and lightning, I mean."

"Seems to me you're scared of thunder, too."

"Please. Satisfy me. You look like a smart a guy. What is thunder?"

"You're easy satisfied, baby. Okay. Lightning makes a vacuum, and the atmosphere or the wind or something rushes back into it and makes a hell of a racket. That's thunder. And thunder never killed anybody yet."

"No kidding? Sure? Boy, I'll win me some bets with that. Nobody seems to know. I been asking for ten years, ever since I was nine years old and my brother got hit."

"Killed?"

"No. Just knocked him flat. He was kind of silly for a while. But he's all right now."

"How can you tell?"

"Oh, a wise guy! Say, why are we going so fast? Somebody after us?"

There was no reply, and the girl looked from one to the other, then fell silent.
From time to time lightning streaked along the horizon, thunder crashed, and
Kit would make a wild grab for Roy and bury her head in his shoulder. But he
seemed almost completely unaware of her presence.

Little by little, the rain slackened. Ahead of them loomed the city. They passed
through sleeping suburbs, and shuttered shopping-centers. The lightning still
flashed and the thunder rumbled, but Kit made no more grabs for Roy. She was
back in the big town now. Out in the open country things were different, ter-
rifying!

"Make the Savoy," said Roy.

Boley turned. "Why?"

"So Kit can pick up a cab. We got no time to trundle her home."

"Well, that's a hell of a note," said Kit. "I live to bejesus and gone from the
Savoy and it'll be just my luck to get a smart-aleck driver."

"I guess you can look after yourself," said Roy.

In a short while, the Savoy, a huge expensive river-front hotel on the edge of
town, loomed before them at the end of a street.

"Anyway," said Kit, as the car pulled up at the all-night taxi stand, "I found
out about thunder."

The rain had stopped, and the fine mist was falling again.

Roy handed her some money as she crawled out over his knees. "Two bucks,"
he said. "That ought to get it."

"Yeah," said Kit. "It's just about two bucks from here to my place. Goodbye,
you spender."

Roy said nothing. Boley looked past Roy out the car window at the beautiful young blond standing there in the mist getting her pretty hair wet. He felt
like hanging himself again.

"Good night, baby," he said in a husky voice. Roy glanced at him, but made
no comment.

3

They saw the Chief's car parked near the front of the vast apartment-house
garage as Boley eased the sedan carefully down the long, wet cement ramp. Nick
Gray, the Chief's driver, was leaning against a pillar, smoking a cigarette, and
talking with a garage hand in a white jumper.

Gray waved at them as they got out, a half salute, then he turned to the house-
phone on the pillar and made a call.

"Everybody's got the jumps tonight—real impatient," Gray explained. "I told 'em you were coming up."

"You stay here, Boley," said Roy, making no reply to Gray's statement, but merely raising his eyebrows.

Roy disappeared around the corner of a long cement corridor, on his way to the elevators.

Nick Gray offered Boley a cigarette, lit it for him. "Where you guys been—catting? The Chief's been rousting Lackey all over the place. This is a real big one."

"Yeah," said Boley.

Gray considered him thoughtfully for a moment. "What's it like working for a son of a bitch like that?" A pause. Gray shifted slightly. "I'm just asking for information. I work for one, too. But a different kind."

"The Chief?"

"Yeah. He's the kind who don't know straight up. So he's the Chief. So a guy's got to have friends—pull."

"Yeah," said Boley.

"You're a talkative bastard, Polack."

Boley's small, slanted blue eyes flashed slightly, then he lowered them and mildly contemplated his cigarette. Gray studied him, then said: "The 'Polack' don't mean nothing. What you sore about? Like you calling me 'Mick'."

"Yeah," said Boley.

In a moment, Gray turned away impatiently, got into the front seat of the Chief's car, slammed the door, turned on the overhead light, and began to read a magazine.

Boley leaned against the pillar, puffing on his cigarette. Always the pump. Always these police regulars trying to get him to talk about Roy. They hated Roy's guts. He'd gone from nothing to captain—had never really been on the force at all. Gray's boss, the Chief, Tom Smith, had been on the force for thirty-five years, and had risen slowly through all the regular grades. But the Chief was an Administration man, too, and seemed to hold no animosity to Roy, though he hadn't the slightest say-so over him.

Boley had heard all the talk about Roy. Oh So Low, the Hatchet Man! The Administration's private gunman! Chad Bayliss' pratt-boy! The political pet who got all the backing and all the plums! Etc., etc. The talk was partly the result of envy and resentment, but Boley had to admit that there was more than a little truth in it.

Roy did as he pleased without supervision or discipline. His nominal boss was Police Commissioner Prell, but the Commissioner was too busy juggling his big real estate holdings to pay much attention to Roy, who had a private office in the City Building, one of the best detectives in the area, Emmet Lackey, for an assistant, a couple of young cop secretaries, and himself, an old Downtown homicide dick, now hardly more than a chauffeur, to run errands and stand by—endlessly to stand by.

Roy had been an Army Cop in World War II—an officer, with a great record. After the war, somebody had introduced him to the big political boss, Chad Bayliss—and that was it. The Administration had a tight grip on the city—had been in power nearly twenty years; but occasionally unfortunate crises arose which caused grave misgivings, civic outcries, and even open rebellions. Bayliss was no one for leaving things to chance. He needed an expert troubleshooter, untainted by police politics, police methods, and perverse loyalties. Roy was the man he'd been looking for.

"Yeah," said Boley to himself, "Roy's the man, all right."

He tossed his cigarette away, then stepped on it. Big Nick Gray had decided he didn't want to read a magazine after all. He got out of the Chief's car.

"Want a drink, Boley? Liquor, coffee, something? Colored boy here we can send out. We may be stuck some time."

"Yeah, Nick," said Boley. "Coffee."

Chad Bayliss's apartment at the Stoneham was large and sumptuous. It was on the fifteenth floor and there were huge view-windows in the living-room.

But tonight no one was paying any attention to the mammoth, rain-bound city sprawling endlessly below them.

Tom Smith, the Chief, a big, calm-faced, gray-haired man, who looked enormously strong and fit in spite of his years—he admitted to sixty—was sitting on the edge of a brocaded chair, obviously ill-at-ease in these surroundings, saying little, and that in a low, gruff, embarrassed voice, and from time to time nervously scratching his chin and smoothing his hair.

Commissioner Prell, a short, slender, wiry-looking man in his middle fifties could not sit still and moved from chair to chair, and occasionally looked at the pictures on the walls, fingered the expensive knick-knacks, and kept taking off his horn-rimmed glasses and putting them back on.

But Prell and Smith were almost imperturbable in comparison with Chad Bayliss, who swung from violent and profane denunciations to tears, actual tears, causing Roy to lower his eyes and stare in grim embarrassment at the oriental carpet.

From time to time Bayliss's tired-looking blond wife—a faded beauty—brought her husband a cup of coffee, and said in a worried voice: "Drink that now, daddy. Drink it up."

Bayliss would glance at her in violent irritation, but would drink the coffee without comment. He was a big, robust man, about fifty, with curly dark hair, a red, rather congested-looking face, and liquid, emotional dark eyes which flashed wildly with an almost insane intensity when he was angry. He was, Roy knew, a tough driver, ruthless, unscrupulous, hard-boiled, but over-emotional, sentimental at times, and always in danger of running off the rails, although so far he'd been sure-fisted, and also maybe a little lucky, in his management of the Administration, which he had inherited ten years ago from his better-known brother, Al Bayliss.

Roy hadn't known Chad then. But he'd heard that after his brother died of a stroke at the dinner table, Chad had refused to eat for days, and had suffered so badly from insomnia and general nervousness that he'd been taken to a sanatorium and treated for two months, the newspapers giving out the story that he was vacationing at Coronado, in Southern California.

Now he'd had another bad shock. His best friend, Frank Hobart, nationally-known lawyer, Administration favorite, and millionaire, had been ruthlessly shot down on a city street like a friendless dog.

"Here, daddy, drink this," said Bayliss's worried wife.

He took the cup with shaking hand, then he looked up at her. "Merle, go to bed, for God's sake. I'm all right. I'm just so goddamned mad...!"

He was in evening clothes, with his coat off, and his tie untied. His evening shirt was wilted and blistered. He demolished it now by spilling half the cup of coffee down the front as he tried to drink it. He jumped up, cursing, and flung the cup and saucer across the room.

"Oh, God, daddy!" cried Merle. "My rug!" She put her hands to her face and burst into tears.

There was an appalled silence in the big, well-lit richly-furnished living-room and they could all hear the rain tapping at the glass of the view-windows, see it running down like tears.

Bayliss, getting hold of himself, was trying to soothe his wife. "There, there, baby. I'm sorry. There, there."

Roy glanced at Merle Bayliss then lowered his eyes. He had heard her referred to as Miss America of 1902—a dirty dig. Actually she was about forty, tall and stately, with a pretty, snub-nosed, rather vacuous face, which was beginning to sag. He'd also heard it said that during the first years of their marriage she'd given "daddy" considerable trouble, making eyes at the boys. Now this was a thing of the past, or so he'd heard. Chad had broken her spirit. Might be, Roy considered. Chad could be very rough going, even for a man.

"Oh, God," sobbed Merle. "My beautiful rug!"

"There, there, baby," soothed Chad, but with a note of irritation in his voice now. It was obvious that he was sick and tired of the rug business.

"I'm going to bed," wailed Merle. "I don't care what happens to you, daddy, after what you did—ruining my beautiful new oriental rug! I'm going to bed."

She ran out, sobbing. Chad looked after her, violently irritated; made a move to follow her, then changed his mind and sat down. "As if I couldn't buy another rug, or fifty of 'em," he grumbled.

But he was calmer now, and big Tom Smith heaved a sigh of relief. Prell polished his glasses for the tenth time and pretended to look at the big oil painting of Merle Bayliss which hung over the fire-place.

"Better off in bed, anyway," Chad grumbled. Then he looked up. "Did you ever notice—you fellows—that women can never tell what's important from what isn't? Frank Hobart's dead, and she's worrying about a goddamned oriental rug that we probably got overcharged two hundred per cent for!"

"Yes," said Prell, judiciously, putting on his glasses and peering thoughtfully at Bayliss. "You're right, Chad. Quite right. And very well put."

Tom Smith's contribution to the conversation was a loud sigh. Roy shifted about uncomfortably. Get to the point, he wanted to say, for the love of God, get to the point!

Now Bayliss looked at him speculatively. "How much do you know about Frank Hobart?"

Roy stared at the oriental carpet in silence for a moment, then he asked: "What kind of an answer do you expect to that question?"

Bayliss wagged his head impatiently. "Never mind the caginess, Roy. It's all in the family. We've got a problem, a serious problem. Speak up."

"Well, I know he made a fortune selling the land for the new high school building."

Big Tom Smith stared, open-mouthed. This was news to him. Prell coughed uncomfortably behind his hand and nervously adjusted his glasses. Bayliss flushed angrily. "Now how in hell, may I ask, Roy, did you get that little bit of information? And why did you bring it up?"

Roy dodged. "You asked me what I knew."

"Yes," said Bayliss, "I did. But that wasn't what I meant, exactly." Now he spoke with heavy sarcasm. "Are you suggesting a member of the School Board was not cut in and knocked him off? Or maybe a slighted real estate firm? Say, Abstein and Preston?"

Prell laughed uncomfortably. Abstein and Preston, Inc. was the oldest, richest, and most conservative real estate company in the state.

"No," said Roy. "I don't know why he was knocked off. If you know, tell me, and I'll get busy right away."

"The point is," said Bayliss, looking about him at Prell and Tom Smith, "we want you to get very busy. Very busy. But, Roy, we don't want you to show any actual results. That's why we took this away from Shellenbarger."

"All right," said Roy. "But I've got to know what I'm doing. If I got it straight, you know who killed him, and you don't want it to get in the papers, or be known at all. Am I right?"

"Practically," snapped Bayliss.

"All right. This is a big one. Every bird-dog on every newspaper will have a nose to the trail. You understand? So I've got to show some phony results. But I might put my foot in it, and bark up the *right* tree just out of general efficiency—so... who killed him?"

There was a long silence. Merle Bayliss appeared in the hall doorway wearing a beautiful red velvet dressing-gown and with a white ribbon in her hair. Prell eyed her appreciatively, then coughed and adjusted his glasses.

"Daddy," she called, "I'm going to bed. Sorry I was bad, but...."

"That's all right, honey," said Bayliss, wearily, then he got up, walked over to her, and they both disappeared down the hall.

"A very beautiful young woman," said Prell.

Roy, who was thirty-five, glanced at Prell in surprise. *Young.* Was he kidding?

Tom Smith nodded emphatically in agreement. "Yes," he said, "a very beautiful young woman."

"Oh, well," thought Roy, "maybe by the time I'm fifty-five or sixty one like that will look young to me."

Bayliss came back smoking a cigar and flung himself into his chair. "She says I'm to apologize for the way she acted," he grumbled. "So I apologize—and to hell with it. Look, Roy. Since you've brought up something extraneous like the high school deal—which isn't as dark as it looks... Prell will back me up on that...."

"Oh, certainly, Chad; certainly," said the Commissioner.

"...all right," Bayliss went on. "Since you brought that up, it seems plain you know quite a bit more than you are saying. Stuff more in your own sphere of interest, you might say. So... Roy?"

"I guess you mean the wire-service deal."

Bayliss winced; Prell coughed and adjusted his glasses; Chief of Police Smith sighed and looked down at his big feet. "Yes," said Bayliss, "that! Frank dealt with some very bad boys on that one. Big out-of-town boys. And he called the tune. He made them knuckle under. He told them just how it was to be handled and what our... well, our emolument was to be."

"Our what?"

"Take! Take, for Christ's sake!" cried Bayliss, angrily. "Don't you understand English?"

"I see," said Roy, mildly. "I'll remember that word. You clip a guy, and what *you* get is an emolument. What *he* gets is a lousy split."

Bayliss regarded Roy speculatively for a long moment. "Look, Roy. We didn't clip anybody. This is our town. The money spent here is *our* money. The books couldn't run without the wire-service, so they pay. But do you suppose we want millions going out of town? So... we asked for, insisted on, and got our emolument. But it wouldn't look good in the papers."

Roy sat lost in thought for quite a while. The wind had sprung up and was throwing the rain at the big view-windows. Thunder rolled far off, like wagons over a wooden bridge. Prell, fumbling nervously, dropped his glasses and almost stepped on them. The Chief sighed heavily and looked down at his ankle-high black shoes which had a mirror-like shine to them.

"What makes you so sure you got the right angle on this killing?" Roy asked.

"First," said Bayliss, "the men we mentioned gave in, it's true, but they never liked the set-up, and they never knew anything about Frank's backing. They knew he was a big lawyer, rich, and all that, and must have a powerful fix, but they didn't know what the fix was, or *how* big. Second, look how he was killed. Strictly hoodlum stuff."

"I'll tell you more about that later," said Roy. "But at least I know what to avoid. All right. But, Chad, you understand I've got to put on quite a show. Not only for the newspapers. But also for Downtown."

"I know." Bayliss looked about him. "We all know."

"Okay," said Roy, rising. "I guess that gets it."

Bayliss got up and shook hands with Roy. "I'm sorry about this in a way. Frank was my best friend. I'd like to see the so-and-so that killed him hang. I'd hang him myself with pleasure. But...."

"Yes," said Prell, "it is all very unfortunate."

"You'll get your show," said Roy.

As Roy emerged from the cement corridor into the apartment-house garage, Boley, who was leaning against the wall, smoking and reading a newspaper, glanced up at once, and jerked his thumb over his shoulder in a warning gesture. Looking beyond him, Roy saw the City Hall reporter, Perce Wesson, a hard-faced fat man, talking with Nick Gray.

Roy compressed his lips and walked past them followed by Boley.

"Hello," called Wesson. "How's tricks?"

Roy ignored him and got into the car. Boley went round to the driver's seat and jumped in. Wesson followed them, moving with surprising speed and agility for a man of his weight.

"Not even a 'no comment'?" he gibed.

"Well, if it ain't 'gorblimey,'" said Roy, pretending that he'd just noticed Wesson. "No comment on the 'no comment.'"

"Things are tough all over," said Wesson, who was of English origin but had come into the Midwest twelve or fifteen years ago from western Canada. "I see by the paper where the boys put the fix in at a beauty contest in New York. It's getting so bad, pretty soon a kid will have to know somebody before he can get his scout-badge."

"Gorblimey, you're right."

"Got any idea who spoiled Frank Hobart's profile and his evening?"

"You been demoted? Seems to me I heard you were a political writer now."

"Hargis—look, it's me; the Toast of Whitechapel. You think this hasn't got something to do with politics?"

"What?"

"Gorblimey," said Wesson, "'e's off 'is blooming, bleeding chump—'e is—'Argis!'"

"Cut the patter. If you know who knocked Frank Hobart off, I'm listening. You could help me out a lot. I just went on the case."

"No theories?"

"No theories." Roy turned to Boley. "All right. Run over him if necessary."

"What!" cried Wesson. "And put dents in the fenders of a car that belongs to the taxpayers!"

Boley drove off. Wesson stood looking after the car for a moment, then he walked back to Nick Gray, humming to himself the song he'd composed, "The Hangman Has No Friends."

"Quite a character," he observed.

"Yeah," said Nick, who was as wary with Wesson as Boley had been with him.

"Does he know something? Own somebody? Have a relative in a high place? Nepotism, in short."

"What?" Nick demanded, looking bewildered.

"How do you explain him?"

"I don't," said Nick. Then he turned away hurriedly. "Go hide some place, will you, for Christ's sake? Here comes the Chief."

But Wesson braced the Chief with effrontery. Good old Chiefie, who was a nice, pliable, thick-skulled figurehead!

"Party upstairs?" he demanded. "I keep seeing you big, important guys coming out."

"Please, Wesson—no jokes," said the Chief, climbing wearily into the back seat of his car and sinking down with a sigh.

"A quote maybe?"

"It's out of my hands. That is, I mean—it's been assigned to Captain Hargis."

The car drove off. Wesson stood watching it climb the ramp. "Chieftie," he said aloud, "I think you had it right the first time."

4

Emmett Lackey, Hargis's special investigator, sat at his desk in the old City Building, looking out the window at the misty, black, windy night. The neon signs were all blurred and distorted, and it was so dark that the tops of the big buildings seemed to disappear into the sky.

Lackey was a huge man of about forty. He was not only excessively tall, six five or more, but also very wide and bulky, weighing just under three hundred pounds. And yet, in spite of his size, there was nothing formidable about him. He looked soft, slack, and weak. Small, evasive blue eyes peered out nervously at the world from behind old-fashioned, gold-rimmed glasses. His complexion was very fair, pink and white, and had an almost babyish look to it. His manner was conciliatory in the extreme and he always seemed to be trying to appease somebody. He was referred to by Wesson as 'the giant pygmy.'

But behind Lackey's weak smiles were strong emotions. He hated both Wesson and Roy Hargis with violence. They were both tough, ruthless, successful in their adjustment to life, and, above all, they were both uncomfortably perceptive. In some intuitive way they were aware of Lackey's life-long inner struggle—the struggle he tried to mask by his kindness, his reasonableness, his ingratiation. Nothing came easy to Lackey. He was nervous, timid, shy, and suffered from an unconquerable feeling of personal inadequacy. His great size and bulk meant nothing to him. He'd never learned how to use it. With men like Roy Hargis and Wesson, he felt small, physically small.

Although he knew that he was rated one of the shrewdest detectives in the city, and was well aware that Roy Hargis, on advice from above, had picked him as assistant from a hundred possible choices, this gave him no feeling of self-confidence, and he felt no touch of the elation other men would have felt in his place. Earlier successes at his chosen trade had meant just as little.

It was not that he was misunderstood. Wesson and Roy Hargis both seemed to understand him too well, if anything. Understanding was not what he wanted. His trouble was loneliness. There was nobody in the world who gave a damn whether he came home or stayed away, whether he was sick or well, happy or sad. It seemed impossible for him to make friends. Boley was a case in point; Boley, the melancholy Slav. He had a fellow feeling for him. But Boley did not return the feeling. Boley brushed off all his advances, laughed at him even, taking his tone from Hargis.

And as for women.... At the thought, Lackey rose from behind his desk, sighing heavily, and walked slowly to the window and stood looking out at the drowned city.

Maybe all his feelings of weakness and inadequacy came from the fact that he had never had a woman in all his life. The mere fact was incredible, impossible, sadly but hilariously comical, and Lackey closed his eyes, as if to blot out an image, and flinched slightly. But what had he to offer a woman? In appearance he was grotesque, and caused ironic comment and merriment when he appeared. His manner was impossible, ludicrous—a mixture of false amiability and shyness: he was well aware of all this. Maybe if he hadn't been so aware...!

Several times, after long debates with himself, he had decided to approach a professional. But how did you go about it? That is, how did you go about it so that nobody under the sun would ever have any knowledge of it? He was morbidly sensitive to ridicule, and could imagine, wincing, the comments from his boss and from Wesson, if they ever found out, and they seemed to find out everything.

Mike Antonelli put his head in the door from the outer office. "Heard anything?"

Lackey pulled himself together with an effort and coughed nervously. Then he gave Mike a kindly smile. "Nothing more. Roy's on his way. Ought to be here. Why?"

"The poor sonsabitching kid's asleep out here. I'd like to let him go, but...."

"No, I'm very sorry," said Lackey. "We've got the transcript, I know. But I think Roy ought to... well, you understand, Mike. I'd like to let him go, too, poor kid."

"I'm getting calluses myself," said Mike, then he sighed and closed the door.

The phone rang on Lackey's desk. He picked up the receiver and an emotion-charged, almost hysterical voice began to yammer at him. "No, I'm sorry," said Lackey. "But he's not here. This is Lieutenant Lackey speaking. Hargis's assistant." The voice yammered on. Lackey's eyes lit up faintly. Putting his hand over the receiver, he threw the switch on the intercom on his desk and whispered into it: "Listen. You there? Trace this. Don't miss. Lackey." Then he spoke into the phone: "Yes, yes. This is all very interesting. I'll certainly bring it to the captain's attention. Now, please. Would you let me have that again, more slowly. Calm down now. More slowly, please." Lackey stalled, holding the man on the phone. Finally when he could stall no longer, he said: "Very kind of you. Thank you. Now would you like to leave your name and address so Captain Hargis can contact you? No? Well, I understand. Thank you again, sir."

As Lackey hung up, Creel, one of Hargis's young secretary-assistants, hurried in. He seemed excited.

"I traced it, Emmett. The call was made from Cipriano's."

Lackey's thick eyebrows rose slowly. Cipriano's was the most expensive and exclusive supper-club on Vanity Row. "But this is Monday," said Lackey. "Cipriano's is dark on Monday."

"How do you like that!" cried Creel. "What do we do?"

"I can't take responsibility on this. Captain'll be here in a minute."

Creel was grinning. "This is something! Something!"

They heard voices in the outer office and Lackey walked over and opened the door. The little newsboy, Rosey, was awake now and was standing in the middle of the anteroom with a cigar in his mouth, cursing Roy Hargis, who was looking at him with mild amusement. Roy turned to Lackey.

"Emmett, what about this kid?"

Lackey explained, and Roy nodded. "All right, Mike. Take him home. All the way. Pick up his goddamn papers, if there are any left. Do what ever he wants. Wait a minute. Did this leak, Mike?"

"To the newspapers? The kid as witness, you mean? No."

"All right. Let it stay that way." He turned to Rosey. "Just keep your mouth shut and your nose clean. We may need you later."

"From now on I keep my mouth shut," said Rosey bitterly. "I always keep my nose clean. I don't care how many more guys get it. Even if they fall right in front of me."

Roy laughed curtly and entered his office followed by Boley, who looked sad, weary, and spent. Creel nodded to Roy, then went down the hall and into another office. Lackey closed the door, then explained to Roy about the mysterious call from Cipriano's.

Roy glanced hurriedly at his wrist-watch. "Hell," he said, "it's after three o'-clock. They close tight at two."

"Anyway," said Lackey, "it's Monday night. Dark."

"That's right. Say, what did this guy sound like?"

"Nervous," said Lackey. "Mad. Kind of crazy. I don't know."

"Call Creel. I'll take him with me. Boley stays with you. He's got to put his feet up for a while."

Boley glanced at Roy in surprise. "Yeah. I'm bushed. How did you know?"

"I'm a detective, remember?"

"Yeah," said Boley, sadly. "I'm bushed. But you're the guy who ought to be bushed."

Lackey had just called Creel on the intercom. He now turned and listened eagerly, flushing slightly.

"No," said Roy. "A doll like that is stimulating."

"What a doll!" said Boley, sadly. "And her standing there all alone getting rained on. That's a sacrilege, or something."

Roy turned and glanced at Lackey, then he laughed. "When you going to let me get you fixed up, Emmett?"

Lackey laughed nervously and made a timid gesture of refusal. "Never. No, thanks."

Boley gave him an ironic glance, then sat on the desk and pushed his hat back. Taking out a handkerchief, he slowly mopped his brow, sighing.

"She was a dream. Real dreamy," said Boley. "The prettiest one I ever saw Roy have." Then turning, he told Lackey about Kit coming up over the seat and how the car had skidded and they'd almost got killed, and how when the lightning flashed, the beautiful doll had flung herself on Roy and hugged him and buried her head in his neck.

"Where's Creel, damn it?" cried Lackey, in sheep-like anger, his face flushed. "Now where is he?" He slapped the intercom key violently.

But at that moment, Creel came in, his hat jammed on sideways, his face eager. Creel was about twenty-five and very much interested in life in general and his work in particular. Roy Hargis awed and delighted him. What a break for little Lenny Creel when Roy had picked him as a helper!

Boley turned and scrutinized Lackey carefully. "What are you so het up about, Emmett?"

"As if we didn't know," said Roy, laughing. Then he turned: "Come on, Creel."

They went out. Lackey sank down into his swivel chair and stared in mild sadness at the top of his desk.

"He's what Wesson calls a human domino," Boley observed.

"Who?" Lackey demanded, glancing up foggily.

"Why, Roy. Just that ride in would have given most guys fits—not counting the girl. It gave me fits. I'm still all tight. We could have got killed half a dozen times. And look at him. Bouncing around."

"This girl...?" Lackey began. "She was frightened? Probably very young."

"Nineteen," said Boley, watching Lackey.

5

Commonwealth Street was short and peculiar. It ran for only five blocks, from the west bank of the river to a deadend one block beyond Blackhawk Boulevard. Near the river, Commonwealth was filled with commission houses, fish markets, and cheap saloons; then, as it traveled westward, came pawnshops and employment offices with blowsy bulletins; then two and three storey brick rooming-houses, with dim lights and crooked blinds, stretched almost to Blackhawk, where they were overshadowed and blotted out by the forty-storey Commonwealth Building. Beyond Blackhawk Boulevard and on to the deadend, Commonwealth really blossomed, and was referred to as Vanity Row.

Vanity Row ran for one block. In this block were three exclusive clubs—Cipriano's, the Gold Eagle, and Merlin's; there was also one of the finest and most expensive restaurants in the state—Weber's; and there were two beauty parlors where, as Wesson said, you were looked out unless you were a debutante or dowager from Riverview, or a mink-bearing Vanity Row whore. Glassman's, the Tiffany's of the Midwest, was at the corner of Blackhawk and Vanity Row. On the other corner was a Cadillac sales-room.

At night, the stylized neons of the Row glittered like expensive jewelry: rubies, emeralds, star-sapphires, diamonds. Just a glance at the façades kept most yokels out. If not, the headwaiters, and other major domos, soon had them in the street, suffering from feelings of awe and humiliation.

Wesson, who occasionally got drunk and abusive on the Row, was ejected regularly. He was not exactly a yokel and of course he had fairly good newspaper connections, all the same he was looked upon as an undesirable. Vanity Row made no special play for the newspapers, needing no publicity. The clubs never advertised, nor did Weber's. Nobody was inviting you to the Row. If you didn't belong there, stay away. The headwaiters were painfully superior autocrats. There was no appeal.

Now, except for the lights in Glassman's and the Cadillac sales-room, the Row was dark, and as deserted as if the street had been suddenly abandoned by the inhabitants in the face of an invading alien army. There was a ringing stillness from Blackhawk to the deadend, beyond which loomed huge office buildings, dark except for their elevator-shafts.

"Park it here," said Roy. "We'll see if we can get in the alleyway. If we drive down the Row we might give somebody a chance to run. Nobody drives down the Row this time of night except the street-sweepers."

Creel parked the car on Endicott, one block down from Blackhawk; they got out and hurried up a dark alley toward the rear of Cipriano's.

"How do you know they haven't gone already?" asked Creel.

"I don't," said Roy. "It's a chance."

At the back of Cipriano's there was a light. Roy peered in through the glass of the door, then suddenly grabbed the knob and rattled it loudly. Creel jumped, startled.

A scared black face appeared beyond the glass, eyes wide, showing a lot of white. Roy took out his badge and held it for the Negro to see. But the Negro was doubtful, his face working.

"You better open up," called Roy, harshly.

"I don't know, I don't know," said the Negro. "The boss, he...."

"I want to see the boss," cried Roy, quickly. "Open up or I'll kick it in."

The Negro took the chain off, and reluctantly opened the door. Roy went in quickly, followed by Creel. The big Negro had on an undershirt, and the lavender and gold uniform pants worn by the staff of Cipriano's. He looked sullenly at Roy and Creel.

"Boss back in his office?" Roy demanded sharply.

"He's busy right now. You sure-enough officers? Why you come in like this?"

"Back this way, is it?" asked Roy, starting hurriedly across the big dark room. Creel followed him.

"Look here," said the Negro. "You can't act this way. This is Cipriano's. You'll get yourself fired if you sure-enough are a policeman."

Roy heard talking and turned to the Negro. "All right, boy. You stay put. Understand? Right where you are. Come on, Len."

"Looks like it's me gets fired," said the Negro, glancing off sullenly after Roy and Creel.

They came out into a short but beautiful corridor which seemed to be lined with velvet and smelled pleasantly of expensive perfume. Pinkish indirect lights gave the place an eerily unreal look. The carpet seemed a foot thick and yielded softly as they walked over it. Several large, stylized nudes hung on the wall and half way down the corridor on a stand was a tall, attenuated, weird-looking figure of a nude woman, carved from black wood. A little further along was a door padded with turquoise leather; a silver plaque in the upper center read: Mademoiselle.

Roy pointed to the sign. "Even in a place like this, they have to do it," he said. "Revolting, isn't it?" Then he went over, opened the door and peered in, then he disappeared. Creel stood staring after him with amazement. In a moment, Roy reappeared. "Yep," he said. "It's just a can after all."

Creel laughed uneasily. He was young and romantically inclined. Roy was embarrassing him very much.

"I always wondered what one of those high-price femme johns looked like. Now I know."

They heard talking again, louder now. At the far end of the corridor was an-

other door; this one of plain blond wood, bearing in silver letters the sign:
PRIVATE.

Roy opened the door and went in. Creel followed. A short, dark, chunky, baldheaded man in his shirtsleeves jumped up from behind a desk and stared wildly. Just beyond him was a blond girl in evening clothes. Between them was a champagne bucket on a stand.

There was a moment of strained silence, then Roy showed his badge.

"You'll get busted for this," shouted the man, sputtering, furious.

"I was told you called me."

"I didn't call nobody."

"Okay, Mr. Sert. Suit yourself. But somebody called from here."

"Call traced, eh?"

"Yeah."

"You Hargis?"

Roy nodded and looked at the girl. She was slender and young and her eyes were woozy with champagne. The man followed the direction of Roy's gaze. "That's my wife," he said. "Tootsie, this is Roy Hargis."

"It's a pleasure I'm sure," said Roy.

"For who?" said the girl. "Drop dead."

"Now Tootsie."

"More champagne. Never expected to see a copper in this joint. You're slipping, pappa."

Creel was staring at the girl, open-mouthed. She looked like an angel and talked like a bum. Very confusing.

"Can I offer you gentlemen something?" asked the man.

"Gentlemen, my butt!" said Tootsie.

Roy began to laugh.

"Go on, laugh," said Tootsie. "With that face, a laugh won't hurt you none. More champagne, pappa."

As the man poured Tootsie's glass full he seemed to feel called upon to explain. "You see, we're on our honeymoon. Only been married three weeks. Tootsie's got a load on. Haven't you, honey?"

"That I have, pappa. That I have. But I won't get falling down on champagne. Don't worry. I'm very ladylike on champagne. On martinis, I promise you nothing."

"I'm Joe Sert," said the man. "I guess you know that. Well, I own this place."

"We own this place," Tootsie shouted, waving her glass. "We own it—Cipriano's. How do you like them apples! Two years ago I couldn't get in the front door. I was picture-girl at Headley's and getting my tookus pinched all over the place. Did I drink champagne then? I did not. Cheap gin."

"You could have got in if I'd seen you, Tootsie," said Joe Sert fondly, "and how!"

"Thanks, Joe. Thanks. You may not look it, but you're a gentleman."

Sert flushed slightly, and Roy looked down at the carpet to keep from laughing. Creel, completely bewildered, merely stared, fascinated by Tootsie.

Joe Sert, one of the old timers, was close to fifty now. In the early 'twenties he'd served time on three separate occasions for bootlegging. That was before the boys got things organized. After 1925 he never served a day, nor was he ever arrested again. At the time of the crash, he had over two million dollars in cash stashed away in various safety-deposit boxes. Since then, he'd been, as he said, on the legit, though at one time he'd operated a big gambling-joint at the Reservoir.

That was now a thing of the past, completely forgotten by Joe, who year by year grew more respectable and settled in his ways: a good citizen, a taxpayer (every nickel owed, he now boasted), and the owner of the finest and most exclusive supper-club in the city. A hundred per cent legit, Joe bragged, a hundred per cent!

Joe kept in the background. Only the real insiders knew that he owned Cipriano's. It was run by a glum-faced, impudent Italian named Attilio Gozza. Out front, Attilio was known as Caesar. The great Caesar, most independent, unappeasable, and insolent Maitre D' in the whole city. Rich women from Riverview approached him timidly, and were almost overcome if he was nice to them. Caesar could make you or break you on the Row.

He had a house on the river, a Cadillac, and a chauffeur. It was said that Joe paid him a nominal salary but that his tips came to almost a thousand dollars a week.

"More champagne, pappa," cried Tootsie. "It really goes down slick, then tickles." She giggled loudly.

Joe poured her glass full without a word of complaint, then he said: "Honeybaby, would you mind going into the next room for a little while? I got business."

"It's our honeymoon—for pity's sake! Business yet!" Tootsie rose uncertainly. She was tall and willowy, with a figure like a model. "You won't be long now, will you, pappa? If you are, I'm coming out and get this young guy here and make him come in and talk to me." She flashed Creel a blinding smile. He seemed to wilt slightly.

"It's all in fun you know, boys," said Joe, with a somewhat sickly look. "All in fun."

"Some fun!" cried Tootsie, whirling around in an access of animal spirits and almost falling down. "Oh, I feel great, wonderful, shupendous! You won't be long now will you, pappa?"

"I won't be long, baby."

Creel hurried over and opened the door for her, bowing slightly.

Tootsie destroyed him again with a smile, and patted his cheek. "You're *cute!*" she cried, then she went into the next room, and Creel shut the door quietly behind her.

"She's not used to drinking," said Joe. "It goes to her head."

"I see," said Roy, looking at the carpet.

Young Creel wiped his brow and pulled nervously at his collar.

Joe fussed about his desk for a moment, then sat down and began to twirl an empty champagne glass in his fingers. He seemed reluctant to speak. But finally he said: "Hargis, I guess I don't have to tell you I'm no fink."

"I know your reputation, Mr. Sert."

"Yeah. Well, back when I was just a young guy and kinda wild—you know how kids are!—I had a big rep for keeping my nose clean. I fell a couple of times, and after that the boys at Downtown used to throw the lug on me when there was trouble around. But never got nothing. I did ninety days once just because I wouldn't help the boys out. You see, I want you to understand."

Roy nodded slowly. He was anxious for Joe to get to talking but he knew it would be wiser to let him do it his own way. Although Joe was a legitimate business man now with not a shadow of suspicion of any kind against him, he still thought like a hoodlum. Only a rat cooperated with the police; only a rat finked!

"You see," said Joe, sighing, "Frank Hobart was the best friend a man ever had." Tears came to Joe's eyes and he compressed his lips and for a moment sat very still and stared down at the top of his desk as if trying hard to get himself under control.

Pretending to gaze off across the room, Roy observed Joe out of the corner of his eye. The old hood seemed obviously sincere in his regard for Hobart—as sincere as hardboiled Chad Bayliss had been; and as surprisingly so. Roy reflected that this Hobart man must have been quite a boy. He had only known him slightly: a tall, handsome, well-dressed, grayhaired man with a young face, who would have made a perfect shill for one of those whiskey pitches: definitely a Man of Distinction.

"Smart, too," Joe went on, "the smartest—and a real gentleman. I mean, real. Not a phony hair on his head. Not like most of these Vanity Row white-tie tramps. He was the real McCoy. Knew all about wine, food. Had his own table here. Came in for dinner almost every night. Whether he did or not, we kept the table for him. Had a sign on it: reserved for Mr. Hobart. Caesar used to wait on him, himself. Only man in town Caesar ever played waiter for—except that rich old son of a bitch up in Riverview—what's his name?"

"Spalding?"

"Yeah. Old Man Spalding—and he didn't know beer from champagne nor chicken from veal. You could give him anything and he'd eat it. Not Mr. Hobart. Pietro, the chef, would cook Mr. Hobart's dinner himself, then he'd have the shakes till he heard how Mr. Hobart liked it. Knew all about sauces. Used to give Pietro recipes. Traveled all over Europe, eating at the swell joints. Me— I don't know from lamb chops."

"Me either," said Roy, encouragingly.

Joe stood up. He seemed excited. "Hargis! Look! How could a man like that let this big, impudent broad get his tail in the door... I'm asking you. How could he?"

Roy masked his sudden interest by keeping his eyes lowered and searching for his cigarettes. "I don't know, Mr. Sert. Strange things happen to guys." Roy remembered Tootsie and wondered how a sophisticated old hood like Joe Sert had ever let her get his tail in the door. But as a rule men were not critical of themselves, only of others.

"I know her well," cried Joe, banging the desk. "She used to swing it at me when she first went to work here, but I didn't bite. I could see in her eyes she was a bad one. She's a bad one, all right. She killed him. By Christ, as sure as I'm a man and no mouse, she killed him." He banged the desk violently.

The inner door opened, and Tootsie put her head in. "Pappa," she chided, "stop yelling at those men and calm down. You know what the doctor said." She turned to Creel and gave him a lovely, woozy smile. "Pappa's got blood pressure."

Joe's face worked for a moment, then his eyes showed concern and he sat down and tried to calm himself. Tootsie came over to him, took out his handkerchief, and gently wiped his forehead. "Thanks, baby. Thanks," said Joe. "Now you go back, please. I'll only be a minute."

Tootsie smiled vaguely, then she fumbled for the champagne bottle. Roy got up to help her and poured her glass full, finishing the bottle.

"Thanks," said Tootsie, studying Roy. "What are you doing on the force? A gentleman like you."

Roy bowed ironically. Tootsie turned and looked at Creel. "And him, too," she went on. "He's cute." Then a shadow of doubt crossed her pretty face, and she looked into her glass. "Or maybe it's just this stuff. Yeah, maybe that's it." She turned to Joe. "Now pappa, remember. Keep calm. You've got blood pressure."

Joe nodded sombrely. Tootsie moved uncertainly to the door. Creel sprang into action at once, opened the door for her, bowed slightly.

"Such service from the coppers. It don't figure. My, my," said Tootsie as she disappeared again. Creel closed the door after her—rather reluctantly, Roy thought.

"So she drinks," said Joe, as if to himself. "She's the kindest-hearted girl I ever met in fifty years. All she worries about is looking after me. I got big insurance. If she was a bitch like that... like that...." Joe rose again, sputtering. "I mean, she'd be worrying how to knock me off. Or trying to get me het up all the time so's I'd pop."

"Yes," said Roy. "Mr. Sert, does Tootsie know anything about this business?"

Joe was silent for a moment, grew calmer, and sat down. Finally he spoke. "Hargis, strictly speaking, Tootsie knows from *nothing*."

Roy wanted to laugh, but refrained. Joe wasn't as bemused as he'd thought.

It was Tootsie's kindheartedness that had got him. And why not? Joe was heading toward old age, and probably knew it.

Making up his mind suddenly, Joe pulled open a desk drawer, took out a picture, and shoved it across the desk to Roy. It was a big professional photo, a shiny print. Roy glanced at it: a fat-faced brunette, big. He glanced up at Joe, whose face was working. Then he looked at the picture again and all of a sudden the unconventional, unexpected beauty of the placid, almost expressionless face struck him hard. It was as if somebody had hit him on the jaw out of the blue.

"Jesus!" he exclaimed.

"You too, eh?" said Joe, grimly. "That cow!"

Creel was looking over Roy's shoulder. Roy glanced at him. Creel seemed to get no reaction at all. He shrugged.

"What do you think, Len?"

"Looks fat. I don't know. Just a face."

Roy was amazed, but said nothing. Joe nodded and glanced gratefully at Creel. "Yeah," said Joe. "Just a face. Just a body. I don't get it. Mr. Hobart, he's been a widower for twenty years. He's been around. He's had his pick."

"I'll keep this," said Roy.

"I got plenty more if you want them," said Joe. "She was trying to promote herself when them were took. Singer, something—I don't know. Couldn't sing a note. My damn fool piano player was coaching her—he knew better. Probably trying to get in the kip with her. Everybody was trying to, I must admit. But not me. I had her number—a no-good, heartless, conniving bitch!"

"Name?" asked Roy curtly.

"Her name is Olla Vinck—and it suits her. She goes by the alias Ilona Vance."

"Alias?"

Joe wagged his head impatiently. "I mean, it's a name she made up. I don't mean she's got no record, nothing like that. At least none I ever heard of. But she's an operator."

"I believe you said she worked here. What did she do?"

"She was one of the cigarette girls. Caesar hired her. He thought she was a beauty. And I must admit in that costume... well...." Joe fumbled about in a desk drawer and came up with another picture. It was a flash, taken in the club. The girl was looking straight into the camera with a petulant, pouting expression. She seemed very tall. Her legs were incased in long, sheer, dark stockings, like tights; they were the most beautiful and exciting legs Roy had ever seen. Her eyes were pale in color, gray or very light blue, and seemed to clash with her coal-black hair. Her face was wide, her cheekbones high. There was a suggestion of... what? Delicate brutality, maybe. Sullenness, for sure. Her lower lip was thick, and rather babyish.

"Look what some silly son of a bitch wrote on the back," said Joe.

Roy turned the picture over. Letters printed in pencil read: The Dark Venus.

"Who?" asked Roy.

"God knows," said Joe, wagging his head impatiently.

"You want to tell me about her?"

"Sure," said Joe, grimly. "And I want her pinched and I want her put away. She killed the best guy I ever knew in my life, and I've known quite a few. Okay. Caesar hired her. Some cheap boulevard hustler introduced her to Caesar. Where she'd been, nobody knows. I always figured she'd been a professional, a big time hooker—but I got no proof. Caesar is a happily married man with six kids; he don't play. It's old stuff to him. He just thought she'd be good for the place. And she was. I never seen so many heated up guys. I'll say this for the big cow, she knew how to handle 'em. No limousine ride, flattery and a couple of orchids for her. The snobs never fazed her. When she found out I owned the place, she made a few passes, and smart ones—no dropping the pants, like some of these young bums... but she give me the shivers. I been took in my time, so I know the answers. She passed it, calm as you please. Smart. See what I mean? Then Mr. Hobart began to let his dinner get cold. The chef was going to hang himself—thought he was slipping. Then I saw her talking to Mr. Hobart every night—and he was giving her big tips and telling her to hide 'em. We cut in on all the tips, in case you don't know."

"I see," said Roy, noncommittally. He knew damn well.

"One night, fifty dollars. Caesar told her to keep it. But when I heard about it, I said no! No exceptions. We had two other girls working. Ain't fair! Both of 'em better looking than her, by God! Or I thought so....

"Well, about this time she decides she's going to cash in on her looks and be a singer. Bob Dumas—he's my piano-player, and a nice quiet handsome boy—but nuts, kinda—well, he takes to coaching her. She can't sing for knucklebones. Flat. And she's got a voice—Christ—like a baritone, lower than Crosby's. Awful!

"I think she was trying to impress Mr. Hobart—make him think she was ambitious, not just a big trollop who wanted to lay in bed and have some rich guy keep her. Well, believe it or not, he fell for it. He sets her up. She's got a big apartment, diamonds, furs—you know, the usual." Joe sighed loudly and shrugged. "Well, that's it...."

"Apartment address?" asked Roy.

Joe gave it to him. "H'm," said Roy. "Ashton Terrace. Pretty plush."

"Yeah. All plush."

"This Dumas—address?"

"I ain't got it," said Joe. "He lives in some fleabag. He'll be here tomorrow night at six. Generally plays in the Tangiers Room till one, sometimes later."

"Thanks. Now, Mr. Sert. We got a few facts. But we're still out in leftfield. Why would she kill him?"

"Well," said Joe, "first, she's got a temper like a wildcat with poison ivy. A waiter here, Giuseppe—inoffensive kind of Italian with an accent, but always ribbing. She belted him, broke a tray full of dishes—knocked him *out*...." Joe looked about him in wonder.

"No kidding?" said Roy.

"Knocked him colder than Kelsey's. Had to restrain her. She really blew."

"So...?"

"Well, lately—last few months—Mr. Hobart's been getting drunk regular. Mr. Hobart, of all people! He and the big broad would come in and sit at his table and never say a word to each other all evening. When they did talk they fought. Giuseppe—he hated her, see—he used to try to listen, and sometimes he'd get an earful. Seems the broad was two-timing Mr. Hobart. Or he thought so. Then they had one big fight in here. It was pretty rough. We couldn't stand stuff like that in Cipriano's. You know how it is. Caesar wouldn't say a word to Mr. Hobart, though. So I had to. It was goddamn embarrassing, me telling a man like Mr. Hobart how to behave. He didn't come back for nearly a month. It was pitiful. He was all alone, drank himself silly. Caesar drove him home, personally...." Joe sighed and stood up. "First, she ruined him, that big cow! Then she knocked him off!"

"Why did she knock him off, though?" Roy probed.

Joe swallowed, rubbed his hand over his face, seemed about to speak, then seemed to change his mind, and sat down again.

"What's the motive?"

"Maybe he left her," said Joe, lamely. "Maybe he cut off the money. Maybe they got into a jealous fight. How do I know? But I'm telling you straight—she did it."

Roy got up, nodded. "All right. Thanks, Mr. Sert. I'll look into this. You don't mind if we have a talk later if necessary?"

"No," said Joe. "But no publicity—please."

"You'll never be mentioned if I can help it. Come on, Len."

They turned to go. Tootsie opened the inner door and came in, smiling, gay, very tight. "By, by, boys," she cried, waving her empty glass. "It's been nice seeing you." She singled Creel out. "By, by, cutie."

"Goodbye, Mrs. Sert," said Creel, politely.

"Oh, God!" cried Tootsie. "I'm always forgetting. You see, we just got married. That's me. Mrs. Joseph Sert, Esquire. How do you like them apples!"

"That's you, baby," said Joe with a weary, indulgent smile.

6

Chad Bayliss did not want to discuss anything as important as the ramifications of the Hobart case over his apartment house phone. The Administration had enemies. Two years back there had been a rash of wire-tapping, and an expert electrician, caught at it and refusing to name his bosses, had been handed a stiff sentence by an Administration judge.

Chad drove to meet Hargis outside the Rollerdrome. The place was closed at this hour and in a part of town that was almost deserted at night. All about loomed gas tanks, warehouses, junk yards. It was past four thirty a.m. The rain had stopped and a brisk east wind was blowing thick, dark cloud-masses across the sky. There was a smell of fall in the air. Far to the eastward, a few stars were showing.

Chad's wife had insisted on coming with him. She sat huddled into a corner of the back seat, wrapped in a big fur coat. She was wearing a dark beret. Her face looked pale and strained.

Creel stayed in the other car. Roy and Chad walked up and down the deserted sidewalk, which was shadowed by the huge, arcaded porch of the Roller-drome. Once a tough-looking bum stepped out from no place and asked for money to buy himself a drink. Roy was going to collar him and kick the impudence out of him, but Chad intervened and gave the bum a fifty-cent piece.

Roy shrugged it off, but didn't like it. "I should have vagged him," he explained. "Next thing, he'll drag a girl up some alley. He's a bad one."

"Stop being a policeman," Chad said mildly. "We've got serious business. All right now, Roy. I've got the picture. But what's the matter with Old Joe Sert— blowing his top?"

"Joe's letting his emotions run away with him. But the girl's a mighty fine pigeon for our purposes. If you don't mind a little scandal in regard to Frank Hobart's name, that is."

"His wife's been dead for years. One thing a man's got to have is women. Wouldn't be much of a scandal. Besides, he's got no kids, nobody. Just keep this in mind. As you know, Frank was my best friend. But I'm not worrying about Frank. I'm worrying about the Administration."

"Did you ever see this girl?"

"No. I guess he left her home when he called on us."

"Was he drinking heavily the last few months or so?"

"Yes, he was, and it worried the hell out of me. He got lushed up at the apartment one night and got out of line for the first time since I've known him. I couldn't believe it. He was abusive as hell. Merle went to bed in tears. Charley Prell was there. I thought he was going to pass away he was so surprised. You see, Frank was a real gentleman, from a fine old family—the last of 'em. Might've been what Joe Sert said—the drinking, I mean. Sometimes bad dames get the whip hand over the unlikeliest guys. Of course, that doesn't mean she killed him. We know who killed him, Roy, and why." There was a brief pause, then Chad went on. "Actually, this is a real break for us. Okay, Roy. Go to it. It'll make the headlines. It'll be a big one. Meanwhile, in the background, we'll figure out how to handle our little difficulty with the out-of-town boys. I've already had a feeler. There will be a conference this week sometime, I think.

But that's not your worry. Get on the ball."

"Okay, Chad. Couple more things. I know Joe Sert's been legitimate for a long time now. I think he's straight. But I don't like to pass up any possibilities. Could he be fronting for this outside mob? Trying to pin it on the girl?"

"Not a chance," said Chad, emphatically.

"All right. Now here's a matter of policy. The girl lives at the Terrace. I don't want to go busting in there. It's strictly four hundred. Why put them on the spot? What do I do?"

Chad whistled briefly. "The Terrace, eh? Okay. I'm going right home. I know the manager. I'll phone him, get him out of bed. You stall around for, say, half an hour, then go over. The manager, or somebody, will be at the desk. No guests will be around at this hour. The whole thing will be nice, polite, and quiet."

"Unless some newspaper bird-dog gets wind of it. Then there will be hell to pay."

"There'll be hell to pay later. We can only do so much for the Terrace. They shouldn't take in dames like that."

"All right, Chad."

"Goodnight," said Chad, then as he started back to his car he turned: "Look at the sky. It's getting gray. I didn't know it was that late. Goodnight."

In a moment the car moved off. Roy walked slowly over to his own car, looking at the sky. Eastward, over the tall buildings, a gray light was spreading; the stars which had just begun to show were already paling. Creel was sitting at the wheel, smoking a cigarette. Roy got in.

"I just happened to think of something," he said. "I haven't eaten since lunch."

"All night joint right down the street. I could stand a cup of coffee myself."

The place was deserted except for a tired-looking counterman in a dirty chef's hat. They sat down and ordered. There was a nickel slot-machine in the corner, and Creel went over and began to play it, cursing his luck.

Just as the counterman came with their orders, a fat man in a raincoat entered and sat down at the counter. It was Wesson. Roy started slightly, then ignored him.

"Ever sing, Hargis?" he called.

"What do you mean?" asked Roy, without looking at him.

"Sing. You know. You open your mouth and music comes out. Not sing as in county jail, or even Sing Sing."

Now Roy glanced at him. "You got a snootful, Wesson. Why don't you go home?"

"Home is where the heart is. And right now my heart's with some bacon and eggs—turn 'em over. Buttered toast. Coffee, with cream and sugar. So, I get fat!"

The counterman gave him a sour look, then went for his order.

"What do you mean—get? You're fat as a pig," said Roy.

"Let's get back to singing. There's an old song—*Waltzing Matilda*. Australian soldiers sing it." He hummed the air for Roy who ignored him and began to eat. "Cute, eh? But I can't remember the words. Only one wonderful phrase I'll never forget. Something about 'jumbuck the billabong.' Great, eh? 'Jumbuck the billabong.' Can't get it out of my head."

He began to sing *Waltzing Matilda*, faking the words he couldn't remember and using 'jumbuck the billabong' every line or two.

Finally Roy said: "Look, Wesson. You've got a voice like a rusty saw. Would you mind jumbucking your billabong some place else?"

Wesson roared with laughter and almost fell off the stool, then he sobered and said: "Well, if you guys insist on playing games, and keeping me up late...."

Roy stopped eating. "What was that?"

"Funny place for you and Chad to take a walk—down by the 'Drome. That's where the fags hang out."

Roy pushed his plate away. "You want me to hand you a newsbeat?"

"Is there an echo in here? I'm going mad. Newsbeat, newsbeat, newsbeat!" Wesson gave a loud scream and gripped the counter.

"Look, buster," said the counterman, wearily.

"I mean it," said Roy. "Just let me alone till tomorrow. Then call me early. You got my hand on it." He offered to shake hands.

Wesson looked at his hand for a moment. "And your word of honor, too?"

"Yes," said Roy. "My word of honor."

Wesson took a quarter out of his pocket and tossed it on the counter. "Two-bits is two-bits," he said. "Even in these times. But what's your word of honor worth?"

Roy hit Wesson with the back of his hand, knocking him off the stool.

"Here. Wait a minute," said the counterman, reaching for a piece of hose under the counter.

Wesson rose slowly, then, suddenly, moving with the speed and agility of a boxer, he grabbed up the ketchup bottle and aimed it at Roy. The counterman calmly hit him with the hose and he fell again.

Roy got off the stool and stood looking down at Wesson, who was a little groggy.

"The deal still goes, billabong. I mean it. Come on, Len."

Roy went out. Creel paid and followed him. Wesson got slowly to his feet. The counterman stood eyeing him mistrustfully.

"You suppose he means it?" Wesson asked the counterman.

"I wouldn't know, buster. But don't start no more fights in my place. I got it busted up one night, dishes and all. I'm still in hock."

7

A faint, yellow hint of day was showing at the end of the wide, deserted, residential street when Creel stopped just beyond the big ornate marquee of the Ashton Terrace, and Roy got out.

"Better come in. I might need you," said Roy.

They climbed the wide stone steps which led up to the huge, terrace-like porch, and to the row of ten-foot high, bronze and glass doors.

Above them, the mammoth apartment house slept, with drawn Venetian blinds. If anybody was awake here at this hour it was from insomnia.

Charwomen were just finishing up in the lobby, which was small for the size of the building, elegant, solid-looking, almost like a bank.

The night clerk had been warned. Before Roy could speak, he said: "Mr. Hargis? Mr. Clemm is waiting for you. To your right. The door marked private."

Roy merely nodded, and he and Creel, who was looking about him with interest, walked down a short, marble-paved corridor to a black door with a brass plate.

Roy knocked, then getting no response pushed the door open and went in, followed by Creel. The door admitted them to a deserted ante-room. They heard voices. The main office door was open and a bald man wearing shell-rimmed glasses put his head round the jamb and looked out at them. His eyes were bloodshot, his face pale.

"Hargis?" Roy nodded. "Mr. Bayliss called. Won't you come in? I'm Mr. Clemm, assistant manager. Mr. Dykes, the manager, is indisposed. Touch of summer flu."

Roy went into the office, followed by Creel. A big redheaded man with a red face was sitting beyond a huge glass-topped desk, smoking a cigar.

"This is Grant, our house detective," Mr. Clemm explained. Then: "I can't tell you how shocked I am to learn that a guest of ours is... well... that the police want to question her."

"Have you seen a morning paper?" asked Roy.

"Why, no; I haven't. I was roused from sleep, and so was Grant. Why? What has happened?"

"Do you know Mr. Frank Hobart?"

"Why, certainly. He...." Mr. Clemm paused, and studied Hargis.

"He... what?" Roy prodded.

"Well, I was going to say... Miss Vance was a sort of protégée of his. He came here often. And I might tell you, never went to Miss Vance's suite. He'd wait for her in the lobby. I'm sure that Mr. Hobart...."

"Well, somebody knocked him off tonight," said Roy, abruptly.

Mr. Clemm suddenly looked sick and reached back for the desk, needing support. Grant stood up as if somebody had built a fire under his chair.

"Killed Mr. Hobart?" asked Grant, incredulously. "That fine gentleman. But, who under the sun...?"

"That's what we're trying to find out. Clemm, how do you want me to handle this? You want to call the girl and ask her to come down here?"

"But that's impossible," said Clemm. "She's gone. Left last night, sometime." He turned. "Grant, I think we'd better.... This is a serious matter."

Grant cleared his throat nervously. "Yes, Mr. Clemm. Well, she was out all evening, I think. Then she came in sometime around two-thirty. There was a young fellow with her, I never saw him before."

"What did he look like?"

"Handsome," said Grant. "Tall, slender, dark hair. Dressed careless. Didn't have any tie on. No hat. Kind of a young Cary Grant, like. Dark-complected, though. Kinda like maybe a refined Italian. No, that's not right, exactly. Maybe French. Although I have seen a few young Irishmen who looked like that."

"All right. Go on," said Roy, after a moment of thought.

"Well, he helped her check out. I thought it was kind of funny. Especially after...." He paused and looked at Mr. Clemm.

"Especially after what?" snapped Roy.

"This is no time to keep anything back, Grant," said Clemm, looking sicker than before, and getting himself a drink from a water-bottle on the desk, his hands shaking.

"Well, we had a funny thing here, Captain," said Grant. "A robbery which wasn't a robbery. I mean, well... I'll tell you. A couple of guys came in here with bonafide building inspector badges: plumbers. They had an order all written out proper to inspect the plumbing, heating pipes, et cetera. Neither Mr. Dykes, nor Mr. Clemm was here. The young second assistant told them to go ahead. They were all over the place. They had a handtruck full of wrenches, pipes, and stuff. Finally a floorman let them into Miss Vance's suite: they said they'd traced some trouble to there. They worked for about an hour, then they left. All of a sudden, a maid comes running into my office. She said Miss Vance's suite had been looted. I went right up. Miss Vance had just got home. It was a darned funny situation. Miss Vance just asked me what I wanted. I didn't know what to say. I asked her if everything was all right. She said it was. All the same, one closet door was open and I could see that it was empty. It was where she kept her fur coats."

"I see," said Roy. "You think those plumbers stripped her suite, then she wouldn't admit it."

"I don't think. I know," said Grant.

"When was that?"

"Saturday. Two days ago."

"All right," said Roy. "Now what about Miss Vance?"

"About her? How do you mean?"

"What was your opinion of her?"

"Well, my opinion was," said Grant, slowly, "that she was a very smart girl who knew how to mind her own business. I don't think she had one visitor while she was here, except Mr. Hobart. Nobody in her suite—ever. Maids know around a place, and we are very strict here with single women. We only have a very few. All highly recommended—as Miss Vance was, by Mr. Hobart."

"You got anything to add?" asked Roy, turning to Clemm.

"No," said Clemm. "Nothing illuminating, I'm afraid. Miss Vance was one of the most beautiful young women I've ever seen, and very polite. She dressed plainly, and in excellent taste. She hardly spoke a word to any of us, but she was always friendly, and smiled. Am I right, Grant?"

The house detective nodded.

"Did she pay her bill?"

"Well, as a matter of fact, she didn't," said Mr. Clemm. "But of course that's no great matter. She only owes for a month and she's sending us a check. Quite all right. She's always been very scrupulous about settling her bill on the dot. And of course, she was vouched for by Mr. Hobart."

Roy took a cigarette and lit it thoughtfully, then he motioned Creel out into the ante-room. "Len," he said, "call Emmett. Two things I want him to do for me. First, find out where Robert Dumas lives. He's a piano player and no doubt belongs to the Musicians' Union. Tell him to get an official out of bed if necessary. Then I want him to come to the Terrace and go over the Vance dame's apartment with a fine-toothed comb. Got it? Okay. Call right there. I'll go back and shut the door."

Roy went back in the main office.

"Has Miss Vance's apartment been cleaned since she left?"

"No," said Clemm. "It will get a routine cleaning some time early this morning."

"Don't let anybody touch it. I'm sending an expert down to give it a going-over."

"All right, Captain," said Grant, glancing at Clemm. "We want to cooperate in every way."

Roy noted the glance. "That suite's as good as sealed, you understand," he said harshly.

"Oh, naturally. Of course," said Clemm. Then after a nervous pause: "Captain—this is all most embarrassing for us. Nothing remotely approaching this has ever happened to us here at the Terrace before. We...."

"What are you worrying about? She checked out last night, didn't she? She's off your hands."

"Thank God for that," said Clemm with a sigh. "But the publicity, I mean. The newspapers. After all, she lived here, and...."

"I'll see what I can do," said Roy. "May not even be a line about it. Do my best."

"Oh, fine, fine, Captain," said Clemm. "And if there is ever anything we can do for you; anything, I mean.... You know. Sky's the limit, as people say." Clemm laughed nervously. He was not used to trying to bribe police officers.

"I'll think it over," said Roy, smiling slightly. "There's always the pension fund. You can make the check out to me, of course. Care City Building. Providing I keep you out, that is. No hurry."

He turned and went out. Grant and Clemm looked at each other in consternation.

"Was he joking, Grant?"

"I doubt it," said Grant, wagging his head. "I doubt it very much."

8

It turned out that Bob Dumas lived at Melton Stairs, a Bohemian section of the town, north of Paxton Square and adjoining the worst slum in the city. It was full of musicians, painters, writers, whores, and drug-peddlers, and dotted with little Italian restaurants in basements, hole-in-the-wall cafés, and many rendezvous where men were women and women were glad of it.

Melton Stairs rose steeply from the west bank and climbed slowly to a height which overlooked a wide bend of the river and the big buildings of the downtown section beyond. In the Civil War days the Foot of the Stairs had been a steamboat landing, and now a brass tablet marked the spot where a few volunteer city militiamen had fought off a raid by a party of Confederate irregulars from down-river, who had tried to steal a woodburning paddle-wheeler. This historic event was known as the Battle of Melton Stairs.

In those days, the Stairs was inhabited by a tough and hardy breed of men: sailors, adventurers, runaway slaves from the Deep South, gunrunners, rivermen—quite a formidable lot, who would have been astonished, amused and saddened by their successors.

Creel drove. The Melton Stairs Hill was almost straight up, with short, flat spaces at the intersections. Roy sat smoking a cigar in silence. He was beginning to feel the strain of the long day, but said nothing.

Behind them, the sun was rising over the tall buildings and scattering gold spangles across the wide bend of the dark, oily river. Windows in the houses on the summit of the hill looked like sheets of burnished copper. The wind had blown all the clouds from the sky. It was going to be a hot day.

Creel pulled up at a dilapidated three-storey brick apartment house. Most of the shades were down. Except for a few trucks and milk carts, the streets were deserted. Bohemia slept as soundly this time of day as the rich guests of the Ashton Terrace.

"It's a flea-bag, all right," said Roy, as he got out. "Come on, Len."

They crossed a pavement littered with newspapers and debris of all kinds, and full of crude drawings in chalk, made apparently by children. Roy pointed.

"I didn't know these people round here *had* kids," he said.

"Lots of Italians still left here," said Creel, "although they're getting crowded out."

"It's a damn shame."

"Yes," said Creel. "Mike Antonnelli still lives around here some place. Told me the other day he'd have to move. Music going all night. Weed parties—dames yelling and screaming and running down the street naked."

"That fathead, Wesson, hangs around here. He would."

They went into a little, dirty vestibule where there was a row of buzzers with card racks beside them. Some of the racks had cards, some did not. Roy finally whistled and pointed. Creel looked. An engraved card read: Robert Bonaventure Dumas.

"He should live at the Terrace with a handle like that," said Roy. "Try the door."

The door leading into the first floor hall was old and sagging. Creel worked at it for a moment, lifting it, pressing his knee against it, and finally it burst open with a groan.

"Second floor," said Roy. "218."

They found the apartment just beyond the head of the stairs. Before Roy could knock, the door was opened from within, and they were confronted by a startled-looking slim, blond girl, who stared, then tried to shut the door. Roy pushed past her, followed by Creel.

"You're up early," said Roy, looking about the dirty, cluttered apartment.

"Who are you? What do you want?" snapped the girl. The sudden entrance of two strange men had apparently startled her considerably, but she got hold of herself at once and now didn't seem in the least perturbed or frightened, merely cold and unfriendly.

"We're looking for Bob Dumas," said Roy.

"He's not here."

"But you're expecting him."

"Am I?"

Roy reached past her and closed the door. "Yes," he said. "Sit down."

The girl merely stared at him defiantly through her glasses. Creel found her very attractive. She was quite tall and slender, and dressed plainly and neatly in a white blouse and dark skirt. Her face was rather delicate at first look, and yet her cheek-bones were wide and her blue eyes, partly masked by the glasses, were slanted slightly. Her hair was an almost white-blond, and natural. In general her appearance was refined and ladylike and yet there were danger signals in her face: indications of temper and determination. She was the only girl Creel had ever seen who looked good in glasses. Of course, the glasses themselves were very much out of the ordinary: they had thick, pinkish plastic rims and were canted considerably, adding to the Mongolian effect.

"You know Bob?" she asked, studying Hargis.

"No, but I want to get acquainted," said Roy, briefly showing his wallet with the badge.

"Oh, policemen," said the girl, then she sat down and lit a cigarette.

Roy looked her over. "Don't tell me you live in this flea-bag," he said.

"Down the hall," said the girl, indifferently.

"How do you keep so clean and neat?"

"My place doesn't look like this one."

Roy glanced around him. Shirts and coats were hanging on the backs of chairs. The blinds were crooked and torn. Magazines spilled from a rickety table and lay dog-eared all over the floor. An upright piano against the wall was piled high with sheet music. The place smelled like the trainshed at the Union Station.

"Once in a while I sneak in and clean this up," she said. "Then he doesn't speak to me for a few days. Says he can't find anything."

"Your name?"

"Ruth Jensen."

"Occupation?"

"I own a little music shop at the corner of Melton Stairs and the Boulevard. I have a partner. Mrs. Andrew Sims."

"The woman in Riverview?"

"The same," said the girl, smiling slightly at Roy's surprise. "She's my aunt."

"Why the hell are you living in a joint like this, then?"

"You mean it's against the law or something?"

Creel turned away, smiling slightly, and stared out the window into the sun-streaked, dirty street.

"When I ask a question I've got a reason."

"Well, I live here because I want to. Does that answer your question?"

Roy studied her for a moment. Fatigue was catching up with him and memories of the long night crossed his mind in a jumble: Kit, lightning, Tootsie, Wesson, Chad Bayliss, Joe Sert yammering and getting purple in the face—people were beginning to run together now, like a tipped-up, wet water-color picture. He rose and stretched.

"Got any coffee around here?"

"Yes," said Ruth, rising. "I just made some."

She went to a little dinette, hidden by a beaver-board partition which was scrawled over with musical notations in pencil and signatures in colored crayon, and in a moment came back with three steaming cups. Creel thanked her politely, and she glanced at him rather curiously. Roy merely took the cup from her hand and began to drink. She sat down, discreetly crossed her legs, and glanced mildly and politely from one to the other. It was, Creel thought, as if she were having tea on the verandah of the Riverview Country Club. It was almost comically incongruous in this littered, stinking place.

"Has Dumas been gone long?"

"I don't know," said Ruth.

"Have you been away this evening?"

"No," said the girl.

"Do you usually get up this early—or stay up all night as the case may be?"

"I couldn't sleep. I woke about four, dressed and came over here to talk to Bob. He never goes to bed, you know, till around six o'clock. He wasn't here. I thought he'd be back any time, so I made some coffee and waited."

"Any idea where he could be?"

"No. There's no telling. Lots of times he just goes out and wanders around. Quite a few little places open all night, you know. Several colored places in Paxton Square. Bob goes and listens to the music."

"Busman's holiday, eh? I think he'd get tired of it, playing every night at Cipriano's."

"That's just a job. That has nothing to do with music."

"How's that again?"

"He plays at Cipriano's only to keep alive. He hates it." She studied Roy for a moment, then she took a sip of coffee and went on. "Bob is a musical genius, or at least I think so. And I must say that he agrees with me a hundred per cent."

She said this solemnly, but Roy caught the intended humor and smiled. "He admits it, eh? I hear the Stairs is full of guys like that."

"Not like Bob, I assure you."

"You sort of look after him—is that it?"

"In a way," said Ruth, then lowered her eyes.

There was a long pause, then suddenly Roy asked: "Miss Jensen—do you know Ilona Vance?" The girl gave a slight jump. "I see you do," said Roy, laconically. Then he turned to Creel: "Go call the Terrace. See if Lackey's at it, and if he's found anything."

Creel went out.

"Yes, I know her," said Ruth. "Has this something to do with her? Has she got Bob into some kind of trouble?"

"You've been expecting it?"

"With a girl like that—naturally."

"Like what?"

"Look," said Ruth. "I think we'd better wait till Bob gets here. I refuse to answer any more questions."

"Suit yourself. But this is serious. Somebody has been killed."

Ruth jumped up at once and turned to stare at Roy in an agitated manner. "Killed? Who—for heaven's sake? Not... *Bob?*"

"Sit down, Miss Jensen," said Roy. "Dumas is okay. Calm yourself. It might be a good idea for you to help me. Then maybe I could help you."

Ruth sat down, her color returning. "How could you possibly help me?"

"Who knows?" Roy finished his coffee and set the cup down. "Now this girl—a character sketch might help."

"How can I give you a character sketch of some one who hasn't any character, or any morals, or any intelligence—shrewdness maybe—but no higher intelligence?"

"It's possible you might be prejudiced."

"Yes, it's more than possible. I *am* prejudiced. You see, she's the kind of person who will not take 'no' for an answer. She's been after Bob for a long time. He is very handsome and also rather indifferent to women."

"Quite a combination."

"Yes, and apparently it was catnip to this person, who has had men falling all over her since she was eleven—no doubt." There was a pause. Ruth looked at Roy thoughtfully. "I don't want you to misunderstand what I said about Bob. His indifference to women, I mean. He's perfectly normal. But he's completely absorbed in his work. Has no idea how handsome he is, and doesn't care at all about his personal appearance. If he wasn't working at Cipriano's I doubt if he'd wash or shave. Half the time he even forgets to eat."

"Just stumbles around, eh?"

Ruth threw Roy a sharp look. "Yes," she said. "I suppose to you it would seem that he just stumbles around."

Roy felt that he had been put in his place. The girl had the famous Riverview manner—a short way with peasants. Roy was tired and irritated; now he lost his temper. "Yes," he said curtly, "to me a bum is a bum, no matter what you call it. The Stairs is full of pretentious bums."

"That's true," said the girl. "But Bob is not one of them. I think I will answer no more questions. Of course, you can twist my arm."

After a moment, Roy said: "He was teaching her to sing, I believe."

Ruth laughed in polite derision. "No one could do that. She has a voice like an effeminate bullfrog."

Roy laughed shortly, and at that moment the door opened and a tall young man entered. His white shirt was open at the neck and he was wearing a worn and faded blue flannel coat patched with leather on the elbows. He was hatless. His face had an olive tinge and his short hair was Indian-black. He was smoothly handsome, his eyes dark, alive, and expressive. He had a newspaper in his hand and he was about to speak when he noticed Roy and froze.

"Who are you?" he asked mildly.

"A policeman," said Ruth, quickly.

"One of your friends, Ruth?" he gibed, then he took off his coat and threw it across the room at a chair, missing it.

Ruth rose, picked up the coat, and draped it over a chair.

"One of my many policeman friends," she said.

"Something interesting in the paper?" asked Roy.

"Yes," said Bob. "There's a serial I'm reading—a western serial."

"He reads nothing but cowboy books," Ruth put in, trying to catch Bob's eye.

"I find it very restful," said Bob. "No psychiatry, no social significance, no bellyaching. Very restful." He sat down and put his feet up on the table, pushing off half a dozen magazines which joined the others on the floor. "Got some coffee, Ruth?"

"Yes, Bob," said Ruth, and she disappeared behind the partition.

Roy glanced down at the newspaper which had also fallen to the floor. The headline read: FRANK HOBART MURDERED.

"Did you know Hobart?" asked Roy.

"No," said Bob. "I've heard of him. Who do you suppose killed him?"

Ruth came with the coffee. "Killed who?" she demanded, looking at no one.

"Mr. Hobart, the lawyer, got killed," said Bob, mildly.

Ruth started and spilled the coffee into the saucer.

"Sloppy Susie—cut it out," said Bob. "Waitresses get fired for that."

"You surprised, Miss Jensen?" asked Roy.

"Why—naturally. Mr. Hobart was a friend of my father's. They were friends for years—till my father died."

"Oh, come on," said Bob, turning to Roy. "Let's stop this pussyfooting. It bores me. What do you want to know?"

There was a tap at the door, then Creel came in. He hurried over to Roy and whispered to him. Roy nodded slowly, and studied a slip of paper Creel handed him.

"Okay," said Roy. "But I'll need a couple of more men. We'll pick 'em up at the Hall." Then he turned. "Get your hat on, Miss Jensen—if you wear one. We're all going downtown together."

"You mean we're arrested?" Ruth demanded.

"No. Held for questioning."

Bob grimaced and got up. "This is a hell of a note. I need some sleep. I'm working tonight."

"I'd like to use the phone," said Ruth, sharply.

"At the City Building, Miss Jensen, if you like," said Roy. "But I wouldn't advise it. This is only a questioning. It's very unlikely you'll be held."

Undecided, Ruth looked at Bob, but he just shrugged indifferently, picked up his coat, and began to put it on.

Outside, Wesson was waiting for them.

"Hello, billabong," said Roy. "Got your car with you?"

"Naturally," said Wesson.

"Leave it here and go with us. I'm going to keep my word."

"I don't know," said Wesson, glancing from Ruth to Bob. "They might find me in the river later. What are you doing with these nice people?"

"Routine questioning," said Roy. "Nothing. So you won't go with me?"

"No, but I'll follow," said Wesson.

"I may make a pinch."

"I feel safer in my own car."

"Suit yourself. But I'm a man of my word."

"I'll never dispute it again, especially when I'm standing near a guy with a rubber hose." He turned to Bob.

"Dumas, can I do anything for you?"

"For instance?"

"You can keep his name out of the paper," said Roy. "For the time being, anyway."

"He plays a nice piano," said Wesson. "Soothes me no end when my dobber's down. You take Cavallaro, I'll take Dumas."

"You fat slob!" cried Bob, angrily.

"Did I say something?"

"One more remark about Cavallaro...."

"Bob!" Ruth cautioned.

"What's going on here?" Roy demanded.

"I think I hurt his professional pride unwittingly," said Wesson. "Always putting my foot in it. The body of Silenus, the face of Socrates—and the mind of an eager child. That's Wesson. You go ahead, Roy. I'll follow."

9

When they reached the City Building, the big town was waking up and traffic was growing in volume on all the main streets. On the river many tugs were already at work, towing barges and bulky river freighters. A dark mass of migratory birds, going south for the winter, flew chirping over the Civic Center park. Fall was at hand, and you could sense it in spite of the still heat.

Roy left Bob and Ruth Jensen with Sid Paul and told him to make them comfortable for a while—but incommunicado. Then he sent Creel to pick up a couple of plainclothes boys at the Special Detail, and get another City car, with no insignia, from the garage pool.

Then he hurried back to his own office. Gert Carlson turned and looked at him with raised eyebrows. She had just arrived and was putting on lipstick at a wall mirror. She was about thirty, plain, divorced, secretive, and efficient.

"What wringer were you pulled through?" she demanded.

"It's beginning to show, eh? Emmett get back?"

"I think so. I hear a crawling and scrambling noise in there some place. But I'm not sure. I just walked in. No kidding, Roy—you look pale and worn out. The Hobart business?"

"Yeah. We got it. I'll get some rest pretty soon."

He pushed open the door. Emmett Lackey was at one of the desks. The big fellow started guiltily, then tried hurriedly to conceal something he'd been looking at.

"Oh!" he said, smiling weakly. "Thought it was Gert."

"What you got there—feelthy pictures?"

"Now you know better than that, Roy." Lackey shuffled some papers about on his desk. "I've got notations here—records. I made quite a survey of that girl's apartment."

"Where's the card?" Lackey handed it to him. It read: Avalon 37135. Ad: 237 Avalon Parkway, Barrington Estates. Mrs. Allen Spencer. Sis. "Well?" Roy demanded.

"Allen Spencer's well known around town," said Lackey. "His name used to be Elmer. Since he's been married he's changed it. Probably the wife didn't like Elmer for a name. He's a kind of fly-by-night promoter: real estate, practically everything. He leased the 'Drome for a while and tried to promote ice carnivals. They flopped. Everything seems to flop for him. Owes everybody, but still manages to live on Avalon Parkway."

"I get the picture. All right. The wife?"

"Nothing. She's from out of town."

"Where did you find this card?"

"It was pasted to the back of a drawer with Scotch tape."

"Anything else of interest?"

"Nothing much. I'll make an exhaustive report, Roy. Might be some leads if you need them."

Roy studied Lackey for a moment. The big man's face was flushed; his eyes more than usually evasive. Roy moved over quickly to the desk, pushed Lackey's papers around for a moment, and finally turned up a large shiny print of Ilona Vance in a French bathing-suit. It was overwhelming, enough to corrupt every soldier in Korea.

"Great day in the morning!" he said. "Where was *this* pasted up?"

"I f... f... found it under one end of the carpet." Lackey was horribly embarrassed. He didn't know where to look or what to do with his hands. Sweat broke out on his forehead.

Roy leaned on the desk and stared piercingly at Lackey. "Answer yes or no," he said, sharply. "If she told you to burn down the Court House and shoot your invalid mother, would you?"

Lackey stammered and sputtered, trying to laugh, trying to make a joke of the whole thing in his hopeless, awkward, heavy-handed way. "I ref... f... fuse to answer for f... f... fear of incriminating...."

"*I* would," said Roy. "And I'd steal from the poor-box, and beat up newsboys." He tossed the picture to Lackey. "I don't need it. And don't file it, Emmett. It's yours, all for your little self. Paste it up over your bed."

Lackey's attempts to appear jovial and man-of-the worldish were pathetic. He sat trying to laugh, shaking his big belly.

"All I can say is," said Roy, "whatever Hobart went through was worth it."

"That's a very cynical statement, Roy. Very cynical."

"You disagree?"

"Of course," said Lackey, patting his palms together in a rather pious manner. "Beauty is only skin-deep, you know. Feminine beauty. It appeals to our lower natures."

"I don't seem to have any other kind."

"That's unfortunate, Roy. Makes it impossible for you to judge others correctly. Just as you are judging, or rather misjudging, me at the moment."

"Lackey," said Roy, "you know what you are? A stinking hypocrite. I'd hate to turn you loose on a desert island with that big bim."

"She'd be absolutely safe with me, Roy. I assure you. You don't understand me at all."

Gert buzzed on the intercom and Lackey answered it, then nodded and turned to Roy. "Creel's all set, Roy. Best of luck."

Roy regarded him piercingly again, leaning forward over the desk. "Look here, Emmett. If I turn up with the big bim, I want you to let her alone. It's not fair taking advantage of a girl in jail."

"Oh, go along with you," said Lackey, feebly, trying to laugh.

"I'm going to put her in charge of the biggest matron I can find."

As Roy went out, Lackey sat laughing, holding his belly. But as soon as the door was closed, his expression changed at once and for a moment a look of wild hatred showed in his small blue eyes, then he rose and began to pace up and down beside his desk, the floor trembling under his giant tread.

In the outer office, Gert, yawning at her typewriter, mumbled: "I wonder what's bothering the big crab in there. Why is he scuttling around so much?" Then she told herself: "He belongs on the bottom of the sea, away from the light." She repressed a shudder and returned to her typing.

Little by little, Lackey composed himself. Finally he sat down, rearranged his papers so that he could hide the picture of Ilona Vance in a hurry if anybody barged in, then sighing he gave himself up to a long and minute examination of the big, shapely, bold-looking, beautiful girl.

10

Barrington Estates was no Riverview but at least it was second best. Broad, winding streets wandered up westward from the river regions of the Avalon Yacht Club and Regatta Pier to the low, mound-like hills of the old Indian Camp Grounds, now a City Recreational Park. Big oaks, elms and sycamores bordered all the thoroughfares, and there were wide, well-kept lawns, flower gardens, and ornamental shrubbery.

It was still early and Barrington Estates was just barely awake. Here and there colored maids in black dresses and white aprons could be seen taking in papers, receiving parcels from delivery trucks, and goodnaturedly bickering with milk men, bread men, and dry cleaners.

The section had a pleasant, sylvan air. Early sunlight slanted down through the tall trees, and the wide streets were checkered with sun and shadow. Some of the leaves had already turned yellow, some ochre and red; but the lawns were still green, and here and there lawn-sprinklers were going, throwing up a fine silvery spray, laced with rainbows. Since the storm, a dry heat had been drifting in from the flat land to the west, and heat shimmers could be seen above the asphalt where there was no shade.

Roy had carefully studied a map of the section. This was necessary as the streets seemed to wander about without plan or final destination. They did not run parallel for any great distance, but wound and curved and crossed each other in unlikely places. It was almost as if the whole plot had been laid out in such a way as to make it nearly impossible to find any given address.

But finally Roy had his plans made, and sent the second car off at one of the cross streets in charge of Creel. He took Ed Reynolds with him. Ed was a big, silent man about forty, patient, casual, dependable, but apparently without ambition. He did his work, drew his pay, and that was that. He rarely spoke.

237 Avalon Parkway was a big old house of brick and wood, vaguely Norman English, situated in the center of a wide, choice corner lot. The lawn was full of ornamental shrubbery, and wide tamped gravel paths led here and there. Toward the back there seemed to be a swimming pool with cabanas. Roy whistled to himself. For an insolvent "promoter," this wasn't bad living, not bad at all.

A shiny new coupé was parked in the driveway, headed out.

"You stay here, Ed," said Roy. "If anybody tries to drive out in that coop, just block the driveway."

Ed did not show a flicker of having heard. Roy got out and strolled up the gravel path toward the front door. Unable to find a bell, he banged the big brass knocker. A tow-headed girl about three looked out one of the windows at him, and when he glanced at her she made a face and put out her tongue; then she disappeared like a puppet which had suddenly been pulled off stage.

Roy waited, then he banged the knocker loudly again. Finally the door was opened by a redheaded maid, whose hair was untidy, whose white uniform was dirty and whose expression was one of guarded hostility.

"Yeah?" she said.

"I want to see Mrs. Spencer," said Roy.

"She's laying down. Headache. Can't see nobody."

"Mr. Spencer available?"

"He's sick. Not up yet. Didn't get in till late. I can't bother him."

"May I speak to Mrs. Spencer's sister?"

"Who? She ain't got no sister that I know of. But I only been here two weeks."

"I understand her sister got in last night."

"Sister? No. Not that I know of. But...."

An agitated feminine voice interrupted her. "Clarice! Shut the door. We don't want to see any one. Understand? Shut the door at once."

The maid raised her eyebrows and shrugged, then she started to shut the door, but Roy pushed past her into a big, gloomy-looking entrance-hall. There was a wide stairway just beyond him, and half way up stood a tall, over-voluptuous blond woman in her late twenties. She had on black velvet lounging pajamas, no make-up, and her thick, pale hair was wound up carelessly and tied with a ribbon. Her face was fat, but pretty. Roy nodded to himself. It was the big kid's sister, all right. There was a definite resemblance, although the younger one had all the best of it.

The woman glared at Roy in silent consternation. Suddenly a tall man in wrinkled pajamas appeared at the head of the stairs. His curly, light-brown hair was on end and he looked pale and bleary-eyed.

"Who the hell are you?" he shouted. "Didn't you hear what the girl said? If you got any business with me take it up with my lawyers, Richmond and Dietz. Now get out of here."

"Police," said Roy. "Both of you come down."

The woman reached out and grasped the railing, then she turned and stared helplessly at her husband, who was nervously hitching at his pajama pants and seemed to be bewildered.

"Wasn't my fault, missus," said Clarice.

"All right. Go back to your work," said the blond woman.

The redheaded maid looked from Mr. Spencer to Mrs. Spencer, then she gave Roy a weak and ingratiating smile, shook her head, and disappeared.

"Have you got a warrant or something?" called Spencer.

"Yes," said Roy. "But not for either of you. Come on down."

Suddenly the blond woman put one hand over her face and began to cry, her shoulders shaking.

"Oh, God!" cried Spencer. "Cut it out, will you, Helene? No use crying just because we got a policeman in the house. Say, I'd better get a robe or something."

"All right," said Roy.

Spencer disappeared, talking to himself. Helene hesitated, then she took out a small lace handkerchief and wiped her eyes, and in a moment she descended the stairway into the entrance-hall. She was very tall, almost as tall as Roy in her high heels, and Roy was just short of six feet.

"I'd like to talk to your sister," said Roy.

Helene repressed a start with difficulty. "Sister? I have no sister. What do you mean?"

"Oh, come on, Mrs. Spencer," said Roy. "The truth won't hurt anybody."

"I simply have no sister. Why do you insist? You don't know me. I never saw you before."

"Have you seen the morning paper?"

"No," said Mrs. Spencer, turning to stare at him. "Why?"

"Do you know Mr. Frank Hobart?"

The woman paled noticeably and looked away. "Hobart? The lawyer? No, I don't know him. I've heard of him."

"He was murdered last night."

Roy thought Mrs. Spencer was going to faint and reached out to help her, but she brushed his hand aside and hurried past him into the living-room. Roy followed her. She threw herself face down on a big lounge and cried hysterically. Roy stood watching her. In a moment, her husband appeared in the doorway and stared at her in disgust. He had on a black silk Japanese lounging-robe ornamented with red and gold pagodas and dragons. With his hair combed and his face tolerably composed, he looked rather handsome but very tired, like a slightly passé matinee idol after a gruelling performance.

"Oh, for Christ's sake, Helene!" he exclaimed wearily.

She raised up, pale and agitated, to look at him. "Al—you don't know. My God! Frank Hobart's been murdered!"

Spencer was staggered. "*What!*" He stared at his wife blankly, then he turned and looked foggily at Roy. "You mean...? Is this true, officer?"

"I'm Captain Hargis," said Roy. "This is so big, I got a special assignment."

"*Hargis*—my God!" cried Spencer, and collapsed into a chair, where he sat looking about him vaguely and pulling at his under lip. Finally he reached out and took a cigarette from a little ivory box, but his hands were shaking so that he could hardly light it.

Now Mrs. Spencer sat up. Her face was tear-stained but calm. "Allen, I'm sorry," she said. "I did the best I could. You know that. Now we're ruined."

"Not necessarily," said Roy.

They both looked at him quickly. "The scandal!" cried Mrs. Spencer. "It will ruin Allen in this town, and just when he's having so much trouble anyway."

"You say she's not your sister," said Roy. "Just turn her over to me. That's all you have to do. No publicity."

Mrs. Spencer studied Roy. "You mean it?"

"Helene!" her husband cautioned.

"All right," said Mrs. Spencer, rising. "She's been a millstone around my neck ever since she was knee-high. She never was any good. I came here to get away from her. I married Allen. Everything was going fine—and then she turned up, hungry as usual. And now this! I won't put up with any more of it. I won't...!" She was shouting now and completely oblivious of her husband who was trying to tell her something.

"Helene!" cried her husband. "Listen to me. She's gone. I... I let her out the back way."

"Oh, my God!" cried Mrs. Spencer and fell down on the couch again.

Roy never moved but sat looking from one to the other. Spencer glanced at him curiously. "You heard me," he said. "She's gone. If you want her, you better go get her."

"Don't worry about it," said Roy. Then he went on: "I just want you to answer a few questions before I go."

"All right," said Spencer, "as long as it's okay with Helene. I'll answer."

"It's okay with me, I assure you," said his wife, with almost hysterical anger.

"When did she get here last night?"

"She phoned about two-thirty, waking us up. She got here about three."

"Anybody with her?"

"Yes. A tall young fellow. He brought her bags in, then left."

"Was his name Dumas?"

"I wouldn't know. I was so goddamned mad I wasn't listening. I've had a real bellyful of Olla." He glanced at his wife.

"Yes, Allen, you have. And I hope this is the last of it." She turned to Roy. "Yes, the young man's name was Dumas. Bob's his first name. He's one of Olla's many boy friends, I think. One of her stooges."

"What they *see* in her..." Spencer began, then he shook his head and broke off.

Roy stood up. "Did anybody mention anything about Frank Hobart?"

"Yes," said Spencer. "Olla told us she'd left him, and was going back to San Francisco in a few days. She was trying to promote me for the fare. But I put my foot down."

"For once," said Helene. "And I was proud of you."

"Is that her car in the drive?"

"No. She hasn't any car now. She had one, but she sold it or something. I don't know. Hobart gave her one. She got here in a taxi."

"All right," said Roy. "I may have to talk to you people again. I'll come out if necessary. See if I can't keep you out of this. Looks like she wasn't arrested on your property."

"She what?" Spencer demanded, standing up.

"She's been taken by now, I'm sure," said Roy.

He started to leave. As he went out into the entrance-hall someone banged at the knocker. He went over and opened the door. It was Ed Reynolds. His eyes looked vacant; he was chewing a match. When Roy glanced at him, he merely nodded.

Roy went out, shutting the door behind him. He felt a rising excitement which he tried to fight down.

11

At first he didn't see her. She was hidden by Creel's car. Beyond the car, he saw Wesson and a photographer arguing with Red Benson, a tough dick from the Special Detail, who would just as lief stuff a camera down somebody's throat as not.

"Here's the Captain. Ask him," cried Wesson, red-faced and excited. "Okay, Hargis?"

"Where'd the lens monkey come from?" asked Roy, looking out of the corner of his eye at the girl. "From the ground like a fish worm?"

"The shutter boys never sleep," said Wesson. "He just happened to be visiting a rich aunt on Avalon Parkway."

"Oh, sure," said Roy. "How do you like the newsbeat, you ungrateful limey bastard!"

"Peace, it's wonderful," said Wesson. "Only baby won't stop playing peek-a-boo." Wesson turned toward the girl. "I *see* you. Hiding behind your pursey-wursey. Look, honey; you can't hide what you've got with a small piece of tanned animal skin."

"Do I have to stand for this?" asked the girl mildly.

"Take some pictures, you idiot," cried Wesson, kicking at the photographer.

The girl was almost as tall as Creel, who was far from short. She was wearing a tight white skirt and a dark-blue turtle-neck sweater. Her raven-black hair was pulled back over her ears and tied with a white ribbon. It was long and thick and lay along her back in a coarse mane. She had on dark glasses, and a black patent-leather purse hid her face. It was apparent that she'd dressed in a hurry and had neglected to put on some of her clothing. The detectives were all trying to appear unconcerned, big lawmen, only doing their sworn duty for city, county, state, and country. Even big Ed Reynolds was being elaborately unconcerned.

"Is the lens big enough to get everything in?" asked Wesson, and the photographer snickered.

She was both tall and big and yet she had the most graceful and attractive-looking build Roy had ever seen.

"Okay," he said. "Put her in the car."

"Put her in the car, he says," sighed Wesson. "It's a mercy I'm queer. Think of all the trouble a normal man can get into."

Creel looked at Roy in surprise. "My car?"

"Yes," said Roy. "Turn her over to Alma. Nobody is to see her or talk to her till I get in. Nobody!"

"Okay."

"All right. What are you waiting for?"

Creel's face was flushed. "That picture," he said. "It didn't do her justice."

"A picture? How could it?" Wesson broke in. "It would take a relief map."

Creel got in and Red Benson jumped in beside him. The girl was sitting in the middle of the back seat alone. Red reached back and locked both the doors.

"A wise precaution," said Wesson. "Of course, they can always jump in through the glass."

Roy went over to the car and looked through the window at the girl. She lowered her purse. There was a flash.

"Got it, by Jesus," cried the photographer.

The girl's face was composed, almost blank-looking. She had a rather short nose, which turned up just a little. Her mouth was beautiful. She seemed to be regarding Roy steadily through her dark glasses. He couldn't see her eyes at all.

Roy stepped back and Creel drove off. Ed Reynolds, who almost never made any kind of comment, suddenly spit out the match he was chewing and observed: "Zing!"

"You can say that again, brother," said Wesson. "Zing! Zing! And a jolly jumbuck to you."

Now Wesson pulled out his notebook and Roy gave him the facts he wanted him to have, and concluded as follows: "She was arrested at the Lackawanna Bus Terminal by Detective Lieutenant Lenhard Creel. Got that?"

"I have, massa."

"Now you're on your own. Everybody will have it in half an hour."

"They're holding on for me—an extra." Wesson put his head on one side and looked at Roy fondly. "Do you happen to have a piece of rubber hose in your pocket that you'd like to hit me with?" Then he turned to the dark-faced little photographer. "Come on, Tarawa. Let's burn it up."

They hurried out and jumped into Wesson's car and were off with a loud banging in a dense cloud of oil-smoke.

"Take me home, Ed," said Roy. "I got to get a little rest. Haven't been in the kip for twenty-four hours."

They got in the car. "I've seen some broads in my day..." said Ed, slowly; then he added: "Zing!"

"Yeah," said Roy.

12

Roy found it hard to relax. His blinds were drawn and it wasn't too hot in his room, but he was so tired that the muscles in his legs kept twitching, and when, from time to time, he managed to doze off, the events of the long night, since he'd left Half Moon Beach in a thunderstorm, came rushing at him out of the darkness in a wild, jumbled, distorted mass: Joe Sert was talking like Chad, Creel like Lackey—nothing made any kind of sense—and then, slowly, he'd come to, sweating and nervous, and sitting up in bed, wiping his naked torso with a towel, he'd become conscious of the loudness of the daytime roaring and clanking of the city, and wonder if he'd ever be able to doze off again.

That girl! The sight of her had numbed him. And at that, he'd hardly managed to see what she looked like—her face, anyway. The rest of her had been obvious enough. So obvious, in fact, that even poor old stultified Ed had said: "Zing!" sadly. Out of Ed's reach.

"And out of yours, you damned fool!" Roy told himself, savagely.

Finally he dozed as the roar of the city gradually faded and he heard nothing except the faint ringing of the surface-car bell, as it turned the corner near his hotel... clang-clang, clang-clang....

The phone rang. He got up, cursing. It was Emmett.

"Roy, good grief," wailed Lackey, "you got to come down. I hate to bother you, but.... Every paper in town's putting the pressure on. Even Mr. Bayliss has called."

"What time is it?"

"It's after four."

"My God! Tell Boley to pick me up right away."

He banged up the receiver and hurried in to take a shower. He'd only intended to rest for a couple of hours. He'd practically lost the whole day.

In the shower he began to sing, but checked himself. How long had it been since he'd sung in a shower? Laughing, he bellowed: "Jumbuck the billabong!" Then, he spoke thoughtfully: "Good old Wesson. What a louse!"

He put on the double-breasted gray suit Sam Brod had given him for some favor he'd done for Sam. It was valued at two-fifty. Quite a suit!

Finally he looked in the mirror at himself. "Great," he observed, "except for the face. When the looks were passed out, I got slighted."

And yet he knew that he was attractive to many women. There was a harsh, virile ugliness about his narrow face and his cool, observant gray eyes that troubled them.

13

As they drove to the City Building Boley explained to Roy that the place was in an ungodly uproar with reporters running wild in the corridors and poor old Lackey going slightly crazy trying to preserve order. A girl reporter from a tabloid had sneaked down to the basement cells, either stealing a work-elevator or bribing somebody.

"Which, of course, is not hard to do," said Roy. "Did she get an interview?"

"No. She got her ears burned."

"How so?" Roy turned and glanced at Boley with interest.

"Alma told me that the girl really read the riot act to the reporter. In ladylike language, too. Not even a damn. Alma threw the reporter out. And Alma got told off by the reporter. But it wasn't ladylike. She said she heard words she didn't know existed. I guess it's all a matter of a college education."

"Yeah," said Roy.

"Wesson told me he was hiding for his life. That beat he got sure raised a stink, a couple of papers lodging a protest. They claim Wesson always gets favored because he's a crook."

"More or less true," said Roy, laughing slightly.

"Never saw one like this before," said Boley. "Look, Roy. I'm going to break down. I sneaked a gander at the broad."

"Zing!" said Roy.

"You ought to see Emmett's face. He...."

Roy broke in. "When did *he* see her?"

"See her!" cried Boley. "He worked her over. Gave her the scientific treatment."

Roy lost his temper for a moment, then his mood changed and he laughed curtly. "Well, I guess there's no reason why poor old Emmett shouldn't get an eyeful. Everybody else has. Nobody pays any attention to my orders, anyway."

Boley sobered and was silent for a moment. "It's like this, Roy. I'm telling you. Things got completely out of hand. This is real Big League stuff. Murder of a rich guy like Hobart—and a doll like that mixed up in it! Why, it'll sell more papers than if Washington, D.C. was burned down by Communists. What an uproar! Reporters getting fired... God knows what! You wait!"

"H'm," said Roy. "Let's go in the alleyway. Let's sneak in through the basement, and take a work-elevator upstairs."

"Okay."

"Any of the reporters get to Dumas or Miss Jensen? If they did, I'll put Sid in for transfer."

"I don't think so. He's got 'em hid some place." Boley was beginning to get a little agitated. Once Roy took to the warpath anything could happen. High brass always backed him up a hundred percent!

A gray-haired turnkey started slightly when he saw Roy and Boley coming down the ramp into the basement from the truck entrance. Then he turned and called: "Alma! Alma! The Captain!"

Alma, in her smart gray uniform, came on the run. She was a tall, rawboned woman, about forty. She'd been on the force for nearly twenty years in one capacity or another; and was now the boss of the matrons and policewomen in the City Building, and highly regarded by all the male personnel, which was more than could be said for a good many of the women in the department. She had dark hair, and a long, plain face, slightly disfigured by burn scars she'd received dragging a would-be-suicide out of a gas explosion. She was imperturbable, hard to impress, and seemingly immune to the emotional storms which lowered the efficiency of too many of the policewomen. But now she looked agitated, and a lock of hair kept falling down over her forehead. Roy noticed this at once because it was unprecedented. Alma was the soul of neatness, tidiness.

"What kind of a girl is that you sent me, Captain?" she cried. "She didn't have a stitch on except that skirt and sweater."

"She dressed in a hurry," said Roy.

"A taxi driver came with three suit-cases full of clothes for her. Awful nice things. Prettiest underclothes I ever saw."

"Did you let her have 'em?"

"Of course not. Who's *she?*"

"You mean she's got the drabs on?"

"Naturally, Captain."

"She in a cell?"

"No. I put her in the restraining-room. It's comfortable. Nice bed and all. I had her in a cell till that redheaded b... well, that redheaded girl from the *Post* sneaked down here."

"What do you think of our prisoner?"

"A raving beauty, of course. And very nice and polite in her demeanor. Couldn't be nicer. She really put that redheaded b... that redhead in her place, and politely."

"Give her her clothes. Let her dress up, and make her as comfortable as you can. No drabs, no routine. She's to do nothing but sit in that room and read or whatever she likes."

"I understand, Captain. Yes sir."

"No contact with any of the prisoners. I'm holding you personally responsible."

"Yes, Captain."

"Now about Lackey. Did he question her?"

"No sir. I don't think so. He was only with her in the laboratory for a little while. He made some tests."

"Okay, Alma."

Roy slipped into his office by a back corridor. Boley went around to the anteroom to help Gert and Ed Reynolds. Roy heard the uproar when Boley appeared, and winced slightly.

In the main room, Lackey was sitting at one desk and Wesson at another.

"Well," said Roy, staring at Wesson.

"I'm persona non grata with my colleagues," said Wesson. "Translated, that means they think that I'm a stinker and a louse."

"Well?"

"Now wait a minute, Roy. It's all in the viewpoint, and the viewpoint depends on the moral climate. The present moral climate, shall we say, leaves more than a little to be desired? What do you want me to do—martyrize myself? Did you ever look in a mirror?"

"Glib," said Roy.

"Thank you. No, when in Rome make like a Roman. I'm the inheritor of an older tradition—a Greek among barbarians, you might say. But I've got a belly to fill."

"And *what* a belly! All right; beat it. I've got work to do."

"May I hide in your private office? Come on, Roy. Just till the heat gets off. I've been threatened."

"No. You think I want you going through my files? There's a store-room down the back hall. And don't fill your pockets with typewriter ribbons."

Wesson grabbed up his coat and a fistful of magazines. "The very thing," he said, and went out.

Roy sat down across from Lackey whose upper lip was beaded with sweat, and whose eyes were more than usually evasive behind his old-fashioned glasses.

"I told Creel nobody was to see that girl," said Roy.

"I know, Roy. But I interpreted that to mean, no newspaper people. No out-siders. I had my work to do."

"Well?"

"Her hands are clear of any indication of firing a gun recently."

"All right. How about gloves?"

"I found two pair in the apartment. One pair in a closet, another pair in a waste-basket. I thought to myself, this may be it. But—nothing."

Roy picked up a phone and dialled. In a moment, Alma answered.

"Alma—any gloves in those suit-cases?"

"No gloves."

Roy hung up. "Emmett, tonight I want you to run out alone to that address on Barrington. Those people are okay. Take a look for gloves."

"Yes, Roy. The girl has quite a bad black eye. Did you notice?"

"No," said Roy, his eyes lighting up slightly. "She had on dark glasses."

"She told me there was a closet door in her apartment at the Ashton that stuck. When she tried to pull it open, it gave all of a sudden and hit her."

"Well?"

"I called the Ashton, got Mr. Clemm. One of the closet doors in her apart-ment sticks. She reported it."

"All right. Now—give me the routine stuff."

"No gun has been found. It was apparently a .38. But only one bullet has been located and it is so mashed up it's hard to tell anything. One shot hit Hobart a glancing blow on the temple. One nicked his shoulder. One went through his left chest, killing him. I don't know which of the bullets we found."

"Anything in the newsboy's transcript?"

"It sets the time, that's about all. Shortly after eleven-thirty. Hobart seemed to appear out of nowhere, according to the boy. A car turned the corner directly before, but it may or may not have had anything to do with the killing. In fact, the boy is vague. Reading the transcript, it seems that Hobart walked some little distance before he fell. When the boy first saw him, after hearing the shots, he appeared to be standing on the corner. There were no more shots. All of a sudden he crumpled up."

"Anything else?"

"Oh, yes. Mr. Hobart's Cadillac was found abandoned about ten blocks from the corner where he was killed."

"Have you looked it over?"

"Yes. Nothing. A picture of the girl was in the glove-compartment. It was autographed to: Frank, my darling daddy."

"'Darling daddy,'" Roy mused. "It's a funny thing how many darling daddies catch lead. Fingerprints?"

"They are not all worked up yet. But I don't expect much. The ones on the wheel were all smeared. Let you know later."

"All right." Roy got up. "I want the Jensen girl. Sneak her up the backway. I'll be in my office."

"Okay, Roy." Lackey reached for the phone. "I hope, Roy, that I haven't offended you. I thought you meant...."

Roy laughed shortly. "You just wanted to get a look at the big bim. Now didn't you, Emmett? Admit something for once."

Lackey cleared his throat uncomfortably. "Well, now, of course, there was a natural curiosity, but...."

"I give up," said Roy, and went into his private office, slamming the door.

Just as Roy sat down at his desk, the phone rang. It was Gert in the outer office. "Mr. Bayliss, Captain," she said.

Chad came on at once. He sounded elated. "You're doing great, Roy. Great! I saw the evening papers. It will be front page from morning till night now."

"It's just starting, Chad. Wait till we cut loose with the real pictures."

"I saw the ones in the *World*—couldn't make out much. Dark glasses, purse in the way. But, good God, Roy, what a figure! Now I know what they mean by pneumatic bliss. Poor old Frank. Didn't think he was capable of it. Anyway, it's great work, Roy. Oh, just a minute. One thing. There is always one silly bastard to darken your day, no matter how bright it is. Chuck Thomas called from the *Post*. Old friend of mine. Raised hell. Put in a complaint against you. Said you always favored the *World*. Told him I'd speak to you about it. Now I have."

"Wait a minute, Chad. The *World's* nothing to me. But they got a man named Wesson. He is so smart it might be a good idea to drown him. He dogged me like a bloodhound on this one. He even brought up the word 'politics.' So I took care of him."

"Good work," said Chad. "Beefs never bother me, Roy. However, if you can do Chuck a good turn, don't pass it up."

"Okay. But you understand about Wesson."

"I do, Roy. Goodbye now. You're a whiz, and...."

"Wait a minute," Roy interposed hastily. "Where you calling from?"

"A pay-phone."

"Fine. Listen, Chad. There are some rather funny angles to this case. We might have the guilty person at that."

"Not a chance, Roy. I'm telling you."

"Sure it's not just a preconceived idea you got? You could be wrong."

"Take my word for it, Roy. It's grapevine. They've been making threats, the boys I've mentioned. I sent a man to contact them nearly a month ago. He got nothing but a quick brushoff. There's been a turnover in the organization. New blood. No, Roy. Just keep on the way you're going, but don't try to kid yourself."

"Okay, Chad."

As Roy hung up there was a light tap at the door, then Alma came in with Ruth Jensen, who did not seem quite as composed as she had earlier in the day.

"Sit down, Miss Jensen," said Roy. "You want to wait in the main room, Alma? I won't be long."

"No, I think I'd better go back. We caught that girl from the *Post* again. She was knocking on Miss Vance's door. How she got down there or knew where to knock, I'll never know."

"Who's on duty at the turntable?"

"Old Pat."

"Tell Old Pat to go and buy his wife a present with the bribes he's been taking, and tell Emmett to put Red Benson on the turntable. Emmett is to inform Red that he can now kick all the reporters he wants to—even female ones, and that he can also smash a few cameras."

Alma smiled slightly. "Yes, Captain. Then I'd better go back downstairs. No telling what will break next."

"Did you give the girl her clothes?"

"I did. And I thought she was going to cry. She just hated the drabs. And I wish you could see the way she looked at our nice shower-room."

"Spoiled, eh? Good thing she's not in the County Jail. All right, Alma. If there's any more trouble, call me. But I doubt if there will be, with Red down there."

Alma went out. Roy rose, walked to the window, and lit a cigarette.

"I had no idea what an important man you were, Mr. Hargis," said Ruth.

He glanced at her, noted the irony. All the same, her face showed the strain of waiting and uncertainty. She had a nice front this girl, but Roy was positive that she was very emotional, very passionate, and that she was blindly infatuated with the tall, careless, arrogant, young musician.

"'Captain' not 'mister,'" he said, smiling slightly. "Did they let you use the phone?"

"Yes. Alma is very nice. I took you at your word, so I didn't call a lawyer. I merely called a girl friend of mine, and asked her to look after the shop for me."

"I see. Well, we won't be long. Then you can go."

"What about Bob?"

"I'm going to talk to him later."

"I know. But he needs that job. He hasn't got a penny."

"I think they'll hold the job for him. That is, if he ever gets out of here."

Ruth rose quickly and came over to Roy, her face showing deep concern. "You don't think that he.... How could you think such a thing? Why, he's gentle as a lamb. He wouldn't hurt a fly. Captain Hargis—listen to me. Just because he happened to get mixed up with a... with a...."

"With a what, Miss Jensen?"

"With a horrible person like that."

"He was having an affair with her. Wasn't he?"

"No. He was not," Ruth shouted. "She did everything in the world to...."

"Including a murder."

"I don't know what you mean." Ruth was very pale and agitated. She got out a handkerchief and began to twist it into a ball, then to tear it.

Roy watched her for a moment, then he came over to her, took her gently by the arm and forced her to sit down.

"Tell me what happened last night."

"I told you, Captain."

"No, you lied. Now I'd like to have the truth."

There was a pause, then Ruth said: "I told you the truth."

"No," said Roy. "But if you *would* tell me the truth, it might help Bob, unless I'm very much mistaken. Don't let your vanity stand in the way. I've known two men who were hung for vanity."

Ruth spoke in such a low voice that Roy could hardly hear her. "I don't know what you mean."

"I'll explain. You were with Bob all last evening. It was Monday, and Cipriano's was dark. You had a nice little party together. You sat and talked. Maybe Bob played the piano for you. Not that Cavallaro stuff he has to play. But stuff he likes—maybe his own music...."

Ruth began to cry.

"He's a nice guy. He may be a damned fool, but that has never yet kept a man from being a nice guy. You're a nice girl. I don't mean you are necessarily a virgin, Miss Jensen. There are other ways of being nice. Anyway, two nice people sitting together enjoying a nice evening. Then what happens? The phone rings. A harpy calls. Your nice boy runs out on you, and you sit there waiting...

and you wait... and it's damn near morning...."

"No," sobbed Ruth.

"Yes," said Roy. "You are a very pretty girl, Miss Jensen. And a refined girl, and a good girl in the sense I mean it. You've got Bob's best interests at heart. You'd do anything to help him. You'd like to marry him, and make things easy for him... wouldn't you, Miss Jensen?"

"Yes."

"Fine. And yet right now, out of vanity, you are denying that the harpy called... and that Bob left you... and stayed away all night. Why is that?"

"I wasn't with Bob. He didn't leave me because she called. I don't know anything about it."

"What time did she call?"

There was a long pause. Finally Ruth looked up. "Could I have a cigarette, Captain?"

"Sure thing, Miss Jensen." He took out a cigarette, lit it, and handed it to her. She smoked in silence, her hand shaking slightly. From time to time, tears showed briefly on her eye-lids and she winked them away impatiently.

"He's such an awful fool in some ways," she sobbed. "I don't know why I... living in that awful place! My aunt thinks I'm crazy, and this will nearly kill her."

"Rich women have a way of hanging on. I wouldn't worry about that."

"She's been very nice to me in spite of everything. You see, I was her pet. She paid for my coming-out party. It was very expensive. She had a nice husband all picked out for me. But I wanted a fling. I opened my music shop, then I met Bob. He was always in looking for old records. He's got a big file on Bix. I was able to help him and...." She broke off, shook her head, and made a gesture as if to say: "Why go on?"

"So it goes," said Roy. "Now you're stuck with him."

"Yes," said Ruth.

"What time did Miss Vance call?"

"It was some time after twelve. Nearly twelve-thirty."

"Thank you, Miss Jensen. You can go home now. Thank you again."

Ruth rose and stood looking rather uncertainly at Roy, who was dialling the phone on his desk. "Alma? Come up and get Miss Jensen. Is Lois there? Okay. Take Miss Jensen out through the truck entrance, and have Lois drive her home. Nobody is to see her, understand? Thanks, Alma."

"I'm sure I don't know if I've done the right thing," said Ruth. "I'm just so... well, nothing like this has ever happened to me before, and...."

"You did the right thing," said Roy. "You've got Bob half way out the door now."

"Oh, thank God," said Ruth.

She seemed on the point of breaking down. Roy lit a cigarette quickly and handed it to her.

Ruth had gone and Roy was pacing up and down, lost in thought, when the door opened slowly and a fat, snub-nosed face was poked around the jamb. Wesson! When he was sure that Roy was alone, he came in and shut the door. Roy ignored him. Leaning on the desk, Wesson began to sing.

O, I loikes a bit of Stilton with me dinner,
O, I loikes a bit of Stilton, that I do.
O, I loikes a bit of Stilton with me dinner,
Loik me grandsire did in 1852.

"I was pretty sure your grandsire was an ape," said Roy.

"Now, now. Temper. I only came in because a thought has been bothering me."

"I didn't know anything bothered you, and I didn't know you ever had a thought."

"The Lackawanna Bus Terminal bothers me very, very much."

"Why?"

"It implies the dolly was on the lam."

"Wasn't she?"

"Not from the Bus Terminal."

"It must be true. I read it in the *World.* 'If it's true we print it.' Remember the masthead?"

"We are really a couple of boys, aren't we?" Wesson turned and started out, singing.

"Stay in that store-room and keep out of trouble."

"You don't have to tell *me.* I even found a phone in there. I've been calling every place. I even called my nephew in Oxford."

"Oxford, Ohio?"

"No, England," said Wesson, as he went out, closing the door softly.

14

Roy was sitting at his desk, eating a sandwich and drinking coffee from a paper carton when Boley opened the door, let Bob Dumas in, gestured briefly, and was going to shut the door, when Roy called:

"How are things out front?"

"Worse than ever. Reporters coming in from out of town now. And there's a big shot CNS guy out there, throwing his weight around," Boley explained.

"Tell 'em all to be patient," said Roy. "We'll have the show in about an hour. Anybody see Dumas come up?"

"No," said Boley. "Just like you said."

"Okay," said Roy.

Boley shut the door. Bob took off his coat and tossed it at a chair. He missed. "Show, eh?" he said. "This is a real circus all right."

He turned his back on Roy and stood looking out the window. Night had fallen, clear and mild, with a cloudless sky and many stars. Neon signs blossomed like night flowers all along the boulevards. The roar of the city was loud.

Roy finished his sandwich, drank the remainder of the coffee, then he pulled some papers toward him, glanced at them briefly, and looked up.

"I see you're 4F, Dumas, according to this questionnaire which some efficient character downstairs had you fill out. Why 4F, if I may ask? Don't answer if you don't want to. It's only curiosity on my part. Has no bearing on anything."

"I doubt that very much, Captain," said Bob. "With you everything has a bearing on something. But I'll answer. In fact it gives me great pleasure. So far, I haven't had much luck in my life, but that 4F business, well.... When I was nine years old I fell off a high wall and broke my left leg in two places. Bad breaks. It didn't knit right so they broke it over. I guess the doctor was a clumsy and incompetent old bastard, God rest his lovely soul! The leg was worse the second time. So I've got a limp, and the Army can't touch me."

Roy looked him over. "You mean you're lame? How could I miss it?"

"I'll admit you don't miss much. But the limp is very slight, and I've learned how to manage it."

"So you consider that a great piece of luck, eh?"

Bob left the window and sat down opposite Roy. "Yes. Let me tell you a story, Captain. You seem to have unlimited time."

"Oh, sure."

"I read this story in a book about Whistler, the painter." Roy looked blank. "You know, *Whistler's Mother*." Roy nodded. "Well, it was 1870, and France had fallen apart. The Germans were in Paris. Seems like Whistler was a fire-eating Southerner—like myself." Bob laughed derisively.

"You from the South?"

"New Orleans. Well, Whistler met this young French painter—can't recall his name—at a party. They got to talking about the plight of France and Whistler was surprised that the young Frenchman didn't seem to give a damn. He asked him what he was doing in England at a time like this, why he wasn't in the French Army. The young Frenchman told Whistler he'd run away to keep from getting put in the Army. 'Why?' asked Whistler. 'Because,' said the painter, completely unconcerned, 'I'm a coward.'"

Roy glanced at Bob in surprise, then laughed. The story interested him. It was so unexpected.

"The point is," Bob went on, "this fellow was a painter, not a soldier. He had something to do in the world and he intended to do it. He just didn't go for that hero crap. He was honest."

"Yeah," said Roy. "In World War II we had the stockade full of guys like that.

Some of them chopped off their toes and fingers."

"Pass it," said Bob. "I see I was just wasting my breath."

"Oh, I don't know," said Roy. "You may have a point." He rose and paced up and down for a while, then he turned to Bob and asked: "What time did Ilona Vance call you last night?"

Bob studied Roy for a moment. "Look," he said, "I don't like the quiz program type of conversation. 'Where was you last night, bud, at midnight?' Sounds comical. What do you want to know?"

"I want to know what time she called you," said Roy, mildly.

"She didn't call me at all."

"Why did you leave Miss Jensen then and go out?"

"Here we go. You tell *me*."

Roy looked at him for a long time. Then he nodded. "All right, Dumas. You can go back downstairs. I see you don't want to cooperate."

"Why should I cooperate? For what? I'm minding my own business. I get arrested, dragged in, shoved around from room to room with reporters yelling like maniacs all over the place. I'm supposed to be at work. Now I probably got no job. Not that I'd cry over that. But Ruth would. Say, where is she, by the way?"

"I sent her home."

"Did you question her?"

"You tell *me*," said Roy.

"Here we go. Quips and comical dialogue. Jesus, I get so sick and tired of it at Cip's. Everybody is a comedian now. They get Lauritz Melchior on the radio. All right, he's a great singer. Do they let him sing? No. He has to get boffs, or he's a bum. What the hell is the reason for all this—will you tell me?"

"It's kind of tough for you to stick to the point, isn't it, Dumas?"

Bob regarded Roy for a long time in silence, then he said: "Look, Captain. The point with me is music. Not wars, not boffs, not who shot who and why. I'll tell you a story." Roy grimaced, but made no protest. Bob put his feet up on Roy's desk and searched himself for a cigarette. Roy pushed Bob's feet down without comment, then lit a cigarette and handed it to him. "You may get *this* one," said Bob, then he went on. "A couple of musicians were walking past St. Dominic's Cathedral. Something happened up above and that great goddamn heavy bell came crashing down on the sidewalk making a hell of a racket— enough to scare a man out of his wits. One of the musicians yelled: 'What in the Jesus was that?' And the other one said: 'E Flat.'"

Roy looked at Bob blankly for a moment, then smiled. "I think I see what you mean."

"For instance," said Bob. "You've got a very interesting voice. Sometimes you talk in thirds—in a low register. It's sort of unusual."

"I understand," said Roy, "that Ilona Vance didn't have much of a voice."

Bob winced. "That poor girl. Tone-deaf. However, things could be worse. She might have turned into a lady baritone. Her voice wasn't so bad. But every note either flat or sharp. It was almost phenomenal."

"Why did you persist with her?"

Bob put his feet up on Roy's desk again, but took them down at once. "Well," he said, "you finally worked the conversation around, didn't you? Like a radio announcer with an embarrassingly far-fetched lead-in to the commercial. I persisted, as you put it, because she... well, she was a goddamned determined young lady."

"What time did she call you last night?"

"That's beginning to sound like a song title."

There was a brief silence, then Roy spoke wearily. "One thing I'd never suspect you of is chivalry."

"Why not? I'm from the Deep South. Magnolias and you-all. We put 'em on a pedestal down there, suh."

"Quips and comical dialogue."

"Yes, damn it. I've caught the disease."

"Dumas," said Roy, after another pause, "do you know what the word 'accessory' means?"

"Yes, I think so. It's something on an automobile, isn't it?"

Roy compressed his lips, turned and picked up the phone. "Boley? Okay. Come get him. Take him out through the front. He's on his own now. All the pictures they want, and let him rassle with the reporters for a while." As an afterthought, he added as he hung up: "Not that he won't do okay."

Bob rose, picked up his coat and put it on, having a little difficulty as the lining in both sleeves was torn. "I thought you guys hit people over the head with blackjacks and things. I'm getting off light."

"You're just starting, son," said Roy, turning his back.

"Know a good lawyer I could call?"

"Ask Boley. He's got a fistful of shyster cards."

"Trouble is, they want a retainer or something. Is that right?"

"The sane ones do. We'll get you one for free if you like. But I wouldn't advise it. You can do better singlehanded."

"Thank you, Captain."

In a moment, Boley looked in. "Come on, handsome," he said. "Lots of broads out here, waiting. Give 'em the profile."

"Always the dialogue," said Bob, going out.

As Boley was shutting the door, it was pushed out of his hand and a small, fierce-looking, redheaded girl rushed in. First, she did a wild take on seeing Bob, then she ran to Roy, grabbed his arm, and shook him. Irritated, he brushed her off.

"Who opened the window?" he asked.

Boley, looking embarrassed, hurriedly closed the door.

"I'm Gay Lucas—*Post*," cried the girl. "And I'm goddamned frigging tired of getting shoved around by you big yokels."

"Such language!"

"Don't give me that crap, Captain. Now, listen...."

"You from Smith or Vassar?"

"State. Look now...." She went on and on denouncing the treatment she'd received in the City Building.

Roy ignored her, went to his desk, opened a desk drawer, took out two shiny prints, and without a word handed them to her. One was a portrait of Ilona. The other was Ilona in her cigarette girl costume.

"Now, honey. Satisfied? They're yours."

The girl's eyes flashed. "Why...!" She stammered, overcome.

"Tell you what," said Roy, "if you are a very, very good little girl and are very, very nice to us, I'll give you a picture of her in a French bathing-suit." The girl grabbed at him excitedly. "Later, later, honey. Take it easy."

"I don't know if I can stand the one in the French bathing-suit," said the girl, thoughtfully. "There's a possibility I may be a borderline case."

"I doubt it," said Roy, winking.

"You're cute. Married?"

"Does that matter?"

"No," said the girl, smiling mischievously.

Roy turned her around and aimed her at the door, then he slapped her lightly on the rear. "You're missing all the fun out there."

She looked over her shoulder at him, gave him a wide, compliant smile, then went out.

Roy sat down at his desk. "What I won't do for old Chad!" he observed aloud. Then he picked up the phone: "Boley? Put him on. Joe? Can you hear me? My God, what an uproar! Take him downstairs now. Then get a car and wait for me at the truck entrance. We're stepping out."

15

It was a little after nine. Vanity Row was just beginning to wake up. The doormen, looking like comic opera admirals in their gold braid, were at their posts; the taxi-stand at the deadend had a full rank of cabs; and big chauffeured limousines were drawing up at Cipriano's, the Gold Eagle, Merlin's, and Weber's. There was a scattering of bobby-soxers and gawky, crop-headed boys, looking for autographs: unawed, raucous, cynical.

Boley parked just around the corner on Blackhawk and Roy got out. "I won't be long," he said. "Stay put."

"You going in the front way?" asked Boley, laughing. "Costs a fin just to check your hat, I hear."

"Why do you think I'm wearing this Sam Brod suit?"

"I was wondering about that," said Boley, snickering.

The doorman at Cipriano's glanced curiously at Roy, and seemed about to make a comment as Roy stood waiting for the door to be opened, but something about the way Roy regarded him steadily with his unfriendly gray eyes apparently nettled the doorman and changed his mind. He opened the door, bowing slightly.

"Evening, sir."

Roy found himself in a lobby which resembled a plush-lined and oppressively sweet-smelling cave. The lights were dim. There was a discreet tinkling of silverware and china in the rooms beyond. From time to time a waiter in mess-jacket, cummerbund and lavender-and-gold trousers would move past one of the tall arched doors, carrying a tray. A piano was playing in the bar, called the Tangiers Room, Bob Dumas's normal stand.

The hat-check girl was wearing some kind of a peasant blouse which was nearly falling off her shoulders and leaving practically nothing to the imagination. She had thick, coarse, bushy blond hair and her eyelids were painted blue. She looked like something out of the Swedish Ballet.

A sleek-haired captain in a Tux approached him. His manner was insolent.

"Sir? Please?" he murmured, his black eyes blankly unwelcoming.

"Are you Caesar?"

The captain flinched slightly, as if Roy had made an indelicate remark. "Oh, certainly not. What, may I ask, is your business with Caesar? Is it about a reservation?"

"I want to talk to him. Tell him to come here."

The captain seemed horrified, and looked about him, trying to locate one of the larger waiters, just in case.

"Oh, quite out of the question at the moment, sir. Now if there is anything that I...."

"Do you want me to embarrass you and pull out a badge?"

The captain started and looked about him involuntarily. People were drifting in now in rather large numbers. It was apparently going to be quite crowded, for Tuesday evening.

"Will you come with me?" said the captain.

Roy followed him down a narrow, dim-lit, padded corridor, at the end of which was a small door. The captain knocked discreetly and when an irritable voice cried: "Well?" he spoke a few rapid sentences in Italian. In a moment, the door opened and a pompous-looking little man in a beautifully-cut dark business suit glanced out angrily.

"But this is outrageous!" he cried.

"Just take a minute," said Roy, pushing past him into the cluttered little office.

The captain hurried away, pale and shaken. Caesar shut the door, then he assumed a Napoleonic pose—arms crossed, feet wide apart—and stared with violent Italian contempt at Roy.

"This I must protest!" he cried. "I protest! I protest!"

"Oh, come on," said Roy. "Save it for the suckers." He showed his badge.

"I will have you broken for this. You will see. One word from me. I will whisper one word to Mr. Spalding. Poof! You'll be without your badge."

"Oh, please," said Roy. "Come on, climb down. They tell me you were a friend of Mr. Hobart's."

Caesar started, stared, then tears came to his eyes. He unfolded his arms. Then he elaborately crossed himself. "God rest him. The finest gentleman I ever knew."

"I'm Hargis. I got the case. I just want to ask you one question."

"But why didn't you tell me you were Captain Hargis? I thought you were merely some underling abusing your authority."

"All right. Who introduced you to Ilona Vance?"

Caesar recoiled slightly and ran his fingers through his thick, kinky, gray hair. "Who introduced me to...? But I don't.... I was going to say I don't see what bearing that has. But I *do* see. Yes, yes. She was introduced to me by Elmer Spencer. Do you know him? I believe he is called Allen Spencer now. A sort of promoter."

"He asked you to give her a job?"

"He begged me to. And I did. The most beautiful girl I have ever seen in my life. I mean it, Captain Hargis. A sad, sad case. Even so, I can't believe that she did it."

"Why?"

"Oh, I just can't. She was so beautiful."

"Any idea who might have?"

"Kill Mr. Hobart—that wonderful man? It could only have been an accident."

"Well, we're getting no place, Gozza. Is Joe Sert here?"

"Yes, he's here. Shall I ring him? See if it's convenient?"

"Will you?"

Caesar called on a house-phone and held a brief conversation, then he hung up, and nodded. "He will be pleased to see you, Captain Hargis."

"Is his wife back there with him?"

"Yes. But she's in bed, ill. There's a large apartment back there, you know. Mr. Sert and his new bride have been living there, having their honeymoon. Sorry we had our little misunderstanding, Captain!"

"It's okay."

"I'll show you the way."

Caesar led him through a narrow passageway to the corridor of the women's lounge. It was the same as before, only not deserted. Beautifully-dressed girls were passing back and forth. The stylized nudes on the walls and the grotesque statue of the naked black woman seemed to fade pleasantly into the surroundings now and not stand out stark and bizarre as they had the night before.

As Caesar tapped at the door, he said: "One question, please. That fine gray suit, Captain. Winslow Smith or Samuel Brod?"

"Sam," said Roy, smiling slightly.

"I must give him some of my business," said Caesar. "He's a fine tailor. There's a new Italian in town. Riggio. You might look him up. Tell him Caesar sent you. Discount. He's trying to get started."

"Thanks."

The door was opened by Joe Sert, who was in his shirtsleeves. "Come in, Hargis. Come in. Thanks, Attilio."

"Your servant, Captain," said Caesar, giving Roy a very expensive bow which was usually reserved for the Babylon Room clientele of Cipriano's.

Joe Sert seemed agitated and somewhat sad. Roy sat watching him as he paced up and down, twisting his sparse hair and grimacing. Finally he turned.

"Funny world, ain't it, Hargis?"

Roy could think of no answer to that one, so he merely nodded.

"To tell you the truth, Hargis, I'm not a well man. I got blood pressure and I just found out a couple months ago I got diabetes, too. Well, Tootsie and me—we been on a real bender since we got married. What a honeymoon! I kept saying to myself: 'Joe, boy. You better watch it. You're going to die if you're not careful.' So? So, I never felt better in my life. And Tootsie's sick in bed—and she's just a kid, and strong."

"So it goes," said Roy.

"Yeah, funny. She just collapsed. I thought it was all that champagne. But, no—she's got a fever. Fever keeps jumping around. Doc wants her to go to the hospital for observation for a week. But, Tootsie—she won't go. I'm goddamned worried about her, Hargis. What should I do? Hell, we can't carry her out screaming and kicking. Doc says if she don't go, we better get another Doc, he won't be responsible, that's all. I'm worried to hell about this, Hargis."

"You've just got to persuade her to go, Mr. Sert."

Joe sat down heavily. "Yeah," he said, then for a long time he stared gloomily at the floor. Finally he sighed and looked up. "Okay. I guess you got your own troubles and don't want to hear mine. How you coming on the case?"

"I need a little help."

"All right. What?"

"I found out from Caesar who introduced the girl to him. It didn't lead any place. I was trying to see if I could establish any hoodlum relationship."

"Why?" Joe demanded, looking up quickly.

"I've got my reasons. A funny thing, Mr. Sert. Somebody stripped her apartment. Took her fur coats and I don't know what all. She never reported it. She even denied it to the house dick at the Terrace. I know how it was done, and it was strictly a professional job if I ever heard of one."

"Yeah," said Joe, vaguely.

"You wouldn't know anything about this, would you?"

Joe got up and walked about for a while, pulling at his hair. Finally he stopped in front of Roy. "How would this help, Hargis? I don't get it."

"Simple. If she thought Hobart was responsible for stripping her—taking all the stuff back he'd given her, it might establish a motive for her killing him. We need a motive, outside of a jealous fight or anything like that. Too vague. Something concrete."

"Yeah," said Joe, then after a moment: "You covering me, Hargis?"

"Hundred percent."

"Okay," said Joe. "Anything to put that big broad where she belongs. She ruined the best guy I ever met. Why, he changed like a... listen, Hargis—it was pitiful. Getting drunk, swearing and carrying on in the club, like some downstate hayneck at a plumber's convention... you wouldn't believe it. I *couldn't* believe it at first. It was like he'd blown his stack. And to tell you the truth, I think that's what happened. But I wasn't smart enough to realize it at the time. You see, I had such respect for this guy. Whatever he said was law to me. If he says it snows here in July, okay, it snows here in July. You get what I mean? Let me tell you about Mr. Hobart. He was the kind of guy who never complained—about *anything*. Too much pride. He could have been dying of cancer, but you'd never get a peep. I'm having a hard time explaining what I mean, and what a shock I got when he began to get drunk and cry around about that broad....

"Look. That last night I told you about. He come in the club all alone. His clothes looked wrinkled, he needed a shave. Caesar was horrified—I mean, he really was. Well, Mr. Hobart got so lushed up Caesar didn't know what to do. People were looking at him, and he was spilling drinks down the front of his shirt. Finally, I told Caesar to bring him back here. So we conned him and said I had a new shipment of champagne, and I wanted his opinion on it. He kind of pulled himself together and when he got back here he wasn't so bad—polite and gentlemanly like he used to be. But after one drink of champagne he was gone again—and, brother, I mean really gone...."

Joe stood in the middle of the room, shaking his head in sadness and wonder. "He began to tell me his troubles, blubbering. It was awful, Hargis, to see a man like that... well, I got madder and madder, but not at him, see?

"Then he really breaks down. He tells me he's going loony, he can't sleep, he wants to die... stuff like that. Then it comes out. The big broad had locked him out, wouldn't let him into the kip with her no more, and he couldn't take it. Instead of realizing he was well-off, he goes to pieces. Then he begins to tell me about all he'd done for her, all the stuff he'd given her—he'd spent a fortune on her. A chinchilla and two minks, not to mention a car and jewelry and stuff. He told her she'd have to give it all back to him if she was going to keep on acting this way. Not because he gave a damn about the money—he was loaded and a very generous guy. He was just trying to get her to start playing ball again. But she really gave him the brush. Told him he disgusted her, stuff like that, and finally she tossed him out of her apartment, slammed the door in his face...."

"They lied to me at the Terrace. Said Hobart never went up to her suite."

"It figures," said Joe, mildly. "They're just covering up for business reasons. So," Joe went on, "here's this great guy, Mr. Hobart, acting like a real joker—a real slob. It got me and now I sure enough had blood pressure. I could feel the top of my head throbbing. So... you want to write the rest?"

Joe went to his desk, took out a bottle of whiskey, and poured himself a drink. Then he looked up. "Oh, excuse me, Hargis. I'm kinda rattled. Want a drink?"

Roy merely shook his head.

There was a brief silence as Joe tossed down the drink. "The car was in Mr. Hobart's name. So that was okay."

"You took her *car*, too?"

"Sure. Mr. Hobart's nephew's got it. We gave her the old stripperoo. We even took all her evening dresses. The boys found thirty-five hundred dollars in cash behind a picture. I let 'em keep it. That way the job cost me nothing. I think the boys swung with some of the jewelry, too. And maybe some panties for their girl friends." Suddenly Joe threw back his head and laughed coarsely and at some length. "She didn't leave the Terrace with much more than she had when she went in. Okay. So it's robbery. You covering me, Hargis?"

"Sure," said Roy, then he stood up. "Well, I think this does it. Or comes mighty close to it. You're out of it, Mr. Sert. Grant, the house dick, has already testified she was stripped. This little girl's in a sack."

"'Little girl!'" cried Joe, his eyes flashing with animosity. "She whipped one of my waiters. She threw Mr. Hobart out of the apartment."

"Yeah," said Roy, mildly, then: "Well, goodnight, Mr. Sert. I hope Mrs. Sert is feeling better tomorrow. Give her my best."

Joe flashed Roy a pleased, friendly smile. It was obvious where his weak spot lay. "Thank you, Hargis. She's mentioned you a couple of times, also the kid that was with you. You guys kinda impressed her, I think. Okay, Hargis. Just so I'm covered."

"You're covered."

16

As they neared the City Building corner, Roy said: "Take me in the front way. Time for the show."

"This I want to see," said Boley, sighing, and shaking his head.

He made the turn, then eased over into an inside lane so he wouldn't get into a jam when he tried to move off the boulevard and onto the City Building ramp.

Traffic was heavy and fast in this part of town. Motor cops kept it rolling to prevent tie-ups and blocks at the Freeway entrances.

It was a warm night, almost like summer. A canted half-moon rode high over
the big buildings in a clear, cloudless, indigo sky. A mild breeze blew up from
the river, carrying the smell of deep water. The atmosphere was light and gave
you a feeling of space and freedom.

Boley sniffed the air as he drove. "This is the kind of night you should've been
up at the beach instead of in that thunderstorm. That gold-headed bim! Wonder where she is tonight?"

Roy ignored him. He hardly knew who Boley was talking about. What was
her name? Kit. Crazy kid—wanted to know about thunder!

The City Building was all lit up as if for a celebration. There were so many
lights burning inside that the floodlights outside were dimmed. Cars were
parked all over the first level above the street; some of them were parked cross-
ways and looked as if they'd been abandoned suddenly. Boley and Roy saw a
couple of uniformed coppers checking the cars.

"Those Press guys," said Roy. "What do they use for brains?"

"Wesson does all right."

Roy glanced at him. "Yeah. But there's a mystery about Wesson. How does
it happen a guy as smart as him makes as little money as he does? He's not even
in a profession where you can steal much of anything. You'd think at least he'd
be in politics."

They got out of the car and started across the wide cement plaza toward the
big entrance doors. "Funny guy, Wesson," said Boley. "No matter how much
he drinks, he only gets so drunk. Never falls down, never even staggers, and he
always knows what's what. However, one night I met him in a bar and we tied
one on. Pretty soon he's telling me about his old home in England, and he's got
tears in his eyes. He's been away seventeen years."

"Yeah, and when he got through crying, I'll bet he went on trying to pump
you."

Boley glanced sideways at Roy as they entered the building and turned down
a wide, marble corridor toward the elevators. "Sure he tried to pump me. He's
always trying to pump everybody. But what I'm speaking about is, them tears.
Wesson with tears in his eyes. It beat me. Wesson puts on the best fag act I ever
seen, but he's a real tough cookie and you know it."

"Sure he is," said Roy. "But the tears are easy. He was trying to soften you up,
so you'd feel sorry for him, and break down and give him some info."

"Think so? Yeah. Probably you're right. Why, that louse! And me wasting
sympathy on him. You see, Roy—sometimes I think about the Old Country.
Makes me sad. I remember a big river, a beautiful big river. And I remember
my grandfather. He was a farmer—had a blond beard."

"I thought you were born here."

"No, Poland. They brought me over when I was nine."

"Well, Joe, if you were back there you'd feel sad about here."

"More than likely," said Boley, thoughtfully. "Yeah, I guess you're right. Wherever you are, some place else looks better, and somebody else's girl, and stuff like that. Why is that?"

"I don't know," said Roy, curtly, as they got on the elevator and were borne upward. Such questions bored him. Nothing but futile, idle speculation.

They stopped in a little empty office on the third floor and Roy made a call to the jail in the basement. Red Benson answered.

"How's it going?" asked Roy.

"I had to take care of a couple of wise guys, pushed 'em around a little—but no harm done, not even a black eye. Nobody's got past since I went on, Cap, and nobody will."

"Nice work. As soon as Alma brings the girl up, you can go home, Red. Get a good night's sleep. You earned it. Get somebody to spell you. Now put Alma on."

After a considerable wait, Alma answered. "Yes, Captain."

"Are you ready?"

"Ready, willing and able, Captain. That girl! She really knows how to relax. She's been dressed to come upstairs for over an hour. Most girls would be nervous. Soon as they get dressed to go some place, they want to *go*. Last time I looked in on her, she was sitting in a chair dozing."

"How does she look?"

"Captain," said Alma, "it's not fair. *Nobody* should look that good."

"Okay. Bring her right up."

Roy hung up, then he and Boley climbed the stairs to the fourth floor. They'd got off at the third so Roy could make his call unobserved.

Before they were half way to the fourth floor they could hear the uproar. It sounded like a cocktail party. There was loud talking and laughing and an atmosphere of nervous tension.

When Roy and Boley reached the head of the stairs there were shouts and men came running toward them. The door of the outer office was open and people were milling in and out: pressmen and women, photographers, City Building employees, who had stayed on for the excitement, and a few strangers who apparently had come in from the street. The hallway was littered with newspapers, magazines, chewing-gum wrappers, matches, cigarette butts, and practically anything else people throw away, including, strangely enough, a pair of women's gloves, a shopping-bag with some canned-goods in it, and a man's hat.

"Looks like Saturday afternoon at the State Fair," said Roy.

Several newsmen began to yammer at him at once. Somebody took a flash picture. One man even grabbed Roy by the arm.

"Take it easy. Take it easy," said Roy. "What's all the excitement?"

"What's all the excitement, he says!" cried a red-faced man in a seersucker suit.

Roy grabbed him by the lapels and shook him gently. "You're a season be-hind in that suit, aren't you, pal?"

"I been going since eight this morning. It was hot as hell then. Look, Captain. When? When?"

"When what?"

There was a wild uproar as Roy tried to go into the outer office, brushing peo-ple aside.

"You know 'what!' Don't you know every editor in town is burning every-body's ass for copy about that beee-yooo-ti-full doll!"

"She never killed nobody, now did she, Captain? How *could* she? It's against nature...."

"Even if she did, she'll get off. Providing her lawyer gets her a man jury...."

"With a woman jury she's a dead duck...."

"Wait a minute," said Roy. "Let's not try her yet."

"Quote? How about a quote?" There were shouts and yells and pushing. An-other flash picture was taken. For laughs, Roy took off his hat and held it in front of his face. He got plenty of laughs, but they sounded hysterical.

Then the elevator stopped in front of the outer office door, and Alma emerged, followed by Ilona Vance.

The hubbub died down immediately.

The girl was wearing a plain, simple black silk dress, beautifully moulded to her figure. Her thick black hair, which shone like glass under the lights, was up, and in a large bun on the nape of her neck. She was wearing no jewelry, not even a ring. She had gardenias in her hair. A faint aura of exquisite perfume began to fight with the cigarette-smoke in the crowded corridor. She had on very high-heeled black pumps, ornamented with gold and silver stitching.

"Holy Mackerel!" cried somebody in an awe-struck voice, breaking the si-lence. There were nervous laughs, then the photographers got busy and flash-bulbs lit up the hallway.

"Plenty of time for that," shouted Roy, and the girl looked at him curiously with her large, almond-shaped, emotionless, pale-gray eyes.

"Inside, miss," said Roy, as Boley and Ed Reynolds made a path for her. "Straight on through into the next office."

With the easy, graceful, artificial gait of a model, the girl walked slowly through the crowd, looking at nobody, calm, collected, and impressive.

When she had passed through, followed by Alma, Roy barred the door. "Now listen," he said, "you're all invited in so take it easy. No crowding. No shoving. Everybody gets in and we play no favorites."

"How about Percy Wesson—that fat English fag?"

"Who?" Roy demanded, smiling ironically.

"He must be sleeping with the Commissioner."

"What a repulsive thought!" cried a girl reporter, and there was a general laugh.

Emmett Lackey was in the main office, which was large, with four desks and many chairs along the walls. He was sweating and wiping his face with a big handkerchief as the girl came in preceded by Boley and Ed Reynolds and followed by Alma.

Lackey tried to fade into the background, taking a place at the far end of the room, but the girl noticed him.

"How do you do?" she said politely, in her deep voice, which seemed to come from her heels and yet was pleasant, soft, and natural. In fact, she seemed to have no affectation about her at all, and no coquetry. Her face was unsmiling, and seemed naturally so, not sullen. She did not dab at her hair, pull at her dress, or make any of those futile gestures most women would have made under the circumstances. She seemed entirely and honestly calm and relaxed.

Lackey looked wilted. "How do you do, miss?" he mumbled, bowing slightly.

Boley was overcome and merely stared sadly at this vision and wondered how he could have thought that the little blond babe, Kit, was so good-looking. Ed Reynolds chewed his match. Finally he said to Boley: "Didn't think she could look better. But she does. Why ain't she Miss America? They like 'em big at them contests, don't they?"

At the main office door, Roy barred the clamoring horde again. "Now take it easy, boys and girls. Plenty of room if you don't stampede. All right now."

Roy stood aside and the pressmen rushed in, pushing and talking.

"Would you mind standing over here, miss?" asked Roy, indicating a place in front of one of the desks.

The girl glanced at him, hesitated, then came over. Now she stared at him. Her eyes didn't seem to wink. It bothered Roy a little.

"I'm Captain Hargis, Miss Vance," he explained.

"Oh," said the girl, "you're the boss man."

"I'm the boss man," said Roy, feeling proud of the fact for the first time in months.

"Then I'd better do what you say."

Roy looked at her, expecting a smile, but none came. She turned away from him and ran her eyes over the jam-packed office.

"What is this all about?" she inquired of no one in particular.

The flash-bulbs were going again. A couple of photographers jumped up on a desk, kicking things about. Boley cursed them, but Roy gestured for him to let them alone. A girl photographer pushed her way through the crowd.

"Won't you sit on the desk there, honey, and give the boys a treat?"

There were wolf-howls, but the girl said calmly: "Sorry. No cheese-cake." There were groans. The girl hesitated, then seemed to consider. She glanced over at Roy. "Unless of course the Captain...."

"You decide for yourself," said Roy, quickly.

"All right then," said the girl. "No cheese-cake." She paid hardly any attention to the argument which followed. She didn't enter into it, or even so much as shake her head. Apparently she had spoken, and that was that!

Now she turned to Roy. "Captain, what is all this?"

"It's a press conference."

"You mean I'm supposed to answer questions?"

"Yes."

"Do I have to?"

"You do not," said Roy. "It's all up to you."

She cleared her throat politely then she said: "Sorry. But I will not answer any questions."

There was a tremendous uproar and quite a bit of shoving and protest.

"But, kids," said Roy, "what do you expect *me* to do about it? She's got rights. If she won't, she won't."

"A sad thought," said one of the reporters.

"You used to work at Cip's, didn't you?" somebody asked suddenly.

The girl hesitated, then nodded slowly. "I worked at Cip's. Now that's all. No more questions. I won't answer them." She turned her back on the semi-circle of newsmen. "I'm sorry," she said over her shoulder.

"All right, boys," said Roy. "We'll be around till late. There'll be some bulletins. I'll look after you."

The girl turned around again and faced the reporters. She had a piece of paper in her hand. "I want to make a statement," she said mildly.

"Go right ahead," said Roy, slightly surprised.

The girl read from the paper. "I want to state that I am entirely and completely innocent in regard to the lamentable murder of Mr. Hobart."

There was a dead silence, then somebody laughed. The girl looked in the direction of the laugh. "I would like to see the person who thinks that is funny," she said, coldly.

Nobody else laughed. Roy moved over beside her and asked in a low voice: "Where did you get that statement?"

"Why, I wrote it myself, Captain Hargis. And it's the truth, and I'll just keep repeating it."

He began to study her. At close range, he noticed that she had done a wonderful make-up job on her black eye. He also noticed that her eyelashes were not faked—the longest and blackest he'd ever seen. Then abruptly he stopped studying her. Poor Hobart! Badly overmatched. His breakdown didn't seem as surprising to Roy as it had to Joe Sert.

"Take Miss Vance in my office, Boley," he said.

It took both Boley and Ed Reynolds to get her through the jam to Roy's office. Reporters crowded round her, trying to startle or anger her into answering a question or making a comment. She looked right through them as she moved along. Finally she disappeared into Roy's private office, followed by Boley and Ed Reynolds.

"Do you suppose the ancient Amazons looked like that?" asked a reporter.

"If they did, what kind of guys were the Greeks, fighting them?"

"Fighting 'em *off*, you mean," somebody else put in, and there was a laugh.

"The crack still goes. Any man who would fight her off...."

"Would be wise," a girl reporter interpolated.

Gradually Roy worked them out, and then finally shut the door. Lackey was still standing back against the wall. When Roy looked at him, he took out his handkerchief and mopped his face.

"Well," said Roy, "I'm afraid my show fell a little flat."

"Oh, no. On the contrary," called a voice from some place.

Roy and Lackey turned. Wesson emerged from a clothes closet. His face was red and he was drunk. Roy came over and stood examining him.

"A snootful, eh? Don't tell me you found that in the store-room."

"No," said Wesson. "As a matter of fact, I sent a nice black boy out for a couple of quarts of gin. He drank one of the quarts. He is now lying on the store-room floor, clutching his broom. I drank the other."

"When do you drop down?"

"Ah, that's the question." Beating time with his forefinger, Wesson intoned:

> "Wine there! Wine.... Tomorrow's fears shall fools alone benumb!
> By the ear Death pulls me. 'Live!' he whispers softly, 'Live! I come.'"

Roy merely stared at him.

"I see you don't appreciate classical poetry. Virgil, no less. Roy, do I sit in?" He jerked his thumb toward the door of the private office.

"You do not, you drunken bum!"

They were alone now. The windows in Roy's office were open and the distant roar and clamor of the city drifted in, accentuating the silence. The girl was sitting in the one comfortable chair, a battered old leather armchair which had been knocking about the City Building for years, shunted from office to office. Roy, at his desk, noticed for the first time that the chair was a disgrace, dirty, torn, with the stuffing showing in places.

The girl sat rather straight with her ankles and knees together and her hands crossed loosely in her lap.

Roy fiddled with a pencil, then a desk-knife, finally he rose and shut one of the windows. "Is that better?" he asked. "Cooling off, I think."

"That's better," said the girl.

"How about the other one?"

"Shut that, too, if you don't mind."

Roy shut it. Something about the way the girl spoke interested him, aside from the voice. She spoke with extreme care, like a foreigner who has just learned the language and is afraid of making mistakes and being laughed at. There was something definitely artificial about her diction. She never spoke carelessly, as most Americans do, educated or not. She separated her words neatly and stressed each syllable. Nevertheless, although it was obvious that she'd been taught to speak this way and not too long ago, it blended into her personality and seemed natural, as did her manner of walking, patently stylized.

"She's a production, all right, by God," Roy told himself, then he sat down at his desk and after a moment asked: "You want to tell me what happened in your own words without me breaking in?"

"I don't want to tell you anything, Captain Hargis. I am very distressed over Frank's death. It is a terrible thing, and I'd rather not talk about it."

There was a pause. "You want a cigarette, Miss Vance?"

"I don't smoke."

Roy rose and paced behind his desk for a moment. He felt nervous, markedly ill-at-ease. Generally, he felt superior to people and contemptuous of them and was careless, offhand in his attitude toward them. But this big girl, relaxed, emotionless, decorative, upset him, made him unsure of himself. How did you penetrate her armor?

"I believe you know Bob Dumas," he began, as if tentatively.

"Yes, I know him."

"What time did you call him Monday night?"

"I did not call him any time Monday night. I haven't called him for, oh, weeks."

"Then how did he happen to be with you at the Terrace when you checked out?"

"Was he?"

There was a long pause. With the windows closed the girl's perfume became more and more noticeable. Roy found it very disturbing. In a moment, he went to his desk, got out a cigar, and bit off the end, then he saw that the girl was regarding him with what looked almost like amusement. It was not that her eyes were so pale in color, he decided; the strange effect came from the fact that her eyelashes were so black, thick, and long. He'd noticed the same effect on blue-eyed trainmen, whose sooty lashes had given their hard, masculine faces a falsely effeminate look.

"You mind a cigar?" he asked.

"Not if you open one of the windows."

Roy threw the cigar down on the desk in sudden irritation, breaking it. "Now look, honey," he cried with sudden heat, "let's cut this out. I've got enough against you right now to hang you—or pretty close. So I would advise you to talk. Now let's start over. I intend to be as polite as possible, but I don't intend to overdo it."

The girl regarded him in silence.

"So you didn't call Dumas?"

"No, Captain."

"Did you check out at the Terrace?"

"Yes, Captain."

"Why?"

"I'd decided to go away."

"Why?"

"I was tired of this town. Besides, Mr. Hobart—poor man—was getting quite impossible."

"Jealous?"

"Oh, no. Nothing like that. He had nothing to be jealous about. It was his drinking. I don't know whatever happened to poor Mr. Hobart. All of a sudden he started to drink whiskey. It got to be very embarrassing. Every time we went out together he got... intoxicated."

"Where did you intend to go?"

"I intended to go back to San Francisco."

"Home town?"

"Yes, Captain. I was born there."

"What did you intend to use for money?"

The girl glanced at him, then glanced down at the floor. "I don't understand that question, Captain."

"Did you have the money to go?"

There was a long pause, then the girl said. "There is something I want to ask you if I may."

"Go right ahead."

"I read it in the *World*. It said I was arrested at the Lackawanna Bus Terminal. Who put that in there? And why?"

"You know as well as I do."

"No, I don't. It's a lie. Makes it look like I was running away."

"Weren't you?"

"No. When a person decides to leave a place, is that running away?"

"Do you want us to correct the error in the *World*? Is that it? Do you want us to state that you were arrested as you escaped from the Barrington Estates home of Mrs. Allen Spencer—your sister?"

"Oh, so she told you," said the girl in surprise.

"I already knew. How do you suppose I knew where to find you?"

"How could you know? *Nobody* knew."

"It's my business to know things, Miss Vance. And I assure you, you are not doing yourself any good by your evasive attitude."

"Captain," said the girl, "I'm on my own. I've got to look after myself. This I intend to do to the best of my ability. I'm sorry."

"You're going about it all wrong."

"I'll have to be the judge of that, Captain. What are you trying to say—that I should trust you?"

Roy turned his back, walked to his desk, and sat down.

The girl went on: "Because if that is what you are trying to say, you are not

as intelligent as I take you to be. I trust nobody. I've learned to trust nobody,
I'm sorry to say."

After a long pause, Roy asked suddenly: "Who do you suppose looted your
suite, Miss Vance?"

The girl started slightly and lowered her eyes. Roy waited for a long time, but
as she showed no signs of answering him, he went on: "A chinchilla, two
minks, a car, evening dresses, lingerie—and thirty-five hundred in cash."

The girl stood up abruptly. Her lips were trembling and her eyes were cold
as ice. Her face grew pale with what seemed to be a very strong emotion of some
kind, perhaps rage, Roy decided. There was a long silence. Finally the girl sat
down and composed herself. She had not uttered a word or made a sound, and
yet the entire atmosphere of the office had been changed.

There was electricity in the air.

"Wow!" Roy said to himself, then he rose, walked over to the girl, and stood
in front of her.

"Do you want me to tell you a few other things I know?"

"You *think* you know," she said, refusing to look at him.

Roy noticed that her long fingers were knotted together on her lap and they
were so tightly clasped that her hands were an unhealthy-looking white.

"I know where you abandoned the Cadillac, for instance," he said. "I know
what time you called Dumas. About twelve-fifteen. By the way, he's downstairs
waiting to talk to me. I know that you checked out of the Terrace about two-
thirty. I know that you refused to admit that your suite had been looted. In fact,
I know quite a lot about you Miss Vance. Quite a lot."

She stood up abruptly. They were very close together. There was a sultry
power in her eyes which disturbed Roy so much that he began to turn pale.

"All right," she said, speaking very rapidly and breathing unevenly. "You
know a lot. I admit it. Yes, you know a lot. But you don't know everything. It's
all a mistake. I swear to you on the grave of my mother, on... on anything you
like, that I am innocent. I didn't kill Mr. Hobart. Captain—please help me."

She flung herself into Roy's arms, put her head in his neck. "Please... please
help me," she implored.

The floor seemed to tip. Roy felt overcome, powerless. Against him her
body was strong, firm, rounded, young, and abandoned. He put his arms
around her, then withdrew them, fighting for control.

Finally, he took her arms from around his neck and gently forced her to sit
down.

"Come on, Miss Vance," he said in a shaky voice. "Let's not get emotional
about this."

"I'm sorry," said the girl, looking at the floor. "But I've never had anybody
to help me... *never*."

Roy sat down at his desk, fought a brief battle with himself, then pressed a
buzzer. In a moment, Lois, Alma's assistant, stepped in.

"Will you take Miss Vance back now? I'll talk to her later tonight."

"Yes, Captain. Come on, dear."

The girl left without looking back. Lois closed the door softly. Roy paced the floor for a while, then he went over and opened both the windows wide.

"That goddamned perfume!" he cried, aloud.

After a moment, he went to a mirror and stood studying himself. His face was pale and drawn. "Look, son," he said, addressing his image. "You're the guy with the air-tight system, remember? You don't get into jams with broads. Remember?"

The door opened behind him and he turned abruptly from the mirror, and flushed like a boy caught in some shameful act.

It was Wesson. He was sniffing the air like a birddog. "Ah," he cried, "what a sexy perfume! Did we get any place, Roy? Murderwise, I mean, of course."

"Wesson," said Roy, "have you sobered up?"

"Sober as a judge. I don't mean Judge Anson, of course. They have to prop him up on the bench."

"She denied everything, Wesson."

"Took her a long time to say 'no.' About the murder I mean, of course."

"You are a louse, Wesson. Beat it."

"Why this change of attitude?"

"I always thought you were a louse."

"No, I mean, why so unfriendly?"

"Go round and join the others, Wesson. I've done you enough favors."

Wesson stood staring at Roy, who grabbed up a phone and spoke to Lackey in the main room. "Emmett? Wesson's to be out in the hall with the others now. Keep him there." He banged up the receiver.

Wesson walked slowly to the door, opened it wide, then observed: "Just because I saw the Great Captain admiring himself in the mirror—practicing faces."

Roy started for him. Wesson ran out, slamming the door. Roy checked himself, then walked back and sat down at his desk with a sigh.

As before Bob Dumas took off his coat and tossed it at a chair, missing. But he did not seem quite as unconcerned as he had earlier. He walked over to one of the windows and stood looking out. After a moment he began to sniff, then he turned.

"Smells like the lounge corridor at Cip's in here," he observed.

"Your friend, Miss Vance," said Roy, who was sitting at his desk, running through some papers.

There was a pause, then Bob asked: "When do you sleep, hawkshaw?"

"Oh, I knock it off here and there. I understand they let you use the phone downstairs. Call a lawyer?"

"No. I called a bim. I'm figuring I'll be out of here before long."

"Did the bim tell you what questions I asked her and what her replies were?"

"Captain," said Bob, smiling ironically, "refer to her more politely. You are speaking of the girl I ought to love."

Roy grimaced and lit a cigar. "Feel like talking?"

"Seems I'm in the well-known sack," said Bob, looking down at the city, listening to the traffic noises. Turning he demanded: "Did you hear that la-de-da horn? Minor triad with a dissonant train-whistle bass. Hear the train?"

Roy merely stared at him.

"You think I'm nuts, don't you?" said Bob. "Well, you got company, including Ruth's aunt. Good old biddy, at that. My personal opinion is that she's been around in her day. She's got such a goddamned comfortable look about her, like a well-layed duck. Most women her age don't look like that. They're off at women's clubs, screaming about something. Never saw a woman who could sit so still and look so contented. She makes me nervous."

"When I asked you if you felt like talking," said Roy, "I didn't mean at random."

"I always talk at random. Sometimes, I hear the damnedest things coming out of my mouth. It's what you might call improvising. If you're good, you often get surprising results."

"Miss Jensen must be a hog for punishment."

"To tell you the truth," said Bob, sitting down facing Roy, "she likes it. She's kind of a Silent Joe, herself. Or at least she used to be. She's loosened up considerably since she met me. She was quite a girl when I first saw her. She didn't know which way was up—finishing school, all that—what the hell could you expect?"

"Poor girl," said Roy, "nothing but disadvantages."

"You think that's a joke, but it's not. When I first met her, she couldn't find her way around town. You know that crack Marie Antoinette was supposed to have made—let 'em eat cake? Some people say the story was put out by her political enemies. I'll bet she said it, and meant it innocently. So, okay—if you're out of bread, eat some cake, what the hell! Ruth said a lot of things like that to me. No kidding. She just didn't know how the other half lived."

"Well, she ought to know by now," said Roy.

"She's learning. And that, dear radio audience, brings us to the commercial. We're back to the case, Captain. What do you want to know?"

"I know what time the girl called you. I just want you to admit it."

"All right. I'll admit it. She called me about a quarter after twelve, maybe twenty after."

"Go on."

"No," said Bob. "We'd save time if you asked me questions."

"Save *time!* Now he wants to save time after telling me all about Miss Jensen's aunt and Marie Antoinette."

"You are certainly a man for sticking to the point. Don't you ever relax and just shoot the breeze?"

"Not when I'm trying to straighten out a killing."

"Yeah," said Bob, thoughtfully. "I keep forgetting about that. All right. She called me at twelve-fifteen, we'll say, and she told me she was in a jam and asked me if I had any money. I laughed lightly at that. *Me? Any money?*"

"All right," said Roy, hastily. "Where did you meet her?"

"First I had a row with Ruth. She was standing right beside me and heard every word that was said. Oh, did she do a burn! But I'm not going to let any girl get a rope on me. They can take me as I am, or the hell with it. So I told her to mind her business, and went out. You see, Ruth's got the wrong idea about me and Lone...."

"Who?"

"The girl, Vance. Ruth thought I was riding in the saddle, but I wasn't. You see, this Lone—she's the kind of kid that has got no friends. Women hate her, which is understandable—brother, what competition! And how can a man be friends with her? A man wants to get in the kip with her—or forget the whole thing. Well... to put it bluntly, I'm no mink. I got the necessary equipment and I'm normal. But sex is something that's never bothered me very much...."

"You lucky bastard," Roy observed to himself.

"... no," Bob went on, after a moment of thought, "never has bothered me. Maybe it's because I'm a kind of fanatic. Ever since I was six or seven years old I've never thought about anything but music. I can play five instruments—and *good!* If you don't think that takes up your time—besides I've written a trunkful of stuff—it stinks, but I'm getting better. Well, Lone—she can't figure me out. I'm friendly with her. That's all. No dirty conversation, no feels. We just sit down and talk, and don't ever think that girl isn't smart. Well... that's how it was with us. Pretty soon she wants me to coach her in singing. Hopeless. I try to tell her, but she won't listen. She thinks it's all a matter of trying hard, practice. But she's tone-deaf. Trouble is, she's read all this inspirational stuff. All a guy needs is the will. You know what I mean? Sometimes I get to thinking about all the millions of poor slobs in this country who believe that stuff, and are knocking themselves out trying to be musicians, and writers, and painters, and even muscle-men.... First thing you've got to have is *talent*. The working and sweating comes *after* that."

"Yeah," said Roy, "all right. Just a minute now. We're getting off the track. You say that your relationship with Miss Vance was platonic. I'll take your word for it. Now you met her. Where did you meet her?"

"At Crandall and 47th. She had Mr. Hobart's Cadillac. We left it there, and went to a bar on 47th where we proceeded to lap up quite a few martinis which she had to pay for. I had a buck, thirty—as usual."

"What about the Cadillac? What did she say about it?"

"She said she'd had a fight with Mr. Hobart and he'd taken a swing at her, blacked her eye. She had a hell of a shiner. She said that was the end. She was going to pack up and go back to San Francisco, but she didn't have any money—not enough, anyway. This I thought was kind of queer. She had fur coats, diamonds. I'd seen her in the club looking like some Brazilian tycoon's girl friend. I asked her why she didn't hock some of the stuff. But she didn't give me any answer to this."

"Now let's go back," said Roy. "Did she say anything in particular about Mr. Hobart? Did she say what happened to him?"

"Yes," said Bob. "She let him out at Commercial Street and Blackhawk. He got so mad at her he wouldn't ride in the car with her any more."

"Why did she let him out there?"

"He wanted to go to Cip's."

"Cip's was closed that night."

"I guess they must have forgot it was Monday. Could happen."

Roy thought this over for a while. "All right. Go ahead. What then?"

"Well, she kept trying to get me to go to San Francisco with her. She said she knew the town and we could both get jobs like breaking sticks. She said she wasn't going to take a job here after riding high the way she had—it would be embarrassing. We shot the breeze till closing time. Then we went out and got a taxi and drove to the Terrace where she packed up her things and checked out. I rode clear out to hell and gone with her—way to hell out to Barrington Estates, around there, anyway, where there was a couple she knew. Brother, did she get a frosty welcome. It was damned embarrassing, and there I was like a fifth wheel, not knowing what was what. I was mighty glad to get her off my hands. She kept telling me she'd raise the dough and we'd go to San Francisco. What a persistent girl! Well, she gave me a ten and I took the taxi all the way back. But I heard a wonderful colored band blasting away in a joint down at the river level of the Stairs, so I got out there. Everybody was full of weed and they were jamming. Terrific! I sat there minding my own business and enjoying myself till a weeded-up black girl chose me—and I had to blow, and fast! I could have got raped...."

Bob rose, walked to a window, and stood looking out. "Yeah," he went on, "and it would have been worth it—just to listen to that band. Boy, could they go—and all for fun. That's the point. All for fun—kicks."

"Look, Dumas," said Roy, wearily, "you've done pretty well here. One point. You say there's nothing between you and the girl. Okay. I'm not disputing it. But why, then, was she so anxious for you to go away with her? Does that make sense to you?"

"Yes," said Bob. "Damn good sense. Look; it's like what I was trying to tell you about those colored boys, jamming. Just for fun. No ulterior purpose. Not for money, not for fame, not for safety or security—just for fun. You see, everybody who approaches a beautiful Juno like Lone has got an axe to grind. She's goddamned sick and tired of axes. With me, she could relax. I'm the only friend she ever had. That's what she told me."

There was a long silence. The clamor of the city came in through the open window.

"All right," said Roy. "You can go home. Stay in town. I may need you again."

Bob grabbed his coat up from the floor and began to put it on. "Oh, goody, teacher. School is out." He turned and walked to the door, then he paused. "Captain," he said. "I'll break down. I'm going to get that girl a lawyer. Just her looks might convict her. Every old biddy in town will be boiling with envy over the way she looks in those newspaper pictures. She's in a spot."

"Yes," said Roy, "she's definitely in a spot. And if you're smart, you'll keep out of this. You may not be in the clear yet, son. I'd keep my head down if I were you."

"Good night, Captain. This has sure been an education to me. I like cops better now. Goodbye."

He went out, carelessly slamming the door. Roy winced, then sat shaking his head.

17

Roy heard the strokes of midnight fall solemnly on the air from the Civic Center clock. He should have been questioning the big girl again, but for the moment he didn't feel equal to it. He had a nagging headache, his stomach felt tight, and his eyes were bothering him. Not enough sleep, too much activity and nervous tension.

He sent out for a bottle of beer and a sandwich, and sat eating and drinking, all alone, looking absently out the window at the blank face of the huge, thirty-storey office building across the street. In the daytime it was bursting with life; at night it resembled a gigantic mausoleum, with its pyramid-like stepping, from floor to floor, its countless ranks of dark, deepset windows, and its mammoth solidity.

"Looks like it'll be there for a long time," thought Roy, then he finished the beer, tossed the sandwich paper in the waste-basket, and stood up.

They'd really bitten off a big one this time. It was one thing to operate in semi-darkness, which was usually what happened when the Administration took over a case, for political reasons, and handed it to him; it was an entirely different thing operating in the full glare of all-out newspaper coverage.

You couldn't afford to stumble. Since he'd been working for the Administration, he hadn't made one mistake. He was the fair-haired boy. He could write his own ticket. All accorded him deference. It was stated that he had a great future before him. The graybeards running the Administration seemed to consider him a mere boy and were astonished at his precocity.

"A mere boy," jeered Roy to himself. "Thirty-five and beat up, and I'm a boy. Some boy!"

No, he hadn't made a single mistake. But he was like a tight-rope walker on the high wire with no net. It only took one mistake.

Roy shook his head, sighed, sat down, and forced himself to think about the possibilities and ramifications of the case. The ethical side of the business he pushed completely into the background. It was not a question of innocence or guilt. To the Administration this was a complete irrelevancy. Staying in office was the main, in fact, the *only* point.

Okay. So much for that. Now—where did the danger lie? At the moment, from his own viewpoint, it lay in two directions. First, the girl. Already she had too much influence over him. That had to be guarded against. Second, Wesson. What a guy! With a brief tilt of the status quo, a momentary opportunity—a disaster, a revolution—Wesson could be running things instead of writing about them. In Roy's opinion, he was as able and astute as Chad Bayliss, the Big Man.

And Roy knew that Wesson wasn't in the least deceived. It was no accident that he had mentioned the word "politics" that night in the Stoneham garage. For the moment, he was playing ball. But tomorrow? His paper, the *World*, was not particularly friendly to the Administration, but it was a conservative sheet and not much given to rant and sensationalism. Nevertheless, the *World* was always dangerous because of its immense prestige. And Wesson was just the boy who could blow the lid off, if, for any reason, he decided that was the thing to do.

Roy picked up the phone and called the main room. Lackey answered. "Wesson still around?"

"Yes, Roy. He's doing card-tricks out in the hall and he's wonderful. You should see how...."

"All right," Roy interrupted; "send Lafe out for half a dozen bottles of beer and a couple of corned beef sandwiches. When he gets back with them, ask Wesson to come in my office."

Wesson disposed of a bottle of beer in three swallows and the second corned beef sandwich disappeared as if, when Roy turned away for a moment, somebody had thrown it out the window. Wesson tilted his chair back, lit a cigarette, and patted his huge paunch. He had a fat, freckled, impudent face, and his sparse hair was a sandy-red. When he was a boy in England, he'd been called "Ginger."

"Ah-hh-hh!" he moaned vulgarly, then he belched. "It's an old Arab custom," he explained. "You no like food—no burp—host insulted—gittee throat cut. Thanks, Roy. It hit the spot. Now if you have no other plans for the rest of that beer...."

"Help yourself."

Wesson complied. Between drinks he talked. "I *thought* you might have a change of heart. Turning on an old friend like that. In the diner it was different. I asked for it. I questioned your word. A very stupid and unhealthy thing to do with any man. But with a rough customer like yourself, plain murder. I apologize. But when it comes to a quip or gag...."

"Okay, fat," said Roy. "Now *I* apologize."

"Well, aren't we a couple of boys," said Wesson. Then looking up shrewdly, he asked: "Any new developments?"

"No," said Roy. "But the girl's in real trouble. No alibi, nothing."

"Lucky for you," said Wesson. "Unlucky for her."

"So it goes."

"You expect to hang this on her, Roy? Off the record?"

"Off the record—it looks very much like it."

"What a pity! Not enough of that kind around. Imagine, that honey-girl languishing in a woman's prison. It's a repulsive, a horrifying thought." Roy said nothing. "Don't you think so, buster?" Again Roy made no reply. Wesson reached out and opened another bottle of beer. "You'll excuse me while I make a pig of myself as usual," he went on. "Great appetites and no self-control, no will—a frightening combination, don't you think so, buster?"

"You seem to get along all right," said Roy, then he added: "In a way."

"You mean you've got a proposition? I'm listening. I'm about—say, fifteen hundred dollars in debt."

"Would that put you in the clear?"

"Well, for two thousand I'd be on easy street—for the time being. That is, in my modest way."

Roy went over and stood looking out the window. Wesson finished the bottle of beer, smacking his lips. Finally he spoke. "But... what's money? It slips through your fingers like sand, and has no ultimate value. You Yanks found that out in '29."

"Us Yanks," said Roy, laughing.

"Okay. Okay," said Wesson, slightly embarrassed. "So I'm a citizen. So I'm a Yank. Occasionally my mind goes back to a happier time when to me a Yank was a fearsome object who chewed tobacco, said 'Waal' every other word, and was in awe of Europe. Anyway, what's money?"

"It's a necessity, among other things."

"Granted. But position is better, much better. Like yourself, for instance. Riding high, and with the High Brass patting your dear little head. Think of all the grateful people you do favors for. Just think of it. Like that suit for instance. Look at mine. Fifteen down and the rest when they catch me. All, me!"

Wesson stood up and yawned. "Wesson, the public relations counsel, working as a lousy political reporter. I have brilliant ideas for columns, but will anybody listen to me? Sad, very sad. I suppose you want to get on with your work, Roy."

"Yes," said Roy, starting slightly.

"Well, back to my card tricks," said Wesson, going out.

Chad seemed nervous and worried. He and Roy sat on a little sofa in the vestibule of Chad's apartment, talking in low voices. Mrs. Bayliss had been given a strong sedative by the family doctor and was now sleeping in the big master bedroom down the hall.

"Merle's driving me crazy," said Chad. "I can't go down in the lobby even any more without her calling me to see what I'm doing. She imagines things! Look, Roy. I'm no angel, but I'm getting along in years, and besides, I haven't got time to be chasing women. It's all in her mind." He hesitated briefly, then added: "Well... almost all of it."

Roy shook his head, but offered no comment.

Chad made an obvious effort to force himself to get down to business. "Now about Wesson. You may have a great idea, Roy. But nothing can be done till this case is settled. And by the way, you're doing a great job. Never saw such a spread in my life. Why, everybody's forgotten about poor Frank already. He hardly gets a line. It's all this girl. Keep it that way. Yes, you may have a great idea about Wesson. Correct public relations—it's a big need for us right now with the '52 elections coming up. We might even create a job. I'll talk to the Mayor. But not till after this case is settled, Roy. Everybody isn't stupid or crazy, you know."

"Could I give him a hint?"

"Not unless the worst comes to the worst. Save your weapons till you need them. I shouldn't have to tell you that, Roy."

Roy stood up. "All right, Chad. I hope I haven't disturbed you. But I thought we ought to get this straight right away."

Chad rose. "By all means. I wish every guy in the Administration was as hard-working and conscientious as you are. But we've been in too long, and we're loaded with fatassed deadheads who think it will last forever without their turning a hand. We know better, Roy. Don't we?"

"Yes," said Roy.

They shook hands. "Keep plugging," said Chad, "and if we win the big one in '52, you won't be sitting in that dirty City Building office long. Goodnight, Roy."

18

Roy decided that he'd have Lois stay in the office with him while he questioned Ilona Vance. But abruptly he changed his mind, and now the girl was sitting once more in the beat-up leather armchair and he was sitting at his desk, fiddling with meaningless papers.

She was a little paler than before and even more beautiful, Roy thought. There was something very strange about her face. Or was it her complexion? At times it seemed to be lit from within. Roy could not think of any other way to express it to himself.

"Don't those people out there ever go home?" asked the girl, gesturing vaguely.

Roy had heard the uproar and had forced himself to stay in his office. He'd wanted to go out and help her through the double line of ruthless harriers. But he'd decided against it. At times it was wise to sit in your office and play the big man, and let the hired help handle the details.

The girl reached toward him with a graceful gesture of her long arm and put a torn piece of paper on his desk. He picked it up and read it.

Dear Miss V: Consolidated News Service will pay you one thousand dollars for your life story. You tell me, I write it, and you get the dough. Can it be arranged?

Roy glanced up. "Well?"

"Well," said the girl, "can it be arranged? I'll give them a story. It won't necessarily be my life story. Who tells their life story? But it might do."

Roy nodded. "Sure. But get the money on the line."

"Oh, I intended to."

"I'll take it up with Alma. She'll arrange it. You might slip her a double sawbuck. Her goodwill's worth twenty times that."

"I'd rather have your goodwill, Captain," said the girl looking at him steadily.

Roy laughed uncomfortably. "Mine comes much higher than that."

"I'm sure it does."

Roy got up and walked to the window. "Miss Vance," he said after a moment, "the last time you were in here you got very emotional. I'd prefer it, if that didn't happen again."

The girl said nothing. Roy waited for a long time. He felt pretty sure she was trying to get him to look at her. Finally he did. She smiled slightly. It was the first expression approaching a smile he'd ever seen on her face. She had dimples. "My God!" Roy said to himself. "All that, and dimples, too!"

"I could tell you, Captain, that I would refrain from all emotion. I could promise it. But... I'm afraid if I felt an emotion coming on...." She waved one hand vaguely.

"Well, let's keep it down to a minimum," said Roy, smiling ironically. "Now, Miss Vance. You've got a story to rehearse. And you might as well let me help you rehearse it."

"What do you mean?"

"I mean there will be a coroner's inquest. You can't just dummy-up there very well."

"Oh," said the girl, "I hadn't thought of that."

"Well, think about it. I can wait. I'm patient."

"You don't look patient, Captain," said the girl. "But I presume you must be."
She was smiling again. More dimples.

Roy turned and looked out the window. Then he began to notice the perfume,
exotic, insidious, disturbing. Cursing under his breath, he turned abruptly from
the window and sat down at his desk.

There was a brief silence. He shoved the prop papers around, trying not to
look at her. But his will failed him. He began to study her. She seemed perfectly
relaxed. In fact almost annoyingly so. She sat as before with her ankles and knees
together and her hands loosely in her lap. The gardenias had a creamy glow
against the blue-black background of her hair. Her eyebrows, he noticed, were
black, not curved much, and looked as natural as a man's. At certain angles, in
repose, her face seemed almost mask-like; and then she'd turn, her lips would
open slightly, and you'd notice the very white teeth, and become aware of the
sensitive aliveness of the rather narrow, pale, black-rimmed eyes. What an as-
sembly job—and yet as natural-appearing as a sunrise.

"You want to tell me a story?" asked Roy. "Any story. Maybe the one you are
thinking about writing for CNS." She said nothing. Roy shifted about, took out
a cigar, fumbled nervously with it for a moment, then put it aside. "I had a long
talk with Bob Dumas. He had the rather curious idea that you wanted him to
go to San Francisco with you because you liked his conversation."

"Not his conversation," said the girl slowly. "It's him I like. In a world of
phonies, he's genuine."

"But a little wacky."

"Not at all wacky. Sane. Not like me. Not like you, Captain. Really sane."

"You don't consider yourself sane then? What you consider me is beside the
point."

"Oh, you're like me, Captain. In there pitching. Get the buck, get the influence. Be big. Bob's being himself. Do you know why? Because he's got values
that we can't even understand. As a person, he's impossible. I mean, for any one
to depend on. All the same he'd never steal from you, lie about you, double-cross
you, or sell you down the river for profit."

Roy lowered his eyes and stared at his desk. "I see."

"He's the only person I've ever met like that in my life. For a while I deluded
myself about somebody else, but I was wrong. Oh, so wrong. But the funny
thing about Bob is... I'm not in love with him. Never was. I don't think he gives
two snaps for me that way. I *know* he doesn't. But he's been a good friend to me.
And whatever he told you I'm sure is the truth."

"I'm positive it is. But it brings up some very peculiar questions. Why, for instance, did you let Mr. Hobart out of the car at Commercial and Blackhawk?"

"Because he wanted to go to Cip's."

"On Monday night?"

"He knew it was Monday night. But he happens to be a very good friend of

Mr. Sert's. Mr. Sert has been living there with that girl he married—Tootsie."

"I see. Why did you abandon the Cadillac?"

"Why not? I abandoned Mr. Hobart. What did I want with his Cadillac?"

"Or he abandoned you, as the case may be."

"In a way, yes—you're right. But not exactly in the sense you mean. You see, Mr. Hobart talked marriage to me quite frequently at first. He took me to meet his nephew—his only living relative; things like that. Yes, he talked marriage quite frequently—that is, until I moved into the Terrace. After that, if it was mentioned, I mentioned it, and he would try to change the subject."

"Oldest gag in the world," said Roy. "Come now, Miss Vance. You're not trying to make me believe you fell for a gimmick like that. I'm disappointed in you."

"Well, it's a funny thing, but I did. Why? Because I thought Mr. Hobart was like Bob. He talked like it."

"That I find hard to believe," said Roy. "Look, Miss Vance. *Nobody* talks like Bob Dumas."

"I mean about values. He talked as if...." She stopped abruptly and much to Roy's surprise blushed faintly. Did dream-girls blush? Dream-girls weren't real—how could one blush? "I see what you mean now when you said you were disappointed in me," she went on, composing herself. "Thinking back on what I said, it sounded like I was the poor, wronged, little virgin. I didn't mean anything like that. God knows I've been around. No. It wasn't that I *demanded* marriage. Nothing like that. But *he* was the one who brought it up. Let's put it plainly. It wasn't at all necessary for him to bring it up. Now do I make myself clear?"

"Yes," said Roy, "and I'm no longer disappointed in you."

"Thanks," said the girl, then she smiled, showing new dimples, and gave him an intimate look which he found rather overpowering.

"All right," said Roy, abruptly. "You were saying?"

After a moment, the girl resumed: "I was saying that it took me some time to find out that Mr. Hobart was just another Vanity Row hustler. They're all hustling something; deals, money, influence, girls. He was a girl-hustler. Never meant a word he said. All a line, a routine. I found out later he'd been hustling girls for years. He gave them the big-gray-haired-gentlemanly-respectable-man pitch. It's a good one. He gave me a little extra, I guess. Possibly because at the time, I had my pick. Or almost.

"All right. I'm no fool. I was comfortable. I had practically everything I wanted. It wasn't that I was so set-up about marriage. I've known quite a few girls who married for money, and it turned out they were getting it the hard way. The best way to get money is to work for it. Nobody can throw it up to you then, and try to make a slave out of you. That was the trouble with Mr. Hobart. He wanted to think for me, breathe for me. He wanted to live his life and mine, too. He got furious if I disagreed with him about anything. All right. I could stand all that. But I couldn't stand his insane jealousy. He would have locked me up in a vault if he'd had his way, and taken me out and put me back at his convenience. He just couldn't understand about Bob, no matter how many times I tried to tell him."

"That's understandable," said Roy. "Bob is a very handsome young fellow, and Mr. Hobart was old enough to be your grandfather."

"Look at it my way, Captain. What do I do with myself when Mr. Hobart's not around? I like to sit down and talk—just gab, you know what I mean. Well, I had a girl friend named Bobby. A very beautiful girl—just as good as I am certainly, and when you come right down to it, just as good as Mr. Hobart. But, no; she was a tramp. She was living with some man. Think of that! My, my! What was I doing? But I had to break off with Bobby. Brush her off when she called, things like that. I didn't like it, but I did it. But when it came finally to Bob Dumas, I put my foot down. I had to make a stand some place. I'm a human being. I can't sleep twenty hours a day, or sit in a room by myself. Well, that was it. The thing was, Mr. Hobart was a very domineering man. You should have seen his nephew. He was terrified of Mr. Hobart. What an awful yes-man, stooge! Mr. Hobart loved it. Kept telling me what a bright boy his nephew was. Why, that poor boy didn't have any more spirit than a worm. He was afraid to be alone in a room with me. If Mr. Hobart went out for a few minutes, he made some excuse and went out, too. He was afraid Mr. Hobart might get jealous. Well, I am not a very good subject for domination, never have been. And maybe that is the whole story."

There was a long pause and for a while Roy seemed to be absorbed in some papers on his desk. Finally he glanced up. "What about the black eye?" The girl made no reply, merely looked at him calmly. "I believe you stated that a closet door in your apartment stuck. You pulled at it and it hit you in the eye. Is that correct?"

The girl's face turned a little paler, her mouth worked for a moment, then she seemed to get control of herself. "No, that is not correct. It's true that a closet door in my apartment sticks, however."

"Will you tell me how you got that black eye?"

"Yes. Mr. Hobart struck me several times. Once on the chest, once in the mouth, and once on the cheekbone. He was wearing a ring." The girl seemed about to go on, then her lips tightened, and she sat still as a statue, her face rigid, but her eyes alive and watchful.

Roy shifted about in his chair and rubbed his hand over his face wearily. The headache had returned and was nagging at him like an uneasy conscience. "Miss Vance," he said, "we are going about this completely backwards. We are getting the cart before the horse, and it's partly my fault. Would you like to tell me the whole story in your own words? Start at the beginning?"

"No," said the girl, looking at the floor.

"All right," said Roy. "Then I'll tell you. Leaving the marriage business out of it—that angle seems irrelevant to me—you let Mr. Hobart set you up at the Terrace. Nothing unusual about that. It's done every day. But he spent a small fortune on you: a car, three very expensive fur coats, jewelry, clothes—anything you wanted. Aside from that, you cost him in the neighborhood of say, fifteen hundred a month, maybe more. That's quite a layout. You agree?"

The girl cleared her throat politely. "I agree, Captain."

"All right. You got bored. That's not very unusual either. Mr. Hobart did not approve of one of your girl friends...."

"My only girl friend," the girl amended, "and she's in New York now."

"Your only girl friend. You brushed her off, but it rankled. Then came the Dumas business. It caused rows, fights, all kind of trouble; and much to everybody's surprise, Mr. Hobart took to drink, a guy who had always handled himself with ease before. But you wouldn't give in. He did his best to argue you out of this rather peculiar friendship. More fights, rows. Then he gave you an ultimatum." Roy paused and glanced at the girl, who showed signs of nervousness, although she was still well controlled. "Is that right, Miss Vance?"

"In a sense—yes."

"All right. He gave you an ultimatum. You ignored it. Either you thought he didn't mean it—or you didn't give a damn...."

"I definitely didn't give a... damn," said the girl in a voice so low that Roy could hardly hear her.

"Maybe you didn't give a damn because you never thought he would make any reprisals. You thought he was all talk. You finally lost your temper, stood on your dignity, and locked him out of your apartment. Maybe even *threw* him out. Am I right, Miss Vance?"

The girl made no reply. She sat staring at the floor as if lost in thought, as if paying no attention to what Roy was saying.

"Locked him out or threw him out—it's all one. You just thought he was a silly old fool. I don't think you really realized that you were driving this guy daffy. But that's what happened, Miss Vance. You drove him daffy. Then... one day when you came home, somebody had stripped your apartment. They'd even taken the mad-money you'd saved up—thirty-five hundred. You were so shocked you didn't know quite what to do. But in the end you acted wisely. You didn't report the robbery. You didn't even admit it. You clammed up, realizing that Mr. Hobart, even a guy like Mr. Hobart, had got fed up with your ruthless, selfish ways, and had pulled a fast one on you, and pulled it in a very smart way. You were on the sidewalk again, with maybe a couple of hundred dollars. You didn't even have enough money to pay your rent, which, I'll admit, is high, so you called Mr. Hobart. He *had* you!"

"He *didn't* have me," cried the girl loudly, her voice rising to a higher register. "You're wrong! He was the one who called. He wanted to start all over again. We drove around for hours, arguing. First he drove, then I drove. We were all over the county. Clear up to the Reservoir and back. He wanted me to move out to his house in Riverview. He said he'd get his nephew an apartment in town. He said he'd give back all my things. He'd get me a new car, a Lincoln convertible...."

"What about Dumas...?"

"I was never to see him again. Or talk to him on the phone, or anything. You're right, Captain. Mr. Hobart was daffy at this time. He didn't make sense when he talked. He was wild, like. I had a feeling he might go completely out of his mind...."

"Nevertheless, you wouldn't give in about Dumas."

"No, I wouldn't. It wasn't that Bob meant so much to me—though he does. After all, when you've only got one friend—one person who really cares whether you live or die, or if you're hungry, or if you've got a headache, or.... No, it wasn't only that. I was fighting for myself. If I gave in to Mr. Hobart this time, did everything he wanted me to do, then I was lost. I was no longer a person. I was a something—a silly stooge, like his silly nephew."

"All right," said Roy, bluntly. "So you wouldn't give in. Then what?"

"We got to town some way or other—I don't remember how, though I was driving. I was so nervous by this time that I hardly knew what I was doing. Mr. Hobart just went on yelling and carrying on. We'd stop at an intersection. There would be cars all around us. Mr. Hobart didn't care; he yelled and screamed and waved his arms. People stared at us like we were beasts out of the jungle. Well, I couldn't take any more of it. I tried to drive into the curb so I could get out, and run some place, any place. I'm not exaggerating. I thought Mr. Hobart was about ready for a straight-jacket. But he grabbed me, held on to my dress, wouldn't let me go. I was afraid we'd wreck the car. Finally I got him calmed down a little and told him I'd take him to Cip's. He likes Mr. Sert. They sit around together and gab and drink champagne...."

"What time was this?"

"I'm not positive, Captain. But it must have been around eleven-thirty. Pretty close to it. We'd been driving around since three in the afternoon. And I hadn't had anything to eat, and I was so weak from nervousness and not eating that I was afraid I was going to faint...."

"Go ahead."

"Well, Mr. Hobart seemed calmer. But when I stopped the car to let him out, the whole business started all over again. He begged me, he pleaded with me, he offered me anything—marriage. But I was really afraid of him now. I just wanted to get him out of that car. I reached across him and opened the door. Then he started to scream at me and hit me. He hit me so hard on the cheekbone that I couldn't see for a moment. Then he lost his balance and sort of slipped out of the car. The door was open. I reached over and shut the door and drove off. He was sort of on his knees. But he jumped up and started down the street after me. I could see him in the rear-view mirror. I was terrified by now. I was afraid he'd get a cab and follow me. I really stepped on it, and took the turn at Blackhawk and the Plaza on two wheels....."

The girl was breathing heavily now and her face was white. She began to wring her hands, but little by little she grew quiet as Roy said nothing, and sat tapping on the desk with a pencil. There was a long silence. In a moment the girl resumed her usual pose: ankles and knees together and her hands loosely in her lap. But Roy noticed that she was trembling slightly.

"Miss Vance," he said quietly, "did you ever own a gun?"

The girl stood up at once. There was a pleading look in her eyes.

"Captain... you don't really think that...?"

Roy rose behind his desk. He noticed that his own hands were shaking. In a sudden flash of insight he realized that systems were useless, that long-range plans were futile, and that when your real fate stared you in the face there was no escape. He felt weak, and leaned on his desk. The girl was looking at him helplessly, as if the world had fallen down about her ears.

"Miss Vance," he said with an effort, "you didn't answer my question. Did you ever own a gun?"

The girl's lips were trembling. After a moment she spoke in such a low voice that he could hardly hear her. "No, Captain. I never did."

He came round the end of his desk. They both acted more like automatons, than people; their movements were stiff and awkward, they stared blankly, they said nothing. Roy merely reached out and took her in his arms. There wasn't a sound, and little by little the distant clamor of the big town drifted into the Captain's private office.

In a moment the girl whispered in his ear. "You've got to help me. I've never had anybody in my life to help me."

"Yes," said Roy. "I'll help you."

Suddenly the door opened, and Lackey appeared in the doorway, staring bug-eyed. Roy sprang back like a fighter ready for the kill. His eyes flashed sparks. He took three steps forward and brought one up from his knees. With a loud groan, Lackey fell in the hallway with a tremendous crash as of a big tree toppling, knocking over a chair, a table, and finally the water-cooler, which tipped and swayed a while before it fell, spilling water all over the place.

"You creeping son of a bitch!" shouted Roy, wild with rage. "This is *my* office."

Lackey began to come around, and sat up. His face was greenish and it seemed for a moment as if he might die of fright. "But, Roy," he bleated, "I just came back. I thought you'd gone."

"You thought I'd gone! Where the hell's Lois?"

Lackey managed slowly to drag his mountain of fat, his powerless bulk, to a perpendicular position. "She is perhaps in the lady's room, Roy. Roy, I'm so sorry. I didn't mean... really, I'm terribly sorry."

"What did you want in my office, anyway?"

"I always straighten it up when you leave; you know that, Roy. I always do."

Lackey spoke like a child trying to avoid another blow from the hairbrush.

Lois came in hurriedly from the corridor, showing a horrified face. "Oh, my God, the water! What happened?"

"Take Miss Vance down the back way," said Roy. "Nobody is to see her or talk to her except yourself and Alma till I get in tomorrow morning. Understand? No exceptions. All right, Miss Vance."

The girl left without looking at him. Roy fought to keep his eyes averted, but lost the battle. He turned. She was disappearing, walking as gracefully as before. His heart sank. A whole night would have to pass before he could see her again.

Lackey went out into the back corridor, and returned in a moment with a colored nightman, who was carrying a mop and a pail. Roy looked on in a daze.

Lackey went into the main room, sat down at his desk, and took his head in his hands. Tears started to run down through his fingers. A large purplish bruise was beginning to show on the left side of his soft, puffy face.

Roy came in and stood looking down at him.

"My God, Emmett, I'm sorry. But you... you startled me so. You see...." He broke off.

Lackey looked up at him, smiling sadly, all martyr. "Oh, that's all right, Roy. I should've knocked. But naturally I thought...."

"The girl—she just went to pieces," said Roy.

"Yes, yes. Of course," said Lackey. "I understand perfectly."

"Boley around?" Roy asked abruptly.

"No. I let him go. He was dead. You want Ed?"

"Yes. I'll be in my office. We'll go out the back way, avoid the newspaper hoodlums. And Emmett—I want to sleep till ten. I don't want to be bothered."

Roy, terribly embarrassed in Lackey's presence, turned on his heel and went back into his office.

Lackey lifted the phone and called Ed Reynolds. Then he sat for a long time, not moving, his face blank, staring off across the dim-lit big office. Finally, a slow smile spread over his fat face. "Captain," he said softly, "that's one girl you are not going to get."

19

As Roy turned out his light and opened the window, he heard a clock some place in the little hotel striking three. He stood looking out at the city. There was a gauze-like haze over the big buildings north of him, and a few blue-white stars were twinkling through it. A delicate plume of steamy smoke trailed from a small stack on one of the skyscrapers, turning from red to blue in the intermittent light from a mammoth electric sign on an adjoining building. The city was silent till you listened more closely, then it seemed to breathe like some fabulous, gigantic, soulless animal.

A faint damp breeze began to blow up from the river. Roy stood leaning on the sill, looking out, letting the breeze cool him. He was so tired he could hardly stand and so nervous that at times he felt that he might fly apart—explode in all directions, like a bomb, leaving nothing but some unidentifiable debris to be hastily swept out of sight. His head ached, there was a constriction in his stomach and at times a mist before his eyes. He was so exhausted he was almost afraid to go to bed. To lie alone in a dark room unable to sleep was one of the worst things that could happen to a man.

A car passed below with the radio going—a dance band, playing a fast tune. A woman's laugh drifted up to him.

Cursing under his breath, berating himself, Roy went to the phone and dialled a number. There was a long wait and Roy stood wagging his head from side to side in furious impatience. Finally Lois came on.

"It's Captain Hargis, Lois."

She sounded very much surprised. "Oh, yes? Yes, Captain."

"I just thought of something. Put Miss Vance on."

"But she's sleeping, Captain. We... Alma and I... gave her a couple of sleeping tablets. She was, well... she was pretty much upset. She was crying quite a lot."

"Oh," said Roy. "Well, in that case... okay, Lois. It can wait till tomorrow."

"I'll wake her if you say so, Captain."

"No, no," he said, hastily. "That's okay, Lois." He hung up quickly and went back to the window. "You fool! You idiot! You slob!" He called himself everything that he could think of, but he was talking to a deaf man, and knew it.

He lit a cigarette and stood looking out at the uneasily sleeping city. "You're hooked, you wise guy," he told himself. "You had all the answers. You had it all figured out. And now you're hooked."

After a while he grew calmer. Finally he flipped the cigarette out the window and stood watching it fall in a long arc to the street below, noticed the miniature shower of sparks when it landed, then he turned and got into bed.

"What do we do now, Roy?" he asked the darkness. "You've really got yourself in the dark tunnel now—and no light at either end."

He turned his head on the pillow—and instantly fell asleep.

...his phone rang. Three-quarters asleep, he bull-headedly refused to answer it. "I told that fat slob to let me alone till ten," he muttered; then he pulled the covers over his head. The phone rang and rang, with an insane persistence. Roy let it ring. Finally it stopped.

...now somebody was pounding at his door, and an agitated voice called: "Roy! Roy! You there? You okay?"

Finally he sat up. It was broad day. Yawning violently, almost dislocating his jaws, he leaned over and glanced at the watch on the night table. Five after ten.

"Good God!" he cried, then he jumped out of bed and opened the door.

Boley looked scared. He stood in the doorway, staring at Roy. He had a folded newspaper in his hand.

"Jesus, Roy," he said, stepping in, "I was worried. The guy downstairs rang your phone for five minutes."

"I thought it was the middle of the night," said Roy, yawning. "I thought it was Emmett, waking me up as usual as soon as I get a chance to.... What've you got that paper for?"

"A big break on the case," cried Boley. "They found the gun."

"Who found what gun?"

"It's all here in the *Sun*." Boley held it out to him.

"Damn the paper! Tell me about it."

"It's a big beat for the *Sun*," said Boley. "A guy from the Water, Power and Light Company was working down in the sewer. Power lines, or something. And he found this gun."

"Where was it?"

"Round the corner from Blackhawk on the Plaza. It's a belly-gun. A thirty-eight. All the numbers filed off. A real hoodlum gun."

A quick smile showed on Roy's face, then he wiped it off. Boley glanced at him curiously. The phone rang. Roy answered it with a curse. It was Wesson, and he was yammering.

"What kind of a double-cross is this, Roy? A newsbeat. A real one. And the first one that seed catalogue's had in twenty years. What's the idea?"

"Fat, I just woke up. Boley's reading the paper to me right now. All news to me, billabong. Get your ass down to my office. I'll be there in twenty minutes."

He hung up, then hurried into the bathroom, threw some cold water on his face and began to dress without a shower or a shave. Boley followed him around, talking.

"Damnedest thing," said Boley. "A prowl rolled up right beside the drain and when the guy with the gun looked out of the man-hole there they were. The prowl was from Downtown, of course. And they are grabbing all the credit. Shellenbarger's making a big thing of it."

"He may get burned for that."

"Well," said Boley, "maybe. I wouldn't know. But there was a *Sun* reporter in the prowl. Can you imagine? He was doing some kind of a survey with the coppers. I don't know what. One of those damn dull things they fill the papers up with—especially the *Sun*. Well, of course these dumb cops in the prowl begin yelling 'murder gun' right away—and they also say it's strictly a hoodlum belly-gun, which it is. We got it now. Emmett's working it over."

Roy was almost dressed. The phone rang. Roy grabbed at it then handed his tie to Boley. "Tie it, Joe—tie it," and as Boley wrestled with the tie, trying to get it right, Roy talked on the phone to Chad Bayliss, who seemed to be frothing at the mouth.

"Seems like I can't turn my back," he was shouting. "I spend half the morning trying to convince my wife I'm really going out to play a round of golf—and then I'm just about to play one, when what happens? Some inconsiderate bastard hands me a copy of the *Sun*...."

"Yeah, yeah. Now wait a minute, Chad... I...."

"*You* wait. Front page headlines. Belly-gun. Hoodlum gun. Great mystery. Why was Frank Hobart shot with hoodlum gun? I'm still going to play golf, damn it; but my score will be as high as my blood pressure."

The Big Man sounded silly. Was he that much disturbed? Of course he was. Naturally. He was practically hysterical.

Roy explained the circumstances patiently, then he added: "Just a bad break, Chad. Bad luck. Nobody could foresee a thing like that. I'm leaving right now. Try to relax. Enjoy your game. We'll see what we can do."

Chad hung up with a crash. Boley was holding Roy's coat for him. He plunged into it.

"I guess this makes the girl look pretty white," said Boley.

"Yeah," said Roy, as they went out. "It would seem so."

He felt an irrational elation. Almost from the first, in spite of himself, he'd suspected the girl. Too many lines of enquiry led to her. And yet—what would she be doing with a hoodlum belly-gun? And then Roy caught himself up short. All right, supposing she was innocent—so what? Nothing was changed. The show had to go on as before. In fact, things had to be stepped up now. The "hoodlum" tag was the very thing the Administration was trying to avoid.

"I never did figure she could've done it," said Boley. "It's not in the cards."

Roy merely grunted.

Newsmen were clustered around the City Building, and many of them were prowling through the corridors, getting in everybody's way. The press-room on the first floor was deserted, except for one reporter, sleeping off a hangover.

Roy fought them off. "I just got out of bed," he explained, again and again. "I've got to sleep some time. Bulletins later, boys."

"Yeah, but can't you just hazard an opinion? Don't this put a new complexion on...?"

"Later, guys. Later!"

In the ante-room Gert and Ed Reynolds were going crazy. Roy shouldered his way through with the help of Boley. "Get Red and Creel," Roy called over his shoulder. "You need help out here. Nobody's to come in the main room unless I okay them first." Then he whispered something to Ed Reynolds in passing.

"He's already in there," said Ed, moving his match from side to side with his tongue as he talked. "Sneaked in, I guess."

Roy entered the main room, followed by Boley. Lackey was sitting at one of the desks; Wesson at another.

Wesson looked up. "A pretty go, this," he said. "When the *Sun* gets a beat, that's news. What goes, Roy?"

"How did you get in here?"

"You invited me."

"I'm just curious."

"Backway. I've got influence. Look at the shiner on poor Emmett. He stepped on a rake and it flew up and hit him. Is that right, Emmett?"

"It... wasn't exactly a rake," said Lackey, slowly. Roy studied the big fellow. There was a change, something new. Today he did not look evasive or conciliatory. There was more than a touch of smugness about him this morning. He seemed quietly pleased with himself.

"Could I see you alone, Roy?" he inquired.

"Certainly," said Roy. "Come right in."

The big fellow rose, took a brief-case from one of the drawers, and followed Roy into his private office. Wesson protested loudly, claimed he was being crucified. "Beat by the *Sun*. Oh, my God!" he cried.

"You get the first quote," said Roy, as he closed the door.

They sat down; Roy behind his desk, and Lackey in a straight chair in front of the desk, holding the brief-case on his knees.

"You got quite a shiner, Emmett," said Roy, wincing slightly.

"Please. Let's forget that, Roy. Let's never refer to it again. It was just one of those unfortunate misunderstandings. All my fault, I'm afraid."

"Okay. But it wasn't your fault, all the same. I blew my cork like a damn fool. What have we got here?" He indicated the brief-case.

Lackey unfastened the flap, took out a small revolver, and put it on Roy's desk. It was a belly-gun, no doubt about it, with a snub-nosed barrel and a heavy grip. Hoodlums often used them for fighting at close quarters, and besides, they were compact, short, and easy to carry.

"Yeah," said Roy, studying the gun. "I see. Well, what about it, Emmett?"

"It's a .38, and three shots were fired from it, three bullets left in the chambers. No fingerprints. It's been in water and mud, and the man who found it smeared it all up besides. Nothing there. Also there is no real way to prove this was the murder gun, ballistically speaking, that is. The only bullet recovered was so smashed, so twisted, we can't prove that it came from this gun. Quite impossible."

Roy nodded, then he reached out to touch the buzzer. But Lackey leaned forward and gently restrained him. "Excuse me, Roy. You were... I presume... going to call for Wesson?"

"Yes," said Roy, looking at Lackey, curiously. "What's the matter?"

"Well, I think before you do that, we should have a little talk."

Roy noted the smugness again. "All right, Emmett."

Lackey giggled faintly. "You see, everybody considers the finding of the gun to be the big break in this case, and we can let them think so. But we've got the big break, the real break, right here under our thumbs."

"That so?"

"Yes. Do you know Whitey Vickers?"

"Sure. He's a police fink."

"I've got him locked up downstairs."

"Why?"

"He's our break. He came in to do us a favor. I listened to him, then locked him up—protective custody."

"I see. What was this big favor?"

Lackey giggled again, then restrained himself. "He identified the gun."

"That so?" Roy stood up and leaned on the desk, staring at Lackey. "How did he do that?"

"He saw the picture of it in the *Sun*—a big close up, fully detailed. Oh, I don't think there is any doubt he's telling the truth about it. I think you'll agree with me when you hear the rest. You see, Whitey was a stooge of Nick Brozsa's. In fact, Whitey was pulled in for questioning when Nick got hit by that car and killed."

"I remember," snapped Roy, impatiently.

"You will recall also that Nick Brozsa owned the Dreamland and the Palais De Dance. The Dreamland advertised the best-looking girls in the world, and in the big private room it was a dollar a dance, remember? Commissioner Prell finally closed it because it was just a come-on for high-priced prostitution. Remember?"

"I remember. I remember," shouted Roy, agitated, a cold premonition nagging at him. "Go ahead."

"Well, this beautiful girl turned up. Her name was Dorothy. She was recommended to Nick by somebody—Whitey doesn't know who. He gave her a job in the private room, dollar a dance, and the men began to fight over her. This enraged all the other girls. She was in a spot. Then to make it worse, Nick, himself, fell in love with her—or whatever you call it with people such as those... those...."

"Such as what?" Roy demanded.

"Scummy people," cried Lackey, harshly, surprising Roy. "Scummy, unwashed, stupid, terrible people."

"All right. All right. Never mind the sermon."

Lackey got hold of himself and after a moment continued: "Well, anyway, Nick fell in love with this Dorothy. She was a tall, beautiful, voluptuous brunette. But Nick already had a girl living with him. A redhaired girl, and she was a bad one; not only had a vicious temper, according to Whitey, but she was a drug-addict, and when she got 'coked-up,' as Whitey put it, she was liable to kill somebody. You remember her? Her name was Carla Drew. She was arrested and held when Nick got knocked down and run over by that car. For a while it looked like they had a police case against her. One witness testified he saw her in a car near the spot. But finally the whole thing petered out. There may have been a fix. Station 12 handled it. Anything can happen out there." Lackey sighed now and took his time, keeping his eyes lowered.

Slowly, Roy began to have the feeling that he was being toyed with. He started to study Lackey narrowly. Was there something behind that marshmallow façade he hadn't suspected, hadn't taken into account? Roy sat down, crossed his legs, glanced briefly at some papers on his desk, then leisurely lit a cigar. He glanced up. Lackey was observing him closely now.

"Well," Lackey resumed, "Nick finally decided to let this big brunette alone—afraid it might cause too much uproar round the place. Then he decided he'd fire her. Beautiful as she was, she was more bother at the Dreamland than she was worth. But, according to Whitey, he had a change of heart one night, and went home and kicked Carla out of the house. Carla had to be restrained, and put in jail for a few days. It's all on the record. But when Carla got out, she made threats all over the place. So Nick gave this big brunette a gun to protect herself. Whitey saw him give it to her. It was a gun Nick carried for ten years, all the numbers filed off—you know what I mean. Yes, Nick gave this Dorothy the gun."

There was a long silence. Finally Roy looked up. "And? So?"

"Well, it's a curious thing," said Lackey, "but this girl's name was Dorothy Vance. She was sometimes called Do Vinck. And Whitey says she came from San Francisco. And, Roy, Whitey says he's certain that she's the same girl as the one we've got downstairs—Miss Ilona Vance. The same girl!"

There was a protracted silence. Roy smoked thoughtfully, trying to keep his hands from shaking. Finally he spoke. "All right, Emmett. Good work. But... let's look at the business closely before we do anything rash. In the first place, Whitey is a rat of the worst description. A liar, a thief, playing both ends against the middle. In the second place, his police record is so bad, so unusually bad, that you'd be laughed at if you brought him into court as a witness. Attorney for the defense would make him wish he'd never been born, and the D.A.'s man would have to go hide his head. Any judge would be prejudiced against Whitey, and what do you think a jury of ordinarily respectable citizens would think of him? Do you imagine for one minute that a jury would convict a beautiful girl like Miss Vance on the testimony of a stinking rat like Whitey?"

"No, I don't, Roy," said Lackey, quailing slightly, beginning to lose his smugness. "But it's a link."

"Conviction is what we want, and I even doubt if it is a link. I doubt it very much. I think Whitey would prejudice our case to such an extent that it might be better to forget the whole thing. Not that I want to, you understand."

Roy pressed the buzzer and picked up the phone. "Boley? Wesson there? Oh, he just blitzed you, eh? Send him in."

In a moment the fat, red, snub-nosed face was pushed round the jamb. "Mother," he said, "I come. I come. On my shield."

"Wesson," said Roy, "you get first dibs. There is absolutely no conclusive proof that this gun here was the murder gun. Am I right, Emmett?"

Lackey swallowed. "Y... yes, Roy. There is absolutely no conclusive proof."

"Thank you, gentlemen. Thank you," said Wesson. "Will you give me a little time? Say, one hour?" Roy nodded.

"Okay, then. I'll play one more hand with the poor sad Slay. You know, Roy, I don't believe you appreciate Boley. You should hear him lament when I beat him at gin. Sounds like Joseph Conrad."

Wesson grinned and left.

"Who the hell is Joseph Conrad?" Roy asked.

"He's a writer of sea stories, I believe," said Lackey, some of his smugness returning.

Roy glanced at him. "How many people know about Whitey?"

"Nobody, Roy, but me. That is, nobody knows about his testimony but me. I may say, nobody knows why he is here but me. I thought you'd like it that way."

"Good, Emmett. Now let's give Whitey a little going-over. I've got an idea or two."

Whitey was an albino with pink eyes, a thin, gnarled little man of about forty. When he talked to you, he stood close and peered at you, his eyes squinting, his face puckered. He readily admitted to Roy that he couldn't see very well, especially in the daytime, but at night, he insisted, he was okay. "I can see like a cat at night, Captain," he whined.

They were in the main room of the basement where the lights were lit twenty-four hours a day. Very little sunshine ever penetrated here.

"How about this room?" Roy asked. "Artificial light."

"Oh, I can see fine here, Captain," said Whitey, edging up close. "Damn fine—like a cat."

"All right," said Roy. "Now listen to me, Whitey. This is a damned serious thing—it might send somebody to the chair. You understand? Now don't make any mistakes. Don't just do us a favor, you know what I mean? Take your time. All I want is the truth. You understand, Whitey?" Roy reached out and put his hand on Whitey's shoulder and squeezed.

Whitey wilted slightly. "Jeez, Captain, what a hand!" he whined ingratiatingly.

"No mistakes now, is that clear? You make a mistake and get me in a jam, and I'll send you up for a long one if I have to railroad you."

"I got you, Captain. I got you. Jeez, what a hand!"

"All right," said Roy. "There's a table over there full of revolvers of all kinds. Pick out the gun."

Whitey started to shake with agitation, moved slowly over to the table, and bending down, began to peer nearsightedly at the bewildering array of revolvers.

They were all well-polished and shining.

Lackey stood in the background, looking on nervously. At the moment, he doubted if he himself could pick out the gun.

After long and painful study, Whitey turned and whined: "It ain't here, Captain."

Roy suppressed a smile. "Okay, Whitey. Now come with me."

He took Whitey by the arm, handling him a little roughly, led him to a door, opened it, and pushed him out into a big cement corridor. Whitey started back violently, then turned to stare uneasily and questioningly at Roy.

Twenty policewomen in neat gray uniforms were lined up at attention in the corridor. Most of them were plain, ordinary-looking women. Some of them, however, were tall, young and attractive.

The girl was third from the far end. The uniform did not fit her very well. She was wearing low-heeled shoes. Her black hair was pulled back tightly over her ears and tied in a horse-tail behind. She had on no make-up whatever, not even lip-stick. She stared straight ahead, face rigid. Her cheekbones looked very high and there was something delicately boyish about her face now.

Whitey prowled up and down the line half a dozen times. Every once in a while he would peer closely at a tall, rather angular brunette with a wide, pretty face. She was in the middle of the line.

Finally, sweating, Whitey turned to Roy and observed sadly. "She ain't here, Captain. At least... I can't pick her out."

Roy waved a dismissal at the policewomen and they broke up, chattering, then he drew Whitey back into the main room.

Whitey was shaking. "Throw me in the clink if you like, Captain," moaned Whitey. "But I couldn't do it. Damned if I could do it."

Roy turned to Lackey, who seemed resigned. "You want Whitey for anything else, Emmett?"

"No. I guess not."

"Okay, Whitey," said Roy. "Go home. Keep your nose clean. And stay in town."

Whitey grinned widely. "Okay, Cap. Right you are. At your service any time. Yes sir." He saluted, and turned to go.

Roy called to Boley, who was leaning against the wall, looking bewildered. "Take him out the back, Joe; and drive him uptown. Duck the scribblers."

"At your service, Cap," called Whitey, grinning, relieved, as he followed Boley. "All you got to do's call me. Lieutenant Lackey's got my number."

He and Boley disappeared. Roy turned to Lackey.

"Well, Emmett? You see what I mean about Whitey? You think he'd help our case?"

"No, I don't. But... I think the business should be looked into further."

"Sure, sure," said Roy. "I'll take care of it."

Roy spent the rest of the day leisurely, pacing himself, as he called it. He wanted to see and talk to the girl so badly that he could hardly restrain himself from having her brought into his office, but the one glimpse of her in the corridor downstairs, looking as beautiful as ever, more so, if anything, in spite of being stripped of all aids, had helped considerably, so he went about his business, practicing patience, biding his time.

She was guilty—guilty as hell, and things apparently were much worse than he'd imagined—the Dreamland, for God's sake and Nick Brozsa!—and yet it didn't seem to matter at all. Useless to remonstrate with himself. It was something beyond reason.

He had lunch at the Regent with Len Creel and took his time about it, drinking several steins of beer. He spent most of the afternoon in routine work: signing the payroll, as head of his unit, okaying reports and memoranda of all kinds, writing bulletins for the papers with the help of Creel and Lackey, and finally conferring with a man from the coroner's office about the inquest. Roy had it held over indefinitely.

At seven o'clock things began to quiet down. He and Wesson went out to a seafood restaurant and had dinner. While they were eating, Wesson said:

"Whitey didn't get much of any place, did he?"

Roy started slightly. Then he looked up at Wesson, who was grinning at him. "No," said Roy.

Wesson sighed and ordered another platter of fish, and when Roy showed surprise, he said: "I always eat two double-orders here. They'd feel hurt if I didn't. Besides, I'm a fool for perch. And then, too, the City's paying for it."

"That's right. But some day, you'll just bust. I don't want to be around when it happens."

"'Is tripes vas spread abaht like ivy wines. Hit vere a sight to see,'" Wesson intoned. Then he said: "You won't believe this, but I'm always hungry. Never full. You see I'm among the frustrated of this earth: a mute, inglorious Al Capone. According to Freud, the man who is frustrated in his most urgent desires consoles himself with food."

"And drink."

"No, drinking is a pleasure. Overeating a necessity. Shall we get back to Whitey?"

"Make it brief," snapped Roy.

Wesson gave Roy a hurt look. "I have only this to say. Protecting a broad is not the ideal way to make a career, unless the broad has ten million dollars, of course. In that case, it's de rigueur."

"It's what?"

"Oh, pardon me. I keep forgetting you're practically illiterate. It's the expected thing. It's done."

After a moment, Roy asked: "Wesson, how old are you?"

"I've got a better chance to see my knees than to see forty-five again."

"How did you ever manage to live that long?"

"Oh, come now, Roy. What's a quip among friends? You're illiterate. I'm fat. We all have our crosses to bear."

They finished their meal in silence, Wesson taking his time, and Roy smoking and fuming.

Finally he said as he rose to pay the check: "I'd prefer not to hear any talk about Whitey floating around."

"Roy," said Wesson, putting his hand on his big stomach, "now you've hurt me."

Boley was waiting with the car. Wesson insisted that they drive him back to the City Building, but Roy brushed him off.

"I'm going straight to my hotel and hit the hay," said Roy. "I got no time to drag you around. Take a taxi. When you get home, put your feet up and relax for a while. You're racing your motor a little too much to suit me."

As the car drove off, Wesson removed his hat and bowed, then he turned, went back into the seafood place, and sat down on a stool at the bar.

"What should follow perch, Lloyd?" he called to the little blackhaired Welsh bartender.

"That's a question, Mr. Wesson, sir," said Lloyd, hurrying back eagerly to talk. "A good brandy, perhaps."

"The very thing, Lloyd."

The bartender returned with the brandy. "Didn't you say one night you'd never been in Cardiff, sir?" Lloyd treated Wesson with exaggerated deference which was very unusual for him. He was considered an expert bartender and for that reason was kept on, but he was a surly, fantastical character. There had been many complaints about him from patrons.

"Never been there, sorry to say."

"And didn't you say your hometown was London, sir?"

"London as ever was," said Wesson, sadly.

"Did it ever occur to you, sir, we're a couple of blinking fools for going away?"

"Don't you read the papers, Lloyd? Haven't you heard about the British austerity programs? Now, Lloyd, while I love the Old Place, austerity would be the death of me."

"Maybe you're right, sir. Does it extend to Wales, sir?"

"I'm sure it does. I'm sure it does." Wesson sat staring moodily into his brandy.

With Wesson out of the way, Roy had Boley drive him back to the City Building. They slipped in through the truck entrance.

"You can take me home in a little while, Boley," said Roy. "We've got one stop to make, then you're through for the night."

"Thank God," said Boley. "Myrt's beginning to get suspicious of me."

"How is Myrt, by the way?"

Boley looked at the ceiling and shrugged sadly. Roy laughed shortly, then said: "Grab a chair. Rest yourself."

Old Pat let him past the turntable, grinning.

"How's the graft, Pat?" asked Roy, over his shoulder.

"Not what it used to be," said Pat. "The newspaper boys ain't got it to spend no more, Captain. They been clamped down on."

Lois saw Roy coming and rose from her chair, where she'd been reading a magazine under the corridor light, and stood waiting.

"I want to see Miss Vance."

"Alma's playing cards with her. We're just crazy about that girl, Captain. Didn't she look cute in the uniform today? Why don't we sign her up? She says she's willing."

"Haven't we got enough trouble already?" Roy laughed and Lois laughed with him.

He followed Lois down the hallway. They stopped at the door of the restraining-room. There was a grille in the door. Lois looked through it, then tapped.

"Who's winning?" she called.

Then she opened the door. At the sight of Roy the girl stood up quickly, dropping her cards. She had on a plain blue velvet bathrobe and blue mules with pompoms.

They'd brightened the bare room for her considerably. There were pictures on the walls, flowers, a throw rug, and a nice spread for the bed, which hid to some extent the fact that the bed was a special one with heavy straps for restraining hysterical or temporarily insane women prisoners. Some one had even found a pinkish lamp-shade which gave the small room a pleasant, homey light.

"Well," said Roy, "wouldn't know the place."

"They've been so nice to me here," said the girl, staring at the floor. "I think I'll stay."

"I understand you want to join the force."

"That was Alma's idea. I don't know. I might."

Roy laughed then he turned to Alma. "I'll just be a minute. You and Lois both wait right outside."

They nodded and went out.

"Sit down," said Roy.

The girl sat down on a straight chair and took up her habitual pose at once. Roy sat opposite her.

"I'm going to ask you a few questions. I'd appreciate it if you'd answer them truthfully."

"Yes, Captain."

Roy tried not to look at her, but found it impossible. Somehow she seemed different and at first he couldn't account for it, then finally he figured out what it was. She was sleepy. Her eyes had a drowsy, dreamy expression, and her face looked softer than ordinarily. She seemed younger. But perhaps that was because her hair was hanging loose.

"Did you ever know Nick Brozsa?"

The girl lowered her eyes. "No, Captain."

"Did you ever work at the Dreamland?"

"No, Captain."

"Did you ever go by the name of Dorothy Vance, or Do Vinck?"

"No, I did not," she said softly.

Roy got up. The girl rose, too, and stood looking steadily at him. Roy turned away quickly and went to the door. It was either that, or take her in his arms. She overpowered him. Nothing like this had ever happened to him before. It was almost like a mania, something you couldn't resist if your life depended on it.

He opened the door. "All right, girls." Alma and Lois were leaning against the opposite wall, smoking cigarettes.

"Well, that didn't take long, Captain," said Alma.

"Just checking a point. Goodnight, girls."

Alma and Lois said goodnight, then Roy disappeared around the end of the corridor.

Alma went into the restraining-room, and Lois stood in the doorway, smiling.

"We better not play any more," said Alma. "Your eyes are falling down."

"I could hardly keep them open when the Captain was here," said the girl. "I hope I gave him the right answers."

"I've got a sandwich all wrapped up for you, dear," said Alma. "You want it?"

"Yes, thanks. I may get hungry in the night. Oh, hell," she went on. "I forgot to tell the Captain I got my thousand dollars."

Roy phoned before he went out to see Allen Spencer. The promoter sounded nervous but ingratiatingly eager to help in any way. "You saved us from such an embarrassment, Captain," he said. "My wife's been talking about you ever since."

Roy and Spencer sat in a handsome little study, panelled with blond wood. A hardly noticeable fire burned in a small corner fireplace. The big house was very still.

"The wife and kid are both asleep," said Spencer. "Thanks to you. That girl! How could she be my wife's sister?"

Roy cleared his throat and shifted about rather uneasily. "You don't mind answering a few off-the-record questions, do you, Spencer?"

"I'll answer anything. Anything that will help."

"Did Miss Vance, to your knowledge, ever work at the Dreamland?"

Spencer paled slightly, smoothed his hair with a distracted gesture, then finally spoke. "I knew this would come out some day. I knew it."

"Take it easy, Mr. Spencer. It's very unlikely it will come out publicly."

"Yes," said Spencer. "She worked at the Dreamland. And of course, got into a terrible jam, as she always does. Imagine, Helene's own sister, working in that gilded whore-house."

"What name did she use?"

"That I don't know. Maybe her own—Olla. This Ilona business came later, when she went to Cipriano's. Would you like me to tell you in my own words what...?"

"Yes, go right ahead," said Roy.

"Well, for a long time I didn't even know Helene had a sister. Then this big tramp turns up at the front door. Her heels are run over. She's got the damnedest looking suitcase I ever saw. I let her in. I felt sorry for her—a big beautiful girl like that in such a state. I thought she was peddling something, like soap. Then Helene came into the hallway, took one look and fainted. "Sis!" cries this big girl, and gets down on her knees and begins to cry. Helene finally came to, then she started to scream and raise the devil, and finally chased the big kid to hell out of the house. But I gave her fifty. She'd call me at my office, and I'd slip her another fifty. She fiftied me to death. Finally I broke down and told Helene about it. Helene threw a fit. She thought Olla had left town. The next time Olla called me I told her Helene wanted to see her. But she said she'd just called to tell me she had a good job now and was making plenty of money and she'd send me my money back. In two weeks she gave me three hundred dollars. This worried me. I told Helene about it. Helene just said, 'Oh, my God!' Well, we couldn't get in touch with her, so we forgot the whole thing. Next thing we know, she turns up at the house dressed like the Queen of Sheba, but carrying a suitcase. She was hiding out. One night she drank a few martinis and broke down and told Helene the story. She'd been working at the Dreamland and doing five hundred clear a week. But the boss's girl friend, who was crazy, Olla said, had taken a terrible dislike to her and was gunning for her....

"She stayed with us for nearly two weeks. In spite of everything, she was Helene's only living relative, and Helene was worried about her. Then we read that Nick Brozsa, the man who owned the Dreamland, had been run over by a car and killed. Olla was pretty much upset, and said that now she could never go back there again. And of course, as usual, was out of a job, and broke. It always runs through her fingers.

"Well, I had to do something. I couldn't have her lying around here, hiding when people came. So I spoke to Caesar about her. He put her to work at Cipriano's and you know the rest."

"Yes," said Roy. "Thanks, Spencer. Thanks very much." He got up and they shook hands. "I don't think it will ever come out that she was your wife's sister. No reason for it to."

"Thank God," said Spencer; then: "Look, Captain. Things are a little rough for me right now. But if I can ever do anything for you...."

"If you can, I'll ask you. I'm not bashful. Goodnight, Mr. Spencer."

A new maid let Roy out. She was as awkward, untidy, and inefficient as Clarice, and Roy wondered how it was that the Spencers were so unlucky as to have two like that in succession.

Thinking it over on his way to the car, he decided that probably Spencer, always out on a limb, was poor pay, and had got in bad with the better employment agencies.

20

Roy was undressing for bed when the phone rang. Weary and irritated, he answered it. To his surprise it was Chad and his voice was agitated.

"Roy—you're going to have visitors. I'm calling you from my apartment, understand? What time have you got, Roy?"

"Almost eleven."

"Meet me at the usual place as near one as possible."

"All right, Chad."

"You've got a conference on your hands. Goodbye, Roy."

Lost in thought, Roy put his shirt back on, then picked up a newspaper and sat down to read the sports page while he waited. The business puzzled him. A conference? Who with? And why all the hush-hush? He found it very difficult to concentrate on the baseball news in spite of the fact that there were hot pennant races going in both leagues and the time was running out. In his teens, Roy had played semi-pro ball and had about decided to make a career of it. But one day he'd consulted a Big League scout who had been looking over the semi-pro teams in Roy's area. The scout told him to forget it and pick out another occupation. "All you've got," the scout said, "is determination. You look pretty good in among these humpties because you try so hard. But if you go into Organized Ball you'll never get higher than Class C. So why beat your brains out?" Roy took the scout's advice.

Soon after a clock somewhere in the hotel struck eleven-thirty, Roy heard footsteps in the hallway, then a tap at his door.

He was on the second floor. Apparently the night clerk had told whoever it was just to come up.

Roy opened the door. Two men were outside. The nightlight was on in the hallway and Roy couldn't make them out very well. They were both short and rather young.

"Hargis?" asked one in a somewhat hoarse voice.

"Yeah. Come on in."

He opened the door wider. They came in, one behind the other. They were very well dressed in expensive, conservative clothes, but to Roy "hoodlum" was written all over them. They were hardfaced, arrogant, sure of themselves. Obviously not local boys. Roy knew all the important local boys, and on the rare occasions when he saw any of them, they were excessively deferential.

The shorter of the two was wearing a dark-blue serge suit and a light-gray Homburg with white piping. "I'm Stan," he said. "This is Tommy."

Tommy nodded curtly. He was dressed in a double-breasted gray flannel suit and a gray snap-brim hat. He had a short, turned-up nose, and a long upper lip. He looked like an Irishman. With a glance of mild amazement, he ran his eyes over Roy's room.

"What's this, Hargis? A hideaway?"

They both laughed.

"You might call it that," said Roy, irritated.

"The way you guys do in this town, you should be living at the Stoneham or the Terrace. Why don't we sit down?"

They selected chairs. Tommy took out a handkerchief and dusted off the chair-seat before he sat down. Roy sat on the edge of the bed, ignoring Tommy's insolent rib.

Stan pushed his hat back, took out a cigar, put it in his mouth and began to chew on it. He was very dark. His face was narrow and sharp-featured and his heavy, black eyebrows went straight across without a break.

Both men studied Roy for a long time. He ignored them.

"Round town here," said Stan at last, "they tell me you're a pretty tough boy, Hargis."

"Oh, I don't know," said Roy. He raised his eyes and looked from one to the other. "A guy can get quite a reputation just *acting* tough."

Neither of the men missed the implication, nor the insolence. They studied Roy again for a long time.

"You know who we are?" asked Stan.

"Yes. I think so," said Roy, mildly.

"You want maybe to climb down and be more friendly... maybe?"

"I'm neither friendly nor unfriendly," said Roy. "Let's just talk."

Stan looked over at Tommy. "Maybe he's got a point?"

"Maybe," said Tommy.

"Okay," said Stan. "All right, Hargis. You think maybe two-three million dollars a year is a lot of money?"

"Quite a lot."

"Yeah. Nobody gets two-three million dollars handed to them they don't do something for it? Am I right?"

"Naturally."

Stan spoke with sudden and extreme harshness now. "All right. Then you guys got to do something for it. Goddamn it. What you think we are, Santy Claus?"

"Such as?"

"You know 'such as,' copper," shouted Stan. "You got to burn that broad and get the heat off. Hoodlum guns, all that crap. Nobody shot Hobart but that broad. I ain't saying he shouldn't be shot, pushing us around and not letting us know how high up he went. Get me?"

There was a pause. Roy rose to find a cigarette. Tommy produced a gold lighter and lit it for him. Roy sat down again on the bed.

"You've already talked to somebody else?"

"Naturally, you bum. You think we come to see *you* first, for Christ's sake!"

"Well, then—why did you come to me at all... Stan? Stan? I believe your name's something like that."

Stan looked over at Tommy. "This guy—he frazzles me, like. You care for him, Tommy?"

"Oh, he's all right. You know how it is in these whistle-stops."

"I guess you mean your *boss* talked to somebody," said Roy. "Is that right? Then the big boys left the details to us—the stooges. Well...?"

Tommy laughed heartily when he saw the look on Stan's face. Stan choked on his cigar. He turned a little pale, then he flung the cigar on the floor.

"He talks stooges," he shouted. "Listen, copper. I can buy and sell your big guy. I can buy the building he lives in. I can buy the biggest building you got in town. Stooges!"

"Well, it was only a manner of speaking," said Roy, mildly. "Everybody's got a boss."

Tommy looked over at Stan. "I see what they mean—he's tough. You care for him, Stan?"

"I don't care for him. I think he's a... you know what I mean?"

"Yeah, and a big one. All the same...."

"Yeah, all the same." He turned to Roy. "Look. It's all in your lap. You deliver or no deal, and it's going to be rough in this town. No matter what happens, we operate here. If it's going to be friendly, okay. If not, okay, too. We just don't care. Only... the smoother it is, the better for everybody. They told us you was the man. We thought—me and Tommy—you'd give us the glad hand. You know, glad-to-see-you pal routine. What do we get? We get opposition. Am I right, Tommy?"

There was a long silence. Roy walked over to the window and tossed his cigarette out. He was all tensed up and tried to calm himself. The unabashed arrogance of these dressed up hoodlums infuriated him, and he could just barely restrain himself from tangling with them—an insane thing just to consider. But that wasn't the worst of it. He was like a man wandering in a dense fog—and without a destination even if he found his way through. He literally did not know, at this moment, what he wanted or intended to do. He had his back to the two hoodlums, who kept glancing at each other, and shrugging. Little by little, Roy calmed himself, and turned.

"Don't you guys read our papers?"

"Only the comics," said Stan.

Roy waited before he spoke again and tried to keep his returning rage from showing. "The story about the weapon being a hoodlum gun appeared in only one paper, the *Sun*. Our least important paper. In fact, the other papers carried stories I gave them that there was no conclusive proof that the gun found was the murder weapon...."

"All right. All right," Stan cut in, impatiently. "But we know it was. We get around, copper. We got friends. We know who gave that heater to the broad. We know the broad killed Hobart. So we want her burned, you understand? That's all there is to it. It's simple. Then when the case is closed we all sit down palsy and make ourselves a nice deal. We ain't hungry. We believe in live and let live, up to a certain point. What's the beef, copper? Burn the girl and everybody's happy."

"So far the evidence won't stand up in court. It depends too much on the word of a stinking rat by the name of Whitey Vickers. A defense lawyer would make hash out of him. As a witness, he'd hurt the case in spite of his testimony. You understand?"

Stan studied Roy for a moment, then nodded. "So you know about Nick Brozsa?"

"I know everything there is to know," said Roy. "But proving it, making it stand up, is something else."

Stan rose. Tommy followed suit. They both stood looking at Roy in silence. Finally Stan spoke. "Let me tell you something, copper. You're in the sack. You produce—and fast, or you're out. We got the hand on that. You're a nothing— for all your toughness. You think anybody's going to let you stand in the way of a two-three million dollar deal? There are ways of railroading. You should know all about that, copper. Get busy."

Stan opened the door and went out. Tommy stood looking at Roy for a moment, then he turned to go, laughing. "Stooges!" he exclaimed. "Stan'll never be the same after that crack."

He went out shaking with quiet laughter....

Roy had dressed completely now and was getting ready to go to meet Chad when there was a light scratching at his door.

There was an old dog around the hotel with the odd name of Franklin. He was owned by somebody on the third floor, and was a real bum, who wandered from room to room, scratching at doors, trying to get a handout. He was big, black and of uncertain lineage. Roy liked him, and often brought him in and fed him and let him lie on the bed for a while.

"It's late for that old bastard," Roy mumbled as he went over to open the door.

Roy gave a start. Wesson was standing in the doorway with his hat on the side of his head. He smelled strongly of alcohol.

"I thought it was *another* dog," said Roy. "Well?"

Wesson began to sing the song he had composed about Roy:

> "The 'Angman 'as no friends.
> A melancholy bloke is 'e,
> Pursuing unfathomable ends—
> A strynger to 'umanity."

Roy turned and walked back into the middle of the room. Wesson shut the door behind him, and followed.

"You have some of the strangest acquaintances, Captain," he said. There was a pause. "Roy, do you remember that night in the garage at the Stoneham?"

Roy kept his back turned. "Yeah."

"Do you remember a slightly pertinent remark I made?"

"Yeah," said Roy.

Wesson walked slowly over to one of the windows and stood looking out. Finally he spoke. "Roy, are you acquainted with the Bible?"

"Distantly," said Roy.

Wesson chuckled and went on: "It's full of very prophetic things like: '... except the Lord keep the City, the Watchman waketh but in vain.' Well, Roy, I very much doubt that the Lord is keeping *this* city, and we all know that the Watchman is fast asleep. So?"

"So?"

"We do what we can in the situation in which we find ourselves."

Roy hesitated for a moment, then he said: "I've got to go talk to Chad. I think maybe that old 'public relations counsel' business can be worked out, Wesson."

Wesson turned. "Oh?"

"Let you know tomorrow. I've already talked to Chad about it once."

"There's a pal," said Wesson. "A real pal."

As before, Chad and Roy paced up and down beside the dark, arcaded porch of the 'Drome. It was a warm night. There wasn't a breath of wind, and yet they could smell the river which was some distance away. Roy had his taxi-cab wait—the fare went on the expense account. Mrs. Bayliss was sitting in the back seat of Chad's big limousine, all bundled up, waiting.

"She got up out of a sick-bed to come along," Chad explained, shaking his head wearily. "It's getting rougher all the time."

They paced for a while. "Well," asked Chad, finally, "what did you think of our friends?"

"Nice boys. I almost chose the one called Stan. I'd like to meet him alone some night and no holds barred, and nothing at stake except pleasure."

Chad laughed briefly. "Roy—I'm surprised at you."

"I'd not only change the direction of his nose, but his tune, too."

"And then some morning you'd wake up dead. Stan's the boss."

Roy stopped, turned, and stared at Chad in amazement. "That guy! He's the *boss?*"

"New crop coming up. Funny thing, Roy—but they're dead certain the girl killed Hobart. Seems to me more behind it than just an alibi. But whether she did or not, the deal hangs on sending her up. Either that, or war. And war is something we don't want. We got the big election to win in '52. We've got enemies. Yesterday the D.A. found his phone was tapped. Shortly we've all got to knuckle down and play for keeps."

"I've got plenty on the girl, Chad. But I haven't got an airtight case. How would you like an acquittal?"

"That would be worse than not bringing her to trial."

"That's what *I* think."

"But that's beside the point, Roy. You've got to bring her to trial and you've got to convict her. It's your baby. It's what we're paying you for."

"I'll need a little time, Chad."

"Take all the time you want, as long as you don't miss when the chips are down."

"Okay."

"We've got great faith in you, Roy. We're counting on you. Don't make bums out of us."

They paced in silence for a little while then Roy told Chad about Wesson.

"Why, that fat bastard!" Chad cried, then he laughed. "But plenty smart, all right. The very kind of guy we want on our side. I'll take care of him, Roy. You have my word."

"You have to take care of him now. He could blow us right out of the water, and nobody knows it better than he does."

"Chad," called Mrs. Bayliss. "It's getting late. Let's go home. I'm cold."

"She's cold," said Chad in a low voice. "I'm sweating." After a pause, he asked: "Anything else?"

"No."

"All right then. Hit it! The sooner the better. This town's a gambling gold mine, always has been. Biggest gambling town in the country on a per capita basis. The big outside boys would just love to gobble it. But they've been playing along for years, for one reason or another. Let's keep 'em playing along. Goodnight, Roy."

They shook hands briefly, then Chad got into his limousine and drove off.

Roy's taxi-driver was holding the door for him. "You like a little fun tonight, mister?" he inquired. "Two new joints just opened on North Baxter. New girls—some from the West Coast. Hollywood poontang."

"Not tonight, pal," said Roy, as he got into the cab, sighing with weariness.

21

Boley drove Roy into the office about ten the next morning. Ed Reynolds was sitting at Lackey's desk, chewing a cigar for a change.

"Did you see Gert on the way in?" he asked.

"No," said Roy. "She must be in the john."

"Well, you're wanted at Boardroom A on the seventh floor at 10:15."

Roy stared in surprise. "Me? What the hell have I got to do with Boardroom A? You sure you got that right? That's where the Planning Commission meets."

"I got it wrote down right here," said Ed. "And Gert, she's got it wrote down outside."

"Where's Emmett?"

"Don't know. Didn't come in this morning. Didn't call either."

"That's damn funny. Old Johnny-on-the-job. Maybe the poor slob's sick. Give him a ring."

Ed got no answer on Lackey's home phone. Roy began to pace the floor. Something was definitely up! In a moment, Gert put her head in the door.

"Oh, there you are, Captain. Did Ed tell you about your appointment upstairs?"

"Yeah. Is that straight?"

Gert nodded. "Boardroom A. 10:15. My, you're getting important."

"Who set it up?"

"A floor secretary called. Word came through the D.A.'s office."

"I see."

He glanced up at the clock. It was twelve after. "Well," he said to nobody in particular, "I guess I better go see what this is all about."

A smart-looking young secretary in the wood-panelled ante-room looked up at him and smiled. "Go right in, Captain Hargis. You're expected."

Roy went in through the swinging-door. He'd never been in one of these boardrooms before. It was long and rather narrow, and in the middle of it was a massive, polished boardmeeting table with a double rank of chairs. There were only two men at the big table. At the moment the room reminded Roy of a ball-park with a poor crowd.

Chad Bayliss was sitting at the head of the table with a few papers in front of him. On his left sat a young man Roy did not know. He was wearing a crew cut, shell-rimmed glasses, and a bow tie. He had blond hair, long lantern jaws, and cold, observant blue eyes.

"Sit down," said Chad, abruptly. His manner was very unfriendly. He did not look at Roy.

Roy sat down, wondering.

Coming to himself, Chad said: "This is Grant Perrin of the D.A.'s office."

Roy nodded and got an answering nod. Neither of them smiled.

"Roy," said Chad, "what do you think you're doing?"

"In what way?"

"Have you slept with this girl yet?"

Roy flushed slightly. "What girl?"

"Ilona Vance."

"What the hell are you talking about?"

"You know what I'm talking about. Putting me off. Making a boob out of me. You've got enough evidence against that girl right now to send her to the chair."

"I disagree. I explained to you last night...."

Chad cut him off. "Be quiet. Want to hear a legal opinion—from the D.A.'s office? All right, Grant."

"With the evidence I've seen, we could get an indictment without the slightest difficulty, and unless something very much out of the ordinary came up, a conviction."

"What evidence did you see, and how did you happen to see it?" asked Roy.

"Everybody's not asleep, you know, Roy," said Chad. "You're not as goddamn smart as you think you are. All right, let's talk about the evidence. The motive is simple. Frank got damned sick and tired of this floosie and told her to get lost. She wouldn't get lost, so he removed all the things he'd given her. This burned her up so she killed him. So far so good. The murder weapon belongs to her and we can prove it. We know who gave it to her. We've got a witness...."

"Such as he is," Roy put in.

"His testimony will stand up," said Perrin. "I'll guarantee it."

"There's a legal opinion, Roy. So far so good. We've got the motive and the weapon, and God knows we've got the body—poor old Frank!"

"Now it's poor old Frank," said Roy, beginning to lose his temper. He'd had a bellyful the last few days. Wesson, the hoodlums, now Chad.

"Don't take that tone with me, Roy," said Chad, "or you may have to face a malfeasance charge yourself."

"I doubt it," said Roy, looking insolently from Chad to Perrin.

"Okay, okay," said Chad, lowering his eyes. "We'll get no place squabbling." He pushed a paper over to Roy. "Have you seen this new ballistic report?"

Roy looked at it in surprise. "No, I haven't."

"How does that happen?"

Suddenly it came to Roy. Lackey! "This is beginning to have the smell of a double-cross," said Roy.

"Oh, sure," said Chad. "This new report proves that the bullet found came from the murder gun. You see?"

"I see," said Roy, pushing the paper away.

"Now here is an interesting little item," said Chad. "A report on powder marks on one of the girl's gloves."

Roy stood up, stunned. "What is this—a rib?"

"Read the report," said Chad. "You'll see that it was signed and okayed by the best man we've got in the city."

Roy sat down and read the report.

"Now I'm going to ask you a question and I want a truthful answer. Why did you suppress this report?"

There was a long silence. Finally Roy said: "I know you've got Lackey hiding around some place, so you can spring him when convenient. Well, spring him."

Chad thought for a moment, then he pressed a buzzer. After a long wait, Lackey came sidling in from a room at the back. His face was pale and sweating; his mountain of fat seemed to be trembling. He was in such a state that he couldn't look at anybody.

"Lackey," said Roy, "did I see this report about the girl's glove?"

Lackey raised his eyes for a moment and looked quickly from Perrin to Chad. "Yes, Captain. You must have."

"Be more specific, Lackey. So you say I must have. Isn't it one of your duties to bring things like this—scientific reports—to my attention?"

"Yes, Captain."

"Did you bring it to my attention?"

Lackey hesitated and looked about him miserably. At last he forced himself to speak. "I put it on your desk, Captain."

"All right, you put it on my desk. Look Emmett. You're not kidding me any, but apparently you're getting away with it with these men. Now, Emmett— wouldn't you say that this is the most important bit of evidence so far turned up?"

Lackey was silent, stared at the floor.

"Answer him, goddamn it," shouted Chad.

"Y... yes, s... sir," Lackey stammered. "I mean, perhaps, sir, it is the most important. It ties things together."

"All right," said Roy. "Why didn't you mention this to me? This is your side of the business. Why didn't you discuss it with me? Why did you just stick a report on my desk—if you did—of a thing as vital as this?"

Lackey said nothing but stood wetting his lips. From time to time he cast a frightened glance back over his shoulder toward the door as if measuring the distance he'd have to travel in order to escape.

"Answer him, Lackey," cried Chad, red in the face, furious.

"I... I don't know...."

"You don't know, eh? *I* know. Did you tell Chad you barged into my office without knocking when I was questioning the prisoner?"

"You were... you were kissing her," shouted Lackey, quivering with emotion, suddenly bold, with a sort of sheep-like, fearful boldness. "I saw him, Mr. Bayliss. I saw him."

"All right," said Roy. "You saw me. Did you tell Chad I belted you for it— knocked you down—blacked your eye?"

"I've decided to prefer charges," said Lackey, tightlipped, his face flushing, then turning pale.

"Now wait a minute," said Chad, calming down. "You can't do that, Lackey. You want to blow the roof off?"

"He won't do anything," said Roy. "Right now, he's lucky he's alive."

Chad turned to Lackey. "Do you still insist that Hargis suppressed this report on the girl's glove?"

"Yes," said Lackey. "I'm no slave. You can't treat me this way. I'll take it up with the Civil Service Commission. I'll... I'll take it to court. He had no right to hit me when I was merely doing my duty."

"Going behind your superior's back is not doing your duty," said Roy.

"Just a minute," Chad interpolated. "In this case, I disagree with you, Roy. All right, Lackey. Wait outside."

"I demand to be transferred," cried Lackey. "I will not return to that office. I will never work for Roy Hargis again."

"All right, all right," said Chad, wearily. "Just wait outside. Stay put."

Lackey turned and shambled out.

After a moment, Chad picked up a letter in front of him and showed it to Roy. "Here's a request for your resignation signed by the Mayor. You want to write out your resignation right now, Roy? Or do you want to argue about it?"

Roy studied Chad for a moment, but the red, rather congested-looking face told him nothing. Roy knew very well that the request for his resignation was Chad's idea, not the Mayor's. Chad had merely pushed a piece of paper in front of the Mayor and told him to sign it. Chad was the boss, and this was it—the showdown. With Roy out of the way, the girl was a goner sure. Conviction was almost a dead certainty now—which meant a long stretch, years, maybe ten, if nothing worse.

The D.A. would make a circus out of it, with all the trimmings. It would be a sensational trial with national newspaper coverage, newsreel shots, sob stories. And then in a few weeks, an iron door would close on the big kid and she would be buried just as effectively as if planted in some lonely cemetery. Buried, and forgotten.

Roy felt a sudden wave of dizziness and nausea, rose from his chair, and stood leaning on the big shining boardmeeting table, staring at nothing. He'd gone very pale. Perrin and Chad looked at him in surprise, then concern.

"What's the matter, Roy?" asked Chad.

"Nothing, nothing," said Roy, then he sat down, took out a handkerchief and mopped his clammy face.

The picture of that big beautiful girl shut away from him for years, maybe forever, sickened him to such an extent that he felt for the moment as if he might die. Little by little, he began to feel better. The dizziness and nausea left him, and he sat limp, staring at the shining table-top as if hypnotized. Chad's voice roused him.

"You want to sign this, Roy?"

The color started to come back into Roy's face now, and his body began to tense up as if for a physical encounter.

"Chad—can I talk to you alone?"

Chad rubbed his hand wearily over his face, then he turned to Perrin. "Do you mind waiting outside for a few minutes, Grant?"

"Not at all, Mr. Bayliss," said the young D.A.'s man, then he rose and ignoring Roy, went out into the front ante-room.

"That's your probable successor, Roy," said Chad, smiling slightly. "What do you think of him?"

"I don't like bow ties."

There was a brief silence, then finally Chad spoke. "If you're thinking about trying to buck us, Roy.... Look, for Christ's sake—what's a big floosie, more or less? You're no kid. I'm surprised at you, Roy. All right—so she's a beauty. But they all got the same equipment—nobody knows that better than you do; and they all end up being a bore. What the hell has happened to you, Roy? From what I hear, you've always played the woman-game smart. Why blow up now?"

Roy said nothing but sat staring off across the room. Every word spoken by Chad struck him as true to experience, and yet it didn't matter in the least. The calm guy, the guy who was not in trouble, could always give you good advice— the cheapest thing in the world, and the most futile.

"It's not a question of me bucking you, Chad. I'm not considering that now, after all you've done for me," said Roy. "However, if I wanted to, if I finally decided to, it might be very uncomfortable for everybody. You'd have your way, all right, Chad; I know that. But you'd get pretty badly scarred up and the whole thing would have a mighty ugly look to it."

"Granted," said Chad.

After a moment, Roy spoke again: "Do you think a big three-ring circus trial is a good idea, Chad?"

"Why do you ask?"

"A lot of dirty things are going to come out of it. Mr. Hobart's not going to look like any lily. For instance, a smart lawyer is going to show in court that Hobart had been wolfing it on the Row for years."

"Completely irrelevant. After all, we'll set the case, Roy. We'll have our own judge. It'll be run more or less as we want it run."

"More or less," said Roy. "But this is a big one. Suppose somebody manages to see that the girl gets Benny Lynch for defense attorney."

Chad winced. "Who would do that?"

"Who?" Roy laughed curtly. "Chad—you've got enemies. You think everybody is asleep? Take one instance: Wesson. I saved your bacon on that. How about all this wire-tapping? Things are rumbling all over the city. Suppose you lose in '52? What do you think is going to happen to a lot of the boys you've got in office now?"

"What?"

"They are going to the Walls—for malfeasance, and a few other little items, such as stealing."

Chad winced again. "Yeah? So?"

"Let's be optimistic for a moment," said Roy. "Let's say that none of your enemies pick up the business. Let's say that. No one gets Ben Lynch—who would just love to blow you out of the water...."

"All right, we'll say that."

There was a pause, then Roy spoke slowly and in a low voice. "In that case, *I'll* get Lynch to protect the girl."

Chad studied Roy for a long time. "I see," he said; then: "You're really hooked, aren't you?"

"Yes," said Roy.

Chad got up and began to pace the floor. Then he lit a cigar and smoked in silence for a while. Finally he spoke. "Roy, I don't get it. You haven't got a Chinaman's chance to get this girl off."

"I know that."

"Then... what the hell is this all about?"

Roy reached across the table, found the letter requesting his resignation, and held it up.

"I don't like a thing like this hanging over my head."

Chad pulled it away from him and impatiently tore it up. "All right. Now what?"

"What you want is a conviction—is that right, Chad?"

"That's right."

"Give me twenty-four hours. No questions asked."

"I don't know, Roy," said Chad. "You act to me like a guy who's suddenly lost his way. Maybe you don't realize it, but that's the way you act. We had big plans for you, son, but that's all out the window now. You blew the big one."

Roy was surprised to discover that this mattered very little to him. He brushed it aside. "Okay, Chad. That's beside the point. Just give me twenty-four hours. I might get it over fast for you."

Chad sat down heavily in one of the leather armchairs by the window. There was a protracted silence.

"Twenty-four hours is not very long, Chad," said Roy. "So I waste it. Then I'm out. I'll sign anything you like. I'll blow for good. You can put your bright boy with the bow tie in my office, and that will be that."

"It's a tough decision to make," said Chad, after a moment. "But then—all top-level decisions are tough to make. Ever think about that, Roy? I'm the guy who says yes or no. I got to say one or the other, right or wrong. I'm like a baseball umpire. In baseball, there is no such thing as a tie. With us, it's the same. I've got to call 'em and take the consequences. Why do you think I got high blood pressure?" There was a long pause as Chad sat turning something over in his mind. "Once in a while," he went on, "the yes or no guy feels he can relax. He gets hold of a man he's got complete confidence in, and he says to himself, 'Well, that end of the business is taken care of.' Then what happens? All of a sudden the man blows up in his face."

"I admit it, Chad. I'm not arguing with you."

Chad stood up suddenly. "All right, Roy. Get rolling. I'm holding the watch on you."

Roy stood up and smiled wearily. "Thanks. Now about Lackey. I want him to clean out his desk and take a vacation till this is over. Then you do what you like with him."

"Pretty good man, don't you think?"

Roy hesitated for a moment before he spoke. "Yes, in a way, he is. Hard worker, bright. Only trouble with him is, he's a slob, knows it, and resents it."

"Well, we'll see. We'll see."

Roy gestured briefly and left. In the ante-room the bright young man in the bow tie was giving the secretary a line, and she was looking at him coquettishly. Roy walked through the ante-room and out the door, ignoring them.

Ben Lynch's office was in one of the oldest buildings in town. A creaky, wobbling cage-elevator took Roy up to the third floor, and after a brief search in the dark, dusty hallway he found Lynch's office door and went in. It was about six o'clock and beginning to get dark. One small light burned in the dingy outer office which was deserted and smelled of dust, ink, and mildewed books.

Roy tapped at the inner office door and a sharp, high-pitched voice called: "Come in."

Roy opened the door. Lynch was sitting at his cluttered desk, smoking a corncob pipe. He was a small, thin man with curly, rumpled brown-gray hair. He had a thin hawklike nose and piercing hazel eyes. His clothes looked as rumpled as his hair. There was an atmosphere of comfortable failure about him, mitigated somewhat by his keen, shrewd, alive glances.

He was a born rebel. Luckily he had never married, but was content to suffer the results of his rebelliousness alone. He was frugal in everything except tobacco—he smoked incessantly. He did not drink; he ate just barely enough to keep him alive; and his idea of a good time was a weekly visit to the zoo, where most of the animals were long-time friends of his.

All his life, he had found it impossible to knuckle under. His temper flared in and out of season. He was born to be in the opposition. Success would have bored him.

"Well, well," he said, looking up over his pipe. "So you're the famous Captain Hargis? Have you gone crazy or something? I always seem to get the lunatics."

Roy tossed a thick manuscript on his desk. "There's everything, Mr. Lynch. Read it and give me your opinion."

"I'll stay right here and read it. May take me an hour or two."

"That's okay. My home phone number's on there. I'll be waiting to hear from you."

"I've already turned this girl down once," said Lynch. "She's guilty as hell, in my opinion. Although I have no right to that opinion as yet, going only on what I read in the papers—God help me!—and what I can deduce."

"Is that so? Who came to you?"

"A damn fool kid named Dumas, or something like that. He didn't make any kind of sense at all. I ran him out of here. Defending whores I find not only unprofitable, but distinctly boring. They are all alike—too lazy to work, and too stupid to keep out of trouble." He slapped the thick document. "Isn't this a little unusual, Captain—not to say unethical?"

"What does that last word mean, Mr. Lynch?"

"The word? Oh. Well, not much of anything at the present time. Forget I mentioned it. All right, Captain. You'll hear from me shortly."

Roy took out his wallet and counted out a thick stack of bills. "One thousand dollars, Mr. Lynch. Okay?"

"What's that for?"

"Well... retainer."

"Wait a minute, Captain. I told you on the phone I had no intention of defending this girl. This is one time I agree with the Administration. She ought to be sent up. Why should I strain myself over a case I can't win?"

Roy studied Lynch for a long time. Did he mean it? Didn't he know that this was one of the Administration's touchiest cases? Apparently he did not. "Losing his grip, I guess," thought Roy. "I heard he was a real sharpie."

"You misunderstand me," said Roy. "I only want an expert opinion, and maybe some advice."

"An opinion's not worth a thousand dollars."

"I think it is," said Roy, shoving the money across the desk.

"I don't understand this at all, Captain."

"All I want is your honest opinion. Then we can talk later about anything else."

"I'd expect a double-cross if I could figure out any way I *could* be double-crossed in this business."

"Don't worry about any double-cross. This is just strictly between ourselves. Nobody knows anything about this but you and me. Is that understood,

Mr. Lynch?"

"Yes," said Lynch, slowly. "But that again brings up that uncomfortable word 'ethics.' Without ethics, I might tell everybody in town that I'd been approached sub rosa by an Administration official on a hush-hush matter."

"But you've *got* ethics," said Roy, grinning.

"Yes," said Lynch, "I've got ethics, which makes me sort of a freak at the moment, like a two-headed calf."

"Anyway," said Roy, "I'm not approaching you as an official, but as an individual."

"All right. All right." Lynch spoke impatiently. "Let's not get into ring-around-the-rosie. I'll give you an opinion, Captain."

Almost two hours later Lynch called Roy.

"I'm ready, Captain," said Lynch.

"On second thought, I think I'll come over to your office," said Roy. "Easier to talk. I'll be there in twenty minutes. Okay?"

"All right, Hargis."

Roy took a taxi. It was nearly eight and they got jammed up in the theatre traffic. He finally paid off the driver and walked the rest of the way.

The building was deserted. After pressing the elevator buzzer a dozen times with no result, Roy climbed the three flights of stairs to Lynch's office.

The outer door was open. Lynch was sitting on his secretary's desk with a small, portable radio beside him listening to a comedy program and laughing.

"It couldn't be that funny," said Roy.

"Be with you in a minute," laughed Lynch. "They're just about to sign off."

Roy gave him an irritated glance, then he began to pace up and down, puffing impatiently on a cigar. Lynch roared with laughter, then he shut off the radio.

"I don't know how they think up those situations, week after week," he said, still laughing. "By God, that was funny."

Roy shrugged and looked at the ceiling in irritation.

"You find me trivial, Captain?" asked Lynch, smiling ironically and studying Roy.

"No, no," said Roy, hastily.

"You have the face of a very serious man. Maybe too serious. Am I right?"

"Oh, I don't know."

Lynch went into his private office. "Okay. Come on. No more gab from me. We'll get down to business."

He sat down behind his desk. Roy sat opposite him.

"I read every word," said the lawyer. "That's the nearest thing to an airtight case you are likely to see, Captain, barring a confession."

"First degree?"

"Any degree you like. Yes, I'd say first degree, if the D.A.'s office doesn't insist on the death penalty. Juries are funny. They get mulish. And then the death penalty is a very ugly thing, in regard to a woman. Especially a beautiful young woman. Knowing the D.A. as I do, I'm sure he wouldn't ask for the death penalty. He'd leave that to the discretion of the jury. Yes, Captain. This girl can be indicted for first degree murder. A hoodlum belly-gun is not exactly what anybody would describe as a normal accessory of a woman's purse. She took it with her for a reason. And she used it."

"Apparently so. But she might have taken it along to protect herself. She had a black eye, Mr. Lynch."

"If every woman who was given a black eye by her husband or boy friend committed murder as a result, the whole country would be decimated. Naturally, the defense will try to prove she always carried a gun. But do you think that would prejudice the jury in her favor? The D.A. will promptly dub her a gun-moll. No, Captain. This girl will be convicted, and she may be sent up for life."

"You don't see any hope at all?"

Lynch shook his head emphatically. "None whatever."

"Suppose she was afraid Hobart was going to kill her? Suppose he'd threatened her?"

"Did you know Frank Hobart?"

"I met him once."

"Well, Captain, such a thing could never be made to stick in a hundred years. I never knew a nicer man. The D.A. would bring up a parade of bankers, politicians, whatever you like, to prove that Frank Hobart was a real gentleman, kind, considerate, mild in manner. This would not only kill whatever story the girl told about being threatened—it would further prejudice her case. Do you see what I mean? The men who would appear as character witnesses would be of such a calibre as to make that girl look very cheap indeed. Do I make myself clear?"

"Yes," said Roy. "No loopholes at all, Mr. Lynch?"

"Not a one. Of course, a really great trial lawyer might make a tremendous circus of the business and confuse the whole thing so much that the jury wouldn't know which way was up. I'm thinking of such a man as Clarence Darrow was in his heyday. Even so, Captain, the D.A. is a pretty wily fellow himself. No—bluntly, there is no hope, and I wouldn't take this case, myself, for fifty thousand dollars."

Roy said nothing. Lynch studied him for some time, then he filled his pipe and lit it.

"Now may I ask what this is all about, Captain?"

"Just wanted an unprejudiced opinion on how we stood," said Roy, then he rose and picked up the bulky transcript. "Many thanks for your trouble, Mr. Lynch."

The lawyer looked at Roy blankly for a moment, then he opened a desk drawer, pulled out a worn old leather wallet, and counted out a stack of bills. "There's your money, Captain. I'm keeping a hundred dollars for my fee. A thousand is ridiculous. I don't do business that way."

"So I see," said Roy, smiling slightly, looking around him.

Lynch grinned pleasantly. "It all depends on what you want out of life, Captain. Believe it or not, I happen to *like* my life—just the way it is." Lynch pulled on his corncob pipe with evident satisfaction.

Roy found himself envying the little lawyer, and turned away somewhat shaken.

"Here," called Lynch. "Your money. Did you think I was joking?"

Roy picked up the nine hundred dollars and stuffed it carelessly into his pocket. Then he abruptly offered Lynch his hand. They pumped arms briefly.

"I may give you a ring later tonight, Mr. Lynch, and then again I may not," said Roy.

Lynch wrote something on a pad and tore off the sheet. "My home phone. It's unlisted. I had too many cranks calling me at all hours. As I said before, I always get the lunatics."

22

Roy slipped into the City Building through the truck entrance. First he phoned Boley upstairs and told him to come down at once, then he walked up the corridor to Alma's little office and stepped in. It was deserted, but in a moment Alma appeared and started slightly.

"Well, Captain! Where did *you* come from?"

"Just got in."

"Captain, maybe it's none of my business—but what in the world is happening upstairs? All kinds of rumors floating around. Lieutenant Lackey gone. I understand it's a regular madhouse."

"Little change of policy, Alma. Nothing for you to worry about. Won't affect you."

"Oh, I'm so relieved. Lois and I like it so much here in the City Building. Always something going on, and then it's so clean and nice."

"Miss Vance hasn't gone to bed, has she?"

"No, she's playing cards with Lois."

"Is she dressed?"

"No. She's got on her nightgown and a robe."

"Tell her to get dressed. She's going with me. I've got some double-checking on her story I want to do. We'll have to make a lot of stops, so we'll probably be gone for quite a while." Then he added: "Boley's driving us. He'll be down in a minute."

"Why, certainly, Captain. I know she'll be glad to get out for a while. We let her walk about in the back corridors as much as we can. But it's not like being out and seeing the lights and the traffic, and like that."

"No," said Roy. "That's right. When she's ready bring her here to your office. I'll be around some place."

Roy went back into the big, deserted main room, and in a moment Boley appeared.

"Good God, Roy, where you been?" he demanded. "We're all half crazy. There's a rumor around you were removed or something, that you had a big fight upstairs. What the hell happened with old silly Emmett? He blew. Gert came in while he was cleaning out his desk. The big slob was crying and sobbing."

"Look, Joe. I picked you out to drive for me tonight because I know I can trust you. Right?"

Boley studied Roy's face which looked pale and drawn. "Hell, yes, Roy. Sure."

"All right. Don't ask any questions, and don't remember anything. Understand?"

"Jesus, Roy," said Boley, "I wish I knew what was going on. It makes me nervous. It makes us *all* nervous. Old Ed swallowed a match this afternoon. Hell, Roy; you don't seem to realize how much we depend on you. It's like our Old Man was in a jam."

"What makes you think I'm in a jam?"

"Well, something's happening. We don't see you. You don't call. And now look at you—all pale."

Roy said nothing. He found himself avoiding Boley's eyes, which angered and irritated him. "See that transcript over there on the table?" he asked at last.

Boley looked and nodded.

"Take it and keep it with you in the car. Go ahead. I'll be out in a few minutes."

Boley seemed hurt, but he said nothing, turned away, picked up the transcript, and plodded wearily up the ramp to the truck entrance.

Roy waited, pacing up and down. Time seemed to stand still. After a while, he went into Alma's office and rang the corridor phone. There was a long pause, then Lois answered it.

"What the hell is taking so long?" Roy shouted into the phone.

"We can't hurry her, Captain. She's so nervous about going out. She drops everything... can't get dressed. Alma's trying to help her, hurry her along."

"All right," said Roy, harshly, as he hung up. Nevertheless, he was deeply pleased. She was nervous. The big girl was nervous! And all because... and then he stopped himself, and laughed sardonically. Naturally, she was nervous. It had nothing to do with him. She was being held for murder, and she'd lied to him repeatedly. As far as she knew, they were going out to check over her story.

"She's guilty—you damned fool!" he told himself. "She's in real trouble. Why wouldn't she be nervous?"

Finally he heard them coming down the corridor, hurrying, high heels clicking on cement. He turned his back quickly and lit a cigarette. Standing outside Alma's office door, he stared off across the big, empty main room with its bleak glare of lights and its harsh, clear-cut black shadows.

He heard them behind him now.

"Captain," said Alma, "sorry we...."

"Took you long enough," said Roy, turning.

When she met his gaze the girl smiled slightly, showing one small dimple; then she sobered. Roy's face looked harsh, pale and strained. The girl dropped her purse, and said: "Oh, damn!" in a distracted voice. Alma picked it up for her.

"Well, come on," said Roy. "I haven't got all night."

"Yes, Captain," said the girl in such a low voice that they could hardly hear her.

"Take good care of her now, Captain," said Alma, sensing the tension in the atmosphere, feeling nervous without knowing why, and trying to speak lightly and facetiously as a result.

Roy nodded curtly, took the girl's arm, but released her at once with a nervous gesture. "Up the ramp, Miss Vance."

She walked ahead of him up toward the truck entrance. She was wearing the same black dress; she had gardenias in her hair. In contrast with her harsh surroundings, she looked even more beautiful than before. Roy's heart kept contracting, worrying him.

He joined her at the head of the ramp. He noticed the perfume now and drew away slightly.

Boley saw them and stared, then pushed his hat back and scratched his head slowly and carefully.

"How do you do?" said the girl, politely.

"Evening, ma'am," stammered Boley, taking off his hat then hastily putting it back on.

"You got the transcript?" asked Roy.

Boley nodded, staring, befuddled. "Yeah. Yeah."

Roy helped the girl into the back seat, then he climbed in after her. Boley's mouth dropped open in surprise and he just stood there beside the car, staring. Roy slammed the door. Boley came to himself and got hastily into the driver's seat.

"Where to?"

Roy leaned forward and spoke to him in a low voice. "The Beach, Joe."

Boley swiveled all the way around and stared at Roy in horror. "Now, look, Roy. You better...."

"You want to drive for me or not?"

"Sure, Roy. But I'm your friend. I...."

"Then drive out to Half Moon Beach. Some place—the alderman's."

Boley swiveled back, drove out of the parking lot, and turned north on Belleview, a main highway. He was so stunned that he sat muttering to himself. Everything was beginning to be clear to him now. The tension around the office—the rumors—Roy's pale, strained look! But, Roy, of all people! The wise boy; the guy with the wonderful system. Boley felt cold sweat running down his back. He had a dark premonition of disaster.

Roy and the girl sat silent in the back seat. After a moment she moved over closer to him. Roy tensed up, his heart contracting as before, then suddenly he relaxed. The girl gently slipped her arm through his and they sat holding hands in the darkness. The girl's hand was like ice.

After a moment Roy asked: "You warm enough? You should have brought a coat."

The girl pressed up against him gently. "I'm not cold. I'm nervous. Oh, God! I'm so nervous, Captain."

"Don't be nervous. Try to relax."

There was a brief pause, then the girl pressed his hand. "Where are we going, Captain? Where are you taking me?"

"To the Beach."

The girl turned. Her face looked very pale in the semi-darkness. "The Beach? But, why?"

"I've got my reasons. Just relax now. Everything is going to be okay."

She pressed up closer to him. "I *thought* you meant it when you said... but I've been so worried all day, so nervous. Nobody had heard from you. Then I heard Alma talking to Lois. Something about rumors. But when Alma told me you were back, and that you wanted me, I... well, I couldn't even get my clothes on. My hands felt numb. What is this with us, Captain?"

"I'll be goddamned if I know," said Roy, harshly.

There was a long pause, then the girl slid down low in the seat and put her head on Roy's shoulder.

Boley glanced into the rear-view mirror, gave a jump, and almost lost control of the car. They were moving through the suburbs now, then they crossed a bridge, and in a little while were in the open country. A yellow moon was up over the fields. Nightbirds flew across in front of the car, cheeping.

Boley sat muttering to himself. "A sucker! Roy Hargis, a sucker. Anything can happen in the world now. Anything!"

The Beach was practically deserted and the string of lights along the shore had an abandoned, melancholy air.

Boley parked the car beside the alderman's sumptuous cottage, and sat waiting, looking at the lights with dead eyes. He remembered the last time, with Kit, the playful young blond kid. He remembered how he'd felt like hanging himself. Now he felt even worse. It was as if there was a continuous earthquake and the ground kept pitching, and worst of all, there was no place to run to. Roy! Ruining himself—over what? A bum! A big tramp! A beautiful one—but even so!

Roy was helping the girl out now. He turned to Boley. "Hand me the transcript." Boley obeyed without a word. "You might as well come in, Joe. We'll be here some time."

Boley got out and followed them to the porch where Roy fumbled with a bunch of keys for a moment, then got the door open. The girl stood close to Roy, holding on to his arm as if he belonged to her. Boley had a strong impulse to give her a swift kick right in her beautiful bottom.

They went in. Roy turned on the lights. The girl looked about her in wonder and surprise at the Hawaiian living-room.

"Why... this is nice," she said.

The place was panelled with varnished matting. There was heavy bamboo furniture. Native throw-rugs dotted the floor, and all the upholstery was of garish island material. There was a huge, well-lighted reproduction of a Gauguin on the wall, native horsemen on a weird pink beach. Carved surf boards and fishing nets decorated the other walls.

As the girl stood looking about her, Roy opened the door of a little library and switched on the lights, then he turned and offered the girl the transcript.

"Sit in there and read this," he said. "Take your time. Make yourself comfortable."

The girl stared at him in surprise and absently took the heavy manuscript from his hand. "But, why...?"

"Because," said Roy, "we have to talk it over right away—as soon as you read it."

"All right," said the girl. "Anything you say, Captain." She took his hand and looked at him lovingly with her pale, almond-shaped, black-rimmed eyes.

Boley turned away, gritting his teeth. This was the end, the finish, the pay-off, the last out!

The girl disappeared into the little study. Roy turned to Boley. "Get the cards, Joe. If Wesson can blitz you, so can I."

Sighing, Boley began to search for the cards.

After a long silence, Boley looked up from his cards and asked: "What's that noise I hear?"

Roy glanced toward the library, but made no comment.

With hand poised to make a play, Boley said: "Sounds like sobbing, or something. Say, Roy—that girl's crying in there."

"She's got something to cry about. Are you going to make that play or aren't you?"

"Huh? Oh!" Boley flung down a card. "Good God, Roy, how can I play cards? You got me nuts with this mystery. What goes?"

"The less you know, the better. Play cards."

Sweating clammily, Boley tried to concentrate on the game, but made mistake after mistake. Finally Roy flung down his hand in disgust and got up.

The crying was worse.

"I can't even stand to hear a dog cry," said Boley. "This bothers me."

"Good God, you been a dick for ten or twelve years," exclaimed Roy, irritably. "You've heard hundreds of people cry."

"Never got used to it. Never liked it. Always wished I could help 'em—do something for 'em."

"You want to do something for *me?*"

"Sure, Roy."

Roy shouted at him. "Then take a walk. Get lost."

Boley stared in surprise at Roy's violence. "Sure, Roy. Okay. Relax. Take it easy."

He went out. Roy heard the screen-door slam. He sat tapping his fingers nervously on the card-table, and looking about him irritably at the Hawaiian living-room. Why did people want to fix up a place to look like this? In Honolulu, okay. But at Half Moon Beach it was silly. He had a sudden impulse to pull the place apart, kick the furniture around, knock down the big stupid cockeyed picture. Who ever saw pink sand?

It was like sitting in some phonied-up night-club. Couldn't people get enough of night-clubs without making their home look like one?

He got up and began to pace the floor. The sobbing had stopped now. Once more time seemed to stand still.

The sobbing started again, then Roy heard a faint scream and the girl cried: "Oh, my God!" to emptiness.

Roy tried to read a magazine he found on a table. He looked at it for fifteen minutes before he discovered that it was a woman's magazine and that he was reading an article on how to increase the size and attractiveness of your "bust."

He threw it on the floor, cursing, then he went into one of the bedrooms and lay down on the bed in the dark. He felt like leaving the world for a little while and finding a cleaner, simpler and more peaceful place. He fought against this irrational notion, trying to laugh at himself...

...he woke with a start. He could hear the big girl shouting: "Captain! Captain!" and running about looking for him, her high heels making a clatter.

He pulled himself to his feet with an effort and went out into the living-room.

She turned. Her eyes were anguished, her face very pale. "Captain, my God," she cried, "what am I going to do?"

Suddenly she seemed to collapse. She fell to her knees beside a couch and bending over it, she put her face in her arms, and cried bitterly.

Roy hesitated, then went over and sat on the couch. After a moment, she looked up at him. There was a shadow of suspicion in her eyes now. "Why did you let me read that?" she demanded.

"I wanted you to see where you stood."

"I don't understand you, Captain. Is this a trick? Is this a double-cross? I don't know what to think."

Roy reached down and stroked her hair. "This is no trick, no double-cross. That's the case against you. They worked it out behind my back in spite of everything I could do."

Hope began to show in the girl's eyes. "You mean you tried? You... *tried?*"

"Didn't I tell you I'd help you?"

"Yes," said the girl, rising slowly to her feet. "You told me. And I... well, I sort of believed you. I don't know why I should. I've been lied to so much in my life." She hesitated then sat down beside Roy. "But, Captain... that... that document! What can we do? They'll put me on the witness stand, won't they?"

"They'll try to."

"They'll ask me hundreds of questions. I can look after myself ordinarily. I've been doing it since I was fourteen. But... I might get mixed up. They just keep asking... and asking. I saw a girl tried once. They made a liar out of her, and a fool—and they convicted her. Captain—what will I do?"

"Tell the truth, for one thing."

The girl looked at him warily, then once more her eyes showed anguish. "How would that help? I mean, for me to tell you."

"*Don't* tell me then," said Roy. "I don't really care, and I think I know the truth, anyway."

"I'll tell you," said the girl. "You may hang me for it—but I'll tell you. I can't stand it any longer. It's so awful to be alone and not have anybody to....." She burst into tears and covered her face with her hands.

"You're *not* alone, honey. Can't you get that through your head?"

She lowered her hands and looked at Roy, then turning suddenly, she flung herself half on top of him into his arms. For Roy, the room seemed to spin. He was kissing her and she was responding wildly, and yet it seemed almost as if it was happening to somebody else.

He lost all sense of time. The girl was whispering in his ear, but he couldn't quite grasp what she was saying. It was something about love, and about fate, and about people meeting seemingly by accident—and yet it wasn't *really* an accident. A nonsensical jumble... and then he heard himself saying:

"But wait a minute. Wait. We've got to talk this over. We've got....."

A certain measure of rationality returned to him by degrees. He was in bed. He had no clothes on. The girl was asleep, with her back to him.

His mind almost a blank, Roy went to the bathroom, took a shower, then walked about the living-room recovering his scattered clothes.

He saw the girl's high-heeled shoes standing upright in the middle of the card-table, and laughed; then he began to whistle as he dressed.

A great peace was slowly descending over him.

In a moment, he lit a cigarette and walked out onto the porch. Boley was sitting in a chair asleep. Roy looked at him indulgently, smiling, then he went over to the screen-door and stood staring out at the water. It was still as glass and the reflections from the lights were as bright as the lights themselves and sharply defined. The moon had set. A handful of stars glittered over the far shore-line in a sky that looked like black velvet.

The sound of the sliding of a foot made him turn. Boley had started awake.

"Roy!" he exclaimed. Then he looked at his wristwatch. "Do you know it's almost two-thirty?"

"Is it?" Roy began to whistle again.

"Roy, you were sure making a hell of a lot of noise in there. I went out and took two or three walks."

"You always wind up with the evening papers, don't you, Boley?"

"Yeah," said Boley, sadly. "But I never wind up in clink."

"Why don't you go sleep in the car? We've got talking to do."

"*Who's* got talking to do?"

"The girl and myself."

"What? Ain't you said everything? You've had plenty of time."

Roy laughed. "We haven't said *anything* yet."

Boley got up wearily. "I don't know," he said. "Maybe it's me. I was only nine when I came over but I guess I'm not Americanized yet." He went out, slamming the screen-door.

Roy heard the girl calling him. "Honey, honey! Where are you, honey?"

He went back into the living-room. "Hurry up and get dressed, Olla. We've got talking to do."

"I *am* getting dressed," she called, "but I can't find my... oh, the hell with it. I've gone without them before."

Roy burst out laughing, then sobered. For the moment, they'd defeated reality, and had created between them an atmosphere of careless lightheartedness as if now they had nothing more serious to face than the normal hazards of living. Yet Roy was never more than half deluded, in spite of his pleasant feeling of returning strength and contentment. But the girl was still remembering the immediate past, and had lost sight of the dangerous, problematical future. He could tell from the tone of her voice.

The girl was all seriousness now. A few abrupt phrases from Roy had brought her back to reality. And yet her attitude was not the same as it had been when they arrived at the Beach. There was nothing tentative about it, nothing wary, groping. She was sure of herself with Roy and looked at him candidly.

She was sitting on the couch, leaning forward, and Roy was sitting in front of her on an ottoman, holding her hands.

"He was crazy," she was saying. "That was it. If you only knew everything! At first he was very nice. I'll admit that. But little by little he changed, and then he started drinking—that was the beginning of the end. I couldn't call my life my own. He phoned me all hours of the night. He hired men to watch me.

When we were out together, he got annoyed if I went to the ladies' room. Oh, you wouldn't believe...! Pretty soon I began to feel a little daffy myself. It wears you down, a thing like that. You feel like you're a prisoner... a... I don't know what!

"...well, about that night. I told you about it, but I... well, I didn't tell you all about it. He acted crazy all evening. Now to tell you the truth I'm not afraid of much of anything. My mother died when I was fourteen and I've had to look after myself ever since, and that makes you tough. But I have a deathly fear of crazy people. Once, when I was a little girl in San Francisco, a man went off his head in our neighborhood and tried to kill his daughter with a hatchet. She got away. She ran over to our house. We couldn't quiet her. She fell down on the floor and had a fit. I was only nine years old. I saw the policemen chase her father up an alley. His face was a funny kind of green color, and his eyes looked all wild, like an animal. Well... Mr. Hobart looked like that, sort of, and I remembered that man in San Francisco.

"... Mr. Brozsa gave me the gun. The Dreamland was a tough place and I was out to all hours. And then there was that trouble with Carla. Well, I got the habit of carrying the gun in my purse. Pretty soon it was like I wasn't dressed if I didn't have that gun in my purse. I didn't even feel safe without it. Can you understand that?"

"I think so," said Roy.

"...well, that night. Finally I thought it was going to be over. I thought Mr. Hobart was going to give up and get out of the car and go see Mr. Sert. You see, maybe I was wrong, but I just couldn't give in to him out of fear. Because then later it would start all over again and it would be worse. But just when I stopped the car at the curb, and opened the door for him, he changed his mind. He said he wouldn't let me go yet. He wanted me to... right there in the car, right there on the street. He talked crazy. He tried to pull my dress off. And when I wouldn't let him, he began to hit me. I only really remember three blows, but there must have been more the way he was flailing his arms. Then he hit me on the cheekbone and I guess I sort of went out for a minute. When I came to he was pulling at me and carrying on... and I was really scared, terrified. I found my purse and got out the gun. When he saw it, he took his hands off me and sort of half fell out of the car on his knees. Then he got to his feet and began to call me everything terrible he could think of. And all of a sudden the gun went off, three times. I don't mean it was an accident. I was so scared and mad I just kept pulling the trigger. He sort of staggered back, so I reached over and closed the door and drove off. I looked back and I couldn't believe my eyes. He was walking down the street, following me. I almost crashed the car, trying to get away....."

She gripped Roy's hands tightly, her lips trembling. Her face was very pale. He saw small beads of moisture on her upper lip. He rose, sat down beside her on the couch, and put his arm around her. She put her head on his shoulder and they sat in silence for a long time.

Later she said: "I never went past the seventh grade in school. When I was twelve years old my father left one day and never came back. He was a Belgian, a big, tall, blond man. Mother always thought he sneaked away and went back to the Old Country. He was always talking about it. My mother was Irish. That is, her father had been born in San Francisco, but of Irish people. She was religious and so is my sister, Ellen—she calls herself Helene now.

"...Ellen never seemed to get in any trouble, maybe because she was fat, like mamma, until she was nearly twenty years old and had gland treatments. She was nearly eighteen when my father ran away so she had an education—at the Nun's school. But I don't think it's education, or I mean, lack of education with me. It was my looks got me into trouble, time after time; and then, let's face it, I'm no big brain. I do things I shouldn't do, always did, just because I felt like it, and the hell with it! Ellen only did what she thought was right. I don't even know what I *think* is right... do you?"

"Only in a very limited sense," said Roy.

"...first time I got in trouble, I was twelve years old—it was not long after my father left. I was beginning to develop and I looked a lot older. It was an arithmetic teacher, of all things—at public school. He was married and had two children. He wouldn't let me alone. I didn't like him at all. I thought he was silly. One night he kept me after school and tried to... well; we had a big fight. I happen to be very strong. I knocked out one of his front teeth."

"I hope that taught him to stick to arithmetic," said Roy, looking at the girl with a certain admiration.

"No," said the girl. "It was worse after that. He just seemed to be berserk. So I ran away from school. I never went back. Anyway, my mother couldn't afford to keep me in school any longer. I got a job in a candy factory. I could pass for sixteen before I was thirteen. Well," said the girl, slowly, "I guess that's enough of that."

"Yeah," said Roy. "I get the general idea."

When they started to drive back, Boley was half asleep, and Roy had just about decided to do the driving himself when Boley took out a cigarette and lit it, then seemed to perk up.

Roy relaxed. The girl was dead for sleep. She wrapped her arms around Roy, put her head on his shoulder, and sighed. Lost in sleep, she grew heavier and heavier, but Roy did not find the burden unpleasant.

When they reached the suburbs, Boley yawned widely and observed: "Well, another day another dollar—getting richer by the minute."

"Yeah," said Roy, absently.

There was nobody awake but Lois. She looked at the three of them with marked relief.

"There she is," said Roy. "Delivered safe and sound."

"I got to go to bed, Lois," said the girl. "Right away. I'm dead."

"Yes, dear," said Lois. "Good Lord, Captain! You kept her out late enough. This girl needs a lot of sleep. We were getting worried. We didn't know what had happened. All these traffic accidents, and things."

"I resent that," said Boley, yawning.

"Goodnight, Captain," said the girl, not looking at him.

"Goodnight, Miss Vance."

The girl turned. Lois put her arm around her and helped her down the corridor. Roy stood watching them go. Finally he sighed and started out.

"All right, Boley. About time we went home."

"About time."

They walked back up the ramp together in silence. As they got in the car, Boley said: "I hope you know what you're doing."

"So do I," Roy replied.

23

It was a bright, hot morning with a burning sun and a lukewarm breeze off the river. Windows were open all over the City Building and although it was not quite ten o'clock people were already complaining about the heat. Indian summer, everybody said.

Roy was back in Boardroom A. Things were not quite so formal this time. They all ignored the big shining table and the double rank of straight chairs. Roy, Grant Perrin, and the great D.A. himself, Bill Wicks, were sitting in leather armchairs near an open window. Beyond them, in the blue, they could see the flag on the Post Office Building fluttering feebly in the half-hearted breeze.

Chad was pacing the floor, smoking a cigar, and dropping ashes down the front of his coat. "I don't know, Roy," he said. "I don't like the feel of it."

"What's your objection?"

Chad turned, stood in front of Roy, and stared down at him for a long time. "My objection, Roy, is as follows: I do not like to be outsmarted by a man who is supposed to be working for me—but isn't. There's such a thing as royalty, you know."

"Excuse me," said Roy. "That's only a personal objection, Chad. I'm talking about a policy objection—a political objection, if you like."

"You haven't any cards, Roy. All you've got is brass, and what brass!"

"Oh, I've got cards, all right. But I don't want to use them unless I have to. In all fairness to you, Chad."

"Oh, thank you," cried Chad, sarcastically. "That's mighty big and generous of you, Captain Hargis."

There was a long silence as Chad paced. Roy noticed that young Perrin was looking at Chad with veiled but marked disapproval. The young jerk! Thought he was much smarter, no doubt. Probably thought Chad had outlived his usefulness and should make way for a new generation of world beaters. Every new generation thought it was a world beater, and yet look at the world! Chad had his faults, all right. He was overemotional and slapdash, but he and his brother, Al, with a little help from the outside, had managed to perpetuate one Administration for nearly twenty years. It was quite a record. Chad could blow his top on occasion and get himself and the Administration into serious trouble, but when he calmed down he knew how to ride with a punch, and he knew how to hold on. The word "quit" had no meaning to him. Perrin would learn!

"Give me your policy objections," Roy insisted. "Your political objections. You want a conviction, and you want a fast one, and you want a sure thing. Okay. I'm offering you all that."

"It will look jobbed," snapped Chad.

Roy couldn't help laughing. Chad's face got red and his eyes flashed wildly, then all of a sudden he began to laugh, too. He roared. In a moment he fell down into a leather armchair and shook all over with laughter, slapping his thigh. Finally he wiped the tears from his eyes, and said to Roy: "You unregenerate bastard! The gall of a door-to-door huckster. Anyway, you misunderstood me. I didn't mean I would object to it looking jobbed. What about the newspapers?"

"All asleep except the *World*," said Roy. "And we've got the *World* in our pocket."

Meanwhile, the great D.A., Mr. William Jennings Bryan Wicks, looked on indifferently, like an old eagle too tired to fly and not interested in anything else; but his young assistant, Perrin, showed his flat disapproval of the entire proceedings by his compressed lips and a certain cold, contemptuous light in his blue eyes. "These bunglers," he seemed to be thinking; "these irresponsible ones. These laughers! Work is one thing. Fun something else."

"I still say it will look jobbed," Chad insisted, then he turned to the D.A. "Bill, what do you think?"

Wicks roused himself. "This girl, Captain—she has legal counsel now?"

Roy nodded.

"And may I ask what lawyer?"

Roy toyed with a book of matches, looking down at it as he spoke. "Ben Lynch."

Chad dropped his cigar on the floor and bending over to pick it up, almost fell forward on his knees. When he straightened up his face was purple and he began to swear at Roy, a long string of profanity which made Perrin wince. "You ungrateful... you rat!" he shouted. "I ought to.... Listen, Roy. This is too much. No deal. Absolutely no deal. It's off. Forget it. We indict the girl and convict her and send her up for life, and you can fight it all you please. We'll ruin you—and

Lynch, too. We'll run you out of town. You want a fight? All right."

There was an appalled silence as Chad struggled ineptly with a handkerchief and a cigar.

After a while Roy said: "Chad, you're just not thinking straight. Nobody's fighting anybody. It's all friendly. I'm friendly. Mr. Lynch is friendly. Miss Vance is friendly."

"I'll bet she is," said Chad. Then: "Roy, did you ever hear the story about the little dog who got the tip of his tail cut off by the wheels of a street car, and then turned his head...."

"Yes," said Roy. "I heard it in the first grade."

"So we are all friendly now. And everybody loves everybody. Especially you and Miss Vance, eh, Roy? I understand *she* loves everybody all right; or maybe only two parties, the Democrats and the Republicans."

Roy said nothing. There was another silence, then Wicks cleared his throat. "Do you mind if I...?"

"No, Bill. Go ahead," said Chad.

"Unless you have some insuperable objection, Chad, I think, to be quite frank, that we ought to consider this proposition of Captain Hargis's. It has its merits. A clear, quick ending. Everybody satisfied. Costs the taxpayers practically nothing. And it will all be forgotten in a day or two."

"You mean you're doubtful that you can convict this girl, Bill?"

"No. I'll convict her, all right—first degree. But it will be a battle—with Lynch and, I presume, Captain Hargis—and it may get a little ugly in the full glare of the newspapers. Don't worry, Chad. If you say convict, I'll convict. But...." Wicks waved his long, thin hands in an ambiguous gesture.

Chad scratched his ear and looked at Roy with distaste. "Roy," he said, "I've been listening to Bill Wicks for almost twenty years, and you could count the mistakes he's made on your thumb. So, whether I like it or not, I feel I ought to entertain your proposition. Give it to me again, fast."

"The girl pleads guilty to manslaughter. The judge gives her one to ten. We don't ask for probation; that would embarrass Mr. Wicks too much. In six months, the girl is paroled, and that's that. She'll do her time at Winona, and be well looked after—some kind of easy job...."

"They don't have the kind of easy jobs she's used to up there," said Chad, going down fighting.

Wicks coughed uncomfortably and ceremoniously offered Roy a cigar which he accepted with thanks. Perrin, who had contributed nothing to the proceedings so far, made himself useful by lighting Roy's cigar for him with a lighter, snapping it on with an ostentatious flourish.

"All right," said Chad. "So far so good. Now what do we get out of this?"

"You get a quick and certain victory, Chad, which will clear the boards for you. You know what I mean. No fuss, no bother—no stoop, squint, or squat."

"Okay," said Chad. "But do we get your resignation, Captain Hargis?"

"Yes," said Roy. "As soon as the case is closed. Meanwhile, I'm still in charge."

Chad turned to the great D.A. "Bill—it's yours. You take care of it."

Wicks stood up. He was long and lean, and aside from the abysmal weariness of his face, he looked surprisingly young and fit for his sixty years. "Chad," he said, "now since it's over I'll give you my honest opinion. We did a good bit of work this morning. Good for all of us. Good for you, good for me, and obviously good for Captain Hargis."

"Yeah," said Chad. "But six months is a long time. And no fence-climbing allowed, Roy." Chad threw back his head and laughed, then he said: "Put that resignation in legal form and sign it. I want it in my hands the minute the girl is sentenced."

"All right, Chad."

Roy went out and crossed the ante-room where the same smart young secretary was no doubt waiting for the boy with the crew cut and the bow tie to come out and give her a treat.

24

The Criminal Courts Building was a madhouse, but Judge Lowdnes's courtroom was almost as quiet as the grave. He had barred all news photographers and closed out the public. No use to complain that he couldn't do a thing like that. He had already done it. From Judge Lowdnes there was no appeal, or hardly any.

He was an institution in the city. In his middle fifties, he was a huge man with an unusually large and impressive head, and he bore a startling resemblance to a well-known portrait of Daniel Webster. He also bore a startling resemblance to a St. Bernard dog. Some invisible and mysterious weight seemed to drag his whole face downward, but it sagged authoritatively and majestically and with an austere solemnity. The Judge had an immense and immovable dignity. Wesson said that he could even pick his nose in a dignified manner.

He looked like a statesman. Real presidential timber, Wesson said, like Warren G. Harding. Al Bayliss had begged him to run for the United States Senate, assuring him of nomination and election, but with great dignity, Judge Lowdnes declined.

He was completely without ambition, and as a result was a very happy man, entirely satisfied with the exaggerated deference shown him in the city. He was kowtowed to by everybody, from newspaper boys to Vanity Row headwaiters. Every time he walked down the street it was a triumphal procession. Caesar in Rome was unpopular compared to Judge Lowdnes in his chosen city.

No one ever argued with him. No one even shook a head in disagreement. He could quiet an obstreperous defense attorney with one sad, penetrating glance. He could have sat for a symbolic picture of the Majesty of Human Justice.

He was the greatest showpiece in the Administration's rather shoddy repertoire. He was famous for political oratory, and in an age which went in for electioneering with coon-skin caps, hill billy bands, and even acrobats and cooch-dancers, the Judge, in black coat and wing collar, lent an incongruous but original and happy note. He could not get warmed up under an hour and a half, and the long, involved, almost Churchillian sentences rolled out of his mouth tirelessly and endlessly with never a bobble nor a grammatical mistake—the Judge was a stalwart remnant of the past. As Wesson said, the news had not yet reached the Judge that Lincoln had been assassinated.

The Judge in his black robe, looked about the sunshiny courtroom with sad dignity, then he gestured toward young Grant Perrin, who stood up quickly, clearing his throat. Perrin was speaking for the D.A.'s office in the case of the State vs. Ilona Vance.

He made quite a long speech, but in short, abrupt, punchy sentences which caused the Judge to frown in disapproval and further compress his already compressed lips.

"And so," Perrin concluded, "for the reasons above given, we are willing, at the discretion of Your Honor, to accept said plea to said offense."

Perrin bowed in the direction of the bench, sat down, and began to rearrange his bow tie which had gone a little askew due to the activities of his Adam's apple.

The Judge nodded majestically, then he glanced over at Ben Lynch, who was fidgetting with a cold pipe and a stack of papers.

"Attorney for the defense?"

Lynch stood up. "We are ready to plead, Your Honor."

"The defendant will please step forward," said Judge Lowdnes.

"If I may say a word, Your Honor," said Lynch.

"You may. Proceed."

"Your Honor," said Lynch, "as we are waiving all appeal from your august decision, whatever it may be, and as we are not asking for probation, we beg, if it please Your Honor, that you pass sentence at once. We ask this for the sake of expeditiousness and convenience, not only of the defendant but of the court and its officers. We are aware of the crowded condition of the docket and we wish to thank the court for its early consideration of our case."

"The court will take the matter under advisement at once, Mr. Lynch," said the Judge. "And now if the defendant will come forward."

The girl rose and moved slowly to a place directly in front of the Judge. She was very pale but looked self-possessed. Every person in the courtroom, from bailiffs to Roy Hargis, effacing himself in a corner of the last row, had their eyes on the girl. She was standing in a pool of sunshine, tall, straight, impressive. The Judge regarded her steadily for a moment, then he cleared his throat loudly, and with portentous dignity slowly took out his shell-rimmed glasses, put them on, and began to read to the girl from a document on the desk in front of him.

The reading went on and on. From time to time the girl wet her lips and made faint sounds in her throat. Finally the Judge concluded.

"You understand the indictment now, Miss Vance?" asked the Judge.

"Yes, Your Honor," said the girl, slowly, in her low-pitched, arresting voice.

"How do you plead?"

"I plead guilty, Your Honor."

There was dead silence as the Judge slowly removed his glasses and put them away.

"Mr. Lynch," said the Judge, "we find your reasons for passing immediate sentence eminently satisfying. As you say, our dockets are crowded as never before. We are faced with a situation such as I had never expected to face in my most melancholy imaginings. Quite incredible. The respect for law has declined to such an extent that I fear for the future of this great country of ours. Lawbreaking has increased a hundredfold since I was a young man. So... our dockets are crowded and we are used to bickering and delaying and all the nefarious practices of those who would escape their well-merited fate, if only for a month, a week, or a day, even, in some cases. So I repeat—your reasons are eminently satisfying.

"And now, by the power invested in me..." and the Judge went off into another speech. Attention wandered. People began to bite their nails, yawn, shift their feet, worry about their gall bladders, their debts, or whatever plagued them most when their minds were not distracted by some vivid interest.

In the far corner of the room, Roy Hargis felt cold sweat running down his back. Good God! Wouldn't the Old Boy ever get it over with?

The girl swayed slightly, then righted herself.

A pigeon flew in one of the windows and had to be eased out by a patient bailiff. But the Judge went on.

And then suddenly he pronounced sentence. Lost in a fog of worry, Roy had missed it. There was a long sigh in the court and a shuffling of feet.

A reporter dashed past Roy, who reached out and grabbed him.

"What did she get?"

"Oh, hello, Captain. She got one to ten—the lucky girl! And she'll be out in six months with good behaviour. And you know her behaviour will be good in a *woman's* prison. Send her to the Walls, and she'd never get out."

The reporter disappeared into the corridor, laughing.

Roy stood up on the seats. The girl was being escorted to the convicted prisoner's door by Ben Lynch. Alma was waiting for her.

All arrangements had been made. The girl was to be driven to the Winona Woman's Prison at once. Lois was to deliver her.

Roy hurried out of the courtroom and took one of the work elevators to the basement. Then he went out into the alley and stood waiting, smoking a cigarette. The prison car was parked only a few feet away from him.

In a moment, the girl came out of a side door, escorted by Alma, Ben Lynch, and Lois. Strangely enough, Alma was crying and wiping her eyes.

The girl looked around her quickly and eagerly, and when she saw Roy her face flushed slightly and she lowered her eyes.

Alma helped her into the car. Ben Lynch shook hands with her and patted her arm. A husky policewoman got into the driver's seat. Lois followed the girl into the car.

Now news photographers began to swarm about the car, snapping pictures from all angles.

Just as Lynch and Alma stepped back from the car Roy walked over to it, and looked in. "Goodbye, Miss Vance," he said. "Good luck."

"Goodbye, Captain," said the girl.

Roy stepped back now. The car drove off and turned the corner at the alley.

"Soon as I get some time off, I'm going up and see her, poor girl," said Alma, whose eyelids were red. "She was like a kid sister to me. I don't care what they say about her, I've never had a nicer girl in my custody."

Roy made no comment.

Boley was waiting for him out in front so Roy went back into the Criminal Courts Building and started for the Boulevard through the lower corridor. Someone grabbed his arm. He turned. It was young Perrin.

"Captain, I've been looking every place for you."

"What's up?"

"Why, Mr. Bayliss said...."

Roy snapped his fingers. "Oh, I forgot. Where is Chad?"

"He's in the Head Bailiff's Office, waiting for you."

"Man of his word, I guess. Thanks."

Roy went off down a side corridor, opened a door, and stepped in. A clerk glanced up at him from a desk. "Captain Hargis? Mr. Bayliss is expecting you. Right through there."

Roy let himself into a little office which smelled of stale tobacco smoke and ancient ledgers. Bayliss was perched on the edge of a cluttered desk, smoking a cigar. He regarded Roy sardonically.

"Well, the farce is over," he said. "For a moment or two I thought the Judge was going to launch out into Speech Number Three. The one he delivers to the American Legion every year or so."

"So you were there."

"Like you, I was hiding."

Roy reached into his inside coat pocket and took out a big envelope. From it he extracted a letter, opened it, and handed it to Chad.

"My resignation," said Roy. "Effective as of now."

Chad took the resignation and read it carefully. "Fancy, fancy," he said. "Ben

Lynch write this for you?"

"Yes."

"I thought I detected his fine, black-Irish hand," said Chad. "Quite a document, yes sir. Nicely put." Chad tore the letter into four pieces and handed it back.

"You don't approve of the wording?"

"Look," said Chad, "a guy can make a mistake. I was a little premature in some of the remarks I made the other day. Roy—on second thought, you are just the kind of son of a bitch we need. Like Wesson."

"Why, thank you, Chad."

They shook hands, then Roy turned to go, but Chad stopped him.

"Got any particular plans for the future? Say, six months from now?"

Roy ran his hand over his face meditatively and studied Chad. "No. Why?"

After a brief hesitation Chad said: "Listen, Roy; that girl's no good. She's a real bad one."

Roy nodded slowly. "I know, Chad," he said. "I know." He started away.

"Well... as long as you know..." Chad called after him.

25

The doorman at Cip's eyed Wesson dubiously as he always did, then he stared. It was a new Wesson in a Sam Brod suit, and a modish gray hat. He was barbered to within an inch of his life and smelled strongly of expensive cologne.

"Evening, Mr. Wesson," said the doorman, bowing slightly, then opening the door.

Wesson ignored him, shrugged and went in. The blond check-room girl with the blue eyelids looked up at him indifferently, then started, and ran her eyes over him.

Wesson went over to her. "Hello, Peaches."

She gave him the teeth. "Why, hello, *you.*"

"How do you like me?"

"I like you fine," said Peaches.

"I'm in the moo now, babe. Things are going to be different."

"Things," said Peaches, "are definitely going to be different—if you're in the moo."

"Oh, I'll prove it—later. Winter's coming on. The coat season, we call it in Knightsbridge."

"Where?"

"Never mind where, babe."

A slim dark captain in a Tux came over to him, carrying a large decorative menu with gilt edges.

"Yes, please, Mr. Wesson?"

"Did Caesar speak to you about my reservation?"

"Yes, Mr. Wesson."

"Two in the Tangiers Room? Nice quiet place? Booth?"

"As to the booth, sir...."

"Goddamn it, I said 'booth,'" shouted Wesson. "And it better be a booth."

"I'll... I'll check with Caesar at once, Mr. Wesson."

He hurried off through the dim-lit, padded lobby. Wesson winked at Peaches, who leaned far over the half-door in her low blouse.

"There's going to be some changes made," said Wesson, eyeing Peaches's display with marked approval.

Somebody tapped him on the shoulder.

"Always interruptions," said Wesson, turning.

Roy, also in a Sam Brod suit, was grinning at him. Wesson looked him over and laughed.

"Aren't we a couple of boys?" he said.

They sat in the favored number one booth in the Tangiers Room, finishing their dinner and listening to Bob Dumas playing his soft, soothing, intimate music.

"I don't know what the hell I'm eating," said Roy, "but whatever it is, I like it."

"I ordered the dinner especially for us, Roy. Sort of a celebration. And I intend to pick up the tab. Now I don't want you to get the idea I'm going to make a habit of this... even though I'm now in a position where I can steal."

Roy laughed curtly.

A bus boy cleared their dishes away, then the waiter appeared with the dessert menu.

"Send the captain over," said Wesson.

"Oui, M'sieu," said the waiter, bowing.

Appollo, the Head Captain of the Tangiers Room, came hurrying over. He was nervous. Caesar had put these two rather dubious gentlemen into his number one booth. He felt that he should salaam, and yet it went against the grain. He remembered too well Wesson's obnoxious antics of the past. A bad drunk, quarrelsome, arrogant.

"You have Stilton?" Wesson demanded.

"Yes, Mr. Wesson."

"Would you like some cheese, Roy, or a sweet?"

"Cheese."

"Very well, Appollo, Stilton, if you can recommend it."

"It is of a fine excellence, Mr. Wesson."

"Water crackers?"

"Oh, yes sir."

"There is a very fine water cracker made by Jacob of London," said Wesson.

"But you wouldn't have that here I don't suppose."

Appollo flushed slightly. "I will have to see, sir."

He bowed and turned away.

"I intend to twist the knife, Roy," said Wesson. "When the worm turns, it's bad enough. But when the lion wakes...."

"Oh, bushwa!" said Roy.

Wesson seemed hurt. "Roy, can't you let me have my little triumph? It's not going to last very long—say about a year—till the next election. You know as well as I do that the boys have finally ridden the Old Horse to death."

"Sometimes Chad pulls off miracles."

"This time, mon vieux, a miracle won't be enough."

There was a short silence, then Wesson sighed and said: "Roy, this triumph of mine is not without its trials. I happened to run into Alden Clarke this afternoon—you know, the stuffy columnist on the *World*. Well, he'd hardly speak to me at first, then we had a drink together. He got very abusive, said I'd sold out, things like that; said my trouble was, I was a cold fish—had no humanity. But I said, 'Look, Alden; you're so wrong. I am a very human man full of outstanding human qualities; such as: lust, cowardice, sloth, and egotism.'"

Roy made no comment.

After a moment, Wesson went on: "It's easy to be wrong about a man. Remember the song I wrote about you? 'Pursuing unfathomable ends—a stranger to humanity.' I was as wrong as Clarke. You're no stranger, Roy. Or if you were, you've now joined the ranks."

Roy looked up, stared at Wesson, his eyes narrowing. "What the hell are you talking about?"

"Humanity. You've joined the ranks, Roy. It may have taken a beautiful doll to recruit you, but you've joined. And here you are like any other stumbling yokel—trapped."

Roy stared at Wesson in silence for quite a while. His thin face looked harsh, pale, strained. Little by little, he seemed to get control of himself. "Wesson," he said finally, "I still don't see how you lived to be forty-five."

He seemed on the point of rising. Wesson laughed expansively and waved his fat hands. "Roy! Roy!" he exclaimed. "We're at Cip's. We've got the world by the tail. Relax. Relax. What's a few quips among friends? Look. Here comes our waiter with the Stilton. Ah!"

Roy sat in tense silence as the waiter served him.

While they were having brandy, Bob Dumas took a breather and lit a cigarette. Wesson motioned for him to come over. He joined them and ordered rum and Coke.

Wesson winced.

Bob sat twirling his glass and studying Roy. The Captain seemed a little off-color tonight, a little nervous, not his usual calm, tough self. "You know," he said to Roy, "it's a funny thing. I've never heard a word from Vance. I always thought bims got lonesome in joints like that. I wrote her twice. Don't you think it's strange she never dropped me a line?"

Roy shifted about uncomfortably, kept his eyes lowered. He wanted to get out of this place—fast. What was he doing here, anyway? Good God! Was he so at loose ends that even the company of Perce Wesson, of all people, was welcome?

"Not that I really give a damn," Bob went on. "Just being a good Samaritan, or something—that's all."

Roy sat tense, trying not to think. The girl wrote him almost every day. Alma had put the fix in for her so she could write as many letters as she liked. Yet the letters helped but little. He wanted to see her, talk to her, hold her in his arms. Time dragged as if somebody had forgotten to wind all the clocks and now they were slowing down and getting ready to stop altogether.

Roy finished his brandy quickly and rose. "Getting late," he said, "and I got a busy day tomorrow."

Wesson glanced up at him shrewdly. "He eats and runs."

"It's on me next time," said Roy, forcing himself to remain for another moment.

"Not at *Cip's!*" cried Wesson, in mock amazement.

"Yep. It's a date." Roy managed an unconvincing smile, gestured goodbye, then went out into the lobby to ransom his hat. Peaches showed a blankly indifferent face as she handed it to him, and did not even glance down at the large tip.

Roy was violently impatient to get out of Cip's—at the moment he felt an unreasonable antipathy to the place, but, as the front door was opened for him, he saw that it was snowing outside—big feathery flakes were drifting slowly down through the light beyond the marquee. At once he was filled with a piercing sense of loneliness and almost changed his mind about going home to the bleak, familiar four walls.

Finally, he went out.

"What's bothering him?" Bob asked.

"Oh, he's got problems," said Wesson, noncommitally. "Like all of us."

At last Bob finished his rum and Coke, sighed, and got up. "Well, back to the tinkling piano. Do you suppose I could get a job with Guy Lombardo?"

Wesson settled himself expansively and sipped his second brandy. After a moment, Bob started to play *L'Amour Toujours L'Amour*, and a good-looking big blond, slightly drunk and wearing a well-filled black evening-gown, began to sing impromptu at the bar in a husky, intimate voice. Her escort applauded and encouraged her.

Wesson regarded her benignly, raised his glass, and bowed in her direction. Smiling, she went on singing.

THE END

W. R. Burnett Bibliography

Novels

Little Caesar (Dial, 1929)

Iron Man (Dial, 1930)

Saint Johnson (Dial, 1930)

The Silver Eagle (Dial, 1931)

The Goodhues of Sinking Creek
 (Raven's Head, 1931)

The Giant Swing (Harper, 1932)

Dark Hazard (Harper, 1933)

Goodbye to the Past (Harper, 1934)

King Cole (Harper, 1936)

The Dark Command (Knopf, 1938)

High Sierra (Knopf, 1940)

The Quick Brown Fox (Knopf,
 1942)

Nobody Lives Forever (Knopf,
 1943)

Tomorrow's Another Day
 (Knopf, 1945)

Romelle (Knopf, 1946)

The Asphalt Jungle (Knopf, 1949)

Stretch Dawson (Gold Medal, 1950)

Little Men, Big World (Knopf,
 1951)

Vanity Row (Knopf, 1952)

Adobe Walls (Knopf, 1953)

Big Stan (as by John Monahan;
 Gold Medal, 1953)

Captain Lightfoot (Knopf, 1954)

It's Always Four O'Clock (as by
 James Updyke; Random, 1956)

Pale Moon (Knopf, 1956)

Underdog (Knopf, 1957)

Bitter Ground (Knopf, 1958)

Mi Amigo (Knopf, 1959)

Conant (Popular Library, 1961)

Round the Clock at Volari's
 (Gold Medal, 1961)

Sergeants 3 (Pocket, 1962)

The Goldseekers (Doubleday, 1962)

The Widow Barony (UK only;
 Macdonald, 1962)

The Abilene Samson (Pocket, 1963)

The Winning of Mickey Free
 (Bantam, 1965)

The Cool Man (Gold Medal, 1968)

Good-bye, Chicago
 (St. Martin's, 1981)

Essays

The Roar of the Crowd
 (Potter, 1964)

Screenplay Contributions
The Finger Points (1931)
Beast of the City (1932)
Scarface: The Shame of a Nation
  (1932)
High Sierra (1941)
The Get-Away (1941)
This Gun for Hire (1942)
Wake Island (1942)
Crash Dive (1943)
Action in the North Atlantic (1943)
Background to Danger (1943)
San Antonio (1945)
Nobody Lives Forever (1946)
Belle Starr's Daughter (1949)
Vendetta (1950)
The Racket (1951)
Dangerous Mission (1954)
I Died a Thousand Times (1955)
Captain Lightfoot (1955)
Illegal (1955)
Short Cut to Hell (1957)
September Storm (1960)
Sergeants Three (1962)
The Great Escape (1963)

Uncredited Screen
Contributions
Law and Order (1932)
The Whole Town's Talking (1935)
The Westerner (1940)
The Man I Love (1946)
The Walls of Jericho (1948)
The Asphalt Jungle (1950)
Night People (1954)
The Hangman (1959)
Four for Texas (1963)
Ice Station Zebra (1968)
Stiletto (1969)